# Time Alone

Veronique Holloway

# Time Alone

## Time and Other Lies
## Volume 3

Veronique Holloway

VH Books

Cover design by David Sorum
Cover Image: St. Paul's Chapel, New York City, NY

Time Alone
Time and Other Lies Volume 3

Printed book ISBN: 979-8-9994779-6-5
ebook ISBN: 979-8-9994779-7-2

VHBooks.net

# Dedication

To the City of New York which has a way of getting under your skin when you least expect it

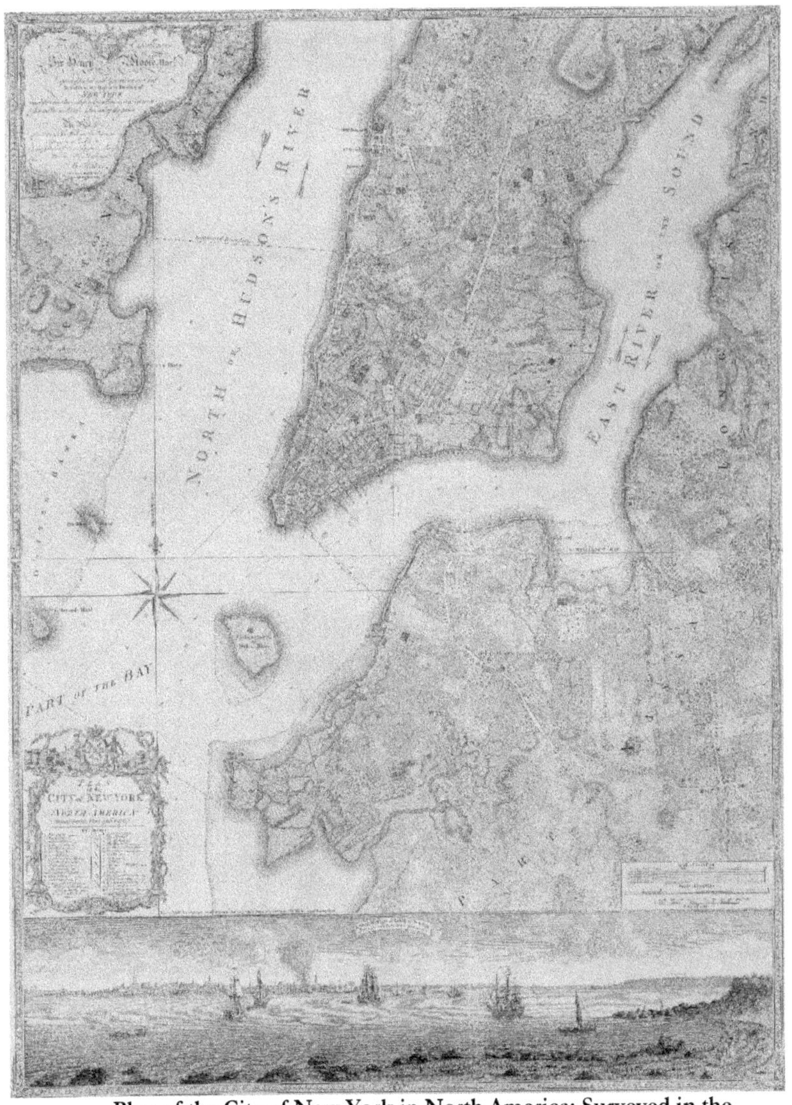

**Plan of the City of New York in North America: Surveyed in the Years 1766 & 1767**

By Bernard Ratzer

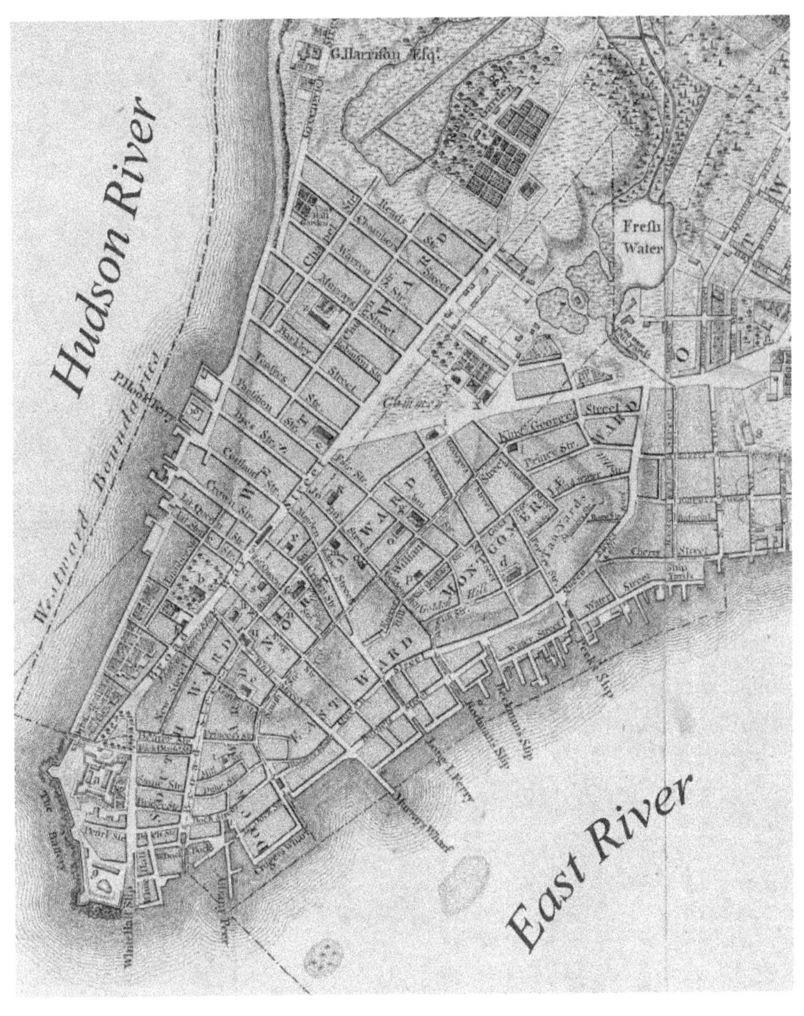



**Tip of Manhattan**

## Chapter 1

Late November 1768

"Are you alright? Are you bleeding?" Ellie dropped the loaf of bread she was holding and ran outside the bakery to the pregnant woman who was doubled over, clutching her stomach.

"Breathe," she told her as she audibly exhaled while holding the woman's gaze. Ellie gave the beautiful young woman a hand to clutch while she supported her back. The woman's curly blonde hair framed her face under her market bonnet while she mimicked Ellie's breathing, their breaths visible in the cold air. There had been little snow thus far, but it was still bitter cold. The young woman slowly started to right herself as the pain subsided, though she continued to clutch Ellie's hand.

"How far along are you?" Ellie asked through the din of the bustling market.

"Six months. I should send for the midwife," the woman said as she glanced around her as though she had lost something.

Ellie's brow furrowed. She continued asking questions while visibly examining the woman. There was no indication that the woman had a fever, and everything looked normal. She wished she had her twenty-first century medicine available to her. Short of that, she asked a nearby outdoor vendor for a chair and guided the woman to sit down.

"It was merely the one sharp pain. I feel well enough now," she said. "I only wish to be certain nothing is wrong with the babe."

"Fetch your midwife if it will ease your mind, but if it helps, I'm a midwife myself." Ellie had no doubt the woman was fine, but she also knew people were reluctant to trust the word of a stranger. If it were her, she would not. "Everything appears to be fine, though you should rest. Is there someone here with you that might escort you home?"

It was Ellie's turn to look around. They were on Duke Street in Manhattan surrounded by shops. Ellie had been out shopping, trying to get herself used to this being the same New York City she had spent so much time in during the covid pandemic of 2020. Eighteenth century New York may as well have been a completely different world. Even the rivers looked somehow different. Though it was far quieter there than in her own time, Manhattan still had an ambient noise due to the hustle and bustle of a city, even if it was only a small city.

The streets were filled with people talking to each other. There were horses, wagons, and carriages rolling past on dirt and cobblestone streets. Outdoor vendors shouted their wares to potential customers while doors to the indoor vendors opened and closed. The women had to strain to hear each other.

"I sent my maid back for my muff after finding I'd forgotten it. After only a few minutes outside, my fingers have already become as icicles."

"If you like, I can escort you," Ellie offered.

"I don't wish to trouble you."

"It's no trouble at all. I don't want to send you off on your own in case the pain comes back."

The woman looked up at her with gratitude. She hesitated, unsure if she was ready to stand, then put her feet under her and pushed herself up with Ellie's help. "In that case, I should make myself known to you. I'm Lucy Byrd."

"It's nice to meet you, Mrs. Byrd. I'm Ellie Russell."

It was easy enough to assume the woman was married given her state. No unwed pregnant woman would be openly wandering the streets unless she was of the lower classes, which this woman was decidedly not.

Ellie escorted the woman home with one hand holding hers and the other on her back, much as she had supported her in the market. They walked slowly, but the woman lived close by. When they got to her door a few blocks away, Ellie grinned.

"We're neighbors," she said, surprised. "I'm only at the end of the block there," she added while pointing to her own door.

Lucy smiled. "How fortuitous. We must have tea sometime."

A young girl threw the door open and came bustling out, nearly knocking them down the steps. "Oh, missus, I'm so sorry. I only just found your muff."

"It's no bother, Jenny. I shall be staying in for the evening."

With brief introductions, Ellie handed off her package to the lady's maid with promises to see her mistress rested.

"Make sure to drink plenty of broth and water," Ellie advised as she headed back to her shopping after making a date for tea. With no plans to stay in the city long, she had no intention of making friends while she was there, but she looked forward to tea with the friendly young woman while she passed the time.

After finding out Dean Russell had left her a substantial estate when he passed, Ellie had gone back to see Walter Coombs in Albany. Dean's factor had been working to find someone to purchase the warehouse and merchandise Dean had owned in order for Ellie to be able to move. When she returned to Albany, he had not yet found a buyer. The economy still had not rebounded from the recession and the warehouse and its contents were worth more than most people in the area were able to part with. Ellie had decided to sign it all away to Walter.

"You can't, Mrs. Russell," he had said in bewilderment.

"I can and I am," she had responded. "Look, there's no telling how long it'll take you to find someone to purchase it all. I don't want to stick around that long. I need to move on. Even if you do find someone, what will become of you?"

"You needn't worry about me, miss. I'll manage well enough."

Ellie had no doubt about that, but she knew he had been with Dean for years. They had been loyal to each other. If anything, she almost felt their history should have put him as Dean's heir rather than herself. He had no other family than the two of them, but Walter had been with him far longer than she had. His estate had been rather opulent, and this was the least she could do. She did not need the added income it would provide.

Walter had helped her any way he could. He had offered a wagon, which she had declined because she did not want to have to fix it along the way if she broke a wheel. She did not have that many things, so a wagon was a little overkill anyway. He then offered a mule, which she considered. It would be better to spread her meager belongings between two animals. In the end, she decided to take only two horses. It would be good to have a spare if it was needed and if it was not, she could sell it if necessary.

After loading up everything she planned on taking with her, Ellie had begun her journey south. She stopped at the Prendergast farm and stayed for a few days, letting her friends know of Dean's death and that she was moving to Boston.

Ellie had gone back and forth over where to live, but in the end, it all came down to the Revolutionary War. She wanted to see history happening. It was 1768 and Boston would be a hub of revolutionary activity over the next several years. Once the war got underway, she would consider moving elsewhere, though she was not sure where she would go. Perhaps she would go south in search of warmer weather. It was a novelty to be able to make the decision for herself. In her own time, she barely managed to scrape by on the wages she earned, leaving her trapped in a job that left little room for extras. Since traveling back through time twelve years prior, her own welfare had been out of her hands entirely. She had been at the mercy of others for far too long and she looked forward to this new opportunity in front of her with excitement.

With the decision made, Ellie had discussed her options with Walter. The weather was turning colder, and it would not be long before the snow began to fall. She hated the cold. She really hated traveling in it. Without a heater and the warmth of the interior of a car, she did not want to be traveling hundreds of miles for days or even weeks until she could reach her destination. Traveling in the winter there was a daunting undertaking.

Ellie could have picked up a sloop and sailed down the Hudson River from Albany, then picked up a ship to Boston from New York City, but then she would have missed seeing her friends before leaving the area. She also would have run the risk of the river freezing over and getting stuck somewhere before she could make it to New York City. It was better to go by land and take the horses. There were three roads that crossed from Albany to Boston without having to go to New York City, but each was in very poor condition. The two oldest roads both passed through country that was not well settled, increasing the dangers to a single woman traveling alone. She would have to go days and days by herself without passing any towns. Of course, it would be dangerous to take any of the three roads. The Old Great Western Road was newly built only fifteen years earlier, but it was quite mountainous with steep, rugged terrain. Ellie imagined the older roads were both just as steep and rugged. Regardless of which road she chose, they were all fraught with treacherous passes and drop-offs.

Her best bet was to go over land on the well-traveled roads that she already knew down to New York City then pick up a ship from there to take her to Boston. She wanted to spend a little time in New York City before continuing the last leg of her journey and decided to stay in Manhattan for the winter. Walter connected her with a couple he knew in the city who were planning on going to visit their daughter in South Carolina for the winter.

Spending the winter in the city would also give Ellie the opportunity to buy some dresses before showing up in Boston with only two. She had continued wearing her Native American tunic and leggings while she was with Dean most of the time, but if she was going to live in a colonial city, she thought it was time to finally purchase more than the two dresses she currently owned. She would give up her White Raven persona and become Ellie once again.

Ellie had pulled out what she thought would be enough money from the stash she had hidden away in the cave on her property in Schoharie. Before leaving Albany, she had enlisted Walter Coombs to help her commission a couple of trunks in various sizes with false bottoms. The man who made them did a fine job and had he not shown her how to access the hidden compartments, she never would have known they were there. He and Walter were the only people who even knew she owned them, which helped her feel safer transporting a large number of coins on her travels. Wanting to have more than one place to store small amounts, she would still have the bulk of it, if anything happened to one stash. Taking as many precautions as she could, she hid the coins inside cloth as well, wrapping them tightly so they would not jingle as the trunks were moved. With the coins buried deep within her things, she set out. The excitement had built the closer she got to the city until she finally arrived in early November.

Thanks to Walter, Ellie had a house in Manhattan and two servants all to herself and she enjoyed the solitude and freedom it afforded her. Having been married for twenty-seven years immediately after graduating high school, then being pulled through time and being at the mercy of others for the last twelve years, she had never been on her own. She relished it now.

## Chapter 2

# December 1768

"I realize we've a visit scheduled, but I wished to show you my gratitude for assisting me of late," Lucy said as she handed Ellie a small bundle wrapped in linen.

Ellie took the offered gift and welcomed the woman inside. Bringing it to her nose for a closer smell, she caught the scent of cinnamon, ginger, nutmeg, and cloves.

"My cook makes the best molasses cookies," she said.

"Thank you." Ellie wanted to dive into them immediately but set them aside as she showed the woman into the parlor. "Would you like some tea?"

"I'm unable to stay long. I only wished to stop by and officially welcome you while I offered my thanks. I'm on my way to purchase a new dress. I'm afraid I'm beginning to outgrow all of the ones I have." Lucy chuckled as she looked down at her belly while placing a protective hand over the bump protruding from her.

"Is your maid with you today?" Ellie asked.

"She is, yes. She's waiting just outside."

Ellie immediately looked out the window. "She doesn't have to wait outside. It's cold out there. She should come in."

"Do not fret. I really must be on my way. The dressmaker shall be awaiting me."

Taking in Lucy's attire, Ellie decided to ask, "Who's your dressmaker? I'm in need of some new dresses myself and yours is lovely."

Lucy beamed. "Well, if you're not overly busy at the moment, you are welcome to accompany me. It would be my pleasure to make the introductions."

"Let me grab my cloak."

The women walked down the street to Fly Market around the corner from them. Lucy made the introductions and Ellie began looking at material options and a few styles. The dressmaker's assistant helped her while she fit Lucy for a new gown. The woman had a small frame but was several inches taller than Ellie. She looked as though she was in her late twenties or early thirties.

"I'm afraid I've already grown bigger with this one than I did with my first. I kept all of my dresses from the last time I was with child, but they all seem to be too snug."

Ellie chuckled. "These things happen."

With fabrics chosen for four new dresses and a new coat, Ellie looked at a few already made options that she could purchase. She tried on a couple of the few dresses in the shop, settling on two that would suit her needs. Her pile grew as she added a muff, gloves, several pairs of stockings, and various other items.

When the assistant gave her a questioning look at both the gloves and muff piled up, Ellie shrugged. "I like having options."

The muff was warmer than gloves but nowhere near as practical. After the dressmaker finished getting new measurements, Lucy came to stand by Ellie, taking in the pile in front of her as her brown eyes grew big.

"That's quite the pile you've amassed."

"It is, isn't it?" Sighing, she added, "I hadn't planned on buying so many right now, but I think this should at least see me through the winter."

Lucy could not help the curiosity that washed over her. "Do you not already have winter dresses to get you through?"

Shaking her head, Ellie said, "Not really. Just this one I'm wearing and one other, neither of which are particularly suited for winter. I haven't really had a need for them."

A laugh escaped Ellie at the confused look on Lucy's pretty face. "I've not been living in a city. I spent most of the last several years traveling with my husband for his trade. During our travels, I always wore the clothing of my Onöndowa'ga:' family. It's only when we went to meetings at home that I ever wore dresses like these."

Lucy's face softened. "Where was home? Am I to assume it was not here?"

Ellie shook her head. "We lived in Schoharie, near Albany."

"How long will you be here?"

"Just for the winter. I'm only passing through but wanted to take the opportunity to see the city while I can."

"It's a beautiful city. It would be my pleasure to show you around."

"Thank you." Ellie smiled her gratitude. Though she had not been planning on becoming close with anyone there, it was hard not to like this woman. Ellie was glad she had agreed to join Lucy on this shopping trip and looked forward to spending winter having her show her around. Maybe it would be more fun than she had originally thought.

---

So shocked by the size of the city the first time she had seen it in this time period that she had nearly cried, Ellie was used to it now as she regularly wandered the streets of Manhattan. Though she had never lived there, Ellie had spent six weeks in Brooklyn working the city morgue during the covid pandemic. It had been during the early days of the virus entering the United States, when the whole world had shut down. She and her team helped manage the influx of dead bodies until the funeral homes could properly dispose of them. Prior to covid she had never had an interest in spending any time in New York, even though she had been there briefly for trainings a couple times before. She did not mind cities, but much preferred nature, something New York City in her time was severely lacking. However, something changed while she had been there during the pandemic. After her time working with the medical examiner's office, she had felt a certain protectiveness over the city. It was in her blood now and had drawn her back there again after she had gone home.

Seeing it as it was now had nearly gutted her that first time. She had taken consolation in the fact that she was seeing the city in the *before* stage of what it would eventually become. She was not certain she would have been able to handle seeing it like this if it were after her time. It was not long before she had separated the city she currently wandered from the one she had once known. It was an entirely different place, and it felt like it. From the tip of the island to the farms in the northeast, the entire city was barely over a mile long. The width was even shorter.

Fort George was located where Battery Park was in the twenty-first century, on the northernmost corner of the convergence of the Hudson River to the north and the East River to the south. The lower barracks were directly to the south of the fort on the East River side of the convergence. Bowling Green was next to the fort and Broadway extended northeast from there. The presence of the fort and the lower barracks combined with the lack of skyscrapers helped Ellie separate the two versions of the city in her mind. There was no mistaking this version for the one she had known, but she had begun to think of them as different places now.

A neighborhood extending between the Hudson River and Broadway was where the wealthiest residents lived, leaving Ellie to avoid the area. With a few exceptions, the rest of the city was fairly mixed. The waterfront along the East River was the most unsavory part of town. In 1724, the city passed an ordinance making it illegal to dump waste into the street which was what they had been doing prior to that time. Once it was illegal, residents without a private waste pit on their property walked to one of the rivers to dispose of their waste, with much of it going directly into the East River. The area closest to the water was a slum filled with taverns, transients, and prostitutes, and debris accumulated on the river leaving the area smelling rather foul. It was also the primary harbor for ships to dock, seeing as how there was only one pier on the Hudson River.

This East River waterfront area was another part of town Ellie typically avoided, though she had found it fascinating to watch the people within it. She had walked through a couple of times upon her arrival but it was obvious that she did not belong there and quickly stopped frequenting the area for fear of her safety. Though she did not wear fancy dresses, her clothing was clean and not worn, setting her apart from the people who lived and worked there. After seeing others robbed or beaten, then becoming aware of how the men looked at her, she thought it best to not linger there.

Queen street ran parallel to the East River and though it was only two blocks from the river, it was a divider between upper- and lower-class residences. The slums were contained closer to the river, but Queen Street was full of upper-class homes. Ellie was in one of them and Mrs. Byrd in another, closer to Wall Street. The upper barracks were located at the far end of the city near the farmland and the Commons was located a block away in front of it. Also called the Fields, it was in the Commons that the Sons of Liberty had erected a Liberty Pole after the Stamp Tax Act was repealed in 1766. Ellie remembered seeing it when she rode into town with Mehitabel Prendergast and Dean Russell a few years earlier. They had ridden in on the Bowry Lane which took them right past the Fields and connected them to Broadway. On previous visits, she had been surprised to recognize Wall Street and Broadway. Many of the streets were the same as those which existed in her time, though most were still unpaved. Though they looked completely different from what she knew, it was nice to at least recognize the names.

Markets were located all around the city with three of them close to the East River near the lower barracks and another one, Fly Market, off Queen Street near Ellie. She loved visiting the markets whenever she could, even if she was not looking to purchase anything. It was fun simply to go and see how everything worked. In addition to the various markets, taverns and merchants were located randomly throughout the city. Artisans worked out of their homes and merchants lived next to counting houses. Laborers lived as close to their work as they could.

The outskirts of town before reaching farmland were considered the industrial district. It was where the more odorous businesses were located. These included distilleries, breweries, sugar houses, more shipyards, ropewalks, two tan yards, slaughterhouses, and animal processing facilities. Ellie usually avoided these areas. If they smelled that horrendous in winter, she could imagine how bad they became in the summer.

The streets were wide with wide sidewalks lined with hitching posts for tying the horses up and no front yards. Some of the houses and shops had small strips of cobblestone or brick running along the front of them, but that was the only frontage anyone had. The buildings often butted against one another, much as they did in her time. Everyone walked to get anywhere, some riding horses, even fewer using carriages. The city was small enough that it was easy to get anywhere on foot. Most of the streets were dirt with a few of them having been paved with cobblestones pulled from the rivers surrounding the island. Though walking the uneven cobblestones could lead to a twisted ankle, it was better than walking through the muddy streets. However, both cobblestone and dirt roads were often spattered with animal feces, leaving Ellie to constantly watch where she was walking. Cattle roamed the streets freely and horses pulled carts and wagons through the busy streets. It may have been a bustling city in the era, but it was still quite agrarian.

The city also contained several churches of various denominations including Trinity Church near Wall Street which Ellie had been to see in her own time. With the Old Dutch Church, the French Church, the New Dutch Church, the Lutheran Church, Presbyterian Meetinghouse, Quaker Meetinghouse, a Synagogue, and Saint George's Chapel to name a few, it seemed as though there was a church on every street, leaving her surprised as to how many there were.

On her first brief visit, Ellie had noted that she could easily walk every street in the entire city in less than a day. She often did so now, while skipping some of the worst or smelliest parts of the city. Ellie had been there for several weeks and had spent much of her time indoors recently due to the weather. Though November had been cold but dry, December was trying to make up for the lack of moisture. It had been cold and snowy for days, but the sun had come out today. It was still cold, but not as bad as it had been. She was tired of being cooped up inside and needed to stretch her legs. Ellie began on her street and headed northwest towards the Fields, walking up and down every street. While she looked forward to her tea with Mrs. Byrd, this was how she preferred to spend her days, passing the time by wandering the city until spring arrived and she could begin her journey to Boston. Pulling her fox fur pillbox hat down over her ears, she was grateful for the warm clothes and boots she had picked up from her Onöndowa'ga:' family the last time she saw them. She would get her fill of the city before she left despite the cold weather.

## Chapter 3

# December 1768

"Mrs. Byrd said you're a midwife?" asked Adelaide Emerson.

Ellie toggled her head. "Midwife, medicine woman, nurse. I've got medical training and experience in a lot of different areas."

Ellie found herself sitting in Lucy Byrd's parlor with her and her sister-in-law having tea. Lucy lived a block away from where Ellie was staying, and the parlor was on the ground floor of a three-story brick house. The room was furnished with settees and chairs occupying the center of the room with end tables between them. Additional seating areas were set off to the sides and sideboards rested against walls covered in light beige wallpaper with a damask pattern. Intricate moulding covered the ceiling and outlined the fireplace which filled the space with a cozy warmth. Ellie had not ventured further into the house, but what Ellie had seen of it reminded her of the home in which she was staying. If she had to guess, she imagined there was a stable to the rear of the property which also housed the household water supply in several barrels, a garden area, and a hole in the backyard where refuse and human waste was thrown. The houses along the street were tall and narrow, butting against one another like they did in her own time. They almost reminded her of the Brownstones so prevalent in her New York City.

"How many women have you delivered of their babes?" Lucy asked.

"Oh gosh," Ellie looked upwards while she thought about it for a minute. "A few dozen now, I think."

"That many? Yet you're so young," Adelaide argued. The woman was close in age to Lucy but was more average in her appearance. Her height was somewhere between Ellie and Lucy and she had light brown hair under a simple linen cap. However, her hazel eyes were shrewd. She appeared to be someone who was loyal to the end to those about whom she cared, but not someone to cross.

"I'm older than I look." Ellie smirked.

It seemed to be a weird side effect of traveling through time. Then again, both attributes might have been magic. Ellie was not entirely convinced they were not. Unsure why or how any of it had happened, when she arrived in the past, she had physically changed. She had been a middle-aged overweight woman with bad eyesight but when she got to the past, her eyesight was perfect, she appeared twenty years younger, and she dropped about forty pounds. She also had some uncanny ability to heal nearly anything within minutes.

"And you're dwelling in the Armstrong residence?" Adelaide asked.

"Yes. Just for the winter though."

"I'm certain they're grateful to you for it. Left empty, the army would take it over to house more troops from England. The Armstrongs would then be charged with supplying everything from firewood and candles to vinegar, salt, and beer or cider. The soldiers would even use their bedding and kitchen utensils," Adelaide tsked.

New York had been the most resistant colony to the Quartering Act passed in 1765 and had refused to adhere to its terms. The colonies were responsible for raising taxes to cover the costs of housing the soldiers they sent, but New York had refused to do so. Barracks had been built in the city, but without enough room for all of them, many soldiers continued to be housed aboard ships. While the army was not allowed to enter the occupied homes of private citizens, they could commandeer any unoccupied buildings, sheds, barns, warehouses, inns, or other buildings.

With New York's refusal to follow the terms of the Act, Parliament had revoked all of their legislative functions including their Assembly. This, combined with the mere presence of the troops led to frequent street fights.

Ellie had been surprised to learn all of this. She had been familiar with some of the resistance to the Quartering Act before coming to the past but had no idea that it went that far in New York. She had learned some of this while with Dean, but since they had been so far away from the cities with little to no troops present, it had not been an issue for them. Since her arrival in the city, it had been a primary topic of conversation for people.

"Yes. The soldiers coming from England have been a difficulty for us all. And how do you know the Armstrongs?" Lucy asked. "Are you a relation?"

"I'm a friend of a friend. My husband's factor knows them and arranged for me to stay with them. It was my luck that I caught them before they left for the winter. Had I been any later, I would've missed them altogether."

Walter had sent her with a letter of introduction asking them to assist her in finding a place to stay until spring. They were preparing to visit family in South Carolina when she had arrived and had not only invited her to stay with them upon her arrival but had offered their home while they would be gone. Two of their servants were staying behind to care for the house and animals, but they preferred to not leave them alone all winter. Ellie was happy to take them up on their offer.

"Your husband?" Adelaide asked. "You're married then?"

It had once again become a habit to say 'husband' and would take a while to break herself of it. The reminder of Dean's death had a shadow passing across her face as she frowned. "Not anymore. He recently passed. That's why I'm here actually." Ellie tried perking herself up, if only a little. "I needed a fresh start and I'm just passing through on my way to Boston."

Both women murmured their condolences. Ellie redirected the conversation away from herself. "You mentioned this is not your first?" she asked Lucy while nodding to her belly.

 

Lucy smiled while rubbing her belly lovingly. "I have one already. If this one is anything like him, I shall certainly have my hands full."

"Oh, but Charles is such an angel," Adelaide said.

Ellie turned the question to her now. "What about you? Do you have any?"

"I have two," she said proudly. "When Mr. Emerson returns home, we may try for a third," she said with a salacious smile.

She giggled knowingly with Ellie while Lucy looked away, uncomfortable.

A small boy came bursting into the room then. "Mama, may I have a cookie?"

"Now Charles, you know you're not supposed to come in here when I've company," Lucy scolded the boy as she quickly put her teacup on the table beside her before he could bump her, spilling the contents.

He shyly turned away from his mother on whom he had laser-focused and looked around the room for the first time. Leaning against his mother, she introduced him. The boy had curly blonde hair, slightly darker than his mother's and cobalt blue eyes that put her in mind of someone else. He definitely did not get his eyes from Lucy, whose were big and russet brown. His sweet face was that of a cherub and Ellie wanted to pull him close and hold him while giving him all the cookies he could ever want.

"How old are you, Charles?" Ellie asked him.

The boy pushed himself further into his mother's side and held up three fingers. Ellie was impressed. She had not been sure if a kid his age would know that but thought she would take a chance.

"Three?" she gasped. "Why, you're practically a man! You'll be in breeches in no time."

The boy still wore the unisex gown of childhood but smiled and nodded emphatically, pulling away from his mother slightly.

"What's your favorite kind of cookie?"

"I like ginger snaps."

"I like that kind, too. Have you ever had oatmeal cookies?"

He shook his head shyly.

"Well, we'll have to see about that," Ellie said, thinking to make some the next time she visited for tea. She continued talking with him for a while until she noticed the room around her had gone quiet. When she looked up, she realized both women were staring at her curiously. Lucy sent the boy on his way.

Ellie smiled. "He's adorable."

"He's usually much better behaved. I must apologize for the interruption."

"Not at all," Ellie waved away Lucy's apology.

The women chatted for some time, getting to know one another. Ellie could see herself becoming fast friends with these two women. Adelaide and Lucy had grown up together, though Adelaide was a couple years older. She had married a ship captain who spent most of his time at sea and when Lucy married Adelaide's brother, a major in the British army, and moved to New York, Adelaide had followed.

Ellie spoke a little of Dean but tried to redirect the conversation whenever it fell onto her. After all this time in the past, it had become second nature to not answer questions about herself, despite Dajoji's advice to open up to people. It was far too easy to let something slip that she should not share with others.

The time passed quickly as they chatted and laughed like old friends.

"Oh, you simply must join us for Christmas. We're to have a ball," Lucy said after inviting Ellie to tea again.

Immediately taken back to the Christmas she spent in Williamsburg with Thomas, Ellie shoved the thought down deep and gave a noncommittal murmur, thanking her for the invite and telling her she would think on it. She thought it might be fun but also thought it might bring back too many memories she wished to keep tamped down. Besides, she would not be there long. Though she enjoyed the company of these women, she was not sure how close she wanted to get to them before leaving in a few months.

Adelaide regaled Ellie with a story about her brother from a previous ball they had held, which caused the women to burst into laughter. It was at that moment that they heard the door open and close as someone came in.

Lucy wiped her eyes as she regained her composure. "There he is now. Darling, come and meet our new neighbor."

"Yes, sweetheart," replied a masculine voice that immediately caused Ellie's pulse to quicken.

The man who walked into the room was more beautiful than she could have imagined. He cut a dashing figure in his British Army officer uniform. Ellie's eyes felt like saucers, and her mouth was suddenly dry while her heart raced, and her teacup trembled in her hand. She came back to herself enough to set the cup down on the table beside her before she dropped it, using the time to try and collect herself.

He stood in the doorway seemingly as stunned as she was.

Lucy was saying each of their names in introduction, but neither heard anything that was said. It did not matter. They did not need anyone else to tell them who the other was.

Ellie stood on shaky legs without even realizing what she was doing, and he was suddenly in front of her. He reached for her but stopped short, taking her hand in his instead. It took everything in him to not pull her into his arms, hold her tight, and never let her go. She felt as though there was no air in her lungs. His cobalt eyes never left hers, but his hand was shaking as much as hers when he brought it to his lips.

He searched her face as if trying to remind himself of all the details. For a moment, it was as if they were the only two people in the room. The astonished Thomas finally spoke in a whisper, breaking the silence. "I thought you dead."

Ellie opened her mouth to speak, but before anything could come out, Lucy spoke up looking back and forth between them. "You know one another?"

The tunnel vision suddenly cleared as Lucy's voice burst their bubble. Ellie had not taken her eyes off of Thomas since he walked into the room, and he had not taken his off of her. Understanding slowly dawned on Ellie that this woman was not Lucy *Byrd*; she was Lucy *Burke*, Thomas's wife. Thomas's *pregnant* wife. The street had been noisy when they met, and she had obviously misheard the name when Lucy had introduced herself. In her certainty that *Byrd* was Lucy's name, Ellie's brain must have caused her to hear it that way every time since.

Thomas's heart was pounding so hard, he could hardly hear anything over the sound. He was suddenly taken back to the side of that road near Halfway Brook and he wanted nothing more than to take Ellie in his arms and keep her there forever. The sound of his wife's voice reminded him of where he was and that he was behaving most improperly.

"We served in the war together," Ellie somehow managed to find her voice, though it was strained. "Well, Thomas served. I sort of just followed along as a nurse and helped where I could."

"Undoubtedly you're far too young to have been a nurse during the last war," Adelaide said while looking Ellie up and down.

"I'm older than I look," Ellie repeated without taking her eyes off Thomas.

Thomas could see Ellie was as surprised and confused as he felt, though he was not certain why she now downplayed their previous relationship. He told himself that she was merely trying to be tactful given the situation, though it was difficult to not be hurt by the distance that now lay between them. He closed his eyes, breaking the connection.

Shaking himself, he released Ellie's hand and turned towards his wife, taking a seat beside her. "Miss Ellie is simply being modest. She was the best nurse I've had the pleasure to work with, and I learned a great deal from her. I'm simply confounded to see her standing here. We were set upon by the French and their savages, and she–" Thomas paused, the emotion choking him, but also suddenly unsure of what had happened that day. She had died in his arms after getting shot in the chest with an arrow. At least, he had thought she had died. He was a physician; he should know when a person was dead. How was she standing there before him, alive? "I had thought her killed," he settled on.

The sound of Thomas's voice was like music to Ellie's ears, even though it sounded choked. She missed him more than she had realized. What were the odds of running into him there? The population was vastly smaller than in her time, but it had still seemed unlikely that she would ever see him again.

Becoming aware that she was still standing, Ellie promptly dropped back heavily into her chair. She had been quiet for too long and knew she was expected to say something in response.

She managed, "Well, as you can see, I wasn't one of the dead that day."

Her voice sounded foreign to her ears.

Adelaide was watching them with suspicion. "Things must be rather informal in the army to display such familiarity with one another."

Thomas attempted to stammer an acceptable response, but Ellie jumped to his rescue. "That's my fault. I'm afraid I'm not used to the formalities here. When I first arrived at the fort, I insisted on everyone calling me by my given name, and it sort of just carried over. It felt weird to be addressed as Mrs. Sorenson all the time by people I worked so closely with."

"Mrs. Sorenson?" asked Adelaide as she cocked her head with her suspicion growing even more. "I thought it was Mrs. Russell?"

Thomas's attention snapped to Ellie before she could respond. "Russell? You married again?"

The questions were already racing through his mind, but now there were so many more. He needed answers, but Thomas was not sure if he wanted them. Worse, he could not ask them with his wife sitting right there.

The pain in his eyes almost gutted her. Ellie had to look away as she replied, "I did."

It was all she could manage in response given their company. There was so much she wanted to tell him, but she did not dare open her mouth to say more. Picking her tea back up for the distraction, she tried to control the shaking in her hands. She was not interested in drinking it, but it gave her something to do with her nervous energy.

Lucy interjected, "Well, saints be praised you weren't killed or maimed by the savages. Such horrible business, war. I can scarce believe you were a part of it, Mrs. Russell. What a harrowing ordeal. You must be rather brave."

Unable to take her eyes off Thomas, she somehow managed to reply. "It wasn't all bad."

The carefree boyishness that had still clung to him during their time together was gone. His long, normally golden brown hair that waved when it was pulled out of the low ponytail he kept it in was darker now with the winter having set in. He was a full-grown man with a wife and a family. She was grateful to see him happy, as this was everything she had wanted for him. Yet, it did not stop a knot from forming in the pit of her stomach.

It had taken years to get over her feelings for Thomas. But seeing him now was bringing everything back up to the surface. Though she did not want to disrespect her hostess, Ellie had the sudden urge to flee. Overcome with emotion, she felt hot and lightheaded and wanted nothing more than to escape this room where Thomas sat beside his pregnant wife. The arrow that had once pierced her heart was nothing compared to the pain she felt there now.

Lucy was either oblivious to the tension between Ellie and Thomas, or she was incredibly good at ignoring it. "You must tell me of your time there and what you did."

"Next time, perhaps. It's getting late, and I've taken up enough of your time." She set her teacup down again and stood to leave, and the others followed suit.

"Are you quite certain?" Lucy asked. "We've only just begun getting to know you." There was a new level of curiosity in her voice. Perhaps the woman was more suspicious than Ellie gave her credit for.

"There will be plenty of time for that." With her feelings toward Lucy having suddenly become conflicted, Ellie had every intention of not allowing another meeting to happen but could not stop the expected response from pouring forth. "I'm just down the street."

She could not believe she managed to say anything to the woman with a smile when irrationally, she suddenly wanted nothing more than to claw her eyes out. Unfortunately, Lucy was all too likable. Ellie could already see what Thomas saw in her. Lucy was beautiful but kind. She was warm and welcoming and had not hesitated to invite Ellie into her home. She had even introduced her to Adelaide and invited her to their Christmas ball. As much as she wanted to hate her, she found she could not. She hoped this woman was everything she herself could not be for Thomas.

Turning to Lucy she said, "Thank you for having me. I enjoyed our visit." She turned to Adelaide and added, "It was lovely to meet you."

Every instinct in Thomas's body told him not to let Ellie leave. He was afraid that if he did, he would never see her again. Yet, how could he ask her to stay?

Ellie nodded to Thomas and gave him a small smile before heading for the door. Lucy stopped her with her next words. "Where are my manners? It's gotten late. You really shouldn't walk home alone. Darling, you should escort our guest and see her to her door safely."

Barely holding herself together, Ellie immediately responded. "Thank you, but that's not really necessary. I'm okay."

Lucy laughed. "Okay? What a peculiar word. Really, it's no bother."

Ellie had gotten better at using words common to the time period, but seeing Thomas had frazzled her brain and her formalities all slipped.

"I'm just at the end of the street. Honestly, I'll be fine."

Thomas was ready to walk Ellie home, but was also afraid that if he did, he may not come back. It took everything in him to let her leave by herself, but he knew it was for the best. Knowing she was not only alive, but there so close was too much for him at the moment. He needed time to regain control over his emotions. Relief and disappointment both flooded him when Ellie declined his escort, and again when Lucy finally acquiesced and bid her a good night.

Ellie fled from the home as if it was on fire. She barely made it inside her own temporary home and closed the door before leaning against it, sliding down to the floor, and sobbing. Thomas looked well and he had the family he had always wanted. Happiness was all she had ever wanted for him and she had moved on years ago. She was happy for him but seeing him had awakened something she had thought long dormant. Content to be on her own since Dean's death, she was now filled with loneliness and longing. How did this man always manage to awaken emotions in her that she had buried deep down for years?

## Chapter 4

# December 1768

Lucy and Adelaide wasted no time in questioning who Ellie Sorenson-Russell was. As soon as the door was closed behind her, they both turned on Thomas, riddled with questions.

"A nurse with whom you served during the last war?" Adelaide asked, her arms across her chest, eyes narrowed in suspicion. Had she been any other woman, he never would have let her question him the way she had. However, as his sister, he gave her some leeway.

"She was at Fort Edward during my time there."

"Who was she there with?"

Adelaide had not been home the winter he had brought Ellie to Williamsburg, having married earlier that year, but the rest of the family had met her and she had left quite an impression on them all. Thomas let out a sigh, knowing his answer would tell Adelaide everything. Yet, how could he lie?

"She was not there with anyone. She arrived with an injury sustained in a battle where she had saved a young soldier's life and came to stay on as a nurse."

On a gasp, Adelaide stepped back, her hand flying to her mouth. "She's the one."

"'The one' whom?" Lucy asked.

Fully expecting Adelaide to tell her best friend what was his business, he was surprised when she left it to him. Lucy looked between the two for a moment, waiting for an answer. It had been obvious by the greeting that there had been something between him and Ellie, but he found himself reluctant to share the extent of it, wanting to keep Ellie for himself rather than sharing this part of his life with his wife and sister.

When the silence stretched out too long, he reluctantly answered. Taking Lucy's hand in his, he turned on the settee to face her.

"Mrs. Sorenson was the woman for whom I mourned when we began our correspondence.

Yanking her hands from his, Lucy stood and turned away from Thomas. She looked to Adelaide for a moment but something passed between them. Patting Lucy on the shoulder, Adelaide walked toward the door.

"I shall be home should you have need of anything," she said as she left. It was not lost on him that she had said the words to Lucy, not to him. It was clear where her loyalties lay.

With Adelaide gone, Lucy and Thomas were alone. Her hand to her chest, she still faced away from him. Perhaps he should not have referred to their courtship as 'correspondence.' Yet, for him it had been. It had taken a rather long time to open up to Lucy. It had been no secret that he mourned a woman whom he had loved dearly, and a relationship with any woman who was not Ellie had been the last he had wanted at the time. A part of him had died and he had struggled to find his way back to the living. Lucy had helped him do so, but it had taken time.

"Well, clearly, she's not dead as you believed." Lucy's tone gave nothing away. He could not tell if she was angry, hurt, or even amused.

"It would appear so," he replied as she turned to face him.

"You've never spoken overly much of her."

"No." He would not do so now, either.

Lucy closed her eyes for a moment, then came to sit beside him once again. "I know not what happened between you, and I've no need to know. But, I do need to know how you feel now."

There was no easy answer to that. Thomas was filled with feelings that he would need to sort through, but this was not the time for it. Now, he would tell his wife what she needed to hear. It was his duty to do so.

"She was important to me once. However, it's been years and she has not been part of my life in all this time. I may have loved her once, but it was long ago and circumstances were not favorable for us. It did not matter then and it certainly has no bearing on you and I now. I've a wonderful life with you and Charles and can scarce wait for my next son to join us."

Putting his hand on her belly, Thomas tried to send her reassurance. They had often teased one another about the sex of the babies. She had always insisted that she would have a boy first to make Thomas happy, followed by a girl on whom she could dote. In return, Thomas had argued, saying he was having nothing but boys. Teasing her now was his way of showing her that nothing had changed by Ellie's sudden appearance. He was not entirely certain he believed it.

Lucy covered his big hand with hers as it rested on her swollen belly. The baby seemed to know they were directing their attention to it as it took that moment to kick, spreading smiles across each of their faces and easing some of the tension between them. It was a strained night between them, but that was nothing new. Ellie's presence was merely one more complication in their already strained marriage, yet had she not always been, even when she had not physically been there?

Riding past the house the next morning in which Ellie now lived, Thomas hesitated, slowing his horse. He was on his way back to the fort after attending business at the upper barracks. Making his presence known to his men and to the citizens of the city, he made a loop every day, going up Broadway and coming back down Queen Street. Sometimes he went the opposite direction or took side streets, but with Ellie's arrival, he had gone up the length of Queen Street, debating on whether or not to stop.

After Ellie's sudden resurrection and abrupt departure from his home, this quickly became a new daily occurrence for him. As the days went on, he continued to vary his route, but always made sure it took him past her house. He was afraid she would disappear again before he had a chance to speak with her and find out what had happened to her all those years ago. Yet, he could not bring himself to stop at her door. He always told himself stopping would not be fair to Lucy and it always managed to urge him forward again.

## Chapter 5

# *December 1768*

So far, Ellie had managed to successfully avoid all of the Burkes, though she wondered how long she would be able to continue doing so. It was a small city after all and they were only a handful of doors apart from one another. It had only been a couple of weeks since her tea and she had gone out of her way to not walk past their home, always taking longer routes in order to avoid it altogether. Ellie had been astonished to have received an invite to Lucy's Christmas ball after their tea. After the greeting her and Thomas had exchanged when he walked into the parlor, Ellie was certain the woman would have wanted Ellie as far away from her husband as she could get. Of course, in this time, extending the invitation may have only been the polite thing to do. Either way, Ellie did not want to go anywhere near either of them.

She had liked Lucy and did not want to give the woman any reason to feel threatened by her, seeing as how Ellie was not a threat at all. It had been ten years since she had last seen Thomas, and he had clearly moved on, as had she. She had told him she wanted him to be happy; to be with someone who could give him the life she could not. Seeing him with Lucy had been a kick in the gut, but she was glad that he had the life she could never give him. However, that did not mean she wanted to see it flaunted in front of her, reminding her how utterly alone she was in the world. She would only be there for a few more months and was confident she could easily avoid them both until she left.

Then the second invite to the ball and RSVP reminder arrived that morning. Ellie sighed when she saw it, thinking to simply ignore it, but now she knew she could not. She sent a reply back declining the invite and renewed her determination to make it through the winter and get to Boston as soon as it warmed up. The Armstrongs would be back in early April, and she would leave as soon as they arrived. Until then, she planned to keep to herself as much as she could. Any free time she had would be spent walking the city, weather permitting, or at the house reading, practicing her knitting, or tending her horses. Spring would come soon enough, and she would be in a new city, starting a new life once again. She had done that so many times, she could not even count what number this was. She sighed at the thought.

Ellie had always enjoyed her semi-nomadic lifestyle and the new adventures it brought. Though as much as she loved seeing new places and experiencing new things, it was difficult to leave everyone she knew behind all the time and continually start over. This time, she was completely on her own and she was finding it difficult. Burying it down deep as she always did with difficult emotions, she focused on the street she was walking down. There was a quiet spot by the water she enjoyed visiting to contemplate life, but she had to navigate her way through the various people working the docks in order to get there.

The tip of Manhattan where the rivers converged was reinforced with a retaining wall, keeping the land from sinking into the water. The top of the wall met with sand that extended up the shore towards another wall which surrounded the grounds of the fort and the lower barracks beyond. Large grassy areas covered the ground between the wall and the buildings. Ellie found herself there often, usually walking towards the East River from her house and going past the Fly Market then through the slums and docks towards the lower barracks to get there. It would have been a straighter path to walk along Queen Street, but going that way meant passing the Burke residence, which she did not want to do. Once she got to Whitehall, she would skirt the wall around the lower barracks and walk along the sandy stretch of beach.

That morning, Ellie made it nearly to the market on Dock Street near the lower barracks when she heard shouting. There was some sort of argument going on between the soldiers and the dock workers. In the short time she had been there, she had already seen that this was a regular occurrence. The colonials thought the soldiers were taking their jobs. Most of the soldiers had come over from England and in their time off, many got part time jobs working to load and unload ships or do whatever other tasks they were able. This did not sit well with the locals, who were already upset by the presence of the soldiers and the

Quartering Act. There was a lot of tension in the city that could be felt all the time. Ellie was a little surprised to learn that the tension had been going on this far back. She had always thought it more prevalent in the last couple of years before the Revolutionary War, but that was still more than six years away.

Walking through the streets of the city on her own often drew attention to Ellie. Sometimes it was from other colonists, often it was from soldiers. People stared, women whispered to one another, and the soldiers were often lewd, or what passed as lewd in this time period. With her long blonde hair, large breasts, thin build, and preference for dressing provocatively, she had always garnered attention in her own time and had gotten used to ignoring it long ago. This time, it was not her attire, but the fact that she walked the streets on her own. Women who walked the streets by themselves were generally considered fair game for the advances of men. Gentlewomen did not go anywhere unescorted, yet since she did not dress like a prostitute or someone from the lower classes, people did not know what to make of her. It did not stop their tongues from wagging.

After making her way through the arguing crowds, Ellie continued toward Whitehall. She did not make it far when she encountered a group of young men using obscene language and crude gestures as a couple of women passed ahead of her. They blocked the women's way forward, causing them to backtrack and pass by the group again while they shouted more obscenities. At least, Ellie guessed they were obscenities by the way the women reacted. She could not quite make out the words from where she was. For a moment, she considered avoiding the scene altogether, but it would mean going all the way around the fort to get to her destination. Deciding

she was not going to let these men bully and intimidate her, she squared her shoulders and walked on,
readying herself for the worst.

A couple of men tried blocking her path, but she
pushed through them. That was when the jeers
started.

"Damned fine, girl, by god," one man said while
leaning in close.

"Where do you lodge, my dear?" asked another.

Ellie stopped walking and looked at the men surrounding her, unable to stop the burst of laughter
that erupted from her lips. Prior to being a stripper,
she had grown up around sailors and marines in the
1980s and 1990s and had been catcalled plenty in her
own time. By comparison, these taunts were rather
juvenile and uninspired. The propositions she had received as a stripper alone would make these men
blush.

Once the laughter started, the men looked back
and forth at each other with confused glances. This
only served to make her laugh even more. It did not
take long before the tears were rolling down her
cheeks and she was doubled over with laughter. The
men did not know what to do with this and stepped
aside to let her pass. Once she regained her composure, she wiped her eyes and started forward. She
placed a hand on the shoulder of one of the men,
patted him a couple of times and continued walking.
Some of the other men in the group doffed their hats
to her and bowed as if in defeat.

It was too cold for Ellie to stay long by the water.
She stopped long enough to take in the air and look
across the harbor to the Brooklyn side. Without

dwelling on it, she walked the beach for a while then headed back, looking forward to the hot stew she knew Hannah Rale would have waiting when she got home. As she passed the men on her way back through, two of them caught her eye and nodded. She smiled and nodded back at them and continued on. She did not make it far before she was stopped by a couple of soldiers returning to the barracks.

"Aren't you a fine miss? What brings you out this way on such a cold day?" one of the men asked while looking her up and down.

"I was out for a walk, but I'm heading home now if you'll excuse me," she replied as politely but curtly as possible. Unlike the dock workers, these men gave off an air of menace.

The other soldier grabbed her arm forcefully. "Why don't you return home with us? We'll keep you real warm."

Ellie tried to jerk her arm free, but the man had an iron grip. "Let me go," she demanded. Ellie's head swam with visions of Elias Blackwell and her heart began to race. She knew she could take care of herself if she needed to but did not want to think about what it would take to do so. A trader on the frontier was one thing; a soldier in the Royal Army was another.

The soldiers laughed but did not release her arm. Before she could try anything else, two of the dock workers that had been in the group taunting her before came over. "Is there a problem here?" one of them asked.

"This is none of your business," the soldier holding her arm said with a snarl.

"I believe it is our business when you lobsterbacks treat one of our women so roughly. Can't you see the lady is not interested in your attentions?"

The soldier was about to reply when something behind Ellie caught his attention. She turned enough to see the rest of the dock workers approaching. They all looked like they were itching for a fight. With the growing tensions between the soldiers and the colonists, they probably were. Finally, he released her arm, pushing her in the process.

"I wouldna' want one of your whores anyway," the soldier spat.

He and his friend turned to leave, and Ellie let out the breath she did not realize she had been holding. She turned to the men who had come to her rescue.

"Are you alright, miss?" the taller of them asked.

Ellie nodded. "I am. Thank you for that."

The man nodded and turned to wave at the rest of the dock workers. They all dispersed, seemingly disappointed that there would not be a fight. The two men who had initially come to her aid remained.

"I'm John Bingham, dockmaster here. This is Dougal McFarrell," the taller man said. He was older with brown hair that was slightly graying. Dougal was probably only a few years behind him. He was slightly shorter with a stocky build. Both of them had forearms that were massive and faces that spoke of a lifetime spent in the sun, likely from their work on the docks. Both men gave off an air of authority.

"Ellie Russell," she replied.

"What brings you down this way, Miss Russell?" Dougal asked.

"I like the exercise and being by the water."

"There's a vast amount of water to choose from," John said. "'Twould be safer for you to walk further away from the barracks and the docks. Perhaps you might try north of the fort?"

"I'll consider it. Thank you again for your help."

The men nodded and headed back to their work while Ellie went on her way. She had no intentions of finding someplace else to visit. She had walked all of the available shoreline, and preferred being at the southernmost tip of Manhattan, looking out over the water towards Brooklyn. The view from that spot was the best she could find. North of the fort looked out over New Jersey, and she was not interested in that. She would continue going there, but would have to reconsider her route, going around the back side of the fort along the water instead of through the streets passing the barracks and dock workers.

## Chapter 6

# January 1769

Christmas came and went, and Ellie had spent it quietly in her temporary home with Hannah and Ezra Rale. The siblings had come over from Ireland and ended up working as indentured servants to the Armstrong family. Hannah was twenty and Ezra was two years younger. Ellie had tried convincing them to spend it at home with their family, but they had none in the colonies. Christmas was not something celebrated by most people in the colonies, anyway. Virginians, who went all out, were an exception to this. Though Ellie had spent the day thinking about her own family and wondering how they were spending the holiday, she treated it as any other day.

Ellie had not only managed to avoid the Burke's Christmas ball, but she had also declined every invite to tea that had come. Lucy had been insistent at first, inviting her every week. After her continued refusals, the invites became more spread out, but they still came. If Lucy wanted to spend time with her that badly, the woman obviously knew where she lived and could come to her. She never did, which told Ellie the invites were nothing more than the woman doing what was proper for her station. Having seen Lucy and Adelaide on the streets a few times, she had always managed to turn and go the other direction before they saw her.

As winter progressed, the darkness seeped in earlier and earlier. Ellie tried to make sure she was indoors when the sun went down. It was one thing to walk around the city in the daytime by herself, but she did not want to risk it at night. Occasionally, she lost track of time and hurried home as the sky began to darken, passing the lamplighters who lit the whale oil streetlamps every night. Some mornings, she was up early enough to see them putting out the torches that burned through the night.

Hannah Rale made Ellie breakfast every day, even though Ellie had insisted she could manage for herself. She had never had someone wait on her and it was an odd experience. The woman was the Armstrong's cook and housekeeper. She also cooked dinner every day, though Ellie had beat her to it on occasion and she slowly convinced Hannah to let her share some of the cooking duties if nothing else. She had grudgingly allowed it but had insisted on doing the cleanup. If letting Ellie assist with the cooking had been a challenge, it was nothing compared to convincing the woman to allow Ellie to eat with her and her brother at the table in the kitchen. The room was typically only where the servants and children ate.

Ezra Rale was a groomsman for the Armstrongs and maintained the animals and household water supply. Since the Armstrongs had traveled by ship, he had stayed behind to tend to the horses while

Hannah maintained the house and the chickens. Ellie was grateful to Ezra since he also tended her horses. He lived in the loft above the stables behind the main house while Hannah stayed inside the main house. Together, they left very little for Ellie to do around the home.

Hannah had not known what to do with Ellie and her strange ways. Ellie considered the meals a small victory, but it had been difficult enough to win Hannah over on them. She did not push too much beyond that. Hannah still maintained the house, which Ellie knew was her job and the reason she had stayed behind. But Ellie never could get used to her making Ellie's bed or emptying the chamber pot that Ellie had begun using. Unlike her home in Schoharie, they did not have an outhouse in the city. There was a waste pit, into which all of the food scraps and household waste not used for other purposes ended up, but it was nothing more than a deep hole in the ground. The chamber pots, however, were not like those at Schoharie or at the fort. They were enclosed inside a small cabinet underneath the seat of a chair, called a closed stool. Much like a toilet, the full seat lifted to reveal another underneath which had a hole in the middle, allowing the user to relieve themselves into the pot which was hidden from view inside the cabinet. It helped contain some of the smell, but only just. With the weather becoming increasingly colder, it was nice not having to go outside.

The one thing Ellie had been more than glad to not have to do herself was the laundry. Everything had to be washed by hand using buckets of water that had to be brought in from the barrels outside. If she wanted warm water, it had to be heated over the fire. After washing, it all needed to be ironed, which was a chore unto itself. Ellie was more than happy to leave this chore to Hannah, giving her more free time to walk around the city.

Ellie did not always go directly to the waterfront on her walks. Some days she walked around the larger streets for quite some time first, passing the various markets or wandering through the sparse parks. After roaming around for over an hour one cold January morning, she made her way towards the East River. Not far from Fort George, Ellie found herself ruminating on her impromptu journey there with Dean and Mehitabel Prendergast. It had been the longest, most grueling trip she had ever done. They had spent eighteen hours in the saddle to go the eighty miles from Poughkeepsie to the fort at the tip of Manhattan, then turned around and flew back immediately after Mehitabel had met with the governor. Ellie had not gone inside the fort with them, opting instead to go get food and provisions for the eighteen-hour return journey.

Pulling her cloak tighter against the cold wind coming off the water, Ellie heard a voice behind her that sent her breaking out in goosebumps all over that had nothing to do with the cold.

"Why do you continuously endeavor to walk around with no escort?"

Her stomach dropping out the bottom, Ellie fought to contain the emotions suddenly flooding her as she turned around. Thomas Burke stood only feet away in his uniform, looking around them. It had not occurred to her that he would be at the fort when she began walking past, but where else would he be?

She huffed out a breath of annoyance and disbelief. After all these years, he had not changed. While she took comfort in knowing he was the same person she once knew so well, it annoyed her as much now as it had then that he thought her incapable of doing anything on her own. She refused to acknowledge the question. It was not only because of her annoyance at his reason for asking it, but also because she did not want to admit that after all these years, she was still just as alone as she had been when they met.

"Good morning, Cap– Major Burke," she said, trying to keep her voice as neutral as possible while remembering his new rank at the last minute. For a moment, neither of them spoke as they stood in the street staring at each other.

Thomas had wanted nothing more than to follow Ellie home the day he first saw her. He walked or rode past that house nearly every day and fought to not go knock on the door, desperately wanting to know what had become of her after she had been pierced by the arrow. How had she survived? Where had she been all these years? Why had she come back now? Why had she never written and told him of her whereabouts? How had she come to be wed after telling him she was incapable of doing so? It took every ounce of willpower he had to continue past the house every day. The only thing preventing him from doing so was that he was afraid of what might happen if he did. He did not trust his too raw emotions to face off against Ellie inside her home. Would she be alone or would he meet her husband? He was not certain he could handle that.

"Where's your escort, Mrs. S–Russell?" he asked again. "You shan't be roaming the streets on your own."

He had seen her walking around before, and she always did so alone. Every time he saw her, he followed her at a discreet distance to make sure she was safe. It gave him some small comfort to know she had not disappeared again and that someone watched over her, even if it meant he was that someone. How could her new husband allow it? What kind of man was he to let her go about unescorted as she did? While he had considered approaching her every time he saw her, he had needed time to collect himself. He still felt raw whenever he saw her, but it did not seem to be improving. Perhaps finally facing her would help.

Instead of answering, she glared at him with her arms folded across her chest. Anger was better than the loneliness and heartache she felt when she looked at him. She shook her head and finally answered with a question of her own.

"Because I'm incapable of taking care of myself?"

"That was not my meaning," he sighed.

It was the same argument in which they had always engaged. His Ellie had always possessed a fierce independent streak and had never been afraid of doing things on her own. He had worried over her on many occasions and tried to remind himself now that she was not his to worry over anymore. It would not stop him from watching over her.

Thomas shook his head and took a fortifying breath. There were questions to which he needed answers. He knew he would not get them if she felt he was questioning her ability to take care of herself.

"The last I saw of you, your chest had been pierced by an arrow during a raid," he said slowly, trying to tamp down the emotions the memory evoked. "I was rendered unconscious, and when I regained my wits, I was back at Fort Edward. I thought you had died."

Thomas paused and Ellie waited for him to continue. She knew he had questions, but she did not have answers and was not about to volunteer anything without him explicitly asking. When she did not respond, he continued.

"I was informed that the wagons were set alight and when they finally got the fires out, they found nothing left but charred remains. They would not let me see any of them." He swallowed hard and quietly added, "I thought you amongst them."

Ellie softened at the tortured expression she saw in his eyes. "Didn't Anwar tell you?"

"He told me you were amongst those burned with the wagons."

"That lying jackass!" she seethed. "Of course he did." Ellie was fuming at Gideon Anwar for not telling Thomas the truth. Why would his surgeon's mate tell him she was dead?

"Mr. Anwar likely knew that had I believed you to still be alive, nothing would have stopped me from coming after you." Thomas answered as if reading her thoughts. He was making excuses, but she could hear the edge of anger in his voice at having been lied to.

Ellie's stomach tightened at his declaration. "Well, I did survive. But perhaps he was right not to tell you. I went with the Onöndowa'ga:' that were there."

"The Onöndowa'ga:'? I understand not. Is that not the Seneca? Yet, was it not the Abenaki who shot you with the arrow? Why would they take you captive if you were near dead?"

"They are the Seneca. The arrow was from the Abenaki, but it was the Onöndowa'ga:'–the Seneca–with whom I went. I wasn't captive, though. I asked them to take me with them."

"How did you do that? You were near dead and unconscious when I last saw you." He paused briefly, then added, "*Why* would you do that?"

Ellie shrugged, trying to avoid answering the questions. She let him think that she had only been *near* dead and unconscious. In truth, she actually had died. It was her strange new regenerative abilities that had brought her back to life, but he had been unconscious when she had come back fully healed.

When she did not respond, Thomas answered one of his own questions.

"Because you had no reason to stay at the fort," he said quietly as realization dawned on him.

It was not a question.

"Not at all." Ellie let out a heavy breath. "Okay, I'll admit leaving the fort was an added bonus at the time. But no, that's not why."

When Ellie did not add more, Thomas asked, "Then why?"

She could have kicked herself for adding that last bit. Ellie really did not want to fill in the gaps of his memory of that day or explain herself to him. He thought she had turned down his proposal because she had not loved him. If he knew how much she had sacrificed for him that day, he would see how much she had loved him. But it made no difference now. They had both moved on from it and she wanted to leave it all in the past.

"It was for the best," she said vaguely.

"That's not an answer," he scolded with a tight set to his jaw. He was standing with his arms across his chest now and Ellie knew he was getting even more annoyed with her. That was fine. She was plenty annoyed with him, too.

"One group of savages tried to kill you, yet you asked another to take you with them? Were you that desperate to get away from me?"

"It wasn't about that, Thomas," she said while looking down the street in an attempt to avoid his accusatory stare.

"Then what was it about? I'm trying to understand here, Ellie. The red man isn't exactly known for keeping captives alive. You had to know they would eventually kill you."

"It crossed my mind," she admitted as she continued looking away.

"Yet you went anyway?"

She did not answer.

"You may have been unhappy, but I would not have thought you wished to die."

"I didn't."

"Then what am I missing?" His voice was starting to rise with every question. Ellie could feel her own emotions bubbling under the surface. Why could he not let it go?

"It doesn't matter. It's in the past and we can't change it. I'll be gone again soon enough. Why don't we just move on and forget it?"

"I can't forget it," he shouted. "I watched you die. Or I thought I had. I knew not what had become of you. I mourned you, Ellie. I tried to move on. Knowing you were dead and that I was to blame was one of the hardest things I've ever had to endure. At least, it was until I discovered you were still alive. Now you tell me that you chose to run away with them after telling me you loved me; that you let me think you dead all this time? That has to be one of the cruelest things a person can do to another."

Ellie did not want to respond at all. She could feel his pain as if it was a living thing. Nothing she could say would change how he felt, even if he was wrong about it being cruel. Under the circumstances, it had been the least cruel option. "I can see where you'd think that."

Thomas closed his eyes, trying to rein in his temper. Was she really trying to justify her actions? His Ellie had been one of the most caring people he had ever known. Perhaps he had not known her at all.

"You disagree?" he scoffed.

"It doesn't matter what I think."

"Do tell; There's nothing for which I'd care more than to know." He said it sarcastically but meant it all the same. "What could you possibly think to be worse?"

"Forget it." Ellie shook her head and tried walking away. Her eyes were burning and if she stayed much longer, she feared she would start crying again. It was the last thing she wanted. "It doesn't matter."

Shouting again, Thomas grabbed her arm and spun her around before she could get away. "It does matter. What are you not telling me? What could possibly have been worse?"

"Letting you die!" she shouted back. "That would have been worse!"

Closing her eyes for a minute in an attempt to regain control of her temper much as he had done only moments before, she lowered her voice before adding on a growl, "They were trying to take you."

Thomas released his hold on Ellie's arm as if burned, unsure how to respond to her confession. He was saved from having to do so by two men approaching.

Ellie looked over her shoulder at the sound of footsteps behind her. John Bingham and Dougal McFarrell came close, having been drawn by their shouting. She looked past them to see the other dock workers all watching closely.

"Are you well, Miss Russell? Are you in need of an escort?" Dougal asked while glaring at Thomas. If she had not been so upset, she would have laughed at the situation. She was grateful to these men for looking out for her but did not want to cause any problems for either them or Thomas.

Ellie put a hand on Dougal's arm and nodded at him. "I'm alright, Mr. McFarrell. Thank you for looking out for me."

The men glared at each other, but Dougal and John made no move to leave. Ellie knew they would stay until they knew she was safe.

"Major Burke is an old friend of mine. We were just having a discussion."

"A discussion?" John asked without moving his gaze from Thomas. "That's not what it sounded *or looked* like from over there." He emphasized the word looked, making sure Thomas knew they had seen him grab Ellie's arm.

Ellie tried to hide her smirk. "I know. I'm sorry if we disturbed you. I promise I'm perfectly safe with Major Burke."

The men looked unconvinced and continued to glare at Thomas for a few more minutes. Their animosity had more to do with the uniform he wore than anything else. Finally, John said, "If you have need of us, we'll be just there." He pointed back toward the water and Ellie nodded.

"Thank you. I appreciate it," she said.

———

Thomas and Ellie watched the men walk away, giving each of them a moment for their tempers to calm down. John and Dougal looked back periodically on their way back to the dock.

"I see you're settling into the city well," Thomas said flatly.

Ellie shrugged. "They're good guys."

Thomas nodded, glad to see she had men looking out for her, even if he was on the outside of it. His mind returned to their conversation before the interruption.

"The savages were trying to take me?" he asked quietly. "I don't recall that." His brow furrowed as he tried to remember.

"That's because you were unconscious. I don't know what happened to you, but they were trying to rouse you."

Ellie kept her answers simple and vague, not wanting to go into details. She had not meant to tell him any of this, but his pushing her had caused it to slip out. Despite having the time out provided by the interruption, his persistence had made her angry and she was not yet ready to fully calm down.

"A Frenchman hit me in the head, rendering me unconscious, but I understand not. How did that become them carrying you off?"

They stood on the street staring at each other for a moment before Ellie finally gave in. Reluctantly, she huffed. "I regained consciousness when they tried to take you. I thought if they took you, they would eventually kill you when you were no longer needed. They needed a medic, so I convinced them to leave you and take me instead. Anwar helped me convince them."

"You went voluntarily, knowing they did not keep their captives alive?" Thomas repeated, not believing what she was saying. His voice had increased in volume again as he fought to keep from yelling at her foolishness.

"Better me than you," she said quietly.

This gave Thomas pause. He turned away momentarily, running his hand over his jaw before taking a deep breath and exhaling slowly. When he turned back to her, he watched her for a moment as she played with her necklace in a gesture so familiar, it made his heart squeeze. He had once thought it a tell that she was being dishonest, but he knew now that it was a sign that she was nervous or uncomfortable.

Thomas was filled with conflicting emotions and did not know what to do with her confession that she had sacrificed herself for him. He had been elated to see her, to know she was alive. She had been his first love and would always have a piece of his heart. Ellie was the one person with whom he could always be himself. He had never felt judged by her, and she had made him a better person. Instead of belittling him about mistakes he made or things of which he knew nothing, she had helped him, and she had taught him. If she did not know something, she was eager to learn it, much as he always had been. They shared a love of learning and had always had an easy companionship. He always thought she was his perfect complement.

The elation he had felt upon seeing her quickly turned to bitterness as the cold truth slammed into him.

She had not wanted him, and now they were each married to other people and could not be together. He never loved Lucy as he had Ellie, but he did love his wife. They had their difficulties, but he would never do anything to hurt her. Not to mention, Ellie's rejection of his proposal still stung even after all these years. Knowing she had gotten remarried to someone else after refusing him fueled the pain he felt over it. It was not only that she had remarried, but that she had done so after telling him she was unable to. He let the anger build up in him again. Could he even believe what she was saying now?

"Why are you here now? Why did you not escape and come back when they took you?"

Thomas was not sure he wanted the answer, but he had to ask. He needed to hear her say that he was the reason she did not come back. Hearing her say that she had taken his place in what she had thought to be a path that only led to death had shaken him deeply. The last thing she had told him that day was that she had loved him. If her story was true, then her actions certainly spoke to that. But he did not want to believe any of it. Believing she had simply chosen to run off to get away from him was easier. He had never been able to let go of her and now that she was there, he could not release the hold she still had on him. Maybe hearing her say that she had not wanted to come back to him would help him finally move on from his feelings for her.

Ellie shook her head. "I gave them my word that I would stay as long as they needed me. I ended up staying a long time. Ultimately, it didn't matter. I had no idea how to find you once the war ended."

This was not what he was expecting to hear. He immediately started filling in the blanks as best as he could. When she had finally escaped her captivity, she wanted to find him. When she could not find him, she married another. Another with whom he would likely have to be sociable now that they lived so close. Yet, he did not want to meet this man who held Ellie's heart. Despite having his own wife, he did not think he could bear to see Ellie in love with someone else. The thought added to his pain, once again turning it to anger. Why was everything with this woman so difficult? Why did it always end up with him in pieces?

"Well, you seem to have found me now," he said with more bitterness than he intended.

Ellie's lips thinned as she pressed them together at his tone. "It would seem so." She looked away, briefly gathering herself, then forced herself to say, "Thomas, I'm really happy for you. I knew you would find someone who could give you everything you want. Lucy seems wonderful. She's so beautiful and she's warm and welcoming and I'm sure she's a great mother."

The words were painful to say, but she meant them regardless.

This did little to assuage the pain he was feeling. *She was happy for him?* Apparently, he really had not meant anything to her after all. He always thought Ellie would have made a great mother, but it had not been what she wanted. Not with him, at least. Did she have children with this new husband of hers? He felt as though he was going mad.

"And what of you, Mrs. Russell? Does your husband give you everything you want? Are you the mother of his children? Does he make you happy?"

He could not keep the venom out of his words, and as much as Ellie tried, she could not overlook it this time. His anger made her not want to share anything with him. She may not have been in love with her latest husband, but she had loved him. Their life together had been filled with adventure and companionship, but also heartache. He had done more for her than she could have ever asked, saving her from both Elias Blackwell and the British. Telling Thomas anything about Dean now while he was this angry somehow felt like a betrayal to Dean's memory.

Instead, she decided it best to leave and said, "Good day, Major Burke. It was good to see you again."

She turned to start walking away again, but Thomas would not be brushed off so easily. He needed somewhere for his anger to go. Grabbing her arm as she began walking away, he spun her back to face him yet again.

"Answer me, Ellie. You told me you weren't in a place to be wed. 'Not here, not now,' you said. Then you went and married as soon as you were away from me. I have to infer that your words meant you only wished to not be wed to me."

The pain in his eyes was hard to see. He was trying to hide it behind anger, and he was lashing out at her, but she refused to feed it. There was nothing she would be able to say to ease that pain.

When she remained silent, he continued, "Tell me how happy you are with him. Tell me how much better he is for you than I would have been. Tell me how perfect your life is without me in it, with him by your side."

Ellie's heart was breaking all over again. She hated seeing Thomas so tortured. But in his anger, she knew there was nothing she could say that would make it any better. Instead, his angry words were like salt being rubbed into the wound of what had happened with Dean.

"It wasn't like that, Thomas."

"Then why, Ellie? Why was I not good enough, but he was?"

"I never said you weren't good enough. If anything, I was the one who wasn't good enough," she yelled.

Her own anger was starting to flare up again now. Why could he not just let her walk away?

The last thing she wanted was for him to see how utterly alone she was. His presence was a constant reminder of everything she once had and lost, everything that always seemed just out of reach for her. She missed being able to touch Thomas or confide in him or see him look at her as though she were everything. Those things all belonged to Lucy now. Ellie had to settle for being alone. She had spent so long being miserable in her first marriage. She had been lonely and never thought she would ever love anyone again. Thomas had changed that. But because she had loved him, she knew that he would be better off without her. It had broken her heart to leave him. It had taken everything within her to turn down his proposal, but had she accepted it, he would have only come to resent her. It was better this way but the years that followed were lonely without him. More than a lover, he had been her friend when she had none.

During her time with the Onöndowa'ga:', then later, when Dean came along, she had felt a little less lonely. They had been her family and Dean had been a good friend to her as well, even if the friendship was nothing like what she had shared with Thomas. But then she had been pulled from her family and Dean had been killed, leaving her alone yet again. She was beginning to think she was destined to walk the earth all on her own forever. She did not know how she had ended up there, in that time, or how she managed to keep healing. Everything from the smallest scratch to fatal stab wounds had healed more quickly than they ever should have. Could she even die? Was she already dead? Was this the afterlife and her punishment was an eternity of loneliness? Nothing but loneliness for her while having to watch the man she once loved love another woman? She could feel the tears pricking her eyes again, and she did not want Thomas to see them. She tried walking away again.

"Ellie don't walk away. Speak with me."

"Leave it alone, Thomas."

"That's what you used to always say to me when I asked about your past. Is that why you married him? Was he a part of your past? Did he come from the same place? Perhaps I should meet him. He must be something special. I'd like to meet the man who has your heart."

"That's not possible," she said shaking her head.

It was all she could do to not tell him he merely needed to look in the mirror to meet the man with that designation. She may have moved on, but he would always own a piece of her.

Before she could say more, he interrupted, "Why not? Do you prefer to keep our past hidden? Are you ashamed of me?"

"Never," she protested.

"Perhaps you're ashamed of him then? Is he away a lot? Does he leave you and the children alone whilst he runs off elsewhere? Does he drink himself into a stupor every night or spend his nights in another woman's bed? Do you even know where he goes, or does he simply scamper off, leaving you ill with worry?"

"Thomas, stop." She was trying to give him the benefit of the doubt, knowing his own emotions were driving him, but she would only excuse so much.

"Here I was under the impression he was magnificent if you deigned to marry him. Perhaps I was wrong. Maybe he is nothing more than a witless toss-pot who treats you poorly and you're ashamed of him. Is that why you don't wish me to meet him, Miss Ellie?"

"You can't meet him because he's dead," she shouted.

This stopped Thomas in his tirade. Dead? That meant she had now been widowed twice. He could not imagine something as awful as that.

"Ellie, I'm so sorry," he said softly. "I knew not."

"No, you didn't," she fumed. "Because you didn't ask. You just assumed you knew everything. But you know what, Thomas? You don't know shit!"

Ellie's anger was overpowering the sorrow she had felt only moments before. She took advantage of his stunned silence and stormed away, leaving him standing alone in the street, too confused, enraged, and heartbroken to follow.

## Chapter 7

## *Early February 1769*

January passed in a slow haze of melancholy. Ellie had been more diligent about avoiding the Burkes after her encounter with Thomas near the fort the previous month. She took measures not only to avoid the street near his home, but also to avoid the streets surrounding the fort. Not that she was able to get out much with winter in full force.

More eager than ever to get to Boston and start her new life, she had no idea what was in store for her but could not wait to find out. Staying in New York for only a few months had seemed like a good idea but now felt like being in limbo. Though even the prospect of finally being in Boston was only somewhat placating. Excited to see history being made, there was nothing there for her personally. She still had no idea if she would ever make it home, though she had long since given up hope of it happening. After her encounter with the lightning outside her village, she no longer knew what to think about how she had ended up there or how to get back home. What did that leave for her? Every time she started a new life there in the eighteenth century, it was snatched away from her. Part of her felt it was pointless to continue trying. She began thinking of herself as a qualitative research analyst, observing life without participating in it. Perhaps her outlook would change with warmer weather and a new location.

Unfortunately, warmer weather was still quite a ways off. February came in cold and snowy, making it difficult for Ellie to get out. Even when she did, there was not much for her to do. She had done a little shopping, purchasing her new dresses, but she did not want to have to transport a lot of things when she left in the spring and had kept her spending light. She resumed practicing her yoga every morning and her tai chi every night after not having done any since her time at the Onöndowa'ga:' village. With Hannah's help, she filled the copper tub every other evening for a soak. She tried to not let the girl wait on her, but she continued to insist on helping Ellie, as did her brother. Ellie compromised by not letting them do everything. Ezra even helped haul the pails of water inside. She had offered to return the favor, but they both wrinkled their noses at her, declining the offer.

Ellie sat by the fire reading a new book she pulled from the shelf in the study, grateful the Armstrongs had a well-stocked collection from which she could choose. After re-reading the same paragraph for the third time, she realized how distracted she was by the howling wind outside and went to sit by the window in the parlor. She wrapped her shawl around herself tighter as the cold seeped in around the window frame. With the latest snowfall, the wind picked up and it was downright blustery outside now. She could not even see the street from where she sat. There was little movement outside as it was far too severe to be out in it.

"Is you needin' more tea miss?" Hannah asked as she came into the room.

"I'm well enough, thank you," Ellie replied, turning her head back out the window.

The girl turned to walk away, but Ellie stopped her. "Why don't you come sit a while. Surely, there can't possibly still be more chores requiring your attention?" It was only the three of them inside the house after all, though she had no idea where Ezra was or what he was up to.

"I'm thanking ya miss, but I couldn't do that."

"Do you read?" Ellie asked. She had tried to connect with Hannah, but the girl had always maintained a distance between them.

"Only what I need to, miss."

Ellie understood that to mean she read the bible and possibly enough to help run the household. Literacy rates had increased slightly since her arrival in the past, but most still had only enough to scrape by.

While Ellie tried getting the girl to relax or open up, there was an insistent knock at the door. It had to be a delivery of some sort, but Ellie was surprised that anyone would be out in that weather for something as trivial as a delivery. Hannah went to the door and the wind opened it wide. Ellie heard the voices from the parlor. Though she could not make out the words, she could hear the urgency in them and stood to go see what the problem was.

Jenny stood inside Ellie's door, bundled in a cloak, a hood over her head. Fat snowflakes covered her and were beginning to melt onto the hallway floor. Surely Lucy had not sent the girl out in this weather for another invite to tea?

Jenny's attention immediately pulled to Ellie when she walked into the hallway and Jenny begged her, "Please, miss, you must be coming quickly."

Ellie's brow furrowed, but she hesitated. "What is it? What's wrong?"

The impatience was apparent as the girl bounced, wondering how she would convince Ellie to follow her. Jenny had been serving tea the day Ellie had been at the house and had likely figured out what had happened. She seemed uncertain and doubtful now.

"'Tis Mrs. Burke, miss. She needs you," she explained urgently.

Ellie could not help but fold her arms across her chest as she dug in. She still had not heard any valid reason as to why she should leave her warm house in this weather, let alone to go see the wife of the man she had once loved so dearly.

"What exactly does she need me for?"

"The time of her travail is upon us and the midwife is not to be reached in this storm. Mrs. Emerson herself is too far away. 'Tis only Mrs. Toole and myself and I've not had any experience with birthing. Please, miss. We can't do this on our own. Major Burke said you'd come."

Ellie saw the pleading and the fear in the girl's eyes and swore under her breath. Her arms fell loose to their sides and Ellie ran up the stairs to gather a few things. Back in minutes, she found herself holding onto Jenny's cloak in order to stay together once they were outside. They were assaulted by the wind and the blowing snow while the cold cut right to their lungs, stealing their breaths. The wind pushed against them, sending the snow into their field of view. Ellie could not tell if the snow was falling from the sky or being kicked up from the ground by the wind. The women battled the blizzard and what should have been a two-minute walk felt as though it had taken an hour.

They finally reached the home and stopped inside the door, catching their breath. Ellie stomped the snow from her boots, opening her cloak. Shaking the wetness from her braided blonde hair, she looked up to see Thomas coming down the stairs holding his three-year-old son. Charles was crying and Thomas was doing his best to comfort him.

Ellie's hand reflexively went to her necklace, and she played with it as she tried to calm her nerves. Every time she saw this man, the butterflies started playing soccer inside her stomach. She told herself it was because every encounter they had since arriving back at Fort Edward that last winter had ended in them fighting. Every encounter except the one in which she had died, anyway. Her body was responding to the stress of impending doom.

"Thank you for coming. She's upstairs," Thomas said.

Ellie nodded and started making her way toward him and the stairs.

"Mommy," Charles cried with an outstretched hand towards the second floor. Thomas bounced him while rubbing his back.

Stopping on the step above them, she turned back to see him. She took his little hand in hers and said, "It's alright, sweetie. I'm going to go take care of your mommy."

Thomas nodded while giving her a pleading look that nearly split her in two.

Ellie followed Jenny upstairs and got to work immediately, pulling things out of her medical bag. She removed the linen bags filled with sand that she frequently used as hot or cold compresses, a pair of scissors, a few other medical tools, and some laces, handing them to Jenny.

"I need you to take these and place the bags outside. You can leave them close by the door where we can easily retrieve them later. Put the tools and the laces into a pot of water and set it to boil. On your way back, I need you to grab a large bowl, a pitcher of very warm water and a basin, soap, and several clean sheets."

Jenny hurried away to do as she was told. Ellie went to Lucy who moaned on the bed. With a clean handkerchief, Ellie wiped the sweat away from the woman's brow. "Mrs. Burke, I need to check and see how dilated you are, alright?"

"Please," Lucy begged, "don't let childbed fever take me or my baby." She clutched at Ellie with her brown eyes big and pleading.

Ellie took her hands in hers. "I promise I'll do what I can to keep you both safe and healthy."

Lucy nodded, but Ellie could still see the fear in her eyes. She assured Lucy that her sweating was natural and not the result of a fever. It seemed to help allay some of her fears, if only a little. She again informed Lucy of her intent to examine her.

The woman nodded her consent and Ellie moved to her feet, lifting her skirt. She asked Lucy questions while examining her cervix and her stomach, ascertaining how far along she was while she worked. The baby seemed to be in the proper position, and everything looked as it should, though just as with every time she did this, she wished she had an ultrasound and all of the equipment and expertise found in a real hospital.

Ellie had mixed feelings about performing deliveries. When everything went well, it was an incredible high to bring a baby into the world. But there were far too many things that could go wrong, and it filled her with anxiety every time. She had only lost one patient since delivering babies in the eighteenth century, but one was too many for her. The baby had died, and she had barely managed to save the mother. It was almost expected in this time period, but Ellie would never accept it. Knowing this was Thomas's wife and child added even more pressure, causing her anxiety to soar to new heights. She wished she could have said no, but with no one else available, she had no choice.

"You're only dilated to about five centimeters. From how far apart your contractions are, I'd say we still have a few minutes."

Mrs. Toole helped Ellie spread a cloth on the floor of the bedchamber. The woman had been tending the fire and making sure the temperature of the room was comfortable. Jenny came back then and took over while Mrs. Toole went back downstairs to fetch some broth for Lucy.

Under normal circumstances, women giving birth would be surrounded by their closest female friends and family. With the storm, all Lucy had were her servants and Ellie. If she were being honest, Ellie much preferred that. She hated having the room full of extra people all trying to help only to end up being in the way.

"Why are we spreading this on the floor, miss?" Jenny asked as they worked.

"It's to catch some of the body fluids and keep them relatively contained. This way they won't seep into everything," Ellie explained.

"Should it not be on the bed, then?"

"If Mrs. Burke was going to deliver on the bed, then yes, but we aren't going to have her do it that way."

Lucy gave her a confused look as they spread the edges, making sure all of the furniture nearby was out of the way and they had room to work. The cloth they spread had been waterproofed using a recipe Ellie had found years before. It had been brushed with a mixture of tallow, hog's lard, turpentine, beeswax, and olive oil. Ellie always kept it in her birthing kit and washed it thoroughly, then reapplied the mixture as needed after each birth, replacing it when it became too worn.

Going over to the bed, Ellie had Jenny stand on the other side. Mrs. Toole came back and had her drink some broth while the women helped her sit up enough to do so. Ellie gave her some ragwort tincture to speed up delivery and hasten dilation of the cervix. Lucy had been in labor for a few hours now and Ellie did not want to draw it out any longer than necessary.

While she drank her broth, Ellie and Jenny helped Lucy remove the outer robe she had on, leaving her in only her shift. They helped her to stand, and Ellie supported her while walking around the room, trying to keep things moving along. There was little to do now but wait. The women all chatted while they waited, talking amiably. Ellie continued to give Lucy the tincture of ragwort every five to ten minutes while they walked slowly around the room. Mrs. Toole periodically went to update Thomas and check on the broth and other items over the fire downstairs.

"Will you be needing your things from the boil miss?" she asked before departing.

Ellie looked up from where she was watching Lucy place one foot in front of the other. "Not until after the baby arrives. Thank you, Mrs. Toole."

"I'm so hot," Lucy complained. "Are you certain I don't have the fever?"

Using the back of her hand, Ellie felt her forehead. "It's a little warm in here, that's all. Jenny, would you mind cracking the window open just a little?"

In a panic, Lucy told Jenny not to do so. Confused, Ellie asked what was wrong.

"The cold air will enter my womb and cause the childbed fever," she said, obviously irritated at having to explain something so simple to someone who was supposed to be a midwife.

Ellie shook her head. "That's not what causes the fever. It's fine. I promise. Go ahead, Jenny."

As a reluctant Jenny rose to do so, Ellie slowly guided Lucy over towards the open window. Though there was still concern in her eyes, Ellie could see the relief on her face instantly as the cold air hit her. The wind was still howling fiercely, and Jenny had to hold the window to make sure it did not fly open and break. After a few minutes, they resumed their walk around the room, Lucy groaning in discomfort.

As they walked, Lucy shared her fears of child-bed fever. Her regular midwife had been afraid of it as were most women of the time. Lucy had a friend who had died from it a few years prior and had been terrified of it when she had given birth to Charles, as she was now.

"You're truly not worried about it? Perhaps I might feel more at ease if you were concerned. It happens all too frequently."

"I'm aware of how real it is and I understand your fears. However, childbed fever is also called puerperal fever and it's caused by infection, not by cold air. It can be prevented with proper management of the birthing environment. I'm always concerned, but I'm also confident that we've done everything we can to sterilize the environment as much as possible."

"Sterilize?" Lucy asked, looking down into Ellie's eyes. The woman was easily several inches taller than Ellie, but at five feet two inches, that was not uncommon for Ellie.

"Everything needs to be as clean as possible. That's why I have Jenny boiling my medical tools. The only other tools I plan on using are my hands." She had also sent a scalpel and a few other items down with Jenny just in case, but she hoped she would not need them.

"And boiling them helps to… sterilize… them?"

"It does," Ellie smiled at her reassuringly. "Since I can't boil my hands, I'll wash them thoroughly with soap and water when it's time for the baby to come." She wanted to explain as much as she could in an attempt to help comfort Lucy. Uncertainty always increased anxiety, so she hoped giving the woman a little knowledge would help put her at ease.

"How does this sterilize prevent the fever?"

Ellie gently corrected Lucy's use of the word, then began to give the woman an abbreviated version of germ theory. "There are organisms that are too small to see with the naked eye, but if we had a microscope, you could see them. These organisms are called germs, and they cause and transmit diseases. Boiling objects, washing with soap and water, and cleaning with alcohol kills them and prevents them from spreading."

"Major Burke told me something of germs." A slow smile spread across her face. "He's meticulous about washing, even immersing himself in water regularly. I've never met anyone who bathes more than he."

She giggled, which caused Ellie to giggle as well, though warmth spread through her chest at the confession, knowing that she was the reason he did so.

Lucy's giggles turned to gasps as she bent over clutching her stomach. Her contractions were beginning to come faster now, and Ellie knew it was almost time. She had Mrs. Toole come over and support Lucy while she went over to the pitcher and basin she had Jenny bring up. Jenny poured the water over her hands above the basin and Ellie scrubbed them thoroughly. When she finished, she had Jenny pour water over them to rinse the soap off. She was just in time as Lucy began to bear down, crying out in pain. With Ellie's instructions, Jenny and Mrs. Toole quickly guided Lucy over to the drop cloth on the floor where Ellie gave her the option to either squat or kneel.

"Whichever is more comfortable for you," she said.

The three women looked back at Ellie doubtfully. "Neither is comfortable. Mrs. Toole, won't you help me over to the bed?" she said between screeches.

Ellie shook her head. "I know it's unconventional, but it does make it easier. This allows gravity to assist, so you have to work that much less."

Lucy looked at her between contractions as she made up her mind. When the pain subsided, she turned to Mrs. Toole and nodded. The women helped her kneel down.

With Lucy in place and Mrs. Toole on one side of her, Ellie sent Jenny downstairs to fetch her tools from the fire. Ellie knelt behind Lucy, lifting her shift up and resting it on her back. "You're fully dilated. The baby's crowning," she said excitedly. Another contraction washed over Lucy, and she cried out in pain.

"Push," Ellie instructed her.

It did not take long for the head to emerge. Ellie felt around, checking to make sure the umbilical cord was not around the baby's neck. With another contraction coming on, Ellie encouraged Lucy to push once again. Within minutes, the remainder of the baby had been delivered. Ellie had Lucy lean back against Mrs. Toole while she checked the airway. As soon as the baby began crying, she handed her off to Lucy.

"Congratulations, mom. It's a girl."

Lucy's face split into a smile and tears rolled down her cheeks as she gazed at her daughter. Jenny was back now and along with Ellie and Mrs. Toole, the women all wore smiles as big as the sky. Ellie continued working, pulling her laces from the now empty pot and tying off the umbilical cord. She cut the cord, tying off the end still attached to the baby and placing the other end into the empty bowl.

With the baby on Lucy's chest, Jenny draped a blanket over them. Ellie encouraged her to try to feed the baby right away while she prepared to deliver the afterbirth.

"But my milk has not yet come in. The liquid there now is not good for her," she protested.

Ellie shook her head. "That's colostrum and it's fine. It won't harm her at all. If anything, it might help keep infection away. It helps boost the baby's immune system."

"Her what?"

"It'll help keep her healthy," she said, too tired to explain further.

Lucy acquiesced and tried feeding the baby.

With another gush of blood from Lucy a few minutes later, she handed the baby back to Jenny and Ellie placed the bowl closer to her, instructing her to push once more. The placenta came out, landing nicely in the bowl, followed by a lot more blood and water. Ellie rubbed Lucy's stomach until the bleeding stopped then cleaned her up.

Jenny cleaned up the baby, put a cloth diaper on her, then placed several sheets on the bed, folding them up in the middle of the bed over the top of another waterproof cloth Ellie had brought. Mrs. Toole and Ellie helped Lucy stand and slowly walk over to the closed stool chair to urinate. Before allowing her to stand, Ellie poured warm water over her.

"You should do this every time you urinate for the next six weeks or until the bleeding stops," she instructed. The bleeding would be significantly less than what it was now but would likely continue for nearly that long.

They slowly walked over to the bed, assisting Lucy with getting in and laying down. Jenny handed the baby back to her and she tried to feed her once again. Mrs. Toole instructed Lucy to drink some broth and eat some of the cheese and crackers she had brought up earlier. Ellie had Jenny retrieve the now cold sandbags she had placed outside and wrapped them in a clean linen before placing them against Lucy's vagina. Even with warning, the woman jumped in surprise when the iciness hit her skin.

"This will help with the soreness," Ellie explained.

With her eyes big, she declared, "If it doesn't freeze everything first."

The women chuckled as Lucy got comfortable on the bed. Satisfied that she had done everything she could for the time being, Ellie left the room to find Thomas and inform him of the news.

## Chapter 8

# Early February 1769

The look on Ellie's face had Thomas on his feet in an instant. He was crossing the room to her, waiting for her to tell him the worst.

"Has something happened? How is she? How's the babe?" he asked with panic in his voice.

Ellie had gone down the hall to find Thomas waiting in the drawing room, Charles asleep on the settee next to him, head on Thomas's lap. She tried to ignore the pull on her heart, but the tears came to her eyes despite her best efforts. It had been an exhausting and highly emotional evening and her defenses were gone.

Giving him as reassuring a smile as she could muster, she answered, "They're both fine. You can go see them."

Relief flooded Thomas. He grabbed her hands to thank her but quickly released them as if burned. He turned to go see his new child but stopped before leaving.

"Thank you, Ellie."

His voice was pained, but all Ellie could do was nod as she watched him go to his wife's bedside.

Ellie stayed for a few hours to keep an eye on Lucy, hoping the storm would pass before she had to make her way home again. If anything, it looked as though it had worsened. Sitting downstairs in the parlor next to the window after checking in on Lucy and the baby, Thomas came in and stood in the doorway.

"I've had Mrs. Toole make up a room for you."

Ellie's eyes got big as she turned away from the window. "Thank you, but that's not necessary." The last thing she wanted was to stay in the house that Thomas lived in with his wife and children any longer than necessary. She had planned to stay a little while longer, but not long enough to spend the night, even though it was already late.

Thomas looked at her, then out the window. "You can't go back out in this storm. You'll never make it home," his voice lowered, "and Lucy still has need of you."

He was right. She could not leave in the middle of the night, and if there were any complications, it would take too long for them to send word and then for her to get back again. Typically, a woman in this time would remain in bed for two weeks to a month. During this 'lying in' period, a neighbor, paid nurse, or family member would stay with her to help with household chores or to see to her needs. In her own time, a woman would remain in the hospital for at least a day or two. Lucy needed to be watched for dizziness, which Jenny or Mrs. Toole could easily do. But her uterus also needed to be observed for firmness every few hours. It was best to make sure the gushes of blood and blood clots stopped, and she also wanted to make sure the baby was feeding every two to three hours. She would need to be changed frequently and the umbilical cord needed to be cleaned with alcohol every time she was changed. Ellie knew she could pass some of these tasks off to Jenny and Mrs. Toole, but frankly, she did not trust anyone else in this time to properly clean things. Boiling a few tools was one thing, but she could easily see someone using alcohol to clean the umbilical cord as instructed, but doing so with dirty hands, not understanding why it was important to take the extra precautions. It was best if she could monitor both Lucy and the baby herself, making sure the umbilical cord did not become infected. If any indications of infection arose, Ellie could catch them early if she was there and hopefully stave it off.

Though Ellie had downplayed it, Lucy's fear of childbed fever was there for a reason. It was the leading cause of death during delivery in this time period and could surface anytime over the next few days, not only during the delivery. Like it or not, she was staying with them for the foreseeable future.

The storm still did not let up the following day. Grateful Ezra Rale was caring for her horses at the Armstrong residence, Ellie did not worry about being away from home for so long. She stayed in her room as long as she could but eventually got up and started her day. Thomas spent most of his time in his bedroom with his wife, the drawing room, or the study, and Ellie was trying to avoid him as much as possible, checking on Lucy only when he was else-where.

She looked for signs of infection, checked to see that Lucy had stopped bleeding heavily, helped Lucy walk to the closed stool chair and clean herself after urinating, then helped her back to bed again. Ellie made sure Lucy was eating and drinking and that Caitlyn was also feeding. Her umbilical cord looked good with no foul smells coming from it. When Ellie was satisfied that both Lucy and Caitlyn were well and did not have any immediate needs, she tidied the room.

Ellie had noticed the painting supplies in the corner of the room the previous night but had not asked about them. They had taken care to move the canvas, paints, brushes, and easel into a corner to make room for the delivery. Ellie eyed the colorful canvas now.

"Do you paint?" she asked Lucy. Ellie had never known Thomas to paint.

Lucy sighed guiltily. "I know it's wicked of me to have such idle pursuits, but Major Burke does in-dulge me so. And I do enjoy it when I may sneak in some time for it."

"It's not wicked at all. May I?" she asked while pointing at the stack of finished canvas leaning against the wall.

When Lucy gestured her consent, Ellie flipped through them. They were a variety of landscapes, some Ellie recognized from Williamsburg, some from New York.

"These are good."

Ellie could see Lucy blushing from across the room. "Thank you."

They talked about where the scenes had come from, and Ellie could see how passionate the woman was about it. She allowed Lucy to gush about her hobby, knowing many women of the time would not understand. Painting was considered an idle hobby and idleness was considered a character flaw.

While Lucy talked, Ellie crossed the room to tend the fire. She stirred the wood, flaring it into a higher flame, and added the last piece of wood from the bin beside the fireplace. While working the fire, Thomas came in to see his wife and Ellie quickly made her excuses and left, giving them some privacy. Stopping in the study, she checked Thomas's fire. If she was restocking one, she may as well do them all. His was still going strong, but his bin was also running low on wood. She made her way down to the basement to gather up enough to begin restocking both fire-places.

Downstairs, Ellie took in the basement. Like the rest of the house, it was much like hers, primarily used for food storage and to store firewood during the winter months, keeping it dry and easily accessible. Another larger stash was piled up outside, but this was for ready use, to be replenished monthly or as needed.

Ellie found a bucket and filled it as full as she could with logs and hauled it back up the two flights of stairs. Seeing that Thomas was still in with Lucy, she stopped in his study first and topped off his wood pile. She went back down and refilled her bucket, stopping to check in the drawing room as well. With that pile low, she emptied her bucket once again and headed back to the basement. By the time she returned from her third trip, Thomas was coming out of Lucy's room. Ellie passed him with a polite smile and a nod, then went into the room to deposit the wood.

Glancing at the bed, she saw Lucy was asleep, so she emptied her bucket as quietly as she could and crept out of the room. In the hallway, she looked up from closing the door to see Thomas standing in the doorway to his study with his arms crossed, watching her. His presence startled her, but she quickly recovered and began walking toward the stairs past him, pail in hand. He grabbed her arm as she passed, stopping her.

"What pray, are you doing?" he asked, annoyance all over his handsome face.

Ellie shrugged one shoulder, immediately on the defensive as he released her. "The firewood was low. I thought I'd refill it."

"Jenny or Mrs. Toole may do that."

"It's fine. No big deal."

Thomas ran a hand over his jaw, trying to find some patience. "I didn't induce you here to wait on us."

"Well, that's good, because I wouldn't have come if you had."

"Next time, call for one of them. I pay them not to allow a guest in my home to perform their labors."

Ellie planted her feet, cocking a hip and throwing her free hand on it. "Look, I saw something that needed to be done and I took care of it. It really isn't a big deal. They're both quite busy and I'm not helpless. I'm perfectly capable of carrying a bucket of wood."

"Several buckets of wood from what I gather," he responded, pointing to his own fireplace. "I never thought you incapable. But that is why I employ them both. You must allow them to perform their duties. If they are unavailable, fetch Mr. Toole or even Hugh. Either may assist you as well."

Ellie huffed. Hugh Pomeroy, a boy of maybe eighteen was Thomas's personal valet. Though he was a servant in the household, he generally did lighter duties, not heavy lifting.

"Whatever," she said noncommittally. Gathering her skirts, she headed back down the stairs, leaving him standing in the hallway.

To spite him, she stopped in the kitchen to check the fire in there and decided to refill Mrs. Toole's wood as well. After refilling the wood, she noticed that the racks that had been placed in the corners of the room were filled with dry laundry. In the summer, laundry would be hung outside, but with this weather, it had to be brought indoors. It must have been hung right before Lucy went into labor. Ellie did not imagine it normally would have been left there very long, but with Lucy bedridden and Jenny and Mrs. Toole picking up the extra chores, it still hung there now, even though it was bone dry.

Dropping the bucket off in the basement, Ellie was annoyed enough at Thomas, not to mention bored enough, that she went back to the kitchen upstairs and placed the three flatirons on their trivets over the hearth. Ellie looked around for the ironing cloth that she knew would be nearby. Finding it in a cabinet, she pulled it out and spread it over the table. As she finished, Mrs. Toole came back in from wherever she had been. Finding Ellie there standing over the table with the ironing cloth spread out, she stopped in her tracks and glared at Ellie.

"Were there something I can help you with, Mrs. Russell?"

Shaking her head, she began pulling down the nearest shift. "No thank you. I can manage."

Mrs. Toole watched while Ellie laid out the garment on the table, still waiting for the irons to sufficiently heat up. "Were Mrs. Burke in need of a clean shift? She should still have a few in her room."

"She's fine. I just thought I'd help."

Mrs. Toole scoffed. "I'll be thanking you miss, but Jenny and I can manage."

Jenny had her hands full with Charles at that moment. "An extra set of hands never goes to waste. I'd rather stay busy if I can."

Mrs. Toole nodded gruffly and turned back to her cooking. After placing a wet cloth over the shift, Ellie grabbed the first iron and began working the fabric in front of her, Mrs. Toole watching her all the while. Ironing with heavy cast iron tools which had to be heated in a fire had taken Ellie some getting used to. She had done very little of it since her arrival in the past. The first several years, she had never needed it, then her and Dean had used a laundry service, so she had not needed to do it herself. When she stayed on the Prendergast farm, Mehitabel had shown her how to use the heavy irons. She had watched Mehitabel several times, asking questions, then had finally tried it with Mehitabel looking over her shoulder the whole time. It had taken some practice, but she had done it. It took having several irons on hand in order to get anything done. As each one was put to use, the others stayed on the fire in order to keep them hot. As the one being used cooled, it was swapped out with one of the others. It was all rather time consuming and Ellie was grateful that Hannah did all of it for her now.

By the time Ellie had completed four or five garments, Mrs. Toole finally stopped checking in on her every few seconds and let her be. Ellie tried talking with the woman, but she was quiet, answering only in short answers, if at all.

"Me children 'ave all grown and Mrs. Burke took me on as her housekeeper and cook," Ellie managed to get out of her. "Me 'usband tends the horses and carriages and the outbuildings." It was the longest string of words the woman said all day.

Ellie trudged away at her task until she had managed to get through all of the clean laundry. It was now ironed, folded, and ready to be put away. She decided the last step was a little too intimate for her liking and left it for Jenny. Despite Thomas's objections, it was common for women to support each other during a childbirth. It was standard practice for a woman to be on bedrest during her entire lying in. Other female family and friends would come and help around the house during that time, but with the storm, no one was coming to assist for a while. Ellie refused to spend the next however many days she was stuck there sitting around doing nothing. This was nothing more than she would do for any other patient and was far less than she had done for Mehitabel. It also gave her something to do while she passed the time.

When Ellie finished all of the tasks with which she could manage to occupy herself, she finally took a break and went to sit in the parlor with a book she had found.

"It's rather cold down here. Would you not prefer to sit by the fire upstairs?" Thomas asked while standing in the doorway looking around the room. He usually made it a habit of not entering a room if she was in it.

The parlor was cold with no fire going. The fire in the drawing room had been kept lit since it was where the family typically gathered, leaving the parlor for guests. But it felt far too intimate for Ellie to be in there.

"I don't wish to intrude, Thomas," she said quietly, her book resting in her lap with a finger marking her page.

He nodded and turned to leave without saying anything, but stopped himself, letting out a deep sigh. "Miss Ellie, come upstairs."

It was not what he had intended to say. He was going to have Jenny make up the fire in the parlor for her, but he hated the thought of her sitting down there by herself. Besides, why waste the firewood to heat both rooms when the upstairs was already warmed nicely?

He turned back to see her studying him quizzically, making no effort to move from her seat. He set his jaw and walked towards her. Towering above her where she sat, he took her hands and pulled her to her feet, then ushered her toward the stairs. The maddening woman just stood there staring at him. He shrugged, shook his head, and walked away, heading back upstairs himself. It only took a moment to hear her soft footsteps on the stairs behind him.

The easy companionship they once shared was long gone. Ellie sat in the drawing room reading while Thomas went back to his study. Occasionally, she would put her book down and watch Charles. When Jenny left to assist Mrs. Toole with other chores, Ellie kept Charles entertained.

## Chapter 9

# *Early February 1769*

Thomas walked into the drawing room after leaving Lucy to sleep to find Ellie lying on the floor face down, leaning up on her elbows, playing with Charles. Her knees were bent, sending her feet into the air, crossed at the ankle. His gaze traveled to her tiny feet which were covered only by her stockings. The woman rarely wore shoes inside the house, and he suddenly remembered her habit of not wearing them outside either if she could get away with it. With one of Charles's toy soldiers in her hand, she was pretending to shoot at the soldier he had in his. She even made the explosive noises as she 'shot' at him.

Thomas cleared his throat as he entered the room, finding a seat nearby. Instead of being embarrassed at being found in such a position as other women would have been, Ellie smiled at him and turned back to Charles to continue playing soldiers. He found it difficult to focus on his book and reread the same words on the page countless times in an attempt to keep his eyes from watching the woman laughing and playing on the floor as a small child.

He should have let her stay downstairs where she would not be so distracting. Though, was that not why he had insisted she come upstairs to begin with? It did not matter where she was or what she was doing, the woman was a distraction. Her being in his home, even more so. It irked him. He did not want to be thinking about her at all, but especially not right now after what his wife had just endured.

Eventually, Charles's attention wandered to something else, and she sat up. Standing, she checked on the baby in the cradle and seeing that Caitlyn was still asleep, she made her way to the settee where she picked up her own book.

Ellie sat with the book unopened in her hands for a few minutes, taking in the scene in front of her. "Your family is wonderful, Thomas."

"Thank you," he said gruffly.

An awkward silence fell while they both focused on watching Charles play with his favorite wooden horse, their respective books forgotten.

"Lucy seems wonderful, too," she said in an attempt to be amicable. "How did you meet?"

Thomas let out an exasperated sigh. "Ellie, don't."

"Don't what, Thomas?" she asked impatiently. She was trying her hardest and he was not making it easy. "Express an interest? Try to understand? See for myself that you're happy?"

He scoffed. "Do not trouble yourself with the false pretense that you care."

Ellie immediately got defensive; a constant state for her when he was around. "I do care!" she exclaimed. "You have no idea..." she stopped herself and took a deep breath, trying to calm herself down. Why could they never seem to be able to communicate without arguing anymore?

She tried again. "I don't want to fight with you. I'm just trying to tell you that I'm happy for you. I'm glad you found happiness. It's all I ever wanted for you."

"Is it?" he asked, disbelieving.

"Yes," she said matter-of-factly. "It is."

"I *was* happy, Ellie," Thomas said quietly while clenching his jaw. "For a time, you made me happy." He turned away. "Then you ripped my heart out."

What could she possibly say to that? 'Sorry' felt woefully insufficient. Telling him that it had broken her own heart as well sounded trite.

He was quiet for a minute. Then, in a soft voice, he said, "Lucy saved my life. I was lost in a sea of despair. She was a candle in the darkness that consumed me, her light flickering in the shadows, her warmth thawing the ice around my heart. She pulled me from the depths even when I thought to never again see the sun."

Thomas had not meant to say as much as he had about Lucy, but he needed the reminder for himself as much as he needed Ellie to hear it.

Not knowing what to say, she said nothing. Thomas was looking away from her, his gaze locked on an abandoned toy soldier on the floor in front of him. Ellie directed her gaze onto Charles, who abandoned his horse now as well. He stood, slowly circling the room, oblivious to the tension between the two adults in there with him. Wandering nonchalantly over to Caitlyn's cradle, he stood beside it for a moment looking down at the sleeping baby inside it.

Charles leaned against the wooden cradle, his chubby hands gripping the lip, then he leaned forward on his tiptoes for a better look. Ellie thought it sweet until he swatted the newborn, who immediately started crying. Without thinking about it, Ellie jumped up and ran over, picking up the baby. She rocked her and shushed her while Thomas handled Charles, swatting the boy on his butt and lecturing him about what he had done. He cried and pouted, with his lower lip fully extended and a scowl on his face.

With the baby no longer crying, Ellie squatted in front of him and gently asked, "Charles, why did you do that?"

"I don't like her," he said as though she were the devil himself. "Can we send her back?"

This broke some of the tension in the room and the adults chuckled.

"Charles, come sit with me," Ellie said, sitting and patting the settee next to her.

Charles looked up at his father, who nodded while eyeing Ellie suspiciously. The boy crossed the room and crawled up next to Ellie. She put an arm around him, and he leaned his back into her slightly. She then set the baby down in Charles's arms while maintaining control so Caitlyn would not be dropped.

Thomas watched with both fascination and horror that Ellie would place a newborn baby in the arms of a three-year-old. Knowing she was maintaining a hold of the girl was the only reason he did not stop it. He was also curious to see what she was doing. She had always done things differently and apparently that had not changed after all these years.

Ellie spoke softly to Charles. "This is your baby now. She needs her big brother to watch out for her. You have to love her and protect her always."

The boy looked up at Ellie with big eyes. "Me?" he asked in a quiet voice.

Ellie's responding smile was warm. "It's a big responsibility. Only the best get to be big brothers. Do you think you can handle it?"

Something shifted in the boy. Charles suddenly seemed proud and nodded solemnly, saying, "I can do it."

Ellie beamed at him. When she looked up, she saw Thomas watching the exchange. "Sorry," she said, the smile easing from her face. "I hope I didn't overstep."

"Not at all," he said.

He had wanted to tell her that she had but could not find it within him to say the words. Had it been anyone else, he would have told them to mind their business. But it was different with Ellie. He thought now that it always would be. He took in the scene before him of Ellie holding both of his children in her arms. It was too much, and he needed an escape. Thomas decided to go check on Lucy.

Charles began fidgeting as he became tired, trying to readjust the heavy baby in his arms.

"Would you like me to take her back now?" Ellie asked.

"Yes, please. She's mine, but I think I need help for now," he said.

Ellie adjusted the baby so she was no longer on Charles's lap. He curled up into Ellie's lap next to the sleeping Caitlyn. With one child in each arm, Ellie's heart wanted to burst. It was all she could do to force herself to stay where she was. Her heart longed for this, but it was only pretend. None of it was hers and part of her wanted to indulge in the fantasy that it was, if only for a moment. The other part of her wanted to run far away, building up the brick wall around her heart, knowing it would never be hers.

As Charles fought sleep, Ellie absentmindedly started humming softly.

"I don't know that song. Does it have words? Will you sing them?" he asked, looking up at her sleepily.

Ellie had to think hard to remember the words to the song she had been humming, but when they came back to her, she started singing *Somewhere over the Rainbow* to him softly.

When Thomas walked in, the picture before him filled him with confusion and longing, more so than the one he had needed to escape only moments ago. How could he long for something he already had? Those were his children; and his wife, whom he loved, was in the next room. Yet, she was not Ellie. Her voice sounded like an angel, and she looked perfect with his children curled up into her. She watched Charles while stroking his hair as she sang. With such a beautiful voice, Thomas had always loved listening to her sing. She was so engrossed in the moment, she had not seen or heard him at the doorway. Ellie started when he came in at the end of the song. Thomas gently picked up the now sleeping Charles to carry him off to bed.

"Where did you ever learn such a song?" he asked when he returned. "I've not heard it before. Such a fanciful idea, flying off into another world."

"Just something I picked up somewhere," Ellie replied, staring down at the baby in her arms.

Thomas jolted, remembering she had been holding Caitlyn for some time. Her arms must be falling asleep by now. He leaned in to relieve her of the sleeping baby.

Ellie shook her arms, then stood and stretched while Thomas put Caitlyn back in her cradle. She headed for the door, unable to be alone with Thomas. He stood when he saw her leaving, and found himself asking, "Stay and have a drink with me?"

She could see the battle waging within him. He was still angry and hurt but was trying to be polite. Damn his breeding. Leaning against the doorframe, hugging it with both hands, she shook her head sadly and said, "Good night, Thomas."

Thomas and Ellie seemed to have developed a tentative truce as the days passed. It was still difficult for each of them to be close to the other and they avoided spending time alone, using Charles as a buffer, but they managed to not fight or yell at each other. Ellie continued to watch the windows for signs that the storm would let up, but it had lingered. It was no longer a blizzard, but it was still coming down steadily. Without snowplows, the snow would pile up in the streets, eventually turning into ice as people moved over it. The soft snow would eventually melt but the icy sheets always took longer and would remain until spring or early summer.

"How's Robert doing?" Ellie asked, grasping at a safe topic.

When she had first seen Thomas, she had been so stunned and his presence had been so all-consuming that she had not even thought about Robert. It was not until much later after she returned to her home that he had crossed her mind. Part of her felt a little guilty for not having thought of him sooner.

"He's well. He's in Williamsburg at the present."

Before she could ask anything else, Charles came running up to where she sat on the couch and asked her to play with him. Instead of dropping to the floor to play with the soldiers he held in his hand, she jumped up, picking him up with her and lifted him up over her head, turning him so he was upside down, carefully holding the skirt of his gown in place as she flipped him. Holding him by the legs, she spun around with him, eliciting squeals of laughter from him. When she stopped spinning, she flipped him back to upright and he wrapped his little legs around her waist. She proceeded to tickle him relentlessly before finally setting him back on the floor. Catching her breath, she rubbed his head and sat on the floor next him, drawing her feet under her to sit cross-legged. Instead of staying on the floor beside her, he sat down on her lap, handing her one of the soldiers.

As he sat there on her lap, Charles kept looking at Ellie. She was not sure what had caught his attention until he reached his little hand up and touched the jewelry above her lip. Suddenly, it made sense. He did not say anything, but she smiled at him, letting him know it was okay to be curious. It seemed to embolden him and he reached for her earrings next. This time as he pointed, he said, "Owie."

Ellie's laughter filled the room. "No. It doesn't hurt."

Satisfied, he went back to his soldiers. Ellie marveled at how easy he was to appease.

Playing with Charles was more fun than Ellie would have thought. She enjoyed the time she got to spend with him. He made her feel young again and she was thrilled that she had the energy to keep up with him. Despite her youthful appearance, she was fifty-seven. It tickled her that she not only looked much younger, but felt younger, too. She had never had kids of her own and wanted to enjoy this time while she had it.

"You needn't indulge him," Thomas said as he watched her, warmth spreading through him at their interaction. "He plays well enough on his own."

"I don't mind at all," Ellie replied. "It's not something I ever get to do."

He wanted to ask her if she had ever had children of her own, but it felt too personal. Every time they tried having those conversations, it ended up in a fight. He was guessing she had not had any, or at least she did not have any with her now. He still knew so little about where she had been all these years and what her life had consisted of, but he could not bring himself to ask, as much as he wanted to.

Thomas watched them play for a while, noting how much Charles adored Ellie. It had only been a couple of days, but his son was smitten with her. Charles took every chance he could get to snuggle up to her, asking her to play with him, read to him, or sing to him. He could not fault the boy. He would do the same if he could. He briefly wondered if he should be allowing it. Ellie had mentioned that she was only to be there for the winter. Would she rip out his son's heart when she left as she had his so long ago? Thomas shook off the thought and told Charles it was time for bed.

Once he got his son settled, Thomas went to his room to turn in himself. He began undressing when he heard the unmistakable sound of little feet running down the hall. Thomas immediately went chasing after his mischievous little boy as he headed back into the drawing room to his new friend.

Ellie looked up from her book as Charles came barreling into the room, his father on his heels. Thomas had long since removed his frock but now, he had also removed his waistcoat and cravat, leaving him only in his breeches, stockings, and loose shirt. The sight immediately had Ellie longing for the familiarity they once shared. She quickly did the math, realizing he would be thirty-eight now. Time had been kind to him. He still maintained his slim waist and broad chest. She could see the muscles in his arms and thighs and admonished herself for having such thoughts. He was firmly off-limits.

Thomas scooped up Charles, flipping him upside down as she had only a little while ago, and carried him back to bed. The boy giggled the entire way down the hall. She could hear Thomas scolding Charles, but there was little heat to it. There was affection in his words that tore at Ellie's heart. She had turned back to her book when he left the room, but now she heard him coming back. He stood in the door, almost shyly.

"I apologize for the interruption. Charles often gives us difficulties at bedtime."

Ellie turned to face him. "I don't mind at all. He really is adorable."

Something on the floor near her feet caught Thomas's attention and brought him into the room. He bent and picked up a toy horse from its position slightly under the settee. Only a few feet from her, in the dim light from the candles and fireplace, it was close enough. Her gaze fell onto his collar when he stood, and she gasped. Thomas stared at her for a moment, at a loss as to what she was seeing. As his hand moved toward his neck he suddenly realized where her eyes had been drawn. He held onto the necklace with the amethyst crystal pendant for only a moment, curling his fingers tightly around it as if it were a lifeline. Releasing the pendant, he removed the necklace from his neck and held out his hand to her. When she did not reach for it, he sat down next to her, grabbed her hand and placed it in her palm, closing her fingers around it. His touch still managed to send her stomach into cartwheels, and she had to fight to maintain control of her warring emotions.

Ellie closed her eyes and took a deep breath, then opened both her eyes and her palm. Turning the necklace over in her fingers, she felt his warmth on it from being tucked against his skin. She looked at it as though it were the most precious thing in the world. Her soft blue eyes were big and questioning when they finally lifted and settled back on his face.

"I thought I lost this forever." Ellie fought the tears that were threatening to spill.

Thomas was close enough to smell her citrus and honey scent. Even in the middle of winter the woman managed to smell like summer. It went straight through him as it took him back to their time together at the fort. His voice was barely a whisper.

"I discovered it in your tent when I cleaned out your belongings after…"

He did not continue the thought, but he did not need to. Ellie could hear the emotion in his throat. He sounded as raw as she felt.

Looking down at her hands, she said, "I'm sorry you had to do that. And I truly am sorry that it happened the way it did. I asked Anwar to tell you. I still can't believe he didn't. I never thought he would tell you anything else."

"*You* should have told me, Ellie." There was more regret than admonishment in his tone. She could feel how much it had hurt him.

"I wish I could have."

"For what it's worth, I regret the manner in which many things happened between us."

It was hard not to wonder what he regretted. Did he regret meeting her altogether and letting her into his life? Or perhaps he only regretted becoming intimate with her? Did he regret proposing marriage? There were so many possibilities, Ellie had to push the thoughts out of her mind before they drove her nuts.

When Ellie looked up, she saw that Thomas had been watching her hands the entire time as she flipped the pendant over between her fingers. Curling up her fist around it, she squeezed, then brought it to her lips and kissed it as if it were a sacred object. She had missed it all these years and it had special meaning for her, tying her to her nieces that she would likely never see again. But now it held deeper meaning, not just for her. She could see Thomas's pain when he spoke of clearing out her belongings. That he had found the pendant tucked deep inside her things meant that he had gone through every inch of her possessions. He had then taken the time and care to change out the cord to one without a broken clasp. The new cord was a black leather thong, knotted in lieu of a clasp. Judging by the wear on it, he had not just put it on for the first time today. She wondered how long he wore it after she left. Had he recently pulled it out again after seeing that she was alive? Instead of asking, she grabbed his hand and turned his palm up, placing the necklace back into it. She curled his fingers around it and when she looked up at him, she said, "You should keep it."

Thomas tried to give it back to her, but she shook her head.

"I want you to have it."

He did not say anything but nodded and put the cord back around his neck.

"Good night, Ellie," he said in a whisper as he stood to leave.

"Good night, Thomas."

Chapter 10

## February 1769

"Mrs. Erwin came to check on me as soon as the storm let up, right after you left," Lucy told Ellie when she came back for a check-up.

The days spent in Thomas's house after his wife gave birth had been some of the longest and most difficult of Ellie's life. Yet, she would not have traded them for anything. After the weather finally cleared and Lucy was out of any immediate danger of infection, Ellie had headed home. She still went to check on her regularly, but she tried to only do so when Thomas was not there. After the first couple days, they had managed to remain civil to one another, but it had been difficult for them both. Seeing him in his domestic bliss cut her deeply knowing that she would never have anything like that. She knew she had made the right decision for him by refusing his proposal of marriage, but it was not because she had not loved him. She wanted the best for him and knew that she was not it. Knowing that did not make it any easier to watch.

Ellie nodded. "Will she be resuming your care now?"

Lucy looked at her with pleading eyes. "I would prefer if you continued. She's a good midwife, but she's already missed everything, and you've taken such excellent care of me."

Sighing, Ellie said, "I'll come back and check on you again in a few days. If you need me before then, send Miss Jenny."

Before leaving, Ellie went to see Mrs. Toole. Pulling a charcoal filtration system out of her medical bag, she handed it to the woman.

"Please make sure everything Mrs. Burke drinks or uses for personal hygiene is cleaned and filtered properly. Same for the baby."

Mrs. Toole took the glass bottle that Ellie handed her and eyed it suspiciously while Ellie explained to her how to use it. She had begun creating the bottles during her time with Dean, making them for herself and sharing them with Mehitabel Prendergast and a few other women. Ellie obtained glass bottles from which she had the bottoms removed and made the necessary activated charcoal. After piercing a cork to create a drainage hole, she stuffed it into the bottle as securely as she could, then began layering the materials into the bottle. First went a thin linen or cotton fabric behind the cork, then her activated charcoal powder, followed by fine sand, a layer of coarse sand, another layer of fine sand, then small rocks. With the bottles filled, she topped them off with another piece of fabric to keep everything in place and begin the first step of straining of any foreign material.

"Once you filter the water, be sure to boil it for at least one minute. Then it's safe to drink or use for personal hygiene. I know the tea water here is good, but I don't want to take any chances with Mrs. Burke or the baby."

Every four blocks or so, there were wooden pumps on the street corners around the city that drew water up from underground springs. With waste from the residents draining into open gutters, despite the ordinance to prevent throwing waste into the streets, the water was often contaminated and undrinkable, though there were a select few of these pumps which brought up good, quality water. These select few pumps were known as tea pumps since they were the ones people went to in order to make a good quality tea. Often, people would stand in line and wait to get their water while others had created a business out of filling barrels from the pumps and delivering them to people around the city.

Ellie returned home and had a visit from Jenny later that same night. Instead of coming inside, Hannah spoke to her at the door, then the girl left. Ellie was confused when Hannah came into the room by herself. She walked over to Ellie and held out a small coin purse. Ellie's brows furrowed as a scowl spread over her face. She put down her knitting and took the purse, looking inside to see thirty shillings.

"What is this?" she asked Hannah.

"Miss Jenny brung it from Major Burke," she replied simply.

"I don't understand."

"That were all she said, miss."

Setting aside her knitting, she stood and ran out the door. "Miss Jenny," she called after the girl who was a few houses away.

Jenny turned and rushed back to Ellie when she saw that she was standing outside in the snow with no cloak or shoes. "What are you doing out here miss? You'll catch your death. You must go back inside at once."

Ellie took the girl's hand and placed the purse back in it. "I don't know what this is for, but you can tell Major Burke it's not necessary."

Jenny shook her head, trying to refuse to take the money. "'Tis for the birthing, miss. 'Tis your fee."

It was Ellie's turn to shake her head. "I don't have a fee. I'm not working as a midwife right now. I was simply helping out an old friend. You tell him that if you need to, but I don't want it."

Jenny looked both confused and a little frightened. Taking the money, she went back to the Burke house.

Ellie went back inside, took off her wet stockings and stood in front of the fireplace, warming up her frozen toes. By the time she resumed her knitting, there was another knock at the door. This time, Ellie stood in the hallway and watched as Jenny shyly pulled the coin purse back out and handed it over to Hannah who looked over her shoulder at Ellie before accepting it.

Ellie folded her arms across her chest and looked at Jenny for an explanation.

"I must not have explained it rightly. The money is for you to keep as payment for delivering Mrs. Burke of her babe." The girl looked as though she had been trying to remember the exact words to re-cite back to Ellie. She imagined Thomas scolding the young woman for having come back with the money.

"Stay here," she told Jenny sternly as she went upstairs to fetch a new pair of stockings.

After putting on shoes and a cloak, Ellie followed Jenny back to Thomas's house. Once they were inside, she left Jenny to her work. The girl was all too eager to be anywhere but where Ellie was headed.

Once on the second floor, she knew exactly where to find Thomas. Lucy was still on bedrest and Thomas would be in his office. She barged in without knocking and stormed up to his desk, dropping the purse on top with a thud.

"I've told you before I don't want your damn money."

Confused, Thomas looked up from his bookkeeping and set down his quill. He said patiently, "It's merely the midwifery fee. It would've gone to Mrs. Erwin had she delivered Mrs. Burke of Caitlyn. As she did not, the fee is yours."

As if she was the hired help? Was this payment for the chores she helped with after delivering the baby? Or was it something Thomas could throw back in her face yet again. Ellie immediately thought of their argument after his proposal when he had accused her of using him to obtain expensive gifts, despite her having tried to reject the gifts at the time. After that, she absolutely refused to accept anything from him now.

With one small act, their tentative truce had faltered once again. Ellie was fuming. She had not done any of it in order to receive any sort of payment. They had not discussed any money exchange between them, and Ellie never would have charged him for the work had they discussed it. At that moment, this was not even her job. She had done it as a favor be-cause there was no one else available. Even had there been, Ellie would have done it as a favor for either of them. She never would have turned Thomas away, nor would she have turned Lucy away. It was who she was. Most of the women she helped while staying with Mehitabel had not paid her either. If there was something she could do to help, she would always gladly step up, even when she did not want to. When it involved people she cared about, she never hesi-tated. Just because she could not be part of their lives, it did not mean that she did not care about them. Even Lucy had gotten under her skin in the little bit of time they had spent together. Ellie did not want to like the young woman, but she did. She could easily see why Thomas was with her.

"This is not what would have gone to Mrs. Er-win. I may not be working as a midwife right now, but I know the going rate. And that," she pointed to the purse still sitting on his desk, "is about double the going rate. Either way, I never sent you a bill or asked for payment."

Thomas leaned back in his chair, placing his el-bows on the armrests and steepling his fingers to-gether over his flat stomach. He had always enjoyed seeing Ellie fired up about something in which she was passionate, though it was not always pleasant be-ing on the receiving end of her ire. He sat back now and watched her, tamping down the amusement threatening to rise. Finally, he shrugged.

"I concede it was not agreed upon ahead of time. However, you did not have to come. Nor were you under any obligation to treat my wife as well as you did, given our history."

"Jesus, just what kind of person do you think I am, Thomas?" Ellie asked, even more insulted than before.

"I thought I knew once, but as it turned out, I was mistaken."

Thomas could not help the bitterness that crept into his words. As much as he enjoyed seeing Ellie riled up, he was constantly reminded of what had occurred between them and how little he knew her. The fact that she could so easily walk away without a word, leaving him to think she was dead for years was something he had never thought her capable of doing. Despite her reasons, it still hurt.

"Keep your goddamn money, Major Burke," she spat. "I don't care what it's for. I wouldn't take your money when I needed it; I sure as hell won't take it now."

Without waiting for a reply, Ellie stomped down the stairs and out the door. She half expected him to follow her and insist that she keep the money, but he did not.

## Chapter 11

## March 1769

The days were slowly warming, and the sun began to peek out more and more. Ellie took full advantage of the warmer days and went out as much as she could. She resumed her walks when it was possible and made her way to her spot down by the water at the Whitehall Slip where she would go and sit by herself, watching the world go by. With the warmer weather, she was happy to linger there, though it was still much colder than she preferred. Sometimes she would meditate or contemplate her situation, and other times, she would watch the ships weave around the bustling port. It never got old seeing the wooden vessels with all of their masts, sails, and riggings. It was times like this that she felt every bit of the period in which she found herself.

On her way back to the house one Sunday, Ellie turned onto her street and nearly ran into a group of people coming from the other direction. She stopped abruptly and looked up into deep chocolate eyes and curly brown hair mostly hidden under a tricorne hat. Her eyes opened wide and a huge smile broke out on her face as she called out excitedly.

"Robbie!"

When Robert Jensen recognized her, he returned one of the biggest smiles she had ever seen, his deep dimples on full display. He began to bow as Ellie threw herself into him and wrapped her arms around his neck for a hug, catching him off balance. Lucy gasped at the forwardness, but Ellie did not care in the least, never having been one for formalities. Had it been any of her friends in her own time, she would have done the same. She was excited to see him and wanted to show it. It had been difficult enough suppressing her complicated feelings for Thomas; there was no reason to do so with Robert. When she had first seen Thomas, she had wanted to throw herself at him, holding onto him with everything she had but given the way things had ended between them, she had not dared. In retrospect, she was glad she had not done so. However, things with Robert were different and she did not hold back now.

The tall man picked her up off her feet and spun her around, kissing her cheek while they embraced. He set her back down then pulled back, still holding her arms.

"Major Burke informed me you had returned to us. And looking as lovely as ever I see. We believed you to have been killed in the ambush. It gives me great pleasure to see we were wrong."

Had she been anyone else, Robert would think her a demon or a witch. But he had always been fond of Ellie and his feelings for her allowed him to put his superstitions aside, dismissing her unusual abilities as anything bad. She had always had a good heart and spent her time helping others, even trying to warn him of the pending massacre of the fleeing garrison from Fort William Henry years ago. A witch or demon could never be as selfless as she was. Though perhaps she was something more; could she possibly be angel? Her very presence there now seemed to indicate some otherworldly explanation.

Ellie took a step back and greeted Thomas and Lucy as well before saying, "Nope. Not dead. Still kicking."

Robert laughed at the strange speech that he had come to love about her. "You always did have a way with words. You must tell me what became of you."

"You first," Ellie said. "I thought you were in Williamsburg. What are you doing here?"

"I recently returned. I was there only for the Christmas season."

When Thomas had mentioned that Robert was in Williamsburg, Ellie had assumed he had returned there for good. It did not occur to her that he might have only been visiting. Neither of the men were in uniform now, so she did not make the connection that he might be there for work.

"So, you live here, in the Big Apple then?" she said lightly, feeling anything but.

Ellie was actually a little giddy at seeing the familiar, friendly face. While she and Thomas had become romantically involved, her friendship with Robert had meant the world to her. When she had turned down Thomas's proposal, she had been afraid she was going to lose Robert too since they had grown up together and were more like brothers than friends. Robert had surprised her by standing by her side, somehow managing to remain neutral between the two of them. She had confided a lot of things in him that she had never told Thomas. Robert had picked up on her accurate foreknowledge of events and had questioned her relentlessly until she told him what he wanted to hear. She had not told him that she had traveled back through time, but when he had asked if she had visions, she let him think that was how she came by her knowledge. She had tried to tell Thomas, but he gave every indication that he would not believe her and would actually think she was ill for thinking such things. She gave up on trying and swore not to tell him.

Robert did not answer. Ellie looked around as three blank faces stared back at her. What did she say?

It was Thomas who asked, "The big apple?"

Ellie tapped her forehead in a '*duh*' gesture, which was also lost on the three of them. "Sorry; just a nickname for New York City."

"What a queer nickname," Lucy said. "I've not heard it before. Wherever did you come by it?"

Ellie shook her head and shrugged. That sounded about right. When had the name first come into use? "I'm not sure where I got it." Looking for an escape, Ellie turned back to Robert, "Well, I'm glad you're here. We must catch up sometime."

"We certainly must," he replied. "I wish to hear everything."

Before she could respond, Lucy jumped on the opportunity to hear the story as well. "Why don't we all go back to the house where we may visit over a fine meal. Mrs. Toole shall have dinner waiting."

Ellie tried arguing there was not much to tell and she did not want to intrude on them, but Lucy and Robert were not having it. She glanced at Thomas, but he showed no reaction. She hesitantly agreed, but only because she wanted to catch up with Robert.

Sitting in the formal dining room, Ellie placed herself next to Robert while Lucy and Thomas sat across from them. Robert pulled out her chair for her like Thomas used to do.

"Do tell us what has become of you these last ten years, Miss Ellie," Robert said as they waited for Mrs. Toole to bring the food. "I wish to hear everything."

Ellie chuckled at his enthusiasm but kept her answer vague. "There's really not much to tell. I lived with the Onöndowa'ga:' until just after the war ended, then I roamed New York selling wares with a trader."

"She refers to the Seneca," Thomas supplied for the sake of Robert and Lucy. "It's the English name for them, though they call themselves the Onöndowa'ga:'."

"That's it?" Robert asked. "That's ten years?"

Ellie could not help the corners of her mouth from turning up. "Okay. I mean, I did a ton of new things, and I learned a lot. I learned how to knit and hunt and process the remains, and I learned how to fish." Ellie paused momentarily, trying to remember everything she had experienced the last several years. She had been ticking them off on her fingers as she spoke and was aware how much she sounded like an excited kid, but she did not care. Suddenly, her eyes got big, and she turned in her seat, grabbing Robert's forearm with both hands as she said excitedly, "Omigosh! And I learned how to milk a cow!"

Three confused faces stared back at Ellie.

"You learned how to milk a cow? And this was exciting?" Robert asked hesitantly.

Ellie nodded, removing her hands from his arm, but keeping her smile in place. "It was. I've never even been close to a cow before. I stayed on a farm for a few months and helped take care of all the animals. One of my jobs was to help milk the cows."

Robert and Thomas could both see how excited she was at having learned this new skill, as if it were some complicated task, only reserved for a select few individuals to learn. Ellie was aware that they saw her excitement but did not understand it. Their confusion only served to amuse her even more. This had been the most amount of time she had been able to spend in Thomas's company without the rush of longing and pain that always accompanied their time together. She wanted to enjoy it while it lasted.

"You've never before been near a cow?" Lucy asked.

Ellie shook her head. "Nope. Never."

"Nor horses, I seem to recall," Thomas added.

He enjoyed seeing her like this. Her almost child-like curiosity and love for learning had drawn him in when he first met her. It gave her an intelligence not often seen, certainly not in women. Those who were intelligent tended to downplay it in order to make themselves more appealing to men. They certainly did not flaunt it like Ellie did. It was not considered an attractive quality in a woman, though he could not help but find it appealing.

"Nor horses," Ellie echoed, looking at him, enjoying his gaze on her. He had been looking everywhere but at her and it had not gone unnoticed. "But also, none of the other animals they had at the farm. I had a neighbor who had goats once, so I've been around them, but none of the other animals they had on this farm. No sheep, pigs, chickens. This was all a first for me."

"You seem rather excited to have been able to spend time on a farm," Lucy said, clearly missing something. She could not understand anyone getting excited over something so mundane, and quite simply, something so lowly.

"I was. I love learning new things. I could never live on a farm permanently, but it was really cool to be able to do it for a little while and learn what goes into it all. I'm practically like any other eighteenth century colonial woman," she preened.

"*Really cool?*" Robert and Thomas echoed.

"Sorry. Um. It was exciting? Quite neat? Is that a better word?"

Robert laughed while Thomas shook his head.

"I nearly forgot how peculiar your manner of speech was," Thomas said fondly, though in truth, he could never forget. But he could not very well say that he had missed it.

"I've been much better, but sometimes I forget," Ellie said shyly.

The truth was, Robert and Thomas felt like family. She had not realized it until she sat at the table there with them both, but the history they shared and the fact that they knew her when she first arrived, teaching her everything she knew about life in the eighteenth century, made it feel as though they had always been part of her life. Sitting there with them made her feel almost as though she had come home, and it was difficult to not think of them as having been from the future as well.

Jenny helped Mrs. Toole bring in dishes of roast venison, vegetables, and bread, going around the table to serve it up to each of them. Ellie had looked around for the kids but knew they would be upstairs with Miss Anne. Jenny and the other servants had helped Lucy with Charles, but now that there were two children and Charles would be starting his education soon, they had hired a nanny. Since children did not often eat at the table with guests, he would be tucked away upstairs with her and his sister.

"So, you milked cows, hunted, and fished. Was that everything in which you've been engaged for the last ten years?" Robert asked. "What did you do with the Onöndowa'ga:'? And how was it you came to be with them? I still understand not how it is you're alive. Major Burke was certain you had expired."

Ellie looked at Thomas for a moment, an apology in her eyes. There was so much she wanted to say to him but had been unable to. Deciding to leave out any mention of her injury, she went with a vague version of the rest of the story.

"They needed a healer, so I went. The braves agreed to leave everyone else at the outpost alone if I went with them and did not try to escape. So, I ended up back in their village and lived there until after the war ended. I was a healer for them, but I also helped with planting and harvesting and that's where I learned to hunt and fish. It was an amazing experience."

By everyone, she had meant Thomas. Both unconscious from their injuries, she had come back to life after having died from hers. Having been laying in his lap, she had felt the movement when they tried to wake him from his head wound. One of the Onöndowa'ga:' in question happened to have been in her hospital weeks before, where she had treated his brother. When she volunteered in Thomas's place, Dajoji readily agreed to her proposition. Of course, she did not share any of this with her friends now. They did not need the details.

Robert nodded. "You sound almost as though you enjoyed your time with the Indians."

There was a question in the statement, as if it was unfathomable to think anyone would enjoy such a fate. Based on the horror stories they had heard from former captives at Fort Edward, she understood his reluctance to believe her experience had been pleasant.

"I did," Ellie replied. "They welcomed me as family. I didn't want to leave them."

"Then why did you?" Thomas asked with barely concealed anger.

The lightness of their conversation was suddenly gone and the pain in his voice had Ellie thinking that there was more to Thomas's question than what was on the surface. It was almost as if he was asking why she had left him instead of the Onöndowa'ga:'. Perhaps it was an accusation that her departure from the village was only to bring him pain now.

Brushing it off, she answered, "I didn't have a choice. The army came in and forced me to leave. They actually took me captive for a while, then threatened that if I was found living in any Native American village again, the army would destroy the village. They told all of us that. They were trying to make sure no 'White' people lived among the Natives anymore, even if they were married to Natives or had children with them. They took the children, too."

Ellie knew she sounded bitter, but it was because she was.

"Native Americans?" Lucy asked. "Do you refer to the savages?"

The phrase had not yet come into popular usage. When she had first arrived at the fort, it was entirely foreign to everyone. Though she had heard it a couple of times in recent years, it was still not common terminology.

"They aren't savages. No more than White men anyway. But yes, I refer to what everyone else calls Indians." Before the conversation could get heated, she tried to change the subject. "But, I feel like I'm dominating the conversation," she said with a chuckle as she speared a roasted potato. "What have you both been up to?" Ellie looked between the men, then added, "Well, I guess I know what Thomas has been up to. What about you, Rob? What have you been doing? You married yet?"

"No. I've not yet married," Robert chuckled. "Thomas and I have gone where the army has assigned us."

"I wondered where you both ended up over the years. I always imagined you both went home after the war."

Robert had a mouthful of food, leaving Thomas to answer. "We both stayed and were stationed here at Fort George after the fall of Quebec."

Ellie almost choked on the bite she was chewing. She started coughing while trying to clear her throat. All this time and they had both been so close.

"You've been here that long?" she eked out after taking a drink.

The men both nodded.

"Nearly eight years now?" Thomas asked while looking at Robert, who nodded.

"I was there," Ellie said excitedly as realization dawned on her.

At the confused looks before her, she added, "At the fort. I mean, just barely, but we were there a couple years ago."

"At Fort George?" Robert asked, sharing a look with Thomas, forks frozen in each of their hands.

Ellie nodded. "Yeah. We rode down from Poughkeepsie. That was one hell of a ride. Eighteen hours straight, then we just turned around and rode right back without stopping. It was rough, but thankfully, I knew how to ride a horse, so I was able to go with."

Ellie looked at Thomas with gratitude for teaching her how to ride. She tried to give him a small smile, but he was distracted and looked confused and upset.

"We?" Robert asked.

"Her husband," Thomas said with venom dripping from the word. At Robert's surprised look, he added innocently, "Did I not mention? She married."

Robert turned sideways in his seat to look at Ellie questioningly. "You married?"

"I did. And yes, he was with us as well."

When the men were too flabbergasted to speak at all of the new revelations, Lucy took the opportunity to say, "It must have been on a day when you were both away, if neither of you saw her." Turning to Ellie, she asked, "What brought you to the fort?"

"We came so my friend Mehitabel could meet with the governor."

"Mehitabel?" Lucy asked on a laugh. "Are you always so informal?"

Ellie chuckled. "Sorry. I am. I forget. We came with my friend, *Mrs. Prendergast.*" Ellie said the formal name with an emphasis.

"Mrs. Prendergast?" The men both shouted the name in disbelief, causing Ellie's and Lucy's heads to turn in their directions.

"Yes," Ellie said hesitantly, her eyes narrowing at the reaction the men displayed at the mention of the name. "We escorted her after her husband's trial so she could meet with the governor."

Thomas was scowling and looked towards the door as if looking for an escape. Robert reached across the table and put his hand on Thomas's arm. Thomas jerked it away, giving him an incredulous look. He knew he had seen Ellie that day, but Robert had convinced him it had not been her. Had he known she was alive then, he would have followed her. He would have chased her down and… And then what? She was there with her husband, and he had already been married to Lucy. Charles had been a year old. As much as he wanted to blame Robert for her slipping through his fingers then, he knew it was not his friend's fault. Truthfully, it was probably for the best. He took a deep breath, trying to calm himself down.

Ellie did not understand what had the men all worked up. She knew the Prendergasts had not been popular in New York City, but she did not understand what had Thomas looking like he wanted to punch someone. It was as if William Prendergast had personally attacked Thomas in some way.

While Ellie and Lucy tried to understand what was passing unspoken between the men, Robert said, "You escorted Mrs. Prendergast, yet you did not come inside the fort with her. Where were you?"

"How do you know I didn't come inside?

"We were there," Thomas said bitterly. "I recall the day all too well."

"Oh," Ellie said in response. "Well, I went to secure provisions for the return trip. I met her and my husband at the gate as they were leaving."

"That's your husband? The man who escorted her?" Robert asked.

Ellie nodded. Thomas seemed even more agitated, though Ellie would not have thought that possible.

When Ellie had refused Thomas's marriage proposal, she had mentioned his age, commenting on how young he was. The man he had met at the fort had to have had twenty years on him. Was that what she had wanted? Someone old enough to be their father? She had always claimed to be far older, but he had never believed it. Had she merely convinced herself she was that old because she preferred men that age?

"He came to the fort another time, before the trial," Robert recalled. "He spoke with the governor on behalf of Mr. Prendergast."

"He's known–knew–the Prendergasts for years. I stayed with Mehitabel in the spring in order to deliver her baby while William was off playing soldier. Mehitabel had not heard from him in some time, so we asked Dean to seek him out. When he found him, William ended up convincing him to speak to the governor for him. He was going to come himself, but knew he'd be arrested if he did." Ellie chuckled at the memory of that year. "I agreed to stay with Mehitabel long enough to deliver her baby, then I was going to return with Dean to continue his trade route for the rest of the summer. I ended up spending the entire summer with her, helping her out on the farm, then trying to figure out how to keep her safe and taken care of while William was sitting in jail all fall."

Ellie had been distracted, but Robert's words sank in now. "Wait. You met Dean? You were there at the fort then, too?"

"Both times." Robert affirmed. He looked at Thomas, who was quiet, but still fuming across the table.

Looking between the two of them, Ellie said, "I wish I'd known. I would have loved seeing you both."

It was true, though Ellie knew it was probably best that she had not run into them at the time. She was not sure how that would have played out with Dean there. She had loved him, but it would have broken her heart to see Thomas while being with Dean. And considering how old Charles was, she was certain Thomas had already been with Lucy then. No; it was best that they had not seen each other on that visit.

"Where is your husband now?" Robert asked.

"He passed away nearly a year ago."

Robert looked remorseful. "I'm sorry."

Ellie merely nodded her thanks.

Lucy added, "Did you not say he had consumption? That must have been difficult for you. My uncle had it and he lingered for rather a long time, suffering for years before passing."

"I'm sorry to hear it," Ellie offered. "Thankfully, that was not the case for Dean."

The woman patted Ellie's hand from across the table. "I'm heartily glad for it. I imagine it was still rather burdensome for you. It's not an easy way to pass. It was quite difficult to watch my uncle in those final months. I can only imagine watching your husband waste away like that."

"Dean didn't waste away. He was murdered before the consumption had a chance to destroy him."

There were gasps around the table.

"Murdered?" Lucy asked. "How dreadful."

"Mm. Another trader ambushed us and tried to take me. Dean fought him off so I could get away and he was stabbed multiple times in the chest and abdomen." Ellie looked across the room, out the window as she recalled that night. She knew she spoke in detached, clinical terms, but it was better that way. She needed the distance it provided her.

"I do hope his murderer was brought to justice," Robert said solemnly.

"He was." Ellie did not elaborate. She did not say that she had killed Elias Blackwell by bashing his head in with a rock, leaving his carcass to be picked clean by scavengers.

After an awkward silence fell over the table, Robert tried to change the subject. "What shall become of you now? Will you work as a nurse here as you did at the fort?"

Shaking her head, Ellie replied, "No. I'm going to Boston as soon as the weather is good enough to travel. I promised the Armstrongs I would stay until they return in a few weeks, but then I'll be gone."

"Boston?" Robert asked, surprised. "Why Boston?"

"I thought you held contempt for the cold and snow?" Thomas asked. He felt as though he was losing her all over again, even though she was clearly never his to begin with.

"I do," she shrugged.

"You are aware it's colder there than it is here in New York?"

Thomas was trying to keep his tone light when being calm was the last thing he wanted to do. He had known her plans were only to be there for the winter, but now as it got closer to her departure, the reality started to set in. It was best if she left, of course, but he could not make himself want her to go.

"I am. But it's temporary," she said while looking down at the food she was moving around her plate with her fork. "I only plan on spending a few years in Boston then maybe I'll head south. I'm thinking maybe Charleston or Savannah." At the last, Ellie looked upwards toward the ceiling as if picturing it.

Ellie wanted to stay in the colonies for the time being. She did not know enough of history to know how populated Florida and Louisiana were or if English was widely spoken in either place that had been settled by the Spanish and French, respectively. It did not help that New Orleans was in turmoil. Having been taken over by the Spanish in 1763, an insurrection had occurred in October of the previous year when Ellie was trying to decide where to go, reinstating the French. Without a more established government in place, it was only a matter of time before the Spanish government returned. Between the French and Indian War and the upcoming Revolution, Ellie wanted no part in that as well. Any further west, she thought would be too unpopulated by any groups other than Native Americans, many of whom did not speak English. Not to mention she had already done that once and did not particularly wish to go back again unless it was to be with her own Onöndowa'ga:' family.

"Why not remove yourself to the south now? There's a great deal of unrest in Boston at the moment," Thomas found himself asking. He may not have wanted her to leave at all, but if she had to go anywhere, he would prefer if she did not find herself in the middle of even more turmoil.

Ellie exchanged a knowing look with Robert.

"There's an awful lot of unrest everywhere. There's nowhere I could go right now to escape what's coming. I just feel a need to be in Boston for a while."

"Pray tell, what, exactly, do you believe is coming?" Thomas asked.

"The only thing that possibly can come of the political climate in which we find ourselves. War is on the horizon."

The conversation was interrupted as Jenny cleared away plates and Mrs. Toole brought in custard. Ellie took the opportunity to change the subject.

"Enough about me. Tell me Rob, why have you not found a woman to settle down with yet?"

Robert laughed at her impertinence. "You always were rather forward. It gives me pleasure to see you've not changed," he said with a smirk. Unlike the surprise she saw in Lucy's face, there was laughter in his eyes.

"And you're avoiding the question."

"I've been waiting upon you to return to us from the afterlife," he flirted as he grasped her hand, bringing it to hold against his chest while he gazed at her, batting his eyelashes. Though he said it jokingly, it was not far from the truth. He had fallen in love with her years before and had only stayed away because of Thomas, but no woman had measured up since.

Pulling her hand away, she slapped him playfully while she laughed. It felt good to have this connection with someone again. This was the first time since her arrival in the past that she felt as though she had a history with another person. Thomas had become distant and formal. She understood why and did not fault him for being so, but she missed having someone to share a past with; someone she could joke with and be herself without having to worry about formalities and proprieties. It felt like she was always on guard, and it was exhausting. Even Dean had her keeping her guard up, unable to fully be herself with him. She had always felt she could be herself around both Thomas and Robert. Now, it appeared she could only do so around Robert.

## Chapter 12

# March 1769

On her walk the morning of March 18, Ellie found herself in the Fields along with a large number of the other inhabitants of the city. They were gathered around the Liberty Pole, celebrating the anniversary of the repeal of the Stamp Act. It amused her to see the celebrations over something like that. She almost understood how people felt, comparing it to the celebrations of the legalization of gay marriage in her own time. What she did not understand, however, was the fact that they were still celebrating it three years later. How long would they continue to do so?

The atmosphere was excited but tense. The people were rejoicing, but the soldiers in the upper barracks on the other side of the Fields watched the gathering closely. Ellie could feel the animosity rolling off of them as they watched the celebrations. However, it did not seem to bother anyone there, and they continued with their festivities.

When Ellie arrived home, she found another invitation to tea from Lucy, causing her to let out an exasperated sigh. The woman was relentless. She appreciated her invite to dinner so she could catch up with Robert, but she still did not want to be the woman's friend. Not only would she be leaving soon, but she also did not want to spend the remainder of her time watching Thomas with his perfect wife and his perfect family, preferring instead to wallow in her solitude.

Ellie ignored the invite, throwing it in the fire Hannah had going in the kitchen.

"She'll only continue to send them, miss," Hannah observed.

"I know. But I'll be leaving soon. She'll stop then." Turning back to watch Hannah prepare dinner, Ellie added, "I'm sorry you keep getting interrupted with them. Did you tell Miss Jenny I was not interested in attending anything with Mrs. Burke?"

Hannah did not bother to answer her. Instead, she only raised her eyes from the dough she was working, giving Ellie a look that asked, "What do you think?"

Ellie knew Hannah had said something. Ellie had also told Jenny herself. After the second time she had told Jenny no, the girl had informed her that Mrs. Burke would not listen. She continued to send the invites and Ellie continued to ignore them. Lucy even stopped by the house a couple of times, but Ellie had not been home. She was glad to have missed her.

When Ellie passed near the Fields the next morning, another crowd was gathered, but this time, it was not celebratory.

"What's happening?" she asked a woman standing nearby.

"The soldiers tore down the Liberty Pole. People are furious. Some of the Liberty Boys are discussing what they should do." The 'Liberty Boys' was how many referred to those involved with the Sons of Liberty.

"So long as they don't attack the soldiers, all shall be well," said a masculine voice behind them.

Ellie spun around to see Robert dismounting from his horse, holding the reins behind him. A smile spread across her face at seeing him. She looked around now, seeing many more soldiers dispersed throughout the gathering. They appeared to be mostly officers on horseback.

"You don't actually think they'll attack, do you?" she asked Robert.

"Are *you* really asking me that?" he asked pointedly. "Do you not already have knowledge of the outcome?"

When she had told him of the Revolution, he had been skeptical, arguing that there was no way a bunch of farmers and merchants would ever attack the Royal Army. She had never tried to convince him anything she said was true, yet the more she told him, the more he had believed her.

"Not for every interaction, no. I only know some of the bigger things," she replied.

The officers were dispersing the crowd now, trying to prevent an escalation. They seemed to be the go-between, keeping the peace between the other soldiers and the habitants of New York City. For some reason, the colonists had far more respect for the officers than the soldiers, though it was still given grudgingly.

"You should remove yourself to home, Ell," Robert said. "Would you care for an escort?"

Ellie smiled up at him. "You know I don't need an escort, but I would welcome the company."

Robert smiled back at her, knowing how independent she was. The woman thought she was indestructible and had no need for a man's protection. It was such an odd thing for a woman to think. Whatever her reasoning for allowing him to accompany her, he welcomed the opportunity.

"I saw the Liberty Pole right after the Stamp Act was repealed," she said as they walked, him guiding his horse along. "It was erected shortly before my journey here with Mrs. Prendergast. I don't remember it looking like that one that was just torn down."

"It was not the same one. This one is the third. The one that you would have seen was either the first or the second one. The first one was erected on His Majesty King George the Third's birthday that June and did not stand for very long. It was quite large with a flag on top that read, 'The King, Pitt, and Liberty.' It was quite a celebration. The soldiers and the people both celebrated together. Even officials came out for the celebration, despite it having been erected by the Sons of Liberty. It represented the colony's opposition to Parliament's authority but quickly became a rallying place for Patriots in the city; a place for people to voice what they believe to be opposition to Parliamentarian oppression. The soldiers were much opposed to that, so they cut it down in August shortly after being erected. It was mere days before another one was erected, but it was also cut down. By the end of September, a third pole was erected and Governor Moore ordered the soldiers not to cut it down that time. That's the one that stood until yesterday."

"It would have been the first one that I saw, then. Unless the second one looked exactly the same?"

Robert shook his head. "Not exactly the same, no."

"Definitely, the first one, then."

They walked in companionable silence for a while, but Ellie wondered about his and Thomas's experience during that time. She remembered reading about the various riots and turmoil around the colonies, both in school, then firsthand in the broadsheets that Dean had shared with her.

"How bad were the riots here?" she asked.

"Well, when the ships first arrived with the stamps, there were perhaps two thousand people at the harbor to protest. Though, that wasn't as bad as the night before the Act was to go into effect. Another two thousand people tried to storm the fort. The Sons of Liberty knew the stamps were being held there and organized a mob to come and destroy them. They tried to urge us to fire on them, and for a time, I feared we would have to. Thankfully, it did not come to that."

Ellie agreed and Robert continued, "There was plenty of carnage that night, though. In plain view of the fort, Lieutenant Governor Colden's coach and several of his sleighs were burned. The fort's commander, Royal Artillery Major Thomas James, had his home ransacked and all his possessions burned. There was rioting and other vandalism throughout the city. When another ship arrived in January, it was boarded, and the stamps were taken off and burned. The mob continued to run the city until the Act was repealed the following March."

"I'm sorry, Robert. That must have been difficult."

"It was. When it was repealed and the Liberty Pole was erected, it brought the people together again, ending much of the violence. But then we received word that William Prendergast was coming to storm New York City only a few weeks later. Unlike the mobs, he had an army. People here were terrified."

Robert looked at Ellie, trying to gauge her reaction. Had she known what her friend had been planning? How involved with the plot was she?

"I can imagine they were," she said. "His fight was always with the patroons. It was never with the people of the city or even the British government. He was merely trying to fight for fair rents. It's unfortunate that the residents here were caught in the middle of it."

Robert gave her a curt nod. 'Unfortunate' was not a word he would have used to describe the situation. But she was not personally involved in the rebellion, for which he was grateful to hear. She had merely helped the man's wife while he was away waging war. He could not fault her for that.

"Once that was behind us, the Quartering Act was passed, which started an entirely new upheaval," he informed her. "Circumstances have been most disagreeable since the end of the last war."

"It sounds like it. And of course, it's not going to end anytime soon. The end of the next war won't be until 1783. That's still fourteen years away." Ellie had to stop for a minute. "Good gods! Just the thought of that is exhausting."

"It is," he agreed on a chuckle. On a whim, Robert turned to look at her. "Let's leave it all behind.

We may board a ship and remove ourselves away somewhere that shan't be affected by it."

Ellie's smile warmed his heart.

"That sounds amazing. We could go to…" she tried to think of someplace she would want to go that would not be affected by any of it. Unfortunately, this war would have a far reach. "Italy," she finally said.

"Italy?" Robert laughed. "Why would you wish to go to Italy?"

"I've always wanted to go there. And they won't be joining in the war. Of course, I know nothing of their history in this time period. Nor do I speak Italian." Ellie frowned. Maybe Italy was not such a good idea after all.

They resumed walking and Robert told her more about the Quartering Act. "When the Provincial Assembly refused to support it, they were discontinued. Fifteen hundred troops arrived from England three years ago, but the Assembly refused to provide money to house them, feed them, or provide them with necessities. They were forced to stay aboard the ships in the harbor."

"The Quartering Act is why the Armstrongs were so eager to allow me to stay in their home while they were away. They didn't want the soldiers taking over the empty house."

"No one does. Most believe the soldiers shall force their way into their homes and take up bedding with their wives and children. They understand not that the Act only allows for them to take over a private residence if it's entirely empty. Otherwise, the army is restricted to warehouses, barns, taverns, and inns. The Armstrongs were right to be concerned, but few others in the city need be."

Ellie's brow furrowed. She did not want to sound unsympathetic to the soldiers who were caught in the middle, but she already knew some of this, in a broader sense of course. Being there in person gave her a different outlook on it. She was reminded of the Vietnam War in which the soldiers took the brunt of the displeasure of the people who did not support the war. They were only doing what they had been ordered to do, but people who were against the war blamed the soldiers instead of the government.

"What did you mean that the Assembly was discontinued? Were they dissolved?" she asked.

"The Assembly at the time was dissolved, but Parliament allowed the governor to re-form a new Assembly that was more sympathetic to Parliament. Unfortunately, many of the men sitting on the new Assembly were also members of the Sons of Liberty. They've recently dissolved another one to re-form it yet again. They've also been prohibited from passing any new laws until they agree to comply with the Quartering Act."

As they approached Ellie's house, they wrapped up their conversation outside her door. Ellie invited him inside, but he had to get back to work. Robert opened her door for her, then took her hand, kissing the back of it before wishing her a good day.

Ellie went inside while Robert stood outside like a guard, waiting for her to close the door behind her before leaving. The formality was odd coming from Robert, but it made her feel good that he had stayed until she was safely inside before leaving. He had always been a good friend to her, and she was relieved to see that he still was. It had felt good to talk to someone she did not have to be on guard with. She was glad he knew she had knowledge of the future, even if he did not understand why or how she had come to be there. She would miss him dearly when she left in a few weeks.

## Chapter 13

## March 21, 1769

While cleaning up after dinner, Ellie, Ezra, and Hannah heard a boom in the distance. Ellie told them to stay inside and ran to the door to see if she could see anything. Of course there was nothing to see. Ezra was right behind her, not listening to her order.

He stopped her from going outside, pulling her back inside by the shoulder. "You'll be stayin' here, miss. I'll go see to what happened."

"You should stay with your sister where it's safe," Ellie argued.

Ezra was not having it. "As the man, 'tis my duty to protect the women. You stay here and I'll go."

Ellie rolled her eyes at the notion but reluctantly let him go. He would have gone with or without her permission. With no further explosions, she decided it must not have been anything too drastic.

It did not take him long to come back and inform them, "The soldiers tried to blow up the new Liberty

Pole. When they couldn't cut it down, they tried setting gunpowder to it."

Another Liberty Pole had been raised by the end of the night after the last one was cut down. However, the new one was much larger and had iron bands wrapped around it in an attempt to keep the soldiers from cutting it down. Ellie laughed at their persistence while the siblings debated whether or not the soldiers would succeed in taking down this new pole. Shaking her head, she left them to their debate.

Wandering around the market the next day, Ellie enjoyed the sunny but chilly day. Winter still lingered, but spring was trying to grace them with its presence. While she looked at the limited variety of produce, she felt someone grab her arm. Startled, she looked up from the asparagus she was sorting through to see Lucy entwining her arm with her own, Jenny standing off to the side a few feet away.

"I dare say you've been avoiding me," she said bluntly.

Ellie turned back to the asparagus, avoiding the woman's gaze. "I've been busy preparing for my departure."

"Busy reading, do you mean?" she chided.

Ellie studied the woman. How had she known that? They had never been that close and while Ellie had mentioned her love of reading at tea the one time she went, she did not think that meant Lucy knew her well enough to know that was how she spent all of her time, even if it was what she had spent much of her time doing after Lucy's delivery.

"What can I do for you, Mrs. Burke?" she asked, getting to the point.

"I took pleasure from our tea together, along with our other visits before and during my travails. I thought we should be good friends, yet you've not returned," she pouted while dropping Ellie's arm so she could finish her shopping.

Ellie stared at her as if seeing her for the first time. Was she for real? How could she possibly want to still be friends with Ellie given her history with Lucy's husband?

Ellie paid for her produce, putting it in the basket she had draped over her arm. Shopping like this was one of her favorite things about being in the past. She much preferred the variety available in her own time, but she had always loved farmer's markets. The markets there reminded her of that. With no grocery stores and no refrigeration, food was purchased daily. Ellie liked that.

Walking away from the vendor, Lucy again took her arm, and they walked as old friends through the streets, Jenny following at a slight distance behind them. Lucy made small talk for a while as they wove through the other people, horses, and carriages.

Ellie was hesitant to relax in Lucy's presence. Though she had been making small talk, Ellie could not help thinking that the woman had something on her mind. It came sooner rather than later.

"I know of your history with Major Burke," Lucy finally said as if discussing the weather.

She let the statement hang in the air between them, waiting for a response from Ellie. There was nothing Ellie could say, so she remained quiet. After a moment, Lucy continued, "You see I've known the Burke family my entire life, having grown up with his sisters. Hence, I heard of the woman for whom he grieved several years ago. When you first saw one another and he said he thought you dead, I assumed that grief had been for you." An assumption which had been confirmed by her conversation with Thomas after Ellie had departed.

She paused again, but again, Ellie remained quiet. There was no accusation and Lucy had not been married to him then. There was nothing to defend or argue and Ellie was not certain what Lucy even expected her to say. She would not deny their relationship. To do so would be pointless.

Lucy stopped walking then, dropping Ellie's arm and turning to face her.

"Have you returned now to steal my husband away?" she asked pointedly.

Ellie laughed. If this woman really knew the history between them, she would know that was not even a possibility. Thomas was not an option for her. She wanted to make it perfectly clear that she was no threat to Lucy.

"I honestly had no idea Thomas was even here. I assumed he had gone back to Williamsburg when the war ended. I'm moving to Boston and only stopped here for the winter before heading north. I hate traveling in the cold and snow and wanted to spend some time here before I left the area. That's the only reason I'm even here. As for Thomas," Ellie shook her head sadly, "That never was an option. I never could've made him happy. I left once because I knew I was not right for him. That hasn't changed, and I don't plan on staying around again now. It's why I've not accepted any further invitations from you for tea. I thought it best to keep my distance. I don't want to cause any issues between you."

Lucy was quiet while she considered Ellie's words. They were in line with what little she already knew. She trusted her husband but did not know yet if she could trust this woman, even if she had plans for her. Finally, she asked, "You left? I thought you to have been taken by the savages?"

Ellie shook her head. "No. I mean, I was, but I volunteered to go. I asked them to take me. I was planning on leaving the fort anyway, so I decided to go with them."

It was not the whole truth, but it was close enough. Ellie thought it best to leave out the part where her departure with them was in exchange for sparing Thomas's life. She had exchanged her life for his, but Lucy did not need to know that.

"Leaving the major to think you dead?"

Ellie's annoyance dripped from her voice, "I did not know he would be led to believe that. His surgeon's mate was there and saw the whole thing, even helped convince the Natives to take me. I thought he would have told Thomas what happened."

"Major Burke does not know you left of your own accord?"

"He didn't." He did now, but she did not think it necessary to share that with Lucy. It changed nothing.

"And you've no interest in rekindling your friendship with him?"

The use of the word friendship did not escape Ellie. She wondered just how much Thomas had told Lucy about her.

When Ellie again shook her head, Lucy smiled, deciding to trust the woman. With a purpose in mind, she needed to gain her friendship in order to carry out her plan. She linked her arm in Ellie's once again, turning back to the market.

Her voice again became light as she said, "Good. Then we shall be friends, and you may join us for tea now."

Ellie laughed at the ease with which this woman viewed the world. She was old and jaded herself, far too cynical to have that kind of faith in people. If she were in Lucy's position, she was certain she would not trust a woman with the history she had with Thomas anywhere near the man she loved. However, she was glad that Lucy did. Despite the fact that she was leaving soon, it would be nice to have a friend, even if it was the wife of the man she once cared so deeply for.

Ellie needed to put her lingering feelings for Thomas aside once and for all. She could think about them again once she was in Boston, but for the remainder of her time there, she needed to distance herself from him. She needed to turn her emotions off once again. Having moved on from him years ago, she could not understand why her emotions continued to reside just under the surface now. He was only a friend; nothing more.

"Fine. I'll come to tea," Ellie relented.

"And you must come to Sunday dinner as well," Lucy pushed.

Ellie shook her head. "I'll come to tea. I don't think I should come for dinner."

"Major Jensen shall be there," Lucy said as she studied Ellie, trying to get a feel for whether her plan could work. She had seen the way this woman had behaved around Robert and his own reaction towards her had also not gone unnoticed. Lucy wanted her husband's friend to be happy and would befriend this woman if she thought it would help. After a brief pause where Ellie did not say anything, she added, "As will Mrs. Emerson. Her husband will be in port and shall be joining us as well."

Ellie sighed. She got the distinct feeling she was being played. "Fine. I'll be there." She looked at Lucy and narrowed her eyes. "This time."

Lucy smiled triumphantly. It was a start.

Later that night, there were more explosions. Ezra again went to check on it and again reported back that the soldiers had returned to the Liberty Pole. Their attempts continued to be unsuccessful.

## Chapter 14

# *March 23, 1769*

*As mankind were made for society, every person who willfully annoys or disturbs that society without any pretense but purely evil, ought to be held in the utmost detestation as a common enemy. And, as in the present case, the cutting this post down can only be done to affront all the Sons of Liberty … the perpetrators would do well to consider the consequences … for they may know that such a body of the people who would not yield to be enslaved by the most august body on earth, will not tamely submit to such a mean, low-lived insult on their liberty, … and if ever the perpetrator is discovered, he may be almost assured New York will be too hot to hold him long.*

Continued attempts at tearing down the Liberty Pole were all thwarted. The Sons of Liberty intervened, making their presence known around the pole. A subtle threat was posted in the newspaper and further attempts to bring down the pole were halted. Whether it was the threats or the fact that the previous attempts had all thus far been unsuccessful, was unknown. But for now, there would be no more attempts to take it down.

Ellie put down the broadsheet and began to ready herself for dinner with the Burkes. She questioned why she had agreed to go and wondered if she could still get out of it. Apparently, Sunday dinner after church was their weekly tradition. Robert and Adelaide both came over nearly every week and her husband joined them whenever he was in port.

When Ellie arrived, everyone was already there. She had not been late, but since they were all coming from church together, it was inevitable that she would be the last to arrive. The men were all in the study upstairs, leaving the women in the parlor to chat while Mrs. Toole finished the meal.

"Mrs. Russell, you should stay," Lucy said to Ellie, startling her with the suggestion.

Ellie would have thought that would be the last thing Lucy would have wanted. Still, she feigned innocence. "Stay where?"

"Here. In New York City. Don't remove yourself to Boston. It's better here."

"That's a horrible idea," Ellie laughed, setting down her tea.

Lucy looked offended. "What's so horrible about it?"

Ellie could not explain it to her and instead replied, "There's nothing for me here."

Lucy was scandalized. "Are we not friends? And what of Major Jensen? Is he not your friend?"

Ellie was skeptical. "I thought men and women were unable to be friends here. Isn't that frowned upon in this society?"

Adelaide piped in curtly with, "That has not seemed to stop you in the past."

"Nor will it in the future," Ellie admitted. "I simply find it odd that Lucy is encouraging it when it goes against your societal standards. I thought adhering to those was everything for y'all." Ellie's use of the word from her upbringing had surprised her, but she stuffed it down, chalking it up to her discomfort.

"Oh, pish. You make me out to be so haughty. I can break the rules when needs be," Lucy said.

Ellie gave a skeptical look to Adelaide, who was giving the same look to Lucy.

Lucy brushed them both off and continued trying to persuade Ellie. "What awaits you in Boston then?"

Ellie had nothing in Boston. She simply wanted to see history being made, nothing more. But she could not say that to these women.

"Adventure. I'm entirely on my own for the first time in my life. I look forward to what comes of it."

"Yet you're on your own here," Lucy said.

Ellie did not know how to explain it to these women. She had been on her own for a very long time. But this was different. This time, she was in control of her life and did not need to rely on anyone else or take care of anyone else. It was only her.

"It's not the same thing. I've been here before. I'm ready to begin again somewhere new. Somewhere I can start over again."

"Is that how you came to be at the fort with my brother to begin with? And what you did when you had your fill of him? How many times have you started anew, Mrs. Russell?"

Ellie scoffed, "That's not what happened at all Mrs. Emerson. I had no choice over either of those situations."

Jenny came in to inform the women that dinner was ready. Mr. Toole had been sent upstairs to retrieve the men and they all met in the dining room. Lucy made introductions between Ellie and Jack Emerson then directed everyone to the table, insisting Ellie sit next to Robert. Though Ellie did not mind at all, and was strangely fortified by his proximity, she again began to think Lucy had ulterior motives for her attendance at this dinner. It did not matter. She would be leaving New York soon enough.

"Tell us of your former husband, Mrs. Russell. How did you meet? Was he a savage?" asked Adelaide once they were seated.

"Oh yes. Do tell. I heard the red men force their captives to marry within a year or die," Lucy added dramatically.

Ellie shook her head while throwing a guilty look at Thomas. She was determined to be on her best behavior and not fight with him for a change. She knew it was possible, but it was far more likely to happen than not. Talking about the man she married after turning him down was a sure way to incite one.

"No, they don't force anyone to marry. In fact, it's quite the opposite. Women have far more freedoms in Native American societies, and they choose their husbands. Men have to convince the women that they are worthy."

There were uncomfortable chuckles around the table as most of the guests looked scandalized.

"You chose to marry, then?" Lucy asked.

"Something like that," Ellie said vaguely. She really did not want to get into all of that at the moment. It felt too personal to discuss in front of a bunch of strangers. She was still uncertain about Lucy, and she did not know the Emersons well, though she was certain Adelaide did not like her in the least.

"How long have you two been married?" Ellie asked while directing her attention to Adelaide and Jack in an attempt to get the spotlight off of her.

Adelaide beamed at her husband. "We were wed twelve years ago."

Ellie congratulated them on having lasted that long, which was a feat in her opinion. The couple still seemed to be happy, but Ellie suspected that was because he was gone all the time.

"Is it difficult to be apart so much?" Ellie asked.

"It can be," Jack answered. "It certainly has its challenges."

Ellie knew the toll it could take on a family when a parent was gone for long periods of time. Her own father had been in the navy and was constantly deploying for six months at a time. It left its mark.

Her attempt to redirect the conversation away from Dean did not last. "You've still not told us about your husband, Mrs. Russell," Adelaide reminded her.

"He was a trader. I met him in the Onöndowa'ga:' village where I lived," she said simply.

"He was not a red man, though, Mrs. Emerson," Robert said, coming to her rescue.

"Major Burke and Major Jensen both met him," Lucy added helpfully. "Apparently he was mixed up in the Rent Rebellion a few years ago."

"He knew the Prendergasts," Ellie defended. "He was not part of the rebellion."

"Russell?" Jack asked. "This wouldn't be Dean Russell would it?"

"You knew him?" Ellie asked excitedly.

"Ah yes. I'm familiar with Mr. Russell. I got my start on one of his family's ships. It's a shame what happened to them. They were good people."

"Yes. It is," Ellie agreed, then explained to everyone else that his family had been murdered when they asked.

"How is Mr. Russell?" Jack asked. "I've not seen him in years."

Ellie looked down at her plate briefly, then said, "He passed away."

"I'm sorry. I'd not heard."

Ellie shook her head sadly. "It just happened last May."

"You say his family was murdered?" Lucy asked. "Is that not what you said happened to him as well?"

"I hadn't thought of that. Isn't that funny," Ellie observed while nodding her affirmation.

Adelaide looked horrified. "Funny?" she admonished while scowling at Ellie. "You find the murder of your husband to be funny?"

"It's an expression, Mrs. Emerson. I only meant that it's ironic. I can assure you; I find absolutely nothing about Dean's murder to be funny."

"Well, one can only assume. We merely have your words and your prior actions to determine what you may be thinking about those who seem to care for you."

The woman had a way of getting under Ellie's skin. She had been pleasant enough when they first met, but ever since, Adelaide had been cold and accusatory toward her. Ellie was not sure what she had done to deserve the woman's wrath, but she suspected it had something to do with her previous relationship with Thomas.

"You don't want to know what I'm thinking," she said while leaning in and glaring at Adelaide. "But let me say again that I find nothing about his death to be funny. Not the fact that it was done while he was defending me from attack. Not the fact that the man who was responsible was the man who caused me to be pulled from my village and my home. Not the fact that I had to sit and watch it happen. And certainly not the fact that I would have died next after being tortured had I not killed his attacker."

Her voice had been getting louder as she spoke, but she was angry at Adelaide's implication that Ellie did not care about Dean or what had happened. She had not meant to share what she had about the situation, but she found Adelaide to be provoking and condescending. Ellie's face had darkened at the memory of Elias Blackwell and everything he had done to make her life miserable. She did not regret taking his life, only that she had not done it sooner. Ellie had not noticed Robert's hand resting on her arm as she spoke. When she finished her tirade, she was shaking. Robert rubbed her arm gently and she pulled her eyes away from Adelaide's face, looking over at Robert. Pulling strength from him by her side, she shut her eyes for a moment, calming herself.

"I must apologize," she said after taking a drink and directing her attention back to Adelaide. "It's a sensitive subject for me. I do not take it lightly as you would suggest."

"My apologies, Mrs. Russell," Adelaide said. "I did not mean to imply such a thing."

A hush had fallen over the table for a moment, and Lucy took the opportunity to say, "Mrs. Russell still has not told us about her time with the savages. I've simply been dying to hear of it."

Ellie sighed while lifting her glass for another drink. "There's really not much to tell. Life with them was actually rather pleasant. I found it much easier to assimilate to tribal life than it was to life at the fort."

"Was life at the fort so difficult for you Mrs. Russell?" Thomas asked pointedly, speaking to her for the first time.

Ellie eyed him over her glass. There was a lot she wanted to say to that, but she was trying really hard to not fight with him. "It had its challenges," she said, echoing Jack from only moments ago.

"Undoubtedly it was easier to assimilate to them as this was not your first time living amongst the red man."

It was a statement, not a question. Thomas had always suspected that she had been born into a wealthy family then was stolen away by the Indians. Since she would never explain where she came from, he could not be certain. Perhaps she would be more open with sharing her past now than she had been then. He was not expecting the questioning look she shot back at him.

"I've never lived amongst them before. Why would you think I had?"

"Have you not? I suppose I always imagined you had. It would have explained a great many things on which you never spoke."

Ellie continued to stare at him questioningly. She had so many questions, she did not know where to begin. Though, she also knew this was not the time nor the place to ask them.

"Mrs. Sor– Russell was a nurse at Fort Edward at the start of the last war," Robert supplied for Jack in an attempt to quell the awkward silence that had fallen over the table. "I'm sorry, Ell, it's difficult to remember you're no longer Mrs. Sorenson," he said while turning to her.

"It's fine, Rob," Ellie said while placing a hand on his forearm. "I have plenty of things I find difficult to remember."

"Such as remembering to not be so familiar with people," Adelaide admonished.

Instead of being embarrassed as Adelaide had intended, Ellie smiled widely. "Exactly," she said and raised her glass in a mock toast to Adelaide.

"She was a marvelous nurse," Robert said. "She easily could have been a physician. The men often sought her out over Mr. Anwar."

Ellie reddened at Robert's praise, but she shook her head. "I believe you're remembering things more favorably than they were. There was plenty I did not know. They only came to me over Anwar because he was such an ass."

Jack and the women all gasped at her language while Robert and Thomas both tried to conceal their laughter. Ellie apologized for being so crass in their company.

"Anyway, much of what I learned about medicine at the fort came from…um… Major Burke." Ellie still struggled with what to call Thomas. She was so used to addressing him and Robert by their first names, it was odd not to do so. Even when she did remember to be more formal, she often forgot that they were both majors now and no longer captains. "He's a fine physician and taught me quite a bit."

Thomas looked at his plate. "I no longer practice medicine."

Ellie dropped her hand to the table, the bite of food on her fork forgotten as she stared at him in shock. "How could you no longer practice? You always wanted to be a physician."

All eyes were focused between her and Thomas. "I grew out of it," he said simply.

Ellie wanted to press the matter but was keenly aware that they had everyone's attention and it somehow felt too intimate a conversation for a dinner with so many other people. She knew by Thomas's tone that he was not going to say any more on the matter. It was something she would have to ask about later when they did not have an audience.

The conversation flowed with only a few awkward pauses. Ellie had to bite her tongue on more than one occasion to not provoke Thomas, but he managed to remain civil, even when she could see she had upset him. Eventually, it came back around to her departure once again.

"The Armstrongs should be home in a few weeks, then I'll be leaving," she said, trying to tamp down equal parts disappointment and excitement.

"Where shall you go?" Jack asked.

"Boston."

"Do you have family there?" he asked.

"I don't." Ellie shook her head.

"Where is your family?" Lucy asked. "I don't believe you've ever mentioned from where you came before the war."

Ellie could not stop from glancing at Thomas again, who was scowling and trying very hard to not look at her. "I don't have any family," she said.

"None at all?" Adelaide asked. "How unfortunate."

"I'm the middle child of five. My older sister died when she was young, but I still have four brothers." Ellie looked down, vanquishing the memories. Looking back up, she corrected herself, "Or at least I did. There's no one now."

"Are you certain you wish to go to Boston, Ell?" Robert asked, redirecting the conversation. He knew this was a touchy subject between her and Thomas and she was grateful to him.

"Why would I not?" she asked.

"Well, with the tensions arising there, I would not think it to be a place you'd wish to be."

"Tensions seem to be arising everywhere, Major Jensen," Thomas said. "Need I remind you of the mobs and riots we've had here ourselves or the recent uprising that came to our doorsteps?"

That was a stab at Ellie, a direct reference to the Rent Rebellion. Ellie wanted to smack him or at least yell at him, but she held her temper and ignored him. When she turned her head away from shooting daggers at him, she saw Robert looking at her.

"Yes, but it seems Boston has more than their share. With the number of Cudgel Boys in the area, the troubles are likely to only continue. It's not safe there right now." Robert shot her a pointed look. "If there is to be another war, it will likely begin there."

"Cudgel Boys?" Ellie asked. Her eyes widened slightly in warning at Robert. When she had admitted to him that she had knowledge of future events, it had led to a long conversation where she had told him of the upcoming Revolution. She did not know many details, but she had told him what she remembered from history classes, namely that most of it seemed to originate in Boston. He had promised to keep the information she had shared with him between them. She had never even told Thomas any of it and she had hoped he had kept her secret.

"Sons of Liberty," Robert provided while giving her a wink and a reassuring smile. Ellie took it to mean that he had not told anyone. She hoped she was interpreting it right.

Thomas did not miss the exchange between them. He knew he was missing something, but he laughed at the absurdity of Robert's prediction. "How can anyone think these colonists would go to war with the British Empire? Riots and rebellions are one thing, but war is something entirely different."

"Exactly," Ellie said nonchalantly. "I'll be just fine in Boston. You're sweet to be concerned, but I'm perfectly capable of taking care of myself."

Robert shook his head doubtfully, knowing why she wanted to be there but not understanding it.

They managed to make it to the dessert course without Ellie and Thomas getting into a fight. It had been difficult, but somehow, they had both managed to hold their tongues. Thomas was not certain how they had managed it, but he thought they had done well. He began to think they might make it through after all.

Thomas could not help from picturing Ellie alone in Boston where there were regular riots and acts of sedition. As much as he wished she was not going to Boston, he knew it was best if she did not stay in New York. He wondered briefly if there was a way to convince her to go elsewhere, maybe to Virginia or Philadelphia.

"I don't plan on marrying again." Ellie choked on the bite she had taken. "Thank you, though."

Thomas turned back to the conversation to find his wife and sister trying to marry Ellie off once again.

"Yet you're still quite young," his wife argued.

"I'm older than I look," Ellie said flatly.

Thomas could not help making eye contact with Robert and exchanging a knowing smile with him at her claim of being older.

"Well, you're still young enough to find someone else. You're beautiful. I'm certain we may find an appropriate suitor for you," Lucy insisted while glancing briefly in Robert's direction.

"Of course we shall," Adelaide joined in. "Leave it to us. We'll find you a new husband in no time."

"I have absolutely no desire to ever be married again. I don't believe in marriage."

The table fell silent at her declaration.

"Yet you've married twice," Thomas pointed out bitterly, breaking the silence.

"Yes," she agreed. "And I'm capable of learning from my mistakes."

Thomas scowled at her.

"Mistakes?" Lucy asked. "Nonsense. We simply need find the right person for you." Her eyes again darted to Robert, who seemed to be amused by the exchange.

Ellie stole a glance at Thomas, who looked pained.

"How have you come to not believe in marriage?" asked Adelaide. "What is there in which to believe?

"I just don't," she shrugged. "It's nothing more than a way to oppress women. Particularly in this day and age. I won't lose my autonomy, and I refuse to be anyone's property."

"Oh, it's not all of that," Lucy argued. "What of love? Would you not wish to marry for love?"

Ellie scoffed. It seemed these women were not going to give up easily. Maybe it was because she would not be there much longer and with any luck would not see them again, but she decided to be brutally honest and tell them how she felt about marriage.

"Love? Love is a myth. It's the worst reason to get married. It's fleeting; doesn't last. Then what happens when it's gone? You're stuck. Trapped in a loveless marriage with someone you can't stand and because you have no rights, no property, and actually belong to your husband by law in this place, you are incapable of leaving. You must submit to his decisions and even his rule. You're in hell for as long as you both shall live. No thank you."

"That's a rather cynical view," Adelaide observed.

Ellie shook her head. "Not cynical, just realistic. I've seen it time and time again. Family, friends, coworkers. Damn near everyone I know has been divorced. People change and they don't change to-gether."

Another silence fell over the room. Ellie took an-other bite of her dessert, letting her words sink in.

When Ellie looked up at the faces staring back at her, there was a mixture of shock, disbelief, and con-fusion. With the exception of Thomas's. On his face, Ellie saw pain but there was more this time. There was pity. Ellie could handle the disbelief, the pain; anything but pity, especially not from Thomas. Ellie set down her spoon and was preparing to make her excuses to go home when Adelaide continued the ef-fort.

"If you harbor no belief in love, why marry twice thus far?"

Ellie sighed. They were not going to let up any time soon. "The first time, I was young and naïve and didn't know any better. The second time, I had no choice. I was taken from my home and the people I loved and forced into captivity with my only choices to become an indentured servant for the rest of my days or marry a trader whom I had come to know and had always treated me well. I chose marriage."

"I thought you said the savages didn't force you to marry?" Lucy asked. "Did they try to sell you?"

Ellie smirked bitterly. "No, the British Army did that. The 'savages' as you call them treated me like family. The British forced me into captivity and would not release me of my own cognizance. I had to be released into someone else's custody like chat-tel. The only concession they allowed me was to choose between marriage or a life of servitude under some cruel master. Marriage seemed the lesser of two evils."

A look of shock and understanding crossed Thomas's face, but now it was also filled with sorrow.

"You say 'The British' as though you are not one of His Majesty's subjects. Do you have no allegiance to the Crown? Did your time with the savages change your loyalties?" Adelaide accused.

"I was never British to begin with, so I can't say I've ever had any allegiance to them."

"Did you not tell me once that your family was English? Thomas asked.

Ellie cursed his memory before responding. "Once upon a time, they were. But that was generations ago. We've not been English in a very long time. And I never was."

"If you were never British, what are you?" Thomas pressed.

Ellie laughed bitterly while shaking her head at the old source of contention between them.

"Surely you're from one of the colonies?" Jack asked.

Ellie again shook her head. "I'm not."

"You don't seem to have a foreign accent," Jack added, intrigued. "From where do you come if not from here?"

Adelaide and Lucy both looked as confused as Jack at Ellie's claim.

"I can't say. I can only say I'm not British," Ellie said evasively.

The conversation continued, with Ellie denying her loyalty to the Crown, yet not being forthcoming about her origins. Thomas put his head in his hands while resting his elbows on the table, proper etiquette be damned. He closed his eyes against the familiar argument and the headache it was bringing on. First the conversation about marriage, now this? Was this not the very thing that had come between them before? She had always kept her past a secret from him, never telling him anything. And now the infernal woman was going to throw it back in his face? As if he needed the reminder.

Without looking up, Thomas suddenly pulled one hand away and slapped it down on the table. The noise of his hand hitting the wood, and the dishes rattling startled everyone into silence.

When he had their attention, he started saying, "Can we please not..." He trailed off for a moment to collect himself. When he finally lifted his head, everyone at the table was staring at him. He started again, directing his attention to Ellie in a cold hard glare. "Mrs. Russell, if you wish to continue the pretense of being unable to divulge your origins, I would appreciate it if you did not discuss them at all. At least not in my presence."

Ellie had the grace to look chastised, but there was something more behind her eyes. Was it hurt? He decided he did not care. She had been the one to inflict the damage this subject brought on. He would not feel guilty about his reaction to it.

She studied Thomas while the entire table sat in silence. The pain in his face immediately took her back to their time together at the fort and all of the arguments they had over this topic. Pasting a smile on her face, she said, "My apologies, Major Burke. I will not speak of such things again."

The words were contrite, but Ellie's nerves were frazzled. She supposed she deserved it, but his response had stung. Would they never be able to be around each other again without fighting? Ellie was suddenly exhausted and glad the evening was nearly over.

Lucy tried to salvage the conversation. "Do you sympathize with the red man, then Mrs. Russell?"

"I have sympathy for any oppressed or marginalized people or those who are displaced from their homes. I know all too well what that feels like and I do not wish it on anyone. I do not approve of their tactics, but I can certainly understand why they feel a need to use them."

"I read of a woman who was taken captive and never was able to resume her life in civilized society," Lucy offered. "Poor dear has struggled for years."

"I would argue that I'm not the norm for captives," Ellie said. "For starters, I was not a captive. I also had a different worldview prior to going into my life with the Onöndowa'ga:' and never quite fit in here to begin with."

Thomas huffed while Robert laughed and said, "You most certainly did not."

More than ready to leave, Ellie set her napkin on her plate and was about to stand when Lucy addressed her, not yet ready to give up on the concept of marriage. "You make marriage sound wretched. Not all of them are so. It is a wife's duty to submit to her husband. In return, he provides her a home, protection, financial support. Is that not a fair trade?"

"No. It's not," Ellie replied. "I can provide those things for myself. A marriage should be an equal partnership, a friendship, companionship. Marriage here is anything but. If I desire companionship, I can find that without tying myself to someone for the rest of my life."

The women were scandalized. Jack looked embarrassed. Thomas looked sad. Robert smirked.

"If I were to ever do it again," Ellie offered, "I would have a partner, not a master."

## Chapter 15

*March 1769*

Robert walked Ellie home after dinner. She had declined his offer, but he had insisted. Having been so drained from the experience, she did not argue with him.

"Have you considered staying, Ell?" he asked as they approached her door.

Ellie eyed him suspiciously. "Have you been speaking with Lucy?"

He looked at her quizzically. "I've not. This is something I've been thinking on since I first saw you again."

Huddling under her cloak, Ellie shook her head. March was a fickle month, and the weather had turned cold again. "I don't think that's a good idea, Rob."

"Stay until I can make arrangements to leave. Then I shall accompany you," he offered.

"Why would you do that?"

This was the last thing Ellie had been expecting. She stopped walking and turned to look at him, seeing the seriousness in his face. They had been friends briefly ten years ago and had not seen each other since, yet he was willing to leave his best friend and his life in New York to come with her to Boston? Ellie was touched, if a little confused.

"I don't want you to go by yourself. It'll be dangerous for you, for any woman on her own."

Ellie felt there was more to his offer that he was not saying, but she did not push him on it, far too tired to think about it. After the way the night had progressed, she would have to wait to ponder it when she could think more clearly.

"I don't know, Rob." She shook her head and continued walking. "You know what's to come. Boston is where it'll all start. You sure you want to be there for that?"

"Why would *you* wish to be there for that?"

"Are you kidding? I've heard about this my entire life. I want to see it happen."

"It'll not be easy, Ell. It will be a dangerous place if what you say is to happen comes to pass. Please wait. I'll accompany you and keep you safe."

"It will be. But it won't really be any safer anywhere else," she countered.

"Most of the battles in the last war took place at the forts," he tried. "If you stay away from them, surely you'll be safer."

Ellie shook her head. "This war will be different. It won't be limited to the forts and military targets. No one will be safe from it."

"Under those circumstances, you really should allow me to accompany you." He paused, sensing her hesitation. "Please, Ell. It's still a few years away.

When did you say the first shots happen? What did you call it; the 'shot heard 'round the world'?"

Ellie nodded. "1775," she said blankly as they approached her door.

"Then there's still time. It shall take time to sell my commission, but I may certainly have it sold long before then and shall come with you."

Ellie was hesitant. "I don't know, Rob. There are still all the events leading up to it: the Boston Massacre, the Tea Party. I'm sure there are plenty others which I don't remember, but the massacre will be happening soon."

"Come now, you don't think those are the only events which lead up to thirteen different colonies staging a revolution? You've seen the tensions already building, even here. This entire city was waiting to be attacked by farmers only three years ago. Stay here and learn of new events."

There was no censure in his voice. Unlike when Thomas had brought it up, Ellie knew he was not making a dig at her over the Rent Rebellion led by William Prendergast. He had a point, but she was still reluctant. She was not even sure why. Maybe it was the thought of allowing someone else into her life again to that degree. What was he really asking her? She did not have the mental capacity to figure it out tonight. It would have to wait for another day.

Turning to go inside, Robert stopped her. "Tell me why you're so insistent on Boston, Ell. I would think you'd had enough of war given what happened to you in the last one. Why should you want to deliberately put yourself in harm's way again?"

She shook her head. "It's history, Rob. I'll be in harm's way regardless of where I am. But how often do we get to see major historical events?"

Ellie could not explain it. The fact was that everyone lived through something historic. She had lived through the fall of the Berlin wall, the 9/11 terrorist attacks, and a global pandemic. But she had always felt cheated that she was unable to have a firsthand experience with either of the first two. She had always wanted to see the wall before it came down, then one day it was gone. Not only was she not in New York when the twin towers fell, but she had woken late in the day, and by the time it was on the news, they had both long since collapsed. She did not even watch it happen in real time. At the time, she was still in school and had only begun her time as a paramedic, so she did not get to assist in any way. Ellie felt like she was always watching life from the rearview mirror. She wanted to see this first-hand, to understand what the colonists in Boston went through in order to create what they thought would be a better world for their children.

Ellie could not tell him that history was not her only reason for escaping. Not American history anyway. She knew she was running again, trying to avoid the pain of having to face her own past every day. Had she not decided when she was with the Onöndowa'ga:' that she would stop doing that? It was time to stop running and be deliberate. Robert was asking her to stay, but her staying would not only hurt her. She could see the pain it caused Thomas every time he saw her. She hated that she was the reason for that pain and wanted to take it away from him. Leaving would alleviate some of it for him.

"Is history not happening here as well? Boston is not the only place these events are occurring. Look around, Ell. People are unhappy throughout all of the colonies. You said yourself that those were only the events of which you were aware."

"I'll think about it," she agreed.

His face split into a dimpled smile and Robert started celebrating, but Ellie paused him with a hand on his arm, "I'm not making any promises."

"For now, I'll settle for a promise that you'll consider it."

Ellie woke Monday morning feeling like she had a hangover, despite not having drunk any alcohol. Grateful she was not working and had nowhere to be, she lingered in bed, trying to alleviate the ache that was splitting her head in two. Despite her best efforts to forget the dinner from the night before, her brain insisted on reliving every conversation, every look from Thomas, every accusation from Adelaide, every cheerful optimism from Lucy, and every confusing interaction with Robert. Ellie groaned into her pillow, rolling over again in an attempt to smother the memories. Instead, she tried to focus on the date and count down the days until she would be able to leave for Boston.

She had no idea when the Armstrongs would be back in New York. With no telephones and letters being sent either by horse or ship, communication was extremely limited and slow. They had told her they were planning on returning in April, which was still another week away. But April could mean anytime during the whole month. It could be a week, or it could be five. Ellie groaned again at the thought.

Her brain returned to Robert's offer when he had walked her home. Ellie told him she would consider it. Was it what she wanted? Did she want to stay long enough for Robert to go with her? Did she even want him to go with her?

Winter had been long and lonely. She had only seen him three times in the last few weeks, but the time she had spent with him had been nice. She missed having someone with whom to talk; a friend who knew her so well. It would certainly make things easier once she got to Boston. On the other hand, would he expect more from her than she was willing to give? After the conversation about marriage last night, she highly doubted it, but people often liked to believe they were the exception to the rule. If she even considered allowing him to go with her, she would have to make it very clear what it was and what it was not.

Ellie finally got herself up and going. Half the day was already wasted away and by the time she made it downstairs, Hannah had long since put breakfast away and was working on the afternoon dinner. It was just as well; Ellie had little appetite. She grabbed a carrot and a piece of bread and sat down at the kitchen table with a thump.

"Dinner were that good were it?" Hannah asked.

Ellie was surprised the girl was asking at all. She must be opening up to Ellie a little.

"It was a disaster," Ellie confessed.

"I'm sure 'tweren't all that," Ezra offered optimistically.

Ellie scowled at his optimism, leaving him to smirk back at her. Unlike his sister, he had no problem following Ellie's lead and treating her as an equal or a friend instead of as someone superior to him. Ellie appreciated that.

"At least I won't be here much longer, and I can avoid a repeat of it," she said, trying to convince herself her plans were still firmly in place, despite not yet having made up her mind whether or not she would extend her stay. Though, she supposed it would also be up to the Armstrongs. Would they allow her to stay on once they returned? If they did not, she would have to find someplace else to live. She was not sure she wanted to do that.

"That reminds me," Hannah said, pulling a letter from her apron pocket. "A dispatch came for you this morn from Mr. Armstrong."

Ellie perked up, reaching out for the letter Hannah offered her. Turning it over in her hands before opening it, she was suddenly nervous about the contents, unsure she wanted to have an end date to her time there. Shaking off her anxiety, she opened the letter and read the contents. Her brow furrowed as she read.

"Do it say when they shall return?"

"Ezra!" Hannah exclaimed, scolding her brother. "That's none of your concern."

One corner of Ellie's mouth turned up at the interaction. She waved off Hannah's concern. "It's alright, Hannah. It actually does speak of their return, though it doesn't say when it will be. Mrs. Armstrong's mother has become ill, and they've decided to stay there for the time being. They've asked me if I'd stay on longer."

Ezra broke out in a smile. "That's wonderful news, miss. How long shall you stay?"

First Lucy, then Robert, now this. Ellie shook her head. It was as if the entire world was conspiring to keep her in New York. What was it about New York City that continuously pulled her back time and again?

"I'm not certain I will stay just yet, Ezra."

"Surely, you will, though? Is you in that much of a hurry to get to Boston?"

"I thought I was," Ellie replied.

"What's waiting there for you?" he asked.

Ellie scoffed. "Nothing but history," she said sadly. Maybe he was right. Maybe she should listen to the universe and stay a while.

While folding the letter back up, Ellie accidently knocked over her water glass, spilling it all over the table. She tried to catch it before it fell, and her attempt only served to leave her arm soaking wet. Hannah hurried over with a linen cloth to sop up the mess and Ellie dried her hand and arm off as well. As she did, her bracelets slid around her wrist exposing the dandelion seed tattoo she had gotten there all those years ago. She paused to look at it now, remembering why she had gotten it in the first place. It served as a reminder of her military upbringing, but also the fact that she always went where the wind took her, and to be open to new possibilities. This was merely one more thing directing her to stay where she was. Ellie had a habit of overthinking a lot of things, but going on a new adventure was never one of those things. She smiled to herself at the prospect. If this was not a new adventure, what was it? Staying did not mean it was forever. She could simply push her trip back and see what happened.

With the decision made, Ellie felt surprisingly lighter.

## Chapter 16

*April 1769*

Despite her decision to stay in New York longer, Ellie did not seek out Robert or Lucy. She had not decided to stay for Lucy and still did not want to be overly friendly with the woman, even if she was all too likable. It simply hurt too much to be near Thomas, seeing the pain she continued to cause him. Had circumstances been different, she would have eagerly accepted the woman's friendship.

Robert, on the other hand, she was not avoiding; she merely did not know where to find him. She had hoped to run into him while out walking or shopping, but she never did. It had only been a couple of weeks since her decision, but if she did not run into him soon, she would break down and go ask Lucy. She was hoping to avoid that possibility.

Ellie stayed busy helping Hannah with the chickens and the garden. They had planted in March and Ellie was out weeding when Hannah came into the backyard to find her.

"You've a guest, miss," Hannah announced.

Sitting back on her heels and still holding the hand shovel, she wiped the back of her hand across her face pushing away the strands of hair that had fallen forward. Looking up at Hannah, she saw Robert standing behind her in his uniform. A smile spread across her face, and she stood. He quickly reached out to help her stand before she made it to her feet. Ellie took the opportunity to give him a hug.

"It's so good to see you," she exclaimed.

Robert held her tight, lingering with her in his arms before letting her pull back. "It's always good to see you, Ell."

"What brings you here?"

"I'd not seen you and was worried you'd left for Boston without saying goodbye."

Ellie cocked her head and put a hand on her hip as if to scold him. "I would never do that to you."

"You did once before," he reminded her.

Ellie had the decency to look chastised. Robert had not meant it to be mean. He only wanted to convey that his concern was valid.

"I'm sorry, Rob. I never meant to do that to you. Everything happened so fast. I didn't even have time to pack my things and take them with."

"I know it was not your intention to leave in that manner last time, nor this time. However, I knew not when you were planning to leave, other than sometime in April."

Robert could not stop staring at the smudge of dirt on her cheek. He wanted to wipe it off, but she was so adorable with it, he debated with himself over doing so. Finally, he reached out and wiped it off. She jerked back in surprise at first but then let him.

"Thanks," she said. "Actually, I'm glad you came. I didn't know where to find you and wasn't quite ready to reach out to Lucy or Thomas and ask them."

With a frown, he asked, "Is it so bad between you? Can you not even be civil to one another?"

She knew he was talking about Thomas, not Lucy. "You were there at dinner. We try. It even works for a while, but we always seem to end up arguing." Ellie laughed bitterly. "I don't think he's forgiven me for still being alive."

Robert did not laugh with her. Instead, he shook his head. "You know not what he went through when we thought you had died. We both blamed ourselves. I think we each blamed one another as well. It was not easy for him."

"I know it wasn't, Rob," Ellie said quietly. She wrapped her arms around herself. "If I could go back and do it differently, I would. And I'm not making excuses, but it wasn't easy for me, either."

Robert put his big hand on her shoulder. "I know, Ell. And I can't tell you how happy I am that we were wrong. To see you alive and well is more than I ever could have hoped for. I know Thomas feels the same. He'll reconcile himself to the circumstances. He merely needs time."

"I doubt that," she said sadly.

Ellie shook herself and dropped her arms, shooing away a chicken who had become interested in her feet. "Anyway, I have news," she said. "The Armstrongs wrote and informed me they'll be staying in South Carolina until further notice. They're unable to get back here anytime soon and have offered me the use of their place as long as I want it."

"Ell, that's fantastic," Robert exclaimed. The smile quickly left him as he paused. "Will you accept their offer?"

"For the time being."

Robert let out a victorious cheer and Ellie could not help the smile that spread across her face. She chuckled at his response but tried to temper it. "I'm not sure how long I'll stay, but for now, I'm postponing Boston."

"That shall have to do, then," he said with a smile.

"We should definitely get together more," she said. "Do you want to come for dinner sometime?"

"It would be my pleasure," Robert said with a smile.

"Good. How do I get hold of you if I need you? I have no idea where you live."

"I live in the officer's quarters at the fort, though I often stay at Thomas's. I know it not to be your preference, but you may always reach me through them if you have a need."

"I thought that might be the case," she said. "Hopefully, it won't come to that."

Robert chuckled and shook his head.

---

Ellie found herself smiling as she walked through the market, swinging her basket. She was looking forward to having dinner with Robert and catching up without Lucy and Adelaide nagging at her or Thomas scowling at her. Her good mood would not last long.

"You shall be staying?" Lucy asked excitedly.

Ellie kicked herself for not paying closer attention to her surroundings. Every time she left the house, she made it a rule to keep an eye out for Thomas, Lucy, or Adelaide. If she saw any of them, she would turn and go in the opposite direction. This time she had been distracted and had not seen Lucy.

"Word travels fast, I see." It had only been the day before that she had spoken to Robert. The only other people who knew were the Rales and the Armstrongs, though the Armstrongs had not likely even received her letter yet.

"Major Jensen informed us. He was rather excited about the prospect."

"He seems to think I need someone to protect me. Apparently, I am incapable of doing anything on my own." Ellie said, rolling her eyes.

She tried to laugh, but the other woman was not laughing with her.

"He merely wishes to see you safe. Do not begrudge him this," Lucy admonished. "Now," she began in a much more cheerful tone, "If you are to stay, there are a few things to which we must see."

Ellie was immediately both confused and concerned. What exactly did this woman have in mind for her? And how was it any of her business?

"You'll need to set up your household, of course," she replied at Ellie's questioning look.

"Oh, I don't need all that. The house I'm in already has everything I need. I've written the owners to let them know I'll be staying on a little longer. They wanted me to stay while they're gone, so they'll be happy to know that I'm extending. I'm still not certain how long I'll be here, though. I don't have a set date, but I still plan on going to Boston before too long."

"Well, you still need a lady's maid. And we should see to—"

Ellie held up her hands to stop the woman.

"Oh no. I don't need all that. It's just me and I'm low maintenance."

Lucy looked confused for a moment but was undeterred. "Mrs. Emerson and I shall take you to the market next week."

"I appreciate the offer, but really, I'm fine. If there's anything I need, I'm perfectly capable of seeing to it."

Lucy huffed. "Very well," she relented. "But you must join us for dinner every Sunday after church. Oh, what am I thinking? Which church do you attend? You're welcome to join us."

Ellie could not help the burst of laughter that erupted from her at the idea of attending church. "No, thank you. I don't do church."

Lucy looked at her strangely. "I see. Well, you shall join us afterwards, then."

"I can't make any promises."

"And I'll send over our schedule. Mrs. Emerson and I get together for our needlework, soap making, candle dipping, and so many other tasks. It goes by so much faster when we're able to keep each other company."

Closing her eyes, Ellie took a deep breath. How did she tell this woman to back off and leave her alone? Maybe she could just avoid her and she would eventually get the hint.

"I'll have to let you know," Ellie said noncommittally.

It was as good as a yes as far as Lucy was concerned. She smiled widely and informed Ellie she would send Jenny over with dates and times. Ellie was more than happy to get back to her shopping, though the lightness she had felt earlier now turned heavy.

## Chapter 17

*May 1769*

With the sun shining down on her, Ellie watched the ships navigate their way around the whales that could be seen popping their heads up out of the water. She was soaking it all up and enjoying the peace of it while her inner turmoil raged a battle of its own. Part of her questioned her decision to stay in New York longer and she considered heading to Boston anyway. Of course, this line of thinking inevitably made her think of her situation and wondered what the point was. Did it matter where she was when she was alone everywhere? She had been excited to finally have a say over her own life for the first time since her arrival in the past, but she found she had periods of loneliness that she had not expected. Every so often, she allowed herself to wallow in her pity and grief for everyone and everything she had lost over the years.

Despite her loneliness, Ellie had successfully avoided Lucy for several weeks. The woman continued to send invites for various gatherings, and Ellie continued to refuse them. When Lucy began checking in on Ellie at home, she always found somewhere else to be. She would not mind spending time with Lucy under other circumstances, but that was not to be.

Robert was all she had there, but he was only a friend, and she only saw him on occasion. Not wanting there to be an appearance of impropriety, he had only come for dinner once. Visiting her at home without a chaperone was inappropriate. He had agreed to come on occasion but would not make it a habit. Ellie had rolled her eyes when he said that, but he agreed to meet her periodically around the city instead. With him working long hours, she did not get to see much of him.

How had she ended up there? After all this time, she still asked herself that. She was no closer to an answer than she had been when she arrived thirteen years ago.

"I thought I might find you here," Thomas said lightly as he approached Ellie sitting on the sandy stretch of shoreline, determined to not fight with her again.

Ellie's gaze was distant. She was staring out over the water at something only she could see while absently twirling the end of her loose blonde braid around her fingers. Lost in her thoughts and not yet ready to let them go, she did not look up when she heard his voice.

"Why would you think to look for me here?"

"I always could find you by the river, Miss Ellie. May I sit?"

Without looking up, Ellie held out her hand to a patch of sand beside her. She had been sitting with her legs and bare feet outstretched before her. Thinking it would have been beneath him to sit directly on the sandy ground, she was surprised he would ask. He never used to take issue with it, but he had been more carefree when she knew him. This Thomas was far more reserved. He sat, pulling his knees up and resting his clasped hands on them.

He sat so close, the smell of leather and wood wafted over her, and she inhaled it deeply. The familiar scent of him was like a stab in her already battered heart. It pulled her into where she could not follow.

"That's a lot of shoreline to search," she observed. "How long have you been looking?"

"This is the first place I sought," he bragged.

Ellie looked at him briefly, giving him a questioning look before turning her gaze back to the water. He prolonged answering, with smugness all over his face. She finally tore her eyes away from the water again to give him a look that said she was not amused. Finally, he sighed and relented.

"In truth, I would have thought to find you to the north of the fort where there are more trees and grass, but I've seen you walking this way often. It's the only place in this direction that isn't teeming with sailors and merchants. Has Brookland caught your fancy?" he asked, noting the direction of her stare.

Ellie's heart tightened that Thomas still knew her so well. She missed having that shared familiarity with another person. Normally, his assessment would have been accurate; she always favored anyplace that was filled with greenery. But the nearest greenery looked across the Hudson River to New Jersey. She was not interested in that view.

"Brook*land*?" she asked, putting emphasis on the second half of the word. She scoffed, "No."

Not expanding on her answer, Ellie turned her attention back out over the water. The spot in which they were sitting was very near to where the ferries departed for the Statue of Liberty in her time, with Governor's Island directly across from her and Brooklyn just beyond. She could make out Ellis Island and Liberty Island to the west, though both were uninhabited now. There was no Statue of Liberty to draw her eye. During the pandemic, the morgue had been in a warehouse in Brooklyn right on the East River. The Statue of Liberty had been visible along the entire drive from their hotel to the morgue and when she had any downtime or was feeling out of sorts, she would always go sit on the dock next to the warehouse and stare out at the water and the statue directly across from them. Despite not having any interest in it before, it had become a symbol of her time there. Now both islands were empty and Brooklyn barely even existed. It was nothing but farmland. It fueled her somber mood.

They were quiet for a time, Thomas giving her space to accept his presence before he tried talking with her. He thought maybe it would help it go more smoothly if they both had time to collect their thoughts. When Ellie finally broke the silence, he was surprised and confused by her words.

"Do you believe in reincarnation, Thomas?" Sitting where she was had Ellie feeling lonely, nostalgic, and introspective. It was a dangerous combination that had her wanting to tell him everything he had ever wanted her to say. Though she knew no good could possibly come of doing so, it would be so easy to tell him where she came from. Instead, she settled for voicing the foremost thoughts in her head at the moment.

"I don't believe I've heard of that. What is it?" he asked.

"It's the belief that when we die, our souls go on to be born again into another being. We have no memories of our past lives, and we could be born into another time and place or even into an animal."

"That sounds rather fantastical," he laughed. "Where do you come up with these ideas of yours?"

Ellie had never ceased to amaze him. He often wondered how she came up with so many of the things on which she spoke.

"I'm serious," she said, her eyes still glued to the water. "What if I was reincarnated? But instead of coming back as a baby, I came back as a fully developed adult with all of my previous memories intact, and in my same body with all my tattoos and piercings. Maybe I really did die when that car hit me, and someone was just trying to cover for the mistake of sending me back home, uninjured. The lightning was a correction which is why it didn't work in the village, and this really is my life, and I'll never make it back home."

Thomas had no idea what she was talking about. His mouth turned down in a frown while his forehead followed. "Miss Ellie, I know not that I understand what you're saying," he said slowly. "Are you well? By car, do you mean to say a carriage? Were you struck by a carriage?"

Ellie could hear the concern in Thomas's voice. Closing her eyes for a moment, she shut off her thoughts and buried everything down deep once again, taking the moment to bring herself back to the here and now. When she reopened her eyes, she finally peeled them off the water and Brooklyn where she imagined she could make out where her warehouse would be. Turning to look at Thomas, she said, "I'm sorry. I'm fine. Was there something I could help you with Major?"

Thomas was not sure what was worse: the previous fixation on something in the distance with the trance-like tone of her voice combined with the strange things she was saying or the cold aloofness with which she addressed him now. He wanted to hear her say his name again, not address him as Major. It was his turn to sigh.

"It's Lucy, actually," he said, reluctant to change the subject.

Before he could continue, Ellie sat up straight as alarm washed through her. "Is she alright? Is it Caitlyn?"

Thomas chuckled, trying to ease her mind and lighten the mood. "Everyone is well. She wishes to invite you to dinner. Again." He looked at her pointedly as he said the last before continuing, "Though she fears you will decline. Again."

Ellie rolled her eyes and shook her head. She had been declining all of Lucy's invitations since her last dinner with the Burkes. It was too much for her and Thomas to sit at a table full of people and not bicker at each other. He was clearly still angry with her and would probably never forgive her, first for turning him down, then for disappearing on him, and now for returning. Their interactions always devolved into an argument or them hurting each other, and they certainly did not need an audience when that inevitably occurred. The next time could easily turn into a yelling match between them.

"So, she thought I'd say yes if she sent you to ask? Tell your wife thank you for the offer, but I don't think it's a good idea."

Thomas sighed. "I'm told you are to stay for a while longer."

There was a question in his voice. "For now," she said. "I'm not sure how long I'll stay, but the Armstrongs have asked me to remain for the time being."

Thomas nodded. Ellie could not tell if he was happy she was staying or upset by the prospect. "Then we're bound to see more of each other. Can we not bury the past and start over, Miss Ellie? Surely, we can declare peace between us?"

Having already moved on from the intensity of her feelings years ago, she wished they could find peace and move forward. Ellie was nothing if not an expert at burying the past, but she desperately missed her friend, the person with whom she could be herself around. It killed her that they could not even manage that. With him being married now, she did not think his version of peace matched hers. She would be happy to rebuild the easy companionship they had once shared but did not think it possible for him. It would be too improper for them to be friends now.

"Is that what you want, Thomas?"

It was not what he wanted at all. He wanted Ellie, but he could not have her. She had made her feelings clear years ago and now he was with Lucy. How had life become so complicated so quickly?

"It's what Lucy wants," he said quietly. "I'd give her what she wants if it's within my power."

Ellie smiled sadly, knowing he would. He had a tendency to put the woman he loved above all else. It was one of the reasons she had fallen in love with him once.

When Ellie remained quiet, Thomas struggled to not fidget. "If you're to be here longer, I think it best. Besides," he added with a lopsided grin, "I'm afraid Lucy is determined to make a friend of you, yet."

Thomas said it lightly, trying to lighten the mood. He knew they were headed for another fight if he did not.

"She certainly is persistent, isn't she?" Ellie said on a chuckle.

Thomas shared in her mirth, agreeing.

"If you are to be friends, I wish not to spend my time fighting with you. It would be best if we could tolerate being in the same room together for more than five minutes."

Was that what this was about? He wanted to be able to tolerate her? Ellie wanted to slap him and tell him to take his truce and shove it. She tamped down the emotions and reminded herself that she had only ever wanted for him to be happy, which she found was still the case even now. If Lucy made him happy, then she would be happy for him. If it meant giving up a few nights to sit at the same table with him and his beautiful family to make him happy, then she would do it. She would sit on the outside and look in on his perfect family while she remained entirely by herself.

Biting back the tears that were trying to form behind her eyes, she said, "You're a good husband, Thomas." Ellie did her best to shake off her melancholy and self-pity. "Fine. I'll behave if you will."

"You shall join us then?"

"I'll try it again. I make no promises that it'll be a regular thing like she wants. But we can take it one visit at a time."

Thomas nodded in agreement. "That's probably best."

## Chapter 18

*Summer 1769*

Ellie did take her visits with the Burkes one at a time. Lucy tried getting her to commit to more, but she only ever committed to one. After getting through a dinner, she agreed to come to the next one. She and Thomas managed to be cordial to each other, mostly by holding their tongues and avoiding discussions of Ellie's past. They both became adept at changing the conversation whenever anything came up that would cause problems. It helped to have Robert there as well. He had always tried to relieve some of the tension that inevitably came up regarding her secrets, and he continued to do so now. After a couple weeks of this, Ellie agreed to tea with Lucy and Adelaide. Soon, she was meeting the women regularly for work tasks as well.

"Charles asks after you often, Mrs. Russell," Lucy informed her while they sat in the drawing room knitting stockings.

Ellie regularly asked after the children, who were not allowed to join the adults for dinner or tea. Those were more formal occasions which children were not permitted to attend. However, when they worked on various tasks, Charles would sometimes sneak away to see them. Lucy always scolded him and sent him away quickly while Ellie always gave him a smile and a wave. His nanny was constantly chasing after him.

Ellie looked up from her stiches, surprised. "Does he?"

"He's been greatly disappointed that you've not been 'round to see him. He asks when you'll come back to read to him and play soldiers with him again."

Lucy and Adelaide smirked at the ridiculousness of a grown woman playing soldiers with a child, but Ellie's heart tightened. "You tell him I'd love to come by and see him sometime."

Lucy stopped knitting and looked up, her hands falling into her lap. "Would you?"

"Of course. He's absolutely adorable. I enjoyed spending time with him while you were recovering from delivering Caitlyn."

As if listening at the door, Charles came running into the room, Anne on his heels. "Charles, you stop it this instant and come back here," his nanny scolded.

Ellie could not suppress the smile that spread across her face. She set her needles and thread down in her lap and held out her hands. "Charles, come give me a hug sweetie."

Charles looked at his mother tentatively, who nodded while speaking quietly with Anne. He smiled and came running over to wrap his little arms around her neck.

"Thanks kiddo. I needed that," Ellie said, hugging him back. "How are you? Are you giving Miss Anne troubles?"

Charles looked guilty for a moment but quickly straightened. "I want to play. Will you play with me?"

Ellie chuckled. "I'm working right now, but what if I tell you a story while I work?"

The boy nodded happily and without waiting for permission, climbed up into Ellie's lap. She had to quickly grab her knitting and set it aside to make room for him.

"What story shall we do?" Ellie thought about it, trying to come up with something. She settled on *Hansel and Gretel* and picked up her knitting to work while she told him the story. When she finished, he wanted another one. She told him *Little Red Riding Hood*, which led to the *Three Little Pigs*.

When he asked for one more, Lucy intervened. "That's enough, Charles. Mrs. Russell is going to run out of stories. It's time for your nap."

Charles clung to Ellie and tried to compromise. "What of a song instead?"

Ellie snickered. She really did not want to sing in front of everyone, but the boy looked up at her with pleading eyes. Letting out a huff, she said, "I'll give you one, but then you have to go with Miss Anne."

He nodded and Ellie began singing *Somewhere Over the Rainbow*.

Hugging the boy one more time, Anne came over to retrieve him. Waving to him, Ellie gave him a wink before he grabbed Anne's hand and left with her.

"That's a peculiar song," Lucy said. "I've not heard it before. Where did you ever learn it?"

Ellie shrugged. "I just picked it up somewhere."

"You're good with him," Adelaide observed.

Her tone was almost accusatory, which Ellie did not understand. Perhaps one day Ellie would figure out why the woman hated her so vehemently. They had gotten off to a decent start. Surely it could not only be Ellie's previous relationship with her brother that had her hackles raised?

"He makes it easy. He reminds me of my nephew." The boy smiled often and was constantly climbing on things in order to jump down when he thought no one was looking. It was easy to picture Charles on a BMX bike in a few years, doing flips and standing on the handlebars, scaring the hell out of her. Maybe it was for the best they did not yet have bicycles.

"You have a nephew? Just one?" Lucy asked.

Ellie nodded, not giving her any more than that. It did not matter, she continued to ask. "Do you have any nieces?"

"I do," Ellie sighed. "I don't really like to talk about my family, though. I can no longer see them."

Instead of closing the door on the subject, it opened it up to more questions. The women began asking why she could not see them, where she was from, and all of the other questions to which she had spent two years avoiding giving Thomas answers.

Ellie shook her head. "They're all gone and I'm the only one left in my family. What do you think?" she asked while holding up her completed stocking in an attempt to change the direction of the conversation.

Adelaide's eyebrows furrowed as she scowled. "I think having Charles here distracted you." She turned her head sideways to view Ellie's crooked stocking from another vantage point, but it did not help. It was as awful as she was trying not to say.

"I'm still learning," she admitted on a laugh.

When Mehitabel Prendergast taught her how to knit, they started with stockings since they were always in need. Ellie had pictured a thick cable-knit sweater in the shape of stockings. She had been surprised to see they were making the thin sock-like stockings she had been wearing since her arrival in the past, never having realized those were hand-knit, but of course, how else would they be made? The yarn used for them was more threadlike, being much finer than what was used to make sweaters. The needles were considerably smaller as well, resulting in around twenty stitches per inch.

Machines were beginning to come into use to make stockings, but most people still handmade them in order to spare the expense. Though Ellie had continued to purchase hers, she wanted to give herself something to work on while she visited with the women and also try her hand at improving her skill. She was not certain it would improve at that point.

"Your tension is off," Lucy offered. "It's tighter some places than it is in others."

That was not the only problem, but Ellie was grateful for the change in subject and let the women show her everything she did wrong.

***

As summer progressed, Ellie found herself settling into life in a colonial city. Without the cold dark days of winter upon her, she began to get out more, taking her time wandering through the outdoor markets, enjoying window shopping in the local shops, and even finding a tavern that held various lectures. Most were not of interest to her, but she managed to find a few on the schedule that she looked forward to attending.

She even began to look forward to spending time with Lucy, though Adelaide was still cold to her. It did not matter. Ellie never needed the approval of others. If the woman wanted to dislike her, it was her problem, not Ellie's. Lucy made her rounds almost every day, visiting people she knew. Ellie often joined her, Lucy introducing Ellie to other people in the community as well. Lucy made a habit of visiting widows or disabled persons, making sure they had everything they needed including companionship. Sometimes Ellie would come for a knitting or sewing circle to find other women there. She enjoyed the camaraderie of it all, though the other women in the sewing circles often had to help her with her stitches or show her how to do a new one. She had learned to sew as a child, but it was only very basic stitches. The ones these women used were far beyond what she had ever learned. The women were all astonished to see how little experience Ellie had with a needle but were quick to help teach her.

Ellie still continued to walk around the city as well. Every now and then Lucy would join her, though she was too busy running her household or visiting neighbors to do it often. Ellie bought more dresses suitable for the warmer weather and a few additional comforts for the house since she was going to be there longer. Though, she tried to keep her purchases to a minimum so she would not have as much to move.

"I know you have Hannah, but a lady's maid would make everything so much simpler for you,"

                                     

Lucy said, trying again to convince Ellie that she needed her own servants. It was an old argument at that point.

"As long as Hannah is willing to keep doing my laundry, I have no need for anyone else," Ellie argued. "I hate doing laundry."

The women laughed and Lucy grabbed Ellie's arm as she often did while they walked through the market or down the street. At first, Ellie had found the gesture strange coming from Lucy, but it had grown on her. She now found it endearing.

As they strode through the Fly Market, the weekly slave auction was in progress. Ellie had forgotten what day it was. She always tried to avoid going on the days of these auctions if she could help it. They were absolutely disgusting. Her nose wrinkled as they heard the announcer describing the slave on the podium as 'seasoned,' meaning that the young girl had been born in the colonies and was therefore accustomed to the local illnesses, customs of the colony, and life of slavery. Ellie was not sure if it was worse that these people described others this way or that she now knew the terminology.

A glance at the girl on the podium showed she could barely be fifteen or sixteen and was covered in old, ratty clothing that barely fit her. Apparently, she was being sold as part of the settlement of an estate after the girl's owner recently died. When they brought her up, they had to pry her from a young boy she had been clutching onto and they both screamed out at the separation.

"Brilliant!" Lucy said following Ellie's gaze. "You could purchase a slave instead of hiring a lady's maid. Though anyone you purchase will likely need to be taught everything, but it shall save you a considerable amount of money."

"Absolutely not. I will not own another human being," Ellie said, aghast.

"This Negro wench even be prime for breeding if'n you so choose," the announcer said, causing Ellie to flinch in disgust. He had been giving a description of the young girl, doing his best to sell her as someone who would be fit for any household chores that could be heaped upon her. Ellie pushed her way through the crowd, wanting to get as far away as possible. She did not get very far when a man ahead of her turned to his associate and snickered about what kind of ride she would give him in bed before bidding on the young girl.

Ellie stopped in her tracks and offered a price slightly above what the man offered. Lucy looked at her in surprise, but a satisfied smile appeared on her face.

The man turned to look at Ellie and bid again, raising his offer. Ellie looked him in the eye, scowling at him, and raised her bid. They had a small bidding war for a few minutes, while Ellie continued shooting daggers at the man each time he made an offer. She wanted to throw a real dagger at him as his vulgar comments had continued. Ellie was no stranger to vulgarity and even preferred it over false niceties, but this man was just plain disgusting. Vulgar was one thing; forced sexual interactions or beatings of a teenage girl were too much. There was no way Ellie was going to let him get anywhere near that girl. Finally, the man turned to Ellie and said, "Take the bitch. She's not worth that much."

Ellie wanted to punch him. She went forward to pay her bill and collect her new property, Lucy following closely behind her.

"Oh, this is a rather inspired idea for you," Lucy said excitedly. "You needn't bother with the expense of a lady's maid when you may simply purchase a slave girl. I mean, why anyone would choose servants over slaves is beyond me. Economics alone makes it an easy decision. I'd prefer slaves myself, but Major Burke does not abide the purchase of them. It does strike me odd, though. I cannot imagine where he came by such a notion. His family has always owned dozens of slaves."

Too stunned by everything that had just ensued, Ellie had no words. As she looked up, she saw them bring out the boy to whom the girl had been clinging. After limping out, he was displayed on the platform as the announcer proceeded to show him off like a prize mule.

"He be no good in the fields with this lame leg, only he do proper good in the house or at a trade. Hire him out as a day laborer to earn your investment back quick."

The attendants were having Ellie sign paperwork as she tried to ignore the ongoing auction. They brought the enslaved girl to her when Ellie saw her watching the boy with tears in her eyes. Ellie asked her, "Is that your brother?"

The girl nodded.

"Damn it," Ellie exclaimed.

The bidding had already started and she did not hesitate. Jumping back from the slave merchant's table, she bid on the boy. There was no bidding war this time and Ellie was able to purchase him for only ten pounds due to his limp. She paid the merchant and waited to collect her new purchases, done shopping for the day. Unable to imagine purchasing anything else more awful than what she had just purchased, there was no more joy in shopping.

As soon as the children were released to Ellie, they clung to each other, looking terrified. Ellie tried to speak to them in as calm and soothing a voice as she could muster.

"What are your names?"

The girl answered for them both, "Tabitha and Harris, mistress."

Ellie cringed. "You don't have to call me mistress. I'm Ellie. It's nice to meet you."

The children looked at her skeptically, but they followed behind her and Lucy as they all headed back toward Queen Street. Ellie saw Lucy home then headed home herself with her new charges in tow.

Once they got back to the house, Ellie asked Ezra to help her draw a bath. Neither of them had any belongings which broke Ellie's heart. They did not even have a change of clothes or a last name. Fighting to keep the rising bile down while they bathed, she put together some clean clothing for them. For Tabitha, Ellie grabbed one of her dresses, but for Harris, she had nothing. He was close enough in size to Ezra that she asked if he would mind parting with some breeches and a shirt until she could go back to the market and buy him some new clothes. She considered going back out that day but could not bring herself to do so. There was no way she could handle going back to that abomination.

With the teenagers bathed and in clean clothes, they all sat down to an evening supper. Hannah was fine with them sitting at the servants table, but now with four lower-class people in the residence, she balked again at Ellie joining them.

"If I don't eat in here with everyone, then you may all join me at the big table in the other dining room," she said.

Hannah was very much against that. "'Twould not do to have indentured servants and slaves sitting in the formal dining room."

"They are not slaves anymore," Ellie said sternly, causing the children's eyes to bulge with disbelief and uncertainty.

Hannah relented and did not say anything else when Ellie sat down with them.

"How old are you two?" Ellie asked. She had guessed Tabitha to be around fifteen or sixteen, and Harris a few years younger, but she could not tell.

"We ain't rightly know, mistress," Tabitha responded with her eyes downcast.

Ellie placed a hand over the girl's for a moment. "Please don't call me mistress. I really would prefer if you called me Ellie."

The children looked at each other, then over at Ezra and Hannah. They were uncertain how to take Ellie's request. She added, "I have no intention of being your new mistress."

Tabitha was immediately alarmed. "Does ya mean to sell us to someone else, mistress?"

Ellie sighed. It was going to take a while before she broke the girl of that. "I absolutely do not. You are not property. I only bought you to secure your freedom. I have no intention of keeping you enslaved. As soon as I figure out what I need to do to emancipate you, I will. And until you become adults, you can live with me. We'll figure out a profession for each of you so you can make your own way in the world."

Neither responded, but they both looked doubtful. Ellie imagined she probably would be in their place, too. Hannah looked downright scandalized.

While they ate, Ellie learned what she could of them, though there was not much to learn. They were born to an enslaved woman who had been brought to the colonies aboard a slave ship and grew up in the house of the people who had originally purchased their mother. She had died from smallpox when Harris was quite young. They never knew their father, though their mother had once said that the same man had parented them both. Neither even knew if he was a man of color or not, enslaved or free. As slaves, they knew no other family. It had only been the two of them.

They had been responsible for all of the household duties in the home in which they were raised. Their previous owners had been shopkeepers, selling various imported household goods. The husband had died during the French and Indian War and the wife remained at the shop, but fell on hard times with the taxes, boycotts, and recession following the war. She could scarcely afford to feed the two kids and had threatened to sell them daily until she passed away unexpectedly a few days ago. They both had a basic grasp on reading, though Harris could not write, and Tabitha could only manage very little.

The first thing Ellie decided she would do after getting them clothed was begin their education. There was going to be a lot to look into and she began making a mental list. She had no idea what kids there did for schooling or if they allowed persons of color to attend. If she could not find anything, she would have to teach them herself. She was fully capable but preferred to supplement a more formal education rather than provide it all herself. There was plenty she could teach them that they would never learn in school.

Ellie was beginning to reevaluate her spur-of-the-moment decision. Angry at the time, she had not been thinking about anything beyond rescuing these two children from the worst kind of life she could imagine. Now that she was beginning to think about everything it would require, she hoped she had not bitten off more than she could chew. Of course, she would not have done it differently if she could do it over again, but it was going to be a big commitment for her. She only hoped she could do the kids some justice.

*Summer 1769*

"You shan't bring them to dinner, Miss Ellie," Robert tried to tell her gently when Ellie tried to bring Tabitha and Harris with her to the Burke's for Sunday dinner. He had stopped by her house to escort her to dinner since she lived along the way from the chapel. Though, she suspected he would have done so even if she had been on the other side of the island. She did not mind. It was nice to spend time with Robert without everyone else there, where they did not have to be so formal.

"Why not? Surely, Lucy won't mind adding two more seats."

"Ell, they're slaves."

Ellie immediately got upset and went on the defensive. "Only until I can make the arrangements to emancipate them."

"Do you have any idea of the costs associated with doing so?"

"I do, actually." She had looked into it already and found that it would not be even remotely cheap. Each of them required a bond of two hundred pounds, which was more than a year's worth of wages for a journeyman in this time who made about 130 pounds a year. She did not care. They were worth it.

"As far as I'm concerned, they're already free."

"Miss Ellie," Robert placed a hand on her arm and waited until he had her full attention. They had some time before dinner would be ready and were having a drink in the parlor before leaving and Ellie had been playing with the glass in her hand. "It matters not what you think. The law does not consider them free until the money has been paid and the paperwork has been submitted. Make no mistake, they are still slaves. As such, they legally cannot be entertained by Whites."

Ellie let his words sink in, knowing the laws might possibly limit what she would be able to do, but thought freeing them would be the easy part. She had no idea it would be illegal to 'entertain' them before they were free.

"Fine. I'll wait until after I've paid their bonds. Then, they'll be free."

"Do you think that wise? What shall they do once they've been manumitted? How will they care for themselves? They're still children, by god."

"I'm not going to just turn them out once I free them, Robert. I'll legally adopt them. Then, they'll be family."

Robert choked on his drink, sputtering and coughing as his face turned red. "Legally adopt? That's not possible."

"I highly doubt that. Though, I'm sure I'm going to need help navigating the courts. You studied law. Can you help me with that?"

Robert shook his head. "There's nothing I can do, Miss Ellie. I'm sorry, but you can't legally adopt them."

"Why not?"

Robert let out a slow breath. "Even were they not slaves, there's no law allowing for children to be adopted."

"None?"

"None."

"What do you do with children who have no parents?" She was perplexed.

"They're oft sent to live with other family if possible. If not, they are turned out to be indentured servants."

"That's awful."

Robert shrugged. "It provides them a place to live, and they learn a trade while being provided for."

His nonchalance at the way things worked annoyed her. She knew it was how things were done in that time, and it probably never occurred to him to think of other ways, but it still bothered her. Ellie shook off the backwards way of handling orphaned children.

"Well, if there's no law, then there's nothing stopping me from doing so," she said stubbornly, lifting her chin.

"I suppose not. It merely won't be supported by any legal backing."

They finished their drinks and made their way down the street to the Burke residence.

"How is your recent purchase working out for you, Mrs. Russell?" Lucy asked excitedly once they all got settled at the table.

She had only purchased the children two days ago, but she had not seen Lucy or Adelaide since, being too busy getting them settled and trying to figure out everything she needed to do for them. Ellie cringed at Lucy's choice of words, but she already knew how the woman felt about servants and slaves. She was born and bred on a Virginia plantation. Thomas and Robert had as well, but apparently Ellie had managed to open Thomas's eyes to another way of thinking during their visit to his home in Williamsburg all those years ago. She was grateful she was able to have had some small influence on him.

"I've had a lot to do. They didn't even have clothes, so we had to go shopping right away. We're still working everything out."

Thomas perked up at the conversation. "What purchase did you make?"

"Mrs. Russell is the proud new owner of two young slaves," Lucy beamed. Ellie wanted to throw her glass of wine at her.

"You purchased two slaves?" he asked, his eyes wide. "I thought you to be firmly against slavery."

"I'm very much against it," Ellie agreed. "Unfortunately, it was better than the alternative. Leaving those children to the men at that meat market would have been cruel and unusual punishment. Once I purchased Tabitha, I could not leave her brother for someone else to purchase. They deserve to be kept together. Now, I just have to figure out how to give them their freedom."

Adelaide and Lucy were both aghast at the thought. "Surely, your intentions are not to simply give it to them?" Adelaide argued. "What have they even done to warrant such a thing?"

"They were born!" Ellie said angrily. "What more reason do they need? They're human beings and deserve to be treated as such. I plan on giving them every opportunity to thrive in life that I can give them."

Robert placed his hand on hers in an attempt to calm her down. She had spent the last several days being angry and irritated over the entire situation and was not about to calm down. Even if she was inclined to do so, him placing his hand on hers was not a good way to get her to do it. She did not hold hands with people. Ellie threw a glare in his direction while jerking her hand free, placing it in her lap. She tried to calm down, reminding herself where she was. Closing her eyes and taking a deep breath, she grabbed her drink to give herself a moment. The conversation continued around her with everyone expressing their opinions. Jack and Thomas were the only ones who had anything even remotely positive to say about it, though Jack was not so much positive as he was neutral.

"Since when do you not believe in slavery, dear brother?" Adelaide asked Thomas after he expressed his opinion.

Ellie did not miss his eyes darting to her before he responded. "Since I realized how abhorrent it is. Consider for a moment that it was you. Would you still be so supportive of it?"

When he used the exact argument Ellie had used on him all those years ago, she became certain that his change of heart had been her doing. It warmed her to think so.

Adelaide laughed. "It could not possibly be me. I'm not a Negro."

Thomas could tell Ellie's patience was quickly running out while she looked adrift in her beliefs, having to defend them to everyone there. He tried to be as supportive as possible.

"Mrs. Russell, have you looked into what it will take to manumit them?"

"I have," Ellie nodded. "As far as I can tell, I think I only need to pay a bond for them. I'm still looking to see if there's anything else, but so far, that's all I've seen."

Thomas nodded. "If we may be of assistance, please ask."

Lucy's eyes went wide at his offer, and she turned to stare at him in horror, though she did not say anything. Lucy was a proper lady of her time and would never dare question her husband at a dinner with guests. Ellie bet he would hear about it later, though. It was unfortunate. She appreciated his offer more than he would ever know. Though she could not imagine any way in which she would need his help, his support meant a lot to her. It seemed he was the only one who did support her decision.

"Thank you. I plan on taking care of it as soon as I can. I already told them what I was planning, but I doubt they believe it. I wouldn't if I were them. But I don't want it hanging over them. I was planning on adopting them as well, but Robert informs me that adoption is not something that happens here."

This was the wrong thing to say. Lucy did not hold back at her latest declaration. "You wish to adopt them? But they're nig—"

"Do NOT finish that statement," Ellie interrupted tersely.

Lucy immediately looked confused. "What did I say?"

"Do not use that word in front of me," Ellie said sternly. "And absolutely not in regard to those children."

"I'd not believed there to be any words that bothered you, Mrs. Russell," Thomas observed curiously.

"There are very few," she admitted. "But that one is at the top of my list."

"I don't understand. What's wrong with it?" Lucy asked innocently.

"It's incredibly racist and derogatory."

All eyes were on her now. She felt the weight of them but did not care. Knowing the word did not carry the same taboo in this time period as it did in hers did not prevent her from feeling the way she did regardless. Whether it was normal to say it or not did not change the fact that it was used to oppress and insult people. Ellie was not about to listen to her friends refer to members of her household that way. It was bad enough they continued to refer to Native Americans as savages or the red man. Ellie drew a line with this.

The rest of dinner passed in false niceties. Ellie had tried to excuse herself early, but they insisted she stay, though it was obvious that she did not want to be there any more than any of them wanted her there. Lucy and Adelaide changed the subject and dominated the conversation, much to Ellie's delight. She kept quiet and barely contributed.

When the men began discussing the current turmoil between the soldiers and the colonists, Ellie's attention was piqued, but only just. She had been interested in seeing history firsthand and had hoped she would be able to see something in Boston, but since she had postponed her departure, she held out hope that maybe something had occurred in New York about which she had never heard. Since she did not know history well, she thought it entirely possible. Apparently nothing eventful had passed yet; only the usual tensions, name calling, and minor altercations.

While the men talked about the tensions, Lucy addressed Ellie and Adelaide. "I am much in need of a new dress for our dear friend's upcoming nuptials at her parents' villa on Long Island in a few weeks. I hope the dressmaker has time to put something together. I do wish to look my best."

"I'm sure you'll look incredible." As much as Ellie was reluctant to admit it, she meant every word. Lucy was beautiful and could easily be a model in Ellie's time. Thomas had chosen well.

"You should accompany us, Ell," Robert suggested, turning back to the women's conversation. "We'll stay on the island for two nights in order to enjoy the festivities."

"Thank you, but I don't think so. I don't know them and wouldn't want to impose." Ellie was also reluctant to join the group for a two-night excursion anywhere, but even more so now after the conversation that had just occurred.

"Nonsense," he and Lucy both said at the same time. After a brief pause, as each waited for the other to proceed, Robert continued, "It would be no imposition at all. On the contrary, it would save me from having to arrive on my own and suffer all the women in attendance trying to push their daughters on me."

Robert chuckled, but Ellie had no doubt that every word he said was the truth. With his curly brown hair and dimples, he was still as good-looking as he ever was. She wondered again why he had never married.

"So, you want me to be your plus one?"

"My what?" he asked in response.

"Your date?"

Robert merely shook his head, indicating he still did not understand what she was asking.

Ellie tried again. "Escort?"

"My armed guard? I don't believe I need one, but if I did, I assure you, I would never ask that of you." He was beginning to understand her meaning but could not resist teasing her now.

Ellie smirked at his response. It was a good thing she did not embarrass easily, or she would be bright red by now. She had no idea what the proper terminology would be in this time for what he was asking her. Thankfully, he was beginning to understand what she was trying to ask.

Bowing low in his chair beside her, he said, "I would be honored if you would be my guest."

Ellie beamed at his request. "How could I possibly refuse when you ask like that?"

After what felt like an eternity, the evening finally ended. Ellie said her goodbyes and was not planning on waiting for Robert to escort her home. Not avoiding him, she simply did not want to wait around for him. The dinner had taken its toll on her and she was exhausted. As she slipped out, Thomas caught up to her on the front step.

"My offer stands," he said. When Ellie looked at him in question, he added awkwardly, "If you find yourself in need of help obtaining freedom for the two children. I know it's not… well. I mean, it can be…"

"Expensive?" she offered, when he could not find a way to say it diplomatically.

"Yes," he said. "I know your preference is to not accept help, but you're doing something that will change their lives. I only meant to make sure you don't run into any difficulty doing so."

Ellie almost laughed in exasperation. How many times had they fought over him trying to give her money? She wondered if he knew exactly how much it was going to cost. If he did, would he still be offering? Biting back her laughter and any scathing remarks she wanted to throw his way, instead she tried to see it as the generous offer it was.

"I appreciate it, Major, but it's not necessary. I'm fully capable of paying the bonds. Though if I run into any non-monetary issues, I'll be sure to ask if it's something you might be able to help with."

Thomas nodded and before it could get awkward, Robert came out. "There you are. I was looking for you and thought I'd missed you."

Ellie pulled her gaze from Thomas and looked at Robert. "Here I am. Are you walking me home?"

"If you'll allow me."

Ellie pasted on a smile and nodded. Though she had not wanted to wait for him, she would not turn him down now that he was there. She wished Thomas a good evening and they headed back up the street, Robert extending his arm for her and placing himself between her and the street as Thomas always used to do.

# *Fall 1769*

The first weeks after Ellie brought Tabitha and Harris home held a learning curve for them all. Ellie had never been a parent and had no idea what to do with kids who were solely her responsibility. Given their ages, she also had a tendency to think of them as being more adult than children. Combined with her desire to give them freedom, she ended up not giving them enough guidance. Without her to tell them what to do, they fell back on their roles as slaves and tried to anticipate Ellie's every need. Hannah tried to insert herself as an overseer and bossed them around, giving them additional chores. When Ellie saw what was happening, she realized she needed to take a more active role in everything. Reluctantly, she stepped up as the head of the household. She had only ever been responsible for herself and her husbands before, so this was new to her.

The first thing Ellie did was implement a chore list. They would all be responsible for something, including her. Hannah and Tabitha both balked at that, but she insisted that they should all be self-reliant, and she did not want anyone waiting on her. Since she did not want to do the laundry or empty the chamber pots, Ellie thought it only fair to take on other tasks to make up for them doing the worst of the chores. It ended up working to everyone's advantage as the work was spread more equitably, allowing each of them to have more idle time.

Ellie also addressed Harris's lame leg that had caused him to fetch a lower price at market than he otherwise would have. To look at him casually, it did not appear that anything was wrong, though he limped when he walked.

"Where does it hurt?" Ellie asked as she examined his right leg.

"'ere, mistress," he said quietly as he pointed at his knee.

It was obviously swollen, but nothing else appeared out of sorts. Pressing gently on various spots around his knee while she asked questions, she determined the pain was at the front of the knee.

"Is it worse when you go upstairs or downstairs?"

"Downstairs, mistress."

Ellie let out an exasperated breath. "Harris, please don't call me mistress. I know it's hard to let go of a lifetime of engrained behavior, but I'm absolutely not your mistress. If you must call me anything, you may call me miss or whatever else is acceptable here, but not mistress."

"Yes, mis–" Harris cut himself off before finishing the word. He allowed himself to raise his eyes only long enough to look for her reaction before dropping them back down again. Ellie would have to work on that as well, but they would have to focus on one thing at a time.

Turning her attention back to his knee, she determined that there were audible clicks of the knee whenever he squatted or kneeled and he experienced increased pain during those times. In the mornings, it was always stiff and painful. It had been going on for years, but his former owners had never bothered to have him seen as he was not deemed worth the expense. Instead, they had allowed him to suffer. Feeling her anger rising again, Ellie had to fight to keep it down.

"Well, as far as I can tell, it looks to me like you have patellofemoral osteoarthritis," she said as she stood. With no advanced medical training, she could not be certain but it seemed in line with everything her former partner had described of her own knee injury when she was still a paramedic.

Tabitha, who had been watching the examination quietly, spoke up now. "What do that mean?"

"It's a fancy way of saying his kneecap is twisted. It causes his calf to rotate outward while his foot rolls inward." Turning back to Harris, she went on to explain his ailment. "There's no cure, but there are some exercises that you can do to strengthen the muscles. We can bind the knee when it hurts, treat it with a cold compress, and make sure you get rest when it's acting up. In time, the pain may go away entirely. The exercises will help the most with that, so you have to make sure you do them."

The siblings looked skeptical, both at the simple treatment, and her suggestion of rest. That was absolutely not something slaves were permitted to do.

Ellie retrieved one of the bags of sand she kept for hot and cold compresses.

"We'll have to go to the nearest water source to cool it off. Ezra, how cold is the water from the tea pumps?"

Ezra had been walking by and Ellie called out to him before he got too far. He maintained the household water supply, filling the barrels from the tea pumps whenever it was needed.

"'Tis cool enough to be pleasurable on a summer day, miss."

"Hopefully, that's cold enough. Would you mind escorting Tabitha for me?"

They all looked skeptical now, but Ellie handed off two of the compresses, hoping the second would still be cool enough when it was time to trade it out with the first. She instructed them to thoroughly soak the pillows while she stayed behind and showed Harris how to wrap his knee then began showing him some exercises her partner used to do, instructing him to do them every morning.

It took longer than she had hoped since she had to make a trip to Schoharie, but Ellie paid the bond for Tabitha and Harris, ensuring their manumission. When she went to pay the bond, the official asked if they had last names in mind. Ellie looked to them for an answer.

"No, mistress," Tabitha responded.

"Most take on the name Freeman to show they are now free, or they use the last name of their owners or any other random name they choose," the official offered helpfully.

The children both looked to Ellie expectantly. "I can't tell you what to call yourselves. It's your name and you should choose it yourself. Freeman is a good name, but there's a world of names out there to choose from. Is there anything you might have thought about or liked in the past?"

They looked to each other, shaking their heads. Tabitha spoke quietly, "Does you think 'twould be fitting if we was to take your name, miss?"

Ellie's heart swelled with pride, spreading to her face in a smile, but worried about the girl's reasons for choosing thusly. "I don't want you to feel obligated to me. I'm more than happy that you'd want to share my name, but if there's another you prefer, please take that one. This is entirely your decision."

Looking at each other again, they nodded without any words passing between them. "That be the name we want, miss."

Pulling them each in for a hug, Ellie nodded. Turning back to the official, she informed him, "Their last name will be Russell."

Ellie received a piece of paper for each of them saying they were free persons. She insisted on getting two copies of each of the documents, wanting to have gotten more, but the official who made them did not even want to make a second copy, let alone anymore. Ellie gave one copy of the papers to Tabitha and Harris, telling them to each keep them on their person and safe at all times. She even made a leather pouch for each of them and waterproofed them the best she could. The second set was tucked away in a locked trunk where she hid extra cash.

Ellie was not taking any chances. Too many free persons were captured and sold into slavery, and she wanted to minimize the possibility of that happening for Tabitha and Harris as much as she could. Having the extra copy of the documents helped ease her mind, if only a little.

"Have you thought about what you want to do with your futures?" Ellie asked the kids over dinner one afternoon.

With their manumission complete, each of them enrolled in school, and them having gotten somewhat settled into their new life with Harris's knee already seeing a vast improvement, it was time to start considering the options. Harris still had a few years, but Tabitha would be an adult soon enough.

Ellie had found a group of missionaries with the Church of England who had set up a school to teach and convert those belonging to non-white races. The Society for the Propagation of the Gospel in Foreign Parts had started out focusing on the Native Americans, whom they referred to as heathens. The group expanded and began teaching Black persons as well, though not very many, as slave owners did not often allow it. Those who did allow it tended to only be interested in their slaves learning to read and write, forbidding them to convert to Christianity, due to the ambiguity surrounding their status as Christianized slaves. As Black persons, they were considered inferior persons, branded as such by God with the color of their skin. However, as Christians, they fell under the New York law stating that "No Christian shall be kept in bond-slavery." The law was modeled after the biblical injunction. Hence, there was a moral quandary with enslaving Christians that owners avoided by not allowing their slaves to convert. Ellie did not care about all that; she only wanted to give the children an opportunity to expand their education. She spoke with the missionaries and enrolled both of the kids in lessons.

Tabitha paused in passing the vegetables to Harris while looking at Ellie with doubt on her face. They were still uncertain about what to expect, thinking that this would not last, and they would have to go back to their old way of life any day. They exchanged a look between themselves before Tabitha answered for them both as she always did.

"No, mistress. We's not yet thought on the matter. What's it you'd like us to do?"

Ellie would have laughed at the girl's response if it was not so sad. Though they were both getting better at calling her miss, more often than not, they still called her mistress. She shook her head.

"I would like if you considered it and gave it some real thought. I know it's going to take some time to get used to the idea, but you're free persons now. Once you're adults, you'll need a way to take care of yourselves."

Though Ellie had every intention of taking care of them as long as necessary, she wanted them to be self-sufficient. Maybe it was her own hyper-independence, but she did not understand or respect anyone who relied on someone else to support them. Whether male or female, she firmly believed everyone should be capable of supporting themselves, unless there were extenuating circumstances like a medical issue. It was probably one of the reasons it had irritated her so much every time Thomas gave her money. She did not want to be reliant on anyone. It had been difficult enough to accept his help in getting her to stay on at Fort Edward as a nurse, then again from Dean when he had agreed to marry her and support her when she had no alternative.

"Yes, mistress," they both said together.

Ellie sighed. "What are you interested in Harris?"

Harris looked panicked and looked to his sister for help. "I... I doesn't know, mistress."

"Alright. What about you Tabitha?"

Tabitha's head went down. "I were always good at helpin' whenevers Mistress Saltonstall got sick," she said in a low voice.

Ellie perked up. "Good. That's a good start. We can work with that. Did you like it?"

Tabitha nodded enthusiastically, which caused Ellie to smile back at her.

"Alright. We'll look into nursing for you. Maybe I can teach you midwifery. Is that something you'd like to learn?"

Tabitha's eyes filled with hope. "Could I, mistress?"

Ellie smiled at her eagerness. "We can certainly make arrangements for it to happen. I'll see if there's any kind of school or training that you could attend, and I'll supplement your training as much as I can." Ellie pondered it for a moment and thought aloud, "I suppose that means I should probably take on some clients here. You'll need firsthand experience."

With that settled, they promised to start thinking about options for Harris as well. They took turns listing off professions, but he shook his head at all of them. When Ellie suggested he consider writing fortune cookies, she had to explain to everyone what it meant. When she did, they all looked at her like she had lost her mind. When she smirked, Harris was the first to pick up on it and he cracked a small smile. It was not much, but Ellie considered it a success. He was still quite shy and it always felt good when he opened up, even if only a little.

"You could... be a dragon slayer."

His smile got bigger, and he started to laugh. His sister was hesitant to laugh, but a smile slowly started to spread across her face as well.

"No? Alright. How about... a spaceman who travels to the moon and all the different planets?"

Hannah and Ezra started to laugh alongside the teenagers and Ellie tried to keep going, wracking her brain for more and more outlandish professions.

"You could milk frogs," Ezra said, joining in.

Everyone began laughing in earnest and soon, they were all throwing out crazy suggestions, trying to outdo one another. Ellie was happy to see them starting to relax a little.

On her next chore day with Lucy, she brought Tabitha along. They were knitting and she wanted to teach Tabitha how to do it. The girl had some basics, but not enough to do much with it. Ellie was still not very good at it herself and had asked Lucy and Adelaide to assist her in teaching Tabitha. They reluctantly agreed.

"What is that you're knitting?" Adelaide asked.

Ellie looked up from the large needles and puffy yarn she was threading together in a long, straight, wide strip to see Adelaide was looking at her. It was not wide enough to be a blanket but had no shape to it otherwise.

"It's a shawl," Ellie replied.

Lucy and Adelaide exchanged a look while Tabitha looked confused but did not say anything.

"What's a shawl?" Lucy asked.

Everyone else seemed to be just as confused when Ellie glanced around the room. "You don't have shawls?"

"I don't believe I've ever heard of such a thing," Adelaide said. Lucy shook her head in agreement.

Ellie held up her nearly completed piece and, careful to not lose her needles, she wrapped it around her neck, demonstrating it. "It's a wrap. Just a little extra something to keep warm when I don't want to put on a cloak. Perfect for around the house."

After trying to find one for sale somewhere and not seeing them anywhere, she had assumed people either made them at home or they were merely not something that was imported there. She had one now that she had made when Mehitabel taught her how to knit but wanted another one.

"It's a blanket?" Adelaide asked.

"No. It's too small for that. Although, you could lay it across your lap, I suppose. It's meant to go around the neck and shoulders like a kerchief."

"Is this something you learned from the sav-ages?" Lucy asked.

Ellie suppressed the urge to smack her friend at her continued usage of the term, but at least she had not referred to Tabitha and Harris in a derogatory manner again. She supposed she should be grateful for small victories.

"No. It's something that was common where I grew up."

"I see. I don't believe you've ever told us where you grew up," Lucy mentioned.

Ellie sighed. She walked right into that one. Thomas would have been proud of his wife.

"Somewhere far, far from here," was her only reply. "With the weather turning, I thought it would be nice to have another one. They're really quite simple to make. And given my aptitude for knitting, I thought it best I stick to less complex projects," she said, trying to change the subject.

The women laughed knowingly. Ellie's skills had not improved, despite having worked at it most of the year.

The change of subject worked, and Ellie took the opportunity to ask about the local midwife.

"Mrs. Erwin is undoubtedly overwhelmed, I'm afraid," Adelaide said.

"Is she the only one in the area?"

After exchanging questioning looks, Lucy offered, "I believe there's a Negro woman who handles some of the births for their people, though Mrs. Erwin is the only one for everyone else."

At least the woman had not called her by the other N-word. Ellie tried to not let Lucy's words get to her.

"Are you planning on working as a midwife again, Mrs. Russell?" Adelaide asked.

"I was considering it. I may pick up a few patients while I'm here. I'm going to teach Tabitha, and I'll need some clients to teach her properly. But I don't want to step on Mrs. Erwin's toes. If there's not enough work for more than one person, I'll leave her to it and see if maybe Tabitha can observe her. It's only until we can move to Boston anyway. It wouldn't be a permanent thing."

"I'm certain there's plenty of work for you both," Lucy said amiably. "There used to be another woman, but she passed away a few years ago. No one has yet come to replace her."

Ellie nodded. "I guess I'll go talk to Mrs. Erwin, then. Maybe she has some patients she's willing to part with."

## Chapter 21

# Fall 1769

The group hired an open carriage that took them through the streets of Long Island. The wedding had taken place the evening before and Ellie had spent the day on Robert's arm, blocking him from the many attempts of women looking to set him up with their daughters, as promised. She had enjoyed her role more than she had expected, laughing with Robert at the disappointed faces they left in their wake. He spent the day introducing her to other guests as his angel. There was something about the way he said it that made her feel like it was not simply an endearment. Ellie had been uncomfortable with the moniker, but even more so with the way he looked at her with reverence and awe whenever he introduced her. After several introductions, she brushed off her unease and decided to enjoy the day. Everyone had been dressed in their best finery, many of the men present in full uniform. It was a beautiful event and Ellie immersed herself in the atmosphere.

The group had decided to take advantage of the occasion and explore the island a little with the free time they had the day after the wedding. Lucy and Adelaide gawked at the massive houses and villas they passed. This was where many of the wealthiest New Yorkers had country homes.

Lucy took it upon herself to play tour guide to the group as they rode, pointing out this house or that, explaining the island to them while their driver assisted.

"The island were near one hundred miles in length and twenty-five in breadth," he informed them. "As we enter into this here middle part of the island, you can already start to see the trees thinning out. 'Tweren't a single tree growing for twenty or thirty miles and there never was."

Looking out across the sea of waist-high grass, the women made amazed noises at the information as if it was the most incredible thing they had ever heard. Ellie was reminded of the long, boring drive across Kansas. It was beautiful to see, but only for the first couple of miles. Driving across the state quickly became monotonous.

"This here plain were the only one of its kind in all of the continent," he continued.

Ellie could not help the snort that came from her. Everyone in the carriage turned to look at her.

"Sorry."

The driver ignored her and continued talking, telling them all about the great curiosity they were seeing.

Back at the inn in which they were staying, the women talked excitedly about everything they had seen on the island. They were sitting around a fire behind the building, enjoying their last night before heading back to children and work.

"What a wonder to see such a place!" Adelaide marveled. "There was not a single tree in all that land today. And the only such place in all of North America. How lucky we are to have been able to see it."

Ellie snickered again at the claim.

"Mrs. Russell, is there something you'd like to share?" Thomas asked sternly.

"I'm sorry. It's just that it's not the only place like that in North America. Much of the country looks like that. Sorry," she quickly corrected herself. "The continent."

"Does it?" he challenged.

Ellie nodded. "It does. There are the great plains in the middle of the coun–continent. They look like what we saw today but over a much larger area. Then there's the tundra up in Canada, which is a frozen wasteland, and of course, the Mohave Desert out west, which is miles and miles of nothing but sand. It doesn't even have grass. Though, much of it is covered with brush and cacti or rocks. But the point is, once you pass the Mississippi River, much of the landscape is treeless."

They all stared at her while she rambled on.

"How do you know of these places?" Lucy asked in awe.

Ellie shrugged. "I've seen them."

They all started talking at once.

Ellie corrected herself, "I mean, I haven't seen the tundra in person, but I have seen parts of Canada that look much like it."

"Yet you've seen the rest of the places you described? You've seen the Mississippi River?" Lucy asked again, still rapt by the prospect.

"You've been past the Mississippi River?" Adelaide added in doubt.

"Several times."

"Was this something you did with your trader?" Adelaide asked.

"No, no. This was long ago. In a previous existence." Ellie's eyes inadvertently traveled to Thomas, who was sitting with his arms crossed, looking at her expectantly, a flash of annoyance on his face.

"I'm sorry," Ellie said, realizing she had probably said too much. "I shouldn't have said anything."

"No, please. Do tell us more. There's nothing else for which I'd care than to hear about all the other places you've been." Lucy was fascinated.

"I don't know. That's a lot of places."

"So many as that?" Thomas asked.

Ellie glanced up at him. "You'd be surprised."

"By all means, then," he challenged.

Dajoji's voice sounded in her head, telling her to let people in. Ellie huffed out a breath. She stood from her seat and looked around to find a stick, then cleared away a patch of dirt near the fire. Kneeling down, the women gasped softly, and Robert immediately tugged at her arm to pull her up again. When she looked up to see the shocked expressions the women wore, she also noted the amused look on Thomas's face. Ignoring everyone's reaction to her kneeling on the ground to play in the dirt, she pulled her arm from Robert's grasp, swatting him away. Using the stick, she drew a rough outline of the United States while adding Alaska and some of Canada. Everyone came in closer, circling around her to see her drawing.

"I've been up here, into Canada," she said while pointing somewhere near what she imagined was Kelowna and Calgary. Then she continued pointing while working her way down and across the map. "I've been to the Pacific Ocean and seen parts of the coast," she said while pointing to several places in Oregon and Northern and Southern California. "The Rocky Mountains run along this part of the continent. I've been several places throughout this region and I've been to the southwest and spent time in the Mohave Desert here. I've also been across the lower half of the continent, across the middle, and across the north from coast to coast, down into Florida, and as far north as the Boston area. Which place would you like to hear about?"

Ellie sat back on her heels, looking up at the group, waiting expectantly. They all looked at her with surprised expressions.

"How is it you've covered so much territory?" Thomas asked. "When we met, you claimed to have never seen a horse up close. Did you do all of this on foot?"

Ellie's eyes widened in momentary panic. Leave it to him to pick up on that. She did not want to lie to him, so instead, she took a deep breath and started describing some of the places she had been while avoiding looking directly at him. With one hand on the stick, her other flew to her necklace as she toyed with it nervously.

"The Rocky Mountains are the highest peaks on the continent. I don't know what the highest peak is, but there are several that reach above fourteen thousand feet. The region is incredibly beautiful. It's full of trees and lakes and opens up into desert to the west. There's an enormous saltwater lake near the western edge that is surrounded by desert and salt flats. The Bonneville Salt Flats are a wide expanse of salt crystals that cover the earth. It's flat and sparkly white for hundreds of miles. Even in the middle of summer, it looks like the ground is covered in snow. Nothing grows there at all. In the distance, the mountains rise up to frame it all. When it rains, the water sits on the surface making it look like a giant lake with the mountains perfectly reflected on the surface like a mirror. I think you'd really like it, Mrs. Burke."

Lucy beamed, her eyes wide and her hands clasped together in front of her. "Oh, I think it would be a great pleasure to see this place," she said excitedly. "Tell us more."

"Past the salt flats is more desert. It's mostly just brush and cacti, but then if you keep going, you cross over the Sierra Nevada Mountains. I think they might actually be taller than the Rockies, but I'm not sure. I think they're pretty close in height. The Rockies cover a much larger area, though." Ellie leaned over her map and outlined the areas with her stick.

"Further south down here, the desert begins to vary a little. The rock becomes red and beautiful. There are areas all along the southwest that have nothing but sand dunes. Again, there's no vegetation at all, just sand as far as the eye can see. But the rocks would really impress you. There's a place called the Grand Canyon, right about here. It's a mile-deep gorge cut into the red rock walls of the desert that stretches nearly three hundred miles. You can see the layers of rock as they formed over millions of years."

"It all sounds rather fantastical," Adelaide said with a frown.

"Indeed, it does," Thomas agreed.

Ellie knew their use of the word fantastical was not meant in the positive way that she was so used to. They did not believe her.

"I think it sounds wondrous," Lucy defended. "I'd not realized so much of North America was inhabited."

Ellie shrugged, but instead of answering, she said, "It's really quite a diverse geography."

"How is it you've had the opportunity to have gone so many places when I dare say only a few men have even covered that much territory?" Adelaide asked as everyone began returning to their seats.

"I guess I've just been lucky," Ellie said before quickly adding, "Here, in the middle, are the plains I spoke of. The Great Plains go on and on for over a million square miles. The terrain is flat with no hills or trees or anything interesting to look at."

"Did any of the places you've been in your *previous existence* include Virginia?" Thomas asked.

Ellie's face dropped along with her stomach. When she did not respond right away, he knew the answer was yes. He added, "Had you been there prior to the time in which I took you?"

There was accusation in his voice. Ellie's mouth went dry, and she felt like she could not speak. Instead, she nodded slightly while closing her eyes against his cold stare.

"You'd already been to Williamsburg, to the governor's palace." It was a statement now, not a question.

Opening her eyes, Ellie could see the hurt in Thomas's face. Unable to look at him, she looked down at her map in the dirt. She was no artist, but she was proud that it at least resembled what the continent looked like. Ellie leaned over it and rubbed her hand in the dirt, erasing it all away before standing and brushing her hands off. She did not want to make matters worse with Thomas and knew it was time to stop sharing her experiences, though she had not shared everything with them. The places she had visited outside the continental United States and Canada had not been included in her discussion. Thomas aside, that might really be pushing the limits of believability with this group. Dajoji would have been proud of her for opening up, but she was not so sure it had been the right thing to do.

Deciding to call it a night, Ellie felt compelled to share one last thing before going. "Of all the places I've been, the forests of the east coast will always be home to me," Ellie said with a sad smile.

Though she had traveled her entire life and did not think of any one place as home, she had grown up along the east coast and always felt more at home amongst the forests and the ocean. She had always missed them when she lived in Utah and Nevada.

As Ellie turned to walk away, Robert escorting her back, Thomas pondered everything she had shared with them. Her confession about having been to Virginia before had upset him immensely. Had she not claimed to have never been there when he took her? He had known something had been off about her during their visit, but he had attributed it to her having been uncomfortable about meeting his family. She had shared more tonight about her past than she had ever shared before. He could not help but wonder why she had decided to finally share that much or if any of what she had said was even true. He still desperately wanted to know more about her, but it also rankled that she never felt that she could do so with him before. What else was she hiding and did it even matter? Could he believe anything she said?

## Chapter 22

# November 14, 1769

A stir by the door of the Burns' City Arms Tavern caught the attention of Thomas and the men with whom he was speaking while waiting for the lecture to begin. It was early and people were still arriving. He ventured to guess many had been held up by the demonstrators that had marched through the streets toward the Coffee House to hear speeches and protest the stationing of troops in Boston. The troops had stood by, waiting to step in if necessary, but it never got out of hand. Once the crowd had burned effigies of the sheriff and Governor Francis Bernard of Boston, they eventually dispersed. He had only just made it to the tavern for the lecture, grateful to leave his responsibilities behind, if only for a few hours.

The initial silence had caught their attention, and all heads turned toward the door, then the murmurs began when they saw the woman who had entered their space. Women were not banned from these lectures, and on occasion, they would show up to hear what was being said, but those occasions were the exception rather than the norm. When they did attend, women were always accompanied by a man or by several other women. It was scandalous for them to attend public functions on their own.

Thomas should have known it was only a matter of time before Ellie attended one. And if any woman would attend a lecture by herself, it would be her. He immediately looked for Robert, but his friend was nowhere to be seen. Ellie had always loved learning new things. Seeing her now in this room full of men waiting to learn something new reminded him of their time in Philadelphia all those years ago. It had been the beginning of the end for them.

It had been on their last night there that Ellie had crawled into bed with him, and they made love for the first time. Though he had been wide awake when she came to him, he had thought he had been dreaming. She had been more surprising than anything with which his imagination could have created. He had cherished the weeks that followed, every spare second spent in each other's arms but on the last day of their journey back to Fort Edward, he had proposed marriage, and she had refused, breaking his heart.

Thomas shook away the memories as he watched her ignore the stares while she crossed the room and found a seat in a row of mostly empty chairs. She sat in the aisle seat as if to make a quick escape yet daring anyone to sit beside her. Head held high, she stared toward the front of the room, her arms folded across her ample chest. Her long golden mane was loosely braided in her usual fashion, remaining uncovered and trailing over her left shoulder. Thomas could not suppress the grin that slowly spread across his lips at the commotion her presence was causing.

As the crowd settled and men began finding their seats, Thomas abandoned his companions and made his way up the aisle a few rows.

"May I?" he asked, gesturing to the open seat next to Ellie. As torturous as it was to sit so close beside her, sitting anywhere else in the room was not an option. Her presence would distract him regardless of where he sat, but this way, he could ensure no one else harassed her.

Looking up to see Thomas in his uniform, standing in the aisle next to her, Ellie had to crane her neck to see his face. He had always towered over her, but with him standing while she was seated, it was an impossible difference in height. Surprised to see him, she merely nodded and swung her legs into the aisle for him to pass by her.

"Is Major Jensen meeting you here?"

"No," she snickered. "He has no interest in these sorts of things."

Thomas chuckled. He knew his friend well and Robert had never been much for learning new things. He would not expect him to come to a lecture such as this, but if anyone could persuade him, it would be Ellie, if only so she did not attend on her own. Though that would never stop her.

The lecture got underway, and Ellie had a hard time concentrating on what was being said with Thomas so close beside her. Their shoulders touched and she found herself leaning slightly into the aisle in order to escape his closeness. She crossed her legs, turning in her seat so her feet were in the aisle. It effectively put her back to him, but she needed the distance it provided.

The speaker had explained the creation and use of steam pumps in mines in order to remove water from mine shafts over seventy years ago. Then, nearly sixty years ago, a man named Thomas Newcomen made the steam engine more efficient by speeding up the condensation process and creating a chain to replace the easily bent straight rod design of the piston. These pumps required constant cooling and reheating of the cylinders, making the technology difficult to apply to anything other than the water pumps. He then went on to describe the latest innovation by a Scotsman named James Watt who developed a condenser only a few years before in 1765. This condenser maintained the cylinder at a constant temperature.

The room broke into a discussion about the practical applications of such a device. Instead of contributing to the discussion at large, Thomas turned to Ellie and asked what her thoughts were on the uses of it. She turned back to face him, bringing her feet back in from the aisle and answered without hesitation.

"Vehicles. Massive, steam-powered locomotives that will transport large numbers of people and goods across the new country."

Thomas tilted his head and studied her, trying to understand what she had said and if she meant it or was simply being fanciful again. He found it becoming harder to tell the difference with her sometimes. He decided to ignore the parts of which he was uncertain and asked about the part he found most intriguing.

"Vehicles? Why would you think that? Horses and oxen would be far more efficient than anything steam could produce."

Ellie shrugged, not wanting to argue or try to explain herself. Saved from having to do so, the lecturer quieted the room to continue his talk. He informed the crowd that most of their guesses had not been put into practice, but one which had been, was that of a self-propelled wagon. It had been developed by a man named Nicolas-Joseph Cugnot. He had developed a steam-powered artillery tractor in France only last month.

"'Tis the first machine to move of its own power," the man said to the amazement of the crowd.

Murmurs spread through the room, followed by questions. He answered them to the best of his abilities, explaining that the Cugnot Steam Wagon needed to stop every fifteen minutes to build power, but it could move at a rate of two and a half miles per hour, being able to pull five tons.

There was a mixed reaction to this from the crowd. Several men were awed by the capability while others laughed.

"Whatever shall one do with the ability to move only two and a half miles per hour, when they must stop every fifteen minutes? That's no better than using oxen," a man in the front suggested, to the agreement of many in the room.

Thomas nudged Ellie at the comment while raising an eyebrow as if to say, "See?"

Ellie merely tilted her head down while arching both of her brows and looking up in an incredulous, "I'm not going to dignify that with a response," gesture. The gesture earned her a smile in return. It was the most natural interaction in which the two had engaged since her arrival in New York City and it felt good. It reminded her of their previous friendship where nothing had felt forced, and they could converse without needing words.

The speaker again gained control of the room and explained that though the Cugnot Steam Wagon did not use James Watt's condenser, the development of both within the last few years indicated that they would be seeing new technological innovations using steam to power a variety of objects.

"Watt has compared the output of his new engine to the pulling power of horses. He calls it 'horsepower.'"

Ellie bit her tongue and struggled to suppress her smirk at the comments and supposition about the future of this new technology.

"For what else shall this engine be used if that's how the inventor is describing it?" the lecturer asked the room.

Thomas watched Ellie throughout the lecture. With her back turned to him, it had been easy to do so without raising her attention. Her face was in profile, though now that she had turned back to the front again, he could see even more of her. As beautiful as ever, there was something more that he was seeing. None of this had taken her by surprise as it had everyone else in the room. Instead, she seemed almost amused by the whole affair. It was the same expression she often had when Charles was telling her about something he had learned, and she was pretending to hear it for the first time.

The lecture ended and men lingered to discuss what they had learned. Thomas introduced Ellie to several people he knew.

"This is my neighbor," he said to several of the men he had been talking with before the lecture began.

Ellie spared him a sideways glance at the label and turned her attention back to the group. She held out a hand to shake with one of the men, but he turned her wrist to kiss the back of it. The others all followed suit. She continuously forgot this custom.

"It's a pleasure, my dear," said the man Thomas had introduced as Cornelius Bogart.

Ellie had to suppress a shudder at the way he was leering at her.

"What did you think of the lecture?" he asked.

"It was rather interesting," she said without clarifying. It had been fascinating to learn the history of steam engines up to this point. She had always thought they had been invented much later. Apparently, that was only when they came into popularity. It must have taken a while to work out the kinks.

"You were able to follow along during the entire lecture?"

Pasting a smile on her face, Ellie reminded herself that it would not do to physically assault this man. In this time period, she would probably end up being jailed or hung or something.

"I followed along just fine, thank you," she said through gritted teeth.

"That's splendid. Your husband allows you to attend such events unescorted?"

"I'm widowed," she said. She was more than ready to leave this condescending ass and head home when he jumped on her declaration.

"You poor dear. I, too, am recently widowed. You must allow me to call on you. I would be happy to escort you to the next lecture or perhaps to something more fitting of a lady, perhaps a ball. I do believe the tavern is hosting one soon."

"Thank you, but I promised Major Jensen I'd allow him to escort me if I decide to attend anything else."

She had no idea if these men knew Robert, but she was taking a chance that either they did or if they did not, the name and rank drop would be enough for them to get the hint. Even in her own time, Ellie had known plenty of men who only seemed to back off of a woman if they thought she was already 'taken.' She hated using Robert that way, but she also knew this man was misogynistic enough that nothing she could say would make him less interested.

Ellie looked up at Thomas to give him a warning look, telling him not to expose her lie. However, what she saw on his face was not amusement or surprise at her dishonesty. It was annoyance. He took her arm, gently pointing her towards the door.

"Gentlemen, it's been a pleasure. But I must escort Mrs. Russell home before the evening draws late. We shall withdraw ourselves from your company."

"I would be happy to see that she makes it home safely," Cornelius drooled.

Before Ellie could decline his offer, Thomas stopped and replied in a clipped tone, "That's rather generous of you, Mr. Bogart, but if my wife finds out I allowed her dear friend to stay out unaccompanied, she would not look too kindly on me."

Thomas's hand now hovered over Ellie's lower back, but he stopped himself at the last minute before making contact. Instead, he moved it up to her shoulder and allowed himself the brief touch as he again turned her toward the door. She graciously took his arm without looking up at him as they exited the tavern.

Thomas tucked Ellie on his side opposite the street and escorted her through the darkness, her hand releasing the hold on his arm once they were away from the tavern. He immediately missed the warmth of it. They walked in silence until they reached Ellie's door. There were so many things Thomas wanted to say, but he thought it best to not say anything. He had once thought that she had cared for him, yet she had so easily walked away. Now that she was back in his life once more, he found himself constantly struggling to contain his emotions, yet she was always perfectly calm and unemotional. Apparently, he had meant nothing to her after all. He had tried to forget her over the years but never could. She had burrowed her way into his heart. Seeing her regularly now only made it that much more difficult and he wished he could hate her or at least be as ambivalent as she was. Wishing he felt as little as she did, that he could so easily move on, he knew he was not built that way. No matter how cold and distant she was, he could not seem to let go of his feelings for her. He did not want to love her. He had been content enough with Lucy before Ellie came back into his life, despite their problems. Thomas reminded himself whatever they might have had or not had was in the past. Needing to focus on the present, he worked to be as polite as he could without betraying himself or his wife.

They reached her door and Ellie turned to him before going inside.

"Thank you for the escort, Major Burke. I appreciate you looking out for me."

After saying goodnight, Ellie paused inside the door to collect herself. It had taken every ounce of control she had to be so close to Thomas all night and not touch him or say anything to him. Though they no longer had the relationship they once did, she dearly missed his friendship and wished they could return to the way things had once been between them before they got too serious. It seemed even friendship with him was no longer on the table and the best she could hope for was cordialness.

———————

"Did you enjoy your lecture?" Lucy's soft voice broke the quiet stillness of the night as Thomas climbed into bed. He had changed into a nightshirt as quietly as he could so as not to wake her, but apparently, it had not mattered. Lying on her side facing away from him, he slid under the covers, wrapping himself around her. His hand went to her hip while he nuzzled her neck.

"I did," he whispered near her ear as his hand roamed freely along her hip toward her breast.

"Now?" she asked. "Darling, it's late."

"It's been an age since we've lain together, sweetheart."

His voice husky with need, he took her mouth when she half-rolled to face him. He remembered exactly how long it had been; not since she had gotten pregnant a year and a half ago. Other couples could only estimate their children's dates of conception, but he knew precisely when each of his children had been conceived. Always skirting the matter, Lucy used pregnancy as a means to avoid it altogether, then had needed time to recover from giving birth, but it had been more than long enough for that. He needed to feel her underneath him, to remind himself that he still loved his wife and why they had married to begin with. The connection that physical intimacy brought would help provide that. It was not about simply satisfying his lust but about showing their commitment to one another and joining together as one.

"Perhaps we could resume this in the morning?" she asked, pulling away from his kiss as she so often did when he felt amorous.

He let out a resigned sigh as his entire body sank, knowing it would not resume in the morning at all. Lucy had been nervous but eager when she came to him on their wedding night, more than happy to let Thomas take the lead. After that, she had been willing, if hesitant. Eventually, she became more and more reluctant to join with him. When she did, it was out of duty or obligation. He had tried to pretend it was not and that she actually wanted him but after a while, he could no longer pretend. It was easier to simply avoid her bed.

As her husband, it was well within his right to take what he wanted from her, but he could not imagine doing so. It was not his way. Of course, it did not help that he had Ellie's voice in his head reminding him of what she had called her right to bodily autonomy. Though he would not admit it, Ellie's voice constantly filled his head, guiding him, challenging him, encouraging him.

"If that's what you prefer, dear."

"It is," she said sheepishly, giving him a placating smile before rolling away from him.

Thomas fell onto his back in frustration, staring up at the darkened ceiling. He loved her, but he wanted her to *want* to be with him. She always seemed to have some excuse for not doing so, and it was difficult to not think of his time with Ellie and her eagerness. He berated himself for having such thoughts as he lay in bed next to his wife.

Since meeting her, every woman had been measured against Ellie and had come up short. She was simultaneously a student and a teacher, challenging him and his ideas, how he saw the world. He loved her views on everything that had always been so different from anyone he had ever known.

Lucy was the opposite of that. Assertive when she needed to be, she was also demure and compliant with most everything he said or wanted–except for sexual relations–leaving no doubt that she was subservient to him, as a dutiful wife should be. The problem was that he did not want a dutiful wife. He had always enjoyed a challenge. There was no question in his mind that Ellie had made him a better person. Turning over onto his side, facing away from Lucy, he tried to wipe memories of Ellie from his mind and get some sleep. It seemed an impossible task.

## Chapter 23

# Friday, December 15, 1769

"The Assembly finally passed the vote to pay for the troops," Robert informed Thomas as he walked his horse into the stable.

"That's fantastic news for the soldiers. I wonder how much trouble the Liberty Boys are going to give us over it."

"I know not, but it's certain they won't be happy about it."

"Is that all they had to say?" Thomas asked.

Robert had just come back to the fort from the meeting at city hall on Wall Street. "They stated that if barracks are not available, all soldiers shall be given adequate housing and provisions at the expense of the colony. They voted to raise eighteen hundred pounds for the soldiers."

Thomas scoffed. "That's not nearly enough. The men shan't be happy about that."

"No," Robert agreed, "Yet the people shan't be happy about paying any amount."

"I don't suppose they shall. They balk at having to pay their fair share of just dues and customs. Do they think security comes free? That wars are not expensive? Who else should pay for our freedom from the tyranny of the French?"

With Robert's horse tended to, the men walked around the fort as they talked, passing soldiers drilling in the yard.

"They think not that the security is necessary, Thomas. The war is over. Why does the Crown continue to send troops from England when the French have fled?"

Thomas looked at his friend in disbelief. "Have you not seen the disagreeable circumstances here, Robert? The Rent Rebellion, the riots over the Stamp Act, people persecuting and harassing customs officials whose only crime is that of doing their duty? I know you have personally been made a target as have the rest of us who wear this uniform. Do you mean to tell me you do not see it?"

"I do see it, Thomas. But had Parliament not passed the Stamp Act in the first place, nor the Sugar Act for that matter, none of the riots and persecution of customs officials would have occurred. It's too much on the people. We've been in recession since the war ended. Asking people to pay extra for everything is too much of a hardship on the poor distressed people. If Parliament had allowed us to represent ourselves in the matter, they would understand that. What do a bunch of people in England know of our plight here? It goes against our rights as Englishmen."

"That does not accord with the facts, Robert. The Stamp Act has been in place in England for over fifty years. It was the least injurious tax Parliament could have proposed. It could have been much worse. The amount they were trying to raise was not unreasonable. Had everyone paid their fair share, it would have cost a single shilling per person per year. How is that unreasonable?"

Robert tried to argue, but Thomas continued. "And the Sugar Act was no less unreasonable. It merely amended the already existing Molasses Act, *lowering* the amount of tax assigned to molasses. The complaint is not with the tax, but with the fact that it's now being enforced where it was not before. With the threat from France over, men wish to forget their responsibilities to the government in favor of personal advantage."

"That's not what it's about. The complaint," Robert corrected, "is with Parliament deciding what is best for us without our input. It's unconstitutional. We have a right to be independent provinces without further injury or neglect from England. These soldiers they send from England are overly bureaucratic, inept, arrogant, brutal, and don't listen to those of us who have spent our lives here. And yet, they believe us to be cowardly, disorderly, and provincial. Are you not tired of being treated as a child from men with less experience than we have?"

Thomas sighed. "Of course I am, Robert. But that does not give me the right to stop paying my dues. We are subjects of the Crown. You would do well to remember that, particularly when in that uniform."

Robert had not yet told his best friend that he was not planning on wearing the uniform much longer. He had been considering Ellie's premonition of the upcoming war for more than ten years now and he always knew on which side he wanted to be, though he had not yet acted on it. With the regular pay and security the army provided, it had been difficult to justify leaving up until now. However, with Ellie back in their lives and the upcoming war looming over them, now looked like a good time to do so. He wanted to tell Thomas before acting on his decision. It would not be right for him to find out that way, but Robert had not yet been able to find a way to tell him.

"I'm thinking on selling my commission."

Thomas stopped walking to look at his friend. "What would compel you to do that?"

Robert did not answer immediately; instead he stood, staring at his friend. Thomas took him by the arm and escorted him outside of the fort without saying a word. They walked around towards the water and Thomas almost expected to see Ellie sitting there on the sand, but she must have been elsewhere at the moment. When they were out of earshot of the other soldiers roaming the area, Thomas looked to his friend for an answer.

Robert looked out over the water, away from his friend. "I'm tired of defending the Crown and an ungrateful Parliament, Thomas. They don't deserve our loyalty."

"Yet we swore an oath that they would have it. Does your word mean nothing to you?" he spat.

"It means nothing to them. What of their oath? Are they not bound to do what's right for us; to allow us our constitutional rights as they instituted?"

Thomas shook his head. "Just because they broke their oath, it does not make it right for us to break ours."

"Which is why I'm selling my commission instead of deserting. Have you not considered it yourself?"

"No, I have not."

"Think on it, Thomas."

Thomas shook his head, yet again. He could not believe what he was hearing from his friend. He had always thought they would serve together for their entire lives, come what may. Combined with what he was saying inside the fort, Thomas began to wonder where his friend's loyalties lay, but was too afraid to ask. He was not certain he wanted to know the answer. What would he do if Robert joined with the Sons of Liberty? He tried not to think on it.

"What shall you do instead?"

Robert ran his hand along the back of his neck. "I thought I'd practice law. I've handled a few things since the war. I could open a practice." Robert did not mention that he would open the practice in Boston. He still needed more time before he brought that up. Thomas was not going to be pleased with that decision and needed to get used to the idea of Robert leaving the army first.

Thomas nodded, unsure what to say. At least he seemed to have a plan. Thomas was not sure whether he found that comforting or not. It meant Robert had been considering this for some time. They had always been of the same mind on everything. When had they become so opposed? Thomas prayed Robert did not have intentions to join the riots and protests against the Crown.

## Chapter 24

# December 16, 1769

To the Betrayed Inhabitants of the City and Colony of New-York.

*My dear fellow-citizens and countrymen,*

*In a day where the minions of tyranny and despotism in the mother country and the colonies are untiring in laying every trap that their malevolent and corrupt hearts can suggest, to enslave a free people; when this unfortunate country has been striving under many disadvantages for these last three years to preserve their freedom, which, to an Englishman is as dear as his life; when the merchants of this city and the towns throughout the colonies have nobly and cheerfully sacrificed their private interest to the public good rather than to promote the plans of the enemies of our constitution, it might reasonably be expected that in this day of constitutional light, the representatives of this colony would not be so audacious, nor be so lost to all sense of duty to their constituents as to betray the trust committed to them. However, this is precisely what they have done in passing the vote to give the troops a thousand pounds out of any monies that may be in the treasury and another thousand out of the money that may still be issued, which the colony will be obliged to pay, whether or not that bill is supported by royal assent. Furthermore, that the representatives have betrayed the liberties of the people will be apparent from the fact that the ministry are waiting to see whether the colonies, under their current distressed circumstances, will divide on any of the ideals under which they are united and contending with the mother country, by which they may carry out their plans against the colonies and remain in administration. If this does not take place, the acts must be repealed, which will be a reflection on their conduct, and will bring the censure and outcry of the nation upon them for the loss of trade which their misconduct has encouraged.*

*Granting money to the troops is implicitly acknowledging both the authority that enacted the revenue acts and that the acts are necessary, as they were enacted for the express purpose of taking money out of our pockets without our consent in order to provide for the defense and support of the government in America. This revenue is insufficient for this purpose, leaving us responsible for providing the deficiency.*

*The Massachusetts and South Carolina Assemblies have both refuted these acts. If they have done right (which every sensible American thinks they did) in refusing to pay this billeting money, then surely we are wrong, very wrong, in giving it. However, our Assembly says it is our duty to give money to the troops, therefore, the Massachusetts Assembly did not do theirs by not obeying the mandate from the ministry. If this is not a division in the ideal, I know not what is. And I doubt not that the ministry will let us know it is to our loss, for it will provide them with argument and fresh courage. This is nothing more than base ingratitude and a betrayal of the common cause of liberty.*

*What other reason can the ministry attribute so cowardly a conduct as this is of the Assembly than the desertion of the American cause? So repugnant and subversive of all the means we and the other colonies have used to oppose the tyrannical conduct of the British Parliament! There is no other reason. Can there be a more ridiculous mockery to impose on the people than for the Assembly to vote that their thanks are given to the merchants for entering into an agreement to not import goods from Britain until the revenue acts should be repealed, while at the same time, they counteract it by approving British acts and complying with ministerial requisitions incompatible with our freedom? Surely they cannot.*

*And what makes the act of the Assembly granting this money even more grievous is that it goes to support the troops kept here not to protect, but to enslave us. Has the truth of this not been shown recently in the audacious, domineering, and inhuman Major Pullaine who ordered a guard to protect a repugnant troublemaker who disobeyed the commendable non-importation agreement of the merchants in order to block the only means left to them under God to disrupt the plans of their enemies to enslave this continent? This example alone ought to be sufficient to persuade a free people to not grant the troops any supply whatsoever. If we had no other dispute with the mother country that made it necessary to not concede anything which might destroy our freedom, reasons of economy and good policy alone suggest that we ought not grant the troops money.*

*Even those who are barely acquainted with English history must know that concessions frequently made to the Crown are not to be refused without some degree of danger of disturbing the peace of the kingdom or colony. This demonstrates the need to stop these concessions now while we are embroiled with the mother country so that after the controversy is settled, we may not have a new bone of contention about the billeting money, which must be the case if we do not put an end to it now. For the colony, in its impoverished state, cannot support a charge which amounts to near as much per year as all of the other expenses of the government without this one.*

*Furthermore, it follows that the Assembly has not been attentive to the liberties of the continent, nor to the property of the good people of this colony in particular. We must therefore attribute this sacrifice of the public interest to some corrupt source. This was apparent in the guilt and confusion covering the faces of the deceitful supporters of this measure when the House was in debate on the matter. Mr. Colden knows from the nature of things that he cannot have the smallest chance of remaining in administration; therefore, he must make the most of his position while he can while receiving a full salary from the Assembly. While he is anxious to obtain his salary, he must attend to his offspring and as some of his own children hold offices in the government, if he did not obtain obedience to his demands or do his duty by dissolving the Assembly in case they refused the billeting money, his children might be in danger of losing their offices. If he dissolved the Assembly, they would not give him his salary.*

*The De Lancy family, knowing the dominance they have in the present House of Assembly and how useful that influence will be to their ambitions to manage a new governor have left no stone unturned to prevent a dissolution.*

*The Assembly have knowingly trampled on the liberties of the people and being afraid of the justifiable resentment of those people from such behavior, are equally careful to retain their seats in the house and fully expect that they can. They imagine that this grand controversy will be settled this winter and they will therefore serve for seven years, in which time they hope that the people will forget the present injuries done to them. In order to secure this objective, the De Lancy family, like true politicians, appeared to be at mortal odds with Mr. Colden and represented him in all companies as an enemy to his country, yet formed a coalition with him to secure them the sovereign lordship of this colony. The effect of this has given birth to the abominable vote by which liberties of the people have been betrayed. In short, they have allowed matters to reach such a point that all of the checks present in our happy constitution have been destroyed. The Assembly may as well save the trouble of formalities and invite the council to take their seats in the House of Assembly and place the Lieutenant Governor in the Speaker's chair. Then there would be no waste of time going from house to house to vote on the position and his honor would have the pleasure to see how zealous his former enemies are in promoting his interest to serve themselves.*

*Is this a state in which to remain when our all is at stake? No, my countrymen, rouse! Imitate the noble example of the friends of liberty in England who, rather than be enslaved, contend for their rights with king, lords, and commons. And will you suffer your liberties to be taken from you by your own representatives? Tell it not in Boston! Publish it not in the streets of Charlestown! You have means yet left to preserve an accord with the brave Bostonians and Carolinians and prevent the plans of tyrants from being accomplished. The vote in the House was so nearly divided on the subject of granting the money to the troops that one vote may have prevented it. Therefore, you have a respectable minority. What I would advise is to assemble in the Fields next Monday where your input shall be taken on this important matter, despite the impudence of Mr. Jauncey in his declaration in the House that he had consulted with his constituents and that they supported giving the money. After this is done, go together as a whole to your members and insist they join the minority in opposing the bill. If they dare refuse your just request, appoint a committee to draw up a summation of the entire matter and send it to the speakers of the several houses of assembly throughout the colonies and to the friends of our cause in England, and publish it in the newspapers that the whole world may know your feelings on the matter in the only way your circumstances will allow. And I am confident it will encourage the friends of our cause and chagrin our enemies. Let the notification to call the people be so communicated that whoever does not participate will be considered to be in agreement with what may be done by those of us who do meet — and that you may succeed is the sincere desire of A SON OF LIBERTY*

## Chapter 25

# December 17, 1769

U NION, ACTIVITY and FREEDOM, OR, DIVISION, SUPINENESS and SLAVERY.

*X My dear Fellow Citizens.*

*In my address to you last night in which I relayed the dangerous consequences that would result to the inhabitants of this distressed colony if you accepted the vote of the Assembly to provide money for the troops as it was passed into a law, I omitted one important consideration which by itself utterly forbids giving them any money. This is always likely to be the headquarters of the troops which will necessarily saddle us with a great disproportion of taxes as compared to the other colonies for supporting those that will constantly be here while they will be*

*exempt from this burden. This will natu-
rally produce two additional grievances.*

>*1.    That all the necessaries of life will
become more expensive, to the great dis-
tress of the poor.*
>*2.    That luxury will be increased and
required of us, which is well known to
be very unfavorable to a country in our
circumstances, whereas if we do not provide quarters for them, money must be
sent from England which will in some
measure    alleviate    the    above    consequences.*

*I hope you have by now considered the im-
propriety and evil tendency of the vote in
question. Need I say more to a free people to
induce them to preserve their freedom and
prevent the most dreadful evils resulting in
slavery? I hope I need not. Therefore, as you
regard all that is dear to Englishmen, you
are requested to meet at the Liberty Pole at
eleven o'clock this morning, to deliberate on
means to preserve your liberties. All that
you have done thus far will be in vain if you
do not persevere until you secure that invaluable necessity on a permanent foundation.
As the intent of this meeting is to get the free
and unbiased sentiments of the people on
this important decision, all of those who are
vying for power are asked to stay at home so
that the people will not be influenced by their*

*deliberations. Therefore, the De Lancys, Livingstons, and Waltons are hereby requested to not give the people any discomfort by their appearance. All other persons who shall not appear will be considered as being in agreement with what will be determined on Monday morning, December 18, 1769.*

*A Son of Liberty*

## Chapter 26

# December 18, 1769

Ellie wondered how many people would show up in the Fields that morning. It became apparent just how many it would be when foot traffic increased outside, and everyone was going in the same direction. With the kids at their lessons, she stepped outside and followed the crowd, making sure to stay on the outer edges of it.

"Mrs. Russell. Good day to you, madam. How lovely to see you."

Ellie turned to see the dockmaster, John Bingham, heading the same direction as her. "Good morning, Mr. Bingham. It looks to be quite a crowd today."

"Indeed," he replied.

"I wasn't sure how many people saw the broadsheets or would actually show up."

"There was another announcement posted around the city only this morning. Did you see it? It was rather spirited," he said while handing her a small piece of paper. "I picked it up at the dock when the wind blew it from its nail."

"I didn't see it," she responded, taking the paper and reading it.

> *To THE PUBLIC. — The spirit of the times makes it necessary for the inhabitants of the city to gather together in order to effectively prevent the destructive consequences of the recent dishonorable and shameful conduct of our General Assembly, who have dared to vote for supplying the troops, without the smallest shadow of an excuse for their insidious allowance, against the loud and collective voice of their constituents, the dictates of sound policy, the ties of gratitude, and the glorious struggle in which we have engaged for our invaluable birthrights. The most eligible place will be in the Fields near Mr. De La Montaigne's, between 10 and 11 o'clock this morning where we doubt not every friend to this country will attend.*

*Spirited indeed*, Ellie thought. The author of this one called out the Assemblymen as being only out for themselves and completely ignoring the desire of the people. Every post or publication she saw seemed to be more and more inflammatory. The constant protests in the streets had not gone unnoticed by her, either. She almost wondered how the colonists managed to make it another six years before the war actually started if things were this volatile now.

John Bingham stayed close to Ellie along the way and did not leave her side once they arrived in the Fields. She did not try to put distance between them, either. He was a kind man who always seemed to look out for her. He never tried to flirt with her or behave inappropriately. Ellie liked him and appreciated his protective instincts toward her that never felt overbearing like Thomas and Robert's often did.

John did not complain or leave Ellie when she said she preferred to stay on the outskirts of the Fields. She gave him leave to go further in, but he stayed by her side. They passed Robert and Thomas and Ellie stopped momentarily, getting a closer look at Thomas's horse.

"Is this Boreas?" she asked, rubbing his muzzle, recognizing the horse she learned to ride on all those years ago. He was a beautiful chestnut quarter horse with black socks fading at the knee and a black mane and tail.

"It is," Thomas said stoically, glaring at the man who had stopped with her.

"I'm surprised you still have him."

"He's been a good companion," Thomas said, leaning forward to rub the side of the horse's face and neck.

Her eyes never met his own, staying locked on Boreas. Marveling at how comfortable she was with the horse, he recalled the first time she went into the stables with him and he learned she had never been near a horse before. Thomas could not resist telling her the fate of her own horse, knowing she would want to know.

"I kept Bella for a time as well but sold her when I left Fort Edward."

"I'm glad she was alright and found her way back. I worried she'd been taken or killed."

Thomas nodded, acknowledging her concerns.

Robert urged his horse closer now and asked her what she was doing there. "I thought you agreed at dinner yesterday to stay away from the area?"

Ellie had agreed to no such thing and told Robert as much now. What she had said when he and Thomas had asked her, Lucy, and Adelaide to stay out of the area was that she would not do anything to jeopardize her safety.

"The meeting may turn violent," Robert said authoritatively. "It's safer for you to stay away from here."

Robert knew she was eager to see 'history in the making' as she called it and would not likely leave, but he had to try. While Thomas was worried not only for her safety, but that she would participate in the events, Robert knew better. He did not think her likely to participate, only wanting to get close enough to watch. But getting close enough may prove harmful. He had been sent out to assist in stopping the soldiers from tearing down the Liberty Pole again Saturday night after the anonymous publication had circulated. It had taken some convincing, making it a late night. The troops were already upset, believing the Assembly had disrespected them by only allowing for eighteen hundred pounds to be directed toward their billeting. Reading the words on the broadsheet saying they were only there to enslave the people rather than protect them had only served to further enrage them. It was anyone's guess as to what would happen today. Every day seemed like a powder keg waiting for a spark.

Thomas laughed quietly to himself at Robert's efforts, knowing how difficult Ellie could be when she thought her safety was not at risk. When she set her mind to something, it was near impossible to change it.

Grudgingly, she pulled her hand away from Thomas's horse, turning back to John. "We should move closer to be able to hear what's happening."

Robert tried again, but Ellie was no longer listening. She said goodbye, leaving them to their duty and making it clear that she made her own decisions. Ellie and John ventured further into the crowd, close enough to hear the speakers.

With a showing of approximately fourteen hundred people, mostly men, the meeting ended up being more peaceful than Ellie had expected. People complained and released some of their anger, but ultimately, it was more productive than Ellie had imagined it would be. She had expected it to be more like a protest, with a select few riling up the masses, but that was not what it was at all. The issues were presented and discussed, more like a town hall meeting. A man named John Lamb acted as moderator of the meeting after introducing himself.

"By a show of hands, is there anyone here who approves of the vote of the House of Assembly, for granting the money to support the troops?" John Lamb asked the crowd.

Maybe six hands raised into the air.

"Are you for giving any money to the troops, on any consideration whatsoever?"

Once again, only a handful of arms raised into the air. Lamb continued, proposing a committee be selected that would take the concerns of the people to the Assembly. The crowd continued to appoint, then vote on the men who would make up the committee. John Lamb was elected as the chairman and several other men were elected as members of the committee. Together, Isaac Sears, Caspar Wistar, Alexander McDougall, Jacobus Van Zandt, Samuel Broome, Erasmus Williams, and James Yan Yaurk would inform the Assembly that the people greatly disapproved of granting the money to the troops, putting them in compliance with the Quartering Act.

With the meeting over and the crowd dispersing peacefully, Ellie headed towards the Burke residence for afternoon tea with the ladies. She relayed the outcome of the meeting to Adelaide and Lucy while they visited and discussed everything that was going on. They were both concerned for Thomas and Robert and hoped things in the colony would soon come to a peaceful end. Ellie almost wished she could tell them things would only continue to escalate, resulting in war. For a moment, she considered trying to find a way to say it. Before she could, the front door opened, interrupting them.

"It seems the Assembly did not like the new handbill that was posted this morn," Thomas informed them as he and Robert arrived, bringing more news with them. Taking off their coats, they entered the parlor. "They were furious over the broadsheet from Saturday and voted in favor of it being an 'infamous and scandalous libel.' They've offered a reward of one hundred and fifty pounds for information about the author. The vote was nearly unanimous."

"Only Philip Schuyler voted against it," Robert added. "John De Lancey himself called for the vote. He was not happy to be defamed in the broadsheets like that."

"I imagine not," Adelaide agreed.

Thomas was not finished. "There was a new one posted this morning, signed only 'A Son of Liberty' giving the location and time of today's meeting. It was also rather libelous, and the Assembly is offering fifty pounds for information regarding the author."

"What of the committee's efforts this morning?" Ellie asked. "Did the Assembly hear them out?"

"They heard them but refused to change their decision," Robert replied. "They shall still provide money for the soldiers."

When Ellie nodded, Thomas could not help but ask if she thought it a good thing. He was curious as to which side she supported and needed the reassurance that she was not favoring the Sons of Liberty.

"I understand the concerns of the residents of New York," she answered. "They have a point that if this is to be the headquarters of the army in the colonies, New Yorkers will harbor more of the cost than the other colonies. But it costs money to billet an army. The troops need sundries to survive here."

"Where do you propose the money come from, if not the residents of the colonies of which they are here to protect?" he asked.

Ellie knew he was baiting her. Instead of getting into it with him, she said, "I'm not a politician, Major Burke. But I do know it will work itself out eventually."

Robert's smirk caught her attention, and he had the grace to look down when she glared at him. Thomas seemed satisfied with her answer and let the matter drop.

A few days later, John Lamb was questioned by the Assembly. They all believed him to have been the author of the broadsheet, or at the very least, abetting the libel by chairing the meeting in the Fields. He was ordered to appear before the House, but most of the other committee members elected that morning wrote to the Assembly saying that Lamb had acted in a manner which was "the undoubted right and privilege of every Englishman." They went on to say that if Lamb had engaged in criminal activity, they were all in the same predicament and should also be summoned to answer for their conduct in a constitutional manner. Their words implied that if the meeting had been illegal, residents were unable to guide their representatives, which was something that had been insisted upon in the previous elections. Recognizing the trap, the Assembly did not issue summons against any of the other committee members and Lamb appeared alone. He denied knowing who the author of the broadsheet was, and the Assembly was satisfied, resulting in his release.

## Chapter 27

# December 1769

"May I have the honor of a dance?" Robert asked as he bowed low in front of Ellie.

Ellie giggled at his display of chivalry. Though it was the norm, and she had seen it for years, she never could fully get used to being on the receiving end of it. Having someone open her doors or pull out a chair were one thing. This was something entirely different. Her husband used to open doors for her when they were young. Johnny's parents never knew where he had picked it up, but Ellie had enjoyed it. For the first several years of marriage, they had worked together, and she did not open a single door in that time. That custom had been easy to fall back into when she had arrived there in the past.

Taking the offered hand, Robert led Ellie out to the dance floor. They were in the King's Arms Tavern, which was a favorite of the garrison officers. It hosted several balls and assemblies throughout the year and their group had opted to attend their

Christmas ball in lieu of the Burkes hosting one that year. Ellie had been grateful for that. She was still not ready to attend one in their home as she was certain it would bring back too many memories for her. At least this was less personal.

"Your dancing has much improved since last I had the pleasure," Robert observed, recalling the balls they had attended in Williamsburg.

"I admit, I've not had much occasion to practice, but Hannah has been giving me lessons."

When Lucy and Adelaide had suggested they attend the ball, Ellie was hesitant. Robert had voiced his desire to escort her and she reluctantly agreed. Once Ellie remembered she still did not know any of the dances of the period, she had turned to Hannah for help. The girl had been more than happy to teach Ellie something so proper.

The dances were all rather formal, beginning with the men in a line on one side across from the women in another line. They each bowed or curtsied to their partner, then each couple would have a turn before everyone on the dance floor intermingled and circled one another, grabbing the hands of whomever ended up across from them for a quick spin as they passed one another. It was so simple but Ellie could not help but enjoy herself. The men in the line were all dressed in the finest coats while the women were all in their best dresses and lace caps, though many wore their hair uncovered. Formal evening gatherings were the one time it was acceptable for women to be in public with their hair uncovered. Several, including Ellie wore no cap or bonnet, opting instead to adorn their hair with feathers, ribbons, pearls, or decorative pins. She had worn her hair half up and half down with curls covering her crown in a popular style that Tabitha had helped her do. Lucy and Adelaide had offered to help her make a new dress, which she attempted, but in the end, she ended up purchasing a new one. Ellie knew her limits and though she could sew, she was no seamstress.

Loose curls fell around Ellie's shoulders as Robert spun her around. She crossed with Thomas and a zing went through her as their hands grasped ever so briefly. She fought to take her eyes from him and ignored the tightness in her stomach.

Focusing back on Robert, Ellie spun around and around. As the night went on, she found herself throwing her head back and laughing as they danced. It was such a simple thing, yet she was having so much fun. Robert watched her intensely all night and stayed by her side. Several other officers tried to interject themselves, but Robert and Thomas both prevented them from doing so. She talked to many people, but none were permitted to stay long. It was not lost on the women.

"Our men seem to be rather protective over you this evening," Lucy observed.

Ellie chuckled uncomfortably. "They can be rather dramatic and overbearing."

"I meant not to imply anything disagreeable. I'm proud to see them doing so. Your status as a young, wealthy widow will draw much attention on its own, yet you're so beautiful as well. It's bound to cause a stir. One can never be too careful under the circumstances."

Ellie shook her head with a laugh. "I'm really not as young as I look."

"Oh, I know you've said so before," Lucy said, waving her hand in Ellie's direction. "But that does not make you old."

Ellie did not tell her she was nearly twice Lucy's age. She certainly did not feel anywhere near that old, nor did she look it. She remained quiet and enjoyed the compliment for what it was.

At the end of the night, the four of them walked home, Ellie and Robert parting ways with Thomas and Lucy at their house while Jack and Adelaide made their own way home. Robert escorted Ellie the rest of the way back to her place and she invited him in, not yet ready for the night to end. Of course, he declined, saying it would not be proper. But, he lingered for a moment, then took her hand and kissed the back of it. The simple gesture warmed her and he wished her a good night before heading home himself.

*January 1770*

"I'd like your blessing to court Mrs. Russell."

A stunned Thomas nearly dropped his drink. He set it down on the table beside him as he steadied himself before turning his full attention onto Robert. The men had been having a pleasant visit in Thomas's parlor when Robert had dropped that bit of news out of nowhere.

"Mrs. Russell is not mine to give permissions over," he said more nonchalantly than he felt. Thomas sat up and leaned forward, resting his elbows on his knees.

"No, but given your previous relationship with her, I wanted to ask out of respect. If you're not amenable to it, I shan't pursue her."

Thomas was quiet, looking toward the doorway guiltily. He knew Lucy was out of earshot upstairs, but could not resist checking, just in case. He did not want to see Ellie courting anyone, particularly not his friend and was at a loss for words. Despite her claims to not believe in marriage, it was likely that she would eventually begin courting someone. Would it be better if that someone was Robert or a complete stranger? Robert would treat her well, though that meant she would always be in his life. Now that he knew she was still alive, he could not imagine her not being in his life again but having her so close was difficult. He was trying to not want her so much. Maybe the problem was intensified by the fact that he knew she was unattached. Perhaps if she belonged to another, he would be able to lose interest.

"Thomas, I'd never want a woman to come between us. I hold deep affection for Ellie. I tried not to, but she's quite wonderful."

"Yes, she is," Thomas nodded. He knew his friend had always cared for her. Thomas had often suspected that was why Robert had never married. No one else had ever been Ellie. She was never Robert's, but Thomas suspected his friend was punishing himself for having feelings for her, knowing how Thomas had felt about her. Now that Thomas was married, it did not matter how he felt.

"How does she feel about the matter?" Thomas asked, even though he did not want to know the answer. If she was against it, Robert would never be asking.

"I've not yet discussed it with her. I wanted to ask you first."

With the new year, Robert had decided it was time to take his chance. He had been holding back, trying to convince himself not to try. She had been Thomas's first love and she had broken his heart. He had always suspected that she harbored feelings for him as well, but he could never act on them because of Thomas. But his friend was happily married now. It was Robert's turn to find his own happiness. And once Thomas accepted that they were together, it would be that much easier for him to accept them both leaving for Boston. He would understand Robert's decision to go with her if he thought Ellie was the only reason Robert was going.

Thomas nodded, leaning back in his seat. He tried his hardest to appear as though he did not care. "You are aware of how she feels on the matter of marriage. What makes you think she'll be open to your advances?"

Robert looked down at the drink still in his hand. "Thomas, what happened with you may not be my fate. She married again. I know she said she was forced into it, yet she stayed with him. How much could she have hated it?"

"Perhaps she only stayed with him for the money?" Thomas suggested, knowing his Ellie would never do such a thing. He was not trying to talk Robert out of it, only trying to make sure he saw every possibility. Then again, maybe he was trying to talk him out of it. What if she broke Robert's heart as she had broken his? Worse yet, what if they married? It was an impossible situation.

Ellie had told him that she left because she had only wanted to see him happy and knew she could not do so. Thomas knew he should afford her the same courtesy. Apparently, she was much stronger than him to be so selfless.

"You believe that not, nor do I," Robert admonished. "We both know she favors me over other men. I've not acted on her familiarity out of respect for you, but I'm asking you now to allow this to take its natural course."

"I'll not interfere, Robert." Thomas took a large drink of his brandy followed by a deep breath. "I wish you all the best," he relented. He even tried to mean it.

## Chapter 28

# January 8, 1770

NEW-YORK

*With the greatest regret, all the real Friends of Liberty and our happy constitution saw at several of our recent elections the most infamous bribery and corruption with the most brutal debauchery and rioting. Many of the poorer people have deeply felt the aristocratic power, or rather the intolerable tyranny of the great and opulent, by being openly threatened with the loss of their employment and to be arrested for debt unless they gave their votes as they were ordered (such is the shocking depravity of the times and the utter contempt of all public virtue and patriotism). It being evident to all impartial men that nothing else can preserve the freedom and independence of elections and prevent the excessive influence of the rich over the poor in the future than a secret method of voting, a motion has accordingly been made in the Honourable House of*

*Assembly for permission to bring in a bill for voting by ballot. This, it was naturally to be expected, immediately alarmed all whose political positions are owed to their wealth rather than their virtue and those men have accordingly exerted the strongest influence that could be made to block the helpful measure. To promote and carry it into completion, the Friends of Liberty decided it was their duty to hear the voice of the people on such an important subject before any of the poorer and more dependent individuals were menaced or coerced by the Corruptors General of the city. Accordingly, they organized a meeting at the Liberty Pole where a majority of freeman and freeholders assembled and declared their approval of voting by ballot in the future. However, the adversaries of the measure disputed, as is their usual custom, the number of persons who met. Another meeting was organized at which a most indisputable majority again voted for appointing a committee to report the desire of the people in favor of securing the freedom of election by ballot to the Honourable House.*

*During all this time until last Thursday night, the promoters of tyranny and despotism were inexhaustible in their attempts to keep the poor in their present bondage by upsetting the patriotic scheme for free elections. Through their customary corrupt practices and unparalleled knack of defamation, they secured as large a body as possible of their own supporters and dependents and gave the public only a few hours' notice of a meeting at the merchant's coffee house last Friday to see how far commercial influence would persuade the common journeymen to accept the present denial of this most invaluable privilege. Here, the great and mighty, the rich, and all manner of wickedness in high places had assembled themselves into a quantity so dense and tremendous, they hoped to awe and intimidate by the very appearance of their size. It was then put forward from the balcony of the coffee house by Mr. Isaac Low, Prolocutor General for the party, that those who were for the old method of voting should remain where they stood and those for balloting should take a step back in order to ascertain the majority vote. This modest proposition was justly opposed by another gentleman on the balcony as it assumed a detestable advantage to the old method, and both parties were equally entitled to hold the ground they occupied. Therefore, he proposed that the different parties should separate different ways. Upon this suggestion, a person in the gallery, who was doubtless incited to commit the horrendous act, came in slyly behind the gentleman who spoke last and endeavored to throw him from the gallery onto the stone pavement below. It was with difficulty that the intended victim by an amazing action and presence of mind saved himself from the intended barbarity. Upon this, the opponents to balloting resorted to their old ploy of getting the people to sign long, fabricated instructions in order to ensnare the ignorant and unwary. However, the people having so recently detected that kind of subterfuge, stopped the speaker by restating 'no instructions.' Silence ensuing again, the person who had just escaped the attempted murder requested that those for balloting move to the left. At that time, a majority of at least three to two (though most people think of two to one) gathered on the left. Having openly given their vote for balloting despite frequent attempts at being silenced by the minority, they immediately proceeded to sign petitions to the House for carrying the said beneficial and important measure into implementation. Still determined to prevent the defeat of tyranny from a few and to restore to the poor and dependent their primitive and constitutional right of voting according to their own judgements, the defeated faction fell back upon their old trick of influencing individuals one at a time to make the poor and distressed sign the said instructions. Furthermore, it is strongly suspected that in order to enhance the list, they intend to procure the contributions of a great number of people who have no vote. However, they may depend on the Friends of Liberty to petition the Honourable House for a copy of the instructions and if in searching the names, they detect such falsehoods, they will expose the contributors and the* perpetrators as such disreputable practice deserves.

As we have had so many sad examples of undue and corrupt influence on the freedom of elections; as the true plan of opposing the Balloting Act be seen as the pretense that it is, namely, to preserve and perpetuate that corrupt influence; as according to the present mode of election, the poor and despondent are evidently reduced to a worse condition than if they had no voices at all by being compelled to give their vote against their own judgement; as it is a most atrocious and villainous violation of our constitutional privilege to bias the poorest man living by threats or promises; as every objected inconvenience to the proposed method can effectually be cured by a Balloting Act, it is hoped that there is still among us sufficient share of public virtue and a sufficient number of incorruptible patriots to erect so impregnable a barricade against the assault of the rich and powerful, and experience has continued to show that the people persevering in a righteous demand have finally proved triumphant.

Mr. Thomas moved for permission to bring in a bill that all elections to be held or made for the election of Representatives to sit in General Assembly for the Colony of New York, shall be by ballot only. After a debate arising from the said motion, the question put forth was carried in the affirmative.

It is therefore so ordered that Mr. Thomas have permission to bring in a bill for that purpose.

## Chapter 29

*January 9, 1770*

To the Public.

Nobody seems to doubt that one day, Great Britain will fall and that glorious constitution which is the envy of the world will crumble into ruin thanks to the corruption seen in elections. A person who buys electors will certainly sell them if he can in order to reimburse himself. As balloting will prevent all the deviousness used in elections to terrify the poor and ruin the integrity of the people, one would imagine that every opponent to patriotism would exert or at least pretend to exert himself in its favour. But unfortunate as it is, the rich are apt to consider their influence upon the poor as part of their advantages and to desire that their money should secure those honours and trusts which instead ought to be the compensations of ability and virtue. Therefore, *when something is proposed to free the tradesman and mechanic, particularly the poor, from a state of dependence upon the lords of the manor, great landholders, the opulent merchant, and the man of figure and fortune, it is not surprising if every trick is utilized to deceive the unthinking part of the community and if possible, to set the poor to work on riveting their own chains. Ever since the motion for bringing in a bill for balloting in elections (which thanks to heaven was carried by a great majority of the House), every effort has been made to attract and trap the unwary. For this reason, the wicked man of wealth claims the balloting plan opens a door to fraud. However, the very design of it is to prevent fraud and that every citizen may be able to expose these devious betrayers of the liberties of the poor. In the outlines of the Balloting Act, it will become obvious that all objections, if there are any, to the practice of balloting in any of the other colonies must arise not from the balloting, but from the imperfection of the laws by which they ballot. And should any defects in the bill be discovered, it will be easy enough to provide a suitable remedy by passing a subsequent law.*

*. . .*

*In elections using this method, the vote of an elector will always remain a secret, for no man's ticket can be divulged. What a noble independency will this give to the tradesman and the poor honest elector! And what innumerable disgust and contention will it prevent. Nor can any man object to it except the wretch who is so uncontrolled as to desire to make a meagre gain by selling his liberty for a dram or a dollar, or the rich landholder who wants a rent out of his tenant's conscience as well as his purse, or the man of mortgages and bonds who most unconscionably threatens to load his debtor with costs for the principal after squeezing seven percent from him for his money or throw him into gaol and starve his children unless he will vote against his country and his conscience for the promotion of this oppressor or his friends.*

*Let all the friends of virtue seize the present moment for the redemption of the poor from slavery. This is the day to establish liberty, and the law now asks for one of the best means to secure it as well as the most accurate test that can be created for discovering those among the rich who are really the friends of mankind at heart. Even should it be granted, he who is against a good Balloting Act may be mistaken through his own misunderstanding and therefore, should be released from the guilt of corrupt ideas. Yet all must recognize that the wealthy man who supports it by denying himself the natural influence of his opulence is in agreement that the poor should be free.*

*This endeavor will prove a touchstone to all. It will try their hearts or the understandings, or both and let every mechanic therefore watch its progress and mark its opposers. It will hardly be possible for them to conceal the cloven foot. Whenever we hear the proud talk of supporting the honour of government by excluding the middle class not only from promotion, but from the power of contributing to the promotion of others, we shall know what they mean. They want a power to enslave.*

PUBLICOLA
*New-York.*

## Chapter 30

# Monday, January 15, 1770

Tempers flared in the streets as Ellie made her way to the cooper on a blustery Monday afternoon. The inflammatory broadsheets continued to be published, with anger directed at the Assembly for supporting the presence of the army, making the citizens pay for them to remain in the colony, and for the state of the elections. Bribery and corruption were seen as running rampant with the poor being threatened to vote for a particular person and electors collecting votes from those ineligible to vote. To combat these, a balloting act was proposed which included, among other things, anonymous ballots. Ellie began to watch the broadsheets daily as the various issues played out in them.

The residents of New York were not the only ones who were angry at the course of events. With unceasing anger at the Assembly over the Military Appropriations Bill, people continued to protest in the streets and tempers continued to flare on all sides. The troops were caught in the middle between a people who did not want them there and the government who was forcing the people to pay for their presence.

That morning, Ellie had her own problem on her hands. She was supposed to be assisting the neighborhood women with the making of a quilt for a young woman who was about to get married, but instead, she was replacing a broken water barrel. Ezra came in early that morning to inform her that while on his return from filling the water barrel from the tea pump down the street, the wheel on the cart hit a pothole and broke, sending the barrel crashing to the ground in pieces. He managed to fix the wheel, but the barrel was unsalvageable. Hannah mentioned that the Armstrongs had left a small bankroll with which to continue running the house in their absence, but something like that had not been factored into the budget. They could certainly make do without the extra barrel as they had several in the stables that Ezra maintained, but Ellie felt that replacing the barrel was the least she could do for the Armstrongs for allowing her to stay on in their home. Tabitha stayed behind to assist Hannah with chores, but Ellie took Harris with her to the cooper.

"The soldiers was at the Pole again Saturday last," said a patron to the shopkeeper as they stepped inside. Ellie welcomed the warmth of the fire in the corner as the woman continued. "Someone passing by saw them and ran into Montayne's Tavern, alerting everyone inside and they all went a-running out to see what is happened."

The shopkeeper, a thin African American woman Ellie guessed to be in her late thirties interrupted the woman from continuing when it seemed she would keep going. Ellie had already heard the tale at dinner the previous day. The soldiers had been frustrated enough to try again to take down the Liberty Pole. When the crowd interrupted their efforts, the soldiers chased them back into the tavern, which was known as the headquarters for the Sons of Liberty in the city.

Once back inside the tavern, the soldiers had drawn their swords and bayonets, insulted everyone inside, and beat a waiter. When that was not enough, they had continued to destroy everything within reach. Robert and Thomas had not been happy to report on the activities of the night in question.

"What could I help you with?" the shopkeeper asked Ellie as the other woman departed.

Ellie informed the woman that she needed a new water barrel. While they discussed her needs, Ellie noticed Harris looking closely at the barrels as if trying to figure out how they were made. The cooper came out from a room in the back and watched him.

"How do the curve get in the wood?" Harris asked, pointing at the outward bow at the middle of the barrel on display.

"We soften de wood wit' a little heat. If we hold it o'er a low fire for 'bout twenty or thirty minute, then we can hammer metal hoops 'round it to make it de shape we wan'."

Amos had been brought over to Maryland as a young boy from Jamaica. He had been enslaved for most of his youth when his master had taught him the trade. Then, he had unexpectedly been granted his freedom in a will when his owner passed away. He took it and fled to New York to start anew, where he met and married Addah only a few years ago.

"And how do the water stay inside? Why it don't leak?"

Ellie had begun working with him and Tabitha on their speech but it would take time to reverse the lifetime of usage and lack of education. Despite this, she did not correct him in public.

The man chuckled at the questions. "Would you like to see how we make dem?"

Harris's eyes lit up. "Could I?"

They looked to Ellie for permission, who nodded with a smile and told them to take as long as they needed. When they went into the back, Ellie turned back to the wife and found the woman staring at her inquisitively.

"He's so curious about everything." Ellie offered. "He wants to know how everything works, and I fear I won't be able to teach him nearly enough."

"Teach him?" When Ellie looked at her with confusion, she added, "Why you would go to the trouble of indulging the whims of a slave?"

Ellie momentarily looked shocked, and the woman quickly added, "Forgive me bluntness. I never seen a White woman care 'bout what her slaves learnt outside what's required of them in they duties."

"Oh, he's not a slave," she said, horrified at the thought. "I mean, I bought him at the slave market, but only to set him free. Him and his sister. I planned to adopt them both, but I was informed there's no legal adoption here, so now I'm just trying to be the best guardian I can to them. Honestly, I hope I can do them both justice so they can be productive members of society, though I admit, I'm still learning how to navigate life in this world myself."

She was rambling and oversharing, but she hated that the woman thought of her as someone who owned slaves. It was not personal, but Ellie wanted to dissuade her of the notion.

The woman eyed her suspiciously. They chatted while Harris got to see the shop. Another customer came in and when the woman stepped out from behind the counter for something, Ellie saw that the woman was pregnant.

"How far along are you?" she asked.

"'Bout four month, I'm supposin'."

"Do you have a midwife?"

"Me sister comes to help during me time. She have seven children of her own."

Ellie nodded. "You should consider someone with proper training."

"Me sister do well enough."

"Harris's sister is training to be a midwife. I've been teaching her what I can, but we need patients. Unfortunately, a lot of White women won't allow her to tend to them so she can gain the experience she needs."

Before Ellie could ask, the woman interrupted. "And you want her to learnt on me?"

"You need a midwife. She needs patients. I can assure you that I'll be there with her throughout the entire process. I've been doing this for years and helped birth dozens. But Tabitha is quite smart and capable."

The woman eyed her for a moment, and Ellie saw when she made her decision. "What were your fee?"

They discussed the cost, which Ellie lowballed since Tabitha was still learning. The woman agreed and Ellie smiled. "I'm Ellie, by the way. Ellie Russell."

"Addah Mawby." Harris and the cooper emerged from the back then and she added, "That there be Amos Mawby."

Ellie greeted the man and asked Harris if he enjoyed seeing the workshop. He beamed at her and nodded. With business taken care of, Ellie informed them she would send Ezra back with the cart to retrieve the barrel and she would be in touch with Tabitha to begin the woman's care.

The whole way home, Harris talked of the cooper's operations and an idea began to form in her mind. She would have to discuss it with Amos before she mentioned it to Harris. She did not want to get his hopes up unnecessarily.

That night, the soldiers again attacked the Liberty Pole, this time being stopped by an alderman.

## Chapter 31

## January 15th, 1770

To The Public

Whoever seriously considers the state of this city and many of the poor inhabitants of it must be greatly surprised at the conduct of those who employ the soldiers when there are a number of poor citizens who want employment to support their distressed families. Every man with any sense amongst us knows that the army is not kept here to protect, but to enslave us, and notwithstanding, our Assemblies have given vast sums of money to provide them with such necessities which many of the good citizens want.

These supplies are paid by a tax on the colony, a third of which is the quota for this city and county. Add to this burden the heavy duty we pay on sugar and other items which so greatly distresses our trade and has so impoverished this city that many of its former inhabitants have moved while others who remain are, for want of employment, unable to support themselves and are thereby becoming a public charge. If the employers or labourers would see to it with that same care and benevolence that a citizen owes to his neighbour by employing him, this might, in a great measure, be prevented, providing comfort to their distressed families and a saving to the community. Is it not enough that you pay taxes for billeting money to support the soldiers and a poor tax to maintain many of the whores and bastards in the workhouse, without giving them the employment of the poor who you must then support if you don't employ them, which then greatly adds to your poor tax? I hope my fellow citizens will take this matter into consideration and not tolerate a set of men who are not only enemies to liberty but at the beck and call of tyrants to enslave. Especially when it will bring on you the just reproaches of the poor. Experience has convinced us that good usage makes soldiers insolent and ungrateful. All the money that you have thus far given to them has only taught them to despise and insult you. This is evident in a great number of them attempting last Saturday night to blow up the Liberty Pole, which they would have succeeded in doing had some of the citizens not discovered them. They had time to saw the braces and bore a hole into the pole which they filled with powder and plugged it up in order to set fire to it. This was discovered by a person at Mr. Montaynes. In resentment, they broke seventy-six squares of his windows, entered his *house, and stopped him in the passageway with swords. They further threatened that if he stirred they would take his life, which intimidated the people in the house so much that they leapt out of the windows. Not satisfied with this atrocious wickedness, they broke two of his lamps and several bowls. In order to better accomplish their desires, they posted sentinels in the roads that lead to the Liberty Pole, to prevent their being discovered. This and worse would be the treatment we might expect if there were a greater number of them. It's hoped that this conduct with the former considerations will be sufficient to prevent any Friend to Liberty from employing any of them for the future. There is a matter of the utmost importance to the liberties of the good people of this colony and the continent now before the Assembly. All the Friends to Liberty that incline to bear a testimony against a literal compliance with the Mutiny Act (Otherwise called the Billeting Act) are desired to meet at Liberty Pole at twelve o'clock, next Wednesday, which will be the 17th, where the whole matter shall be communicated to them.*

*New-York,*
*BRUTUS*

## Chapter 32

# Tuesday, January 16, 1770

"The soldiers was at it until the wee hours of the morn, but they finally took down the Liberty Pole."

Ellie woke to the news that the soldiers had finally succeeded in their goal of the previous month. When Ezra and Harris went to fill the water barrels at the tea pump that morning, everyone was talking about it. They were excited to come back and share the news with everyone else in the house.

"Them used gunpowder to do the job," Harris picked up the telling where Ezra left off. "When it were down, them chopped it into pieces and dumped it on the steps of Montayne's Tavern. People is heading to the Fields now. Could we go, mistress?"

Ellie knew emotions would be elevated and riots could easily break out. She wanted to be there herself, but felt it was too unsafe for the children to go. How could she justify going while telling them to stay behind? Was this one of those parental prerogatives that people always used? Could she tell them to do as

I say, not as I do? She could put off the quilting for a little longer, could she not? Lucy would understand her absence. They often joked that her skill with a needle was better suited for skin than fabric. Ellie was certain they had only invited her out of propriety and friendship, rather than what she could bring to the project.

Tabitha and Hannah picked up on her hesitation and jumped in, telling the boys it was unsafe to go. "Asides," Hannah said, "we need you both here. What if a riot breaks out and we was here all alone?"

Ellie breathed a sigh of relief at her quick thinking.

When they finally all went back to their tasks, Ellie slipped out and headed to the Fields. It was a bitterly cold day, and she bundled up as much as she could. Upon her arrival, she could see there had to be at least three thousand angry people there with soldiers from the nearby barracks skirting the edges of the gathering. Officers on horseback were gathered as well. Ellie looked for Thomas and Robert but saw neither. She was certain they were there, but there were far too many people, and she could not see through the crowd.

There were shouts and protests, everyone trying to talk at once. John Lamb again chaired the gathering, trying to control it as much as possible. People threw out suggestions as to how they should proceed, and each was discussed and debated. Finally, they settled on a possible solution.

"Hereafter, we will treat any soldiers found abroad after dark as enemies to the peace of this city and we will petition the city council to demolish the barracks here in the Fields," Lamb announced.

At the proclamation, several soldiers nearby watching the proceeding drew their swords and dared the crowd to do it themselves. Already inflamed tempers soared to new heights. Those closest to the soldiers began to challenge them, but the officers and city magistrates stepped in and prevented a riot.

Ellie continued to watch, not sure how long she had been there. It was long enough that she was frozen. She decided to head to the quilting party and along the way, heard more shouting coming from the docks. She headed that way before going to Lucy's and discovered that seamen were chasing away the soldiers who had been working there.

## Chapter 33

# January 19, 1770

*God and a Soldier all men doth adore*
*In Time of War, and not before:*
*When the War is over, and all Things*
*righted,*
*God is forgotten, and the Soldier*
*slighted.*

WHEREAS *an uncommon and riotous disturbance courses throughout this city by some of its inhabitants who call themselves the Sons of Liberty but instead should more appropriately be called real enemies to society. And whereas the army, now quartered in New York are represented in a heinous light to their officers and others for having raised a disturbance in this city by attempting to destroy their Liberty Pole in the Fields, which, has now been completed without the assistance of the army, we have reason to laugh at them and beg the public to see how chagrined those pretended Sons of Liberty look as they pass through the streets, especially as these great heroes thought their freedom depended on a piece of wood, and they may be compared to Esau, who sold his birthright for a mess of pottage. And although these shining Sons of Liberty have boasted of their freedom, surely they have no right to defame the army since it is out of the power of military discipline to deprive them of their freedom. However, notwithstanding, we are proud to see those elevated geniuses reduced to the uncomfortable position of having their place of general rendezvous made a Gallows Green, a vulgar place of execution for murderers, robbers, traitors, and rebels, to the latter of which we may compare those famous Liberty Boys who have nothing to boast of but the flippancy of tongue, although they openly and routinely assemble in multitudes to stir up the minds of His Majesty's good subjects to sedition in defiance of the laws and good government of our most gracious sovereign. They have in their recent seditious libel, which was signed BRUTUS, expressed the most villainous falsehoods against the soldiers. But as ungrateful as the soldiers are regarded, it is well known since their arrival in New York, they have watched night and day for the safety and protection of the city and its inhabitants; who have suffered the rays of scorching sun in summer and the severe colds of freezing snowy nights in winter, which must be the case and would be fifty times worse had there been a war, which we sincerely pray for, in hopes those Sons of Liberty may feel the effects of it with famine and destruction pouring on their heads. 'Tis well known by the officers of the 16th Regiment, as well as by several others, that soldiers of the sixteenth always gained the esteem and good will of the inhabitants of whatever quarters they lay and have never been accused of being neither insolent nor ungrateful, except in this city. And the same could be said of the Royal Regiment of Artillery, who always behaved with gratitude and respect to everyone. But the means of making your famous city, which you so boast of, an impoverished one, is your acting in violation to the laws of the British government. But be mindful that you do not wait too long to repent, for if you boast so mightily of your famous exploits, as you have done thus far (as you did with the late Stamp Act), we may allow you all to be ALEXANDERS, and lie under your feet, to be stepped upon with contempt and disdain. But before we submit so meekly, be assured we will stand in defense of the rights and privileges due to a soldier, and no farther. But we hope, while our officers act for us, they'll do so, and we shall leave it to their discretion, to act impartially for us in hopes they and every honest heart will support the soldiers' wives and children, and not the whores and bastards, as they have been so maliciously, falsely, and audaciously labelled in the recent impertinent libel addressed to the public, for which, may the shame they mean to place upon us lay on them.*

*Signed by the 16th Regiment of Foot*

## Chapter 34

# *Friday, January 19, 1770*

Ellie and Adelaide met at Lucy's along with several other women in their small community to work on the quilt. The Burke residence always seemed to be the center of activity, but Ellie had gotten used to it by then. Their home almost felt like a second home to her.

With the women gathered around the outer edges of the parlor, a large basket of fabric had been gathered to which all of the women had contributed. Much of the contents were old shirts or dresses cut down into smaller pieces. They had spent most of the week designing the project and cutting small shapes of fabric to attach together. With so many women working together, the piece was coming along quickly, and it was starting to stretch across the quilting frame now.

Ellie watched more than she contributed, but she had managed to assist here and there. Mostly, she assisted in keeping Charles occupied and out of the way. While reading the third story to Charles, who was sitting on her lap, the women all paused in their work and turned their eyes towards the front window. They could hear shouting in the street and several people were running past the house. Alarm immediately spread through the women, but none made any move to go see what was happening. Ellie set Charles down and stood, making her way to the door. Charles tried to follow but she stopped him, telling him to hold their place in the book.

Opening the door, she could see that the people running by were all carrying sticks or makeshift weapons of some sort. They looked to have been pulled from nearby sleighs, ladders, and even chairs. No one was stopping, but as they went past, several shouted a call-to-arms.

"The Liberty Boys need our help. The lobsterbacks are attacking."

Ellie heard the gasps behind her. She turned to see Lucy standing behind her, shaking. She had gone pale. Grabbing the woman gently by her arms, Ellie guided her back to her seat as quickly as she could.

"Major Burke," was all she could say. Adelaide was nearly as stricken as the women both worried over husband and brother.

"Major Burke is well-trained for this," Ellie assured them. "He'll be fine." Not as certain as she wanted to be, she put every ounce of confidence into her voice as she could muster in order to comfort the women.

The other women gathered closer around them now, lending their support. After making sure the women were alright, Ellie made her way toward the door.

"Stay here and keep the door locked," Ellie instructed them.

"Mrs. Russell," Adelaide called out sternly. "Just where are you going?"

Ellie was impatient to leave. "I'm going to help."

There was a chorus of voices trying to tell her not to go.

"You can't possibly."

"It's dangerous."

"What can you possibly do to help?"

"I'll be alright. If there really is an attack, people are going to be injured. They're going to need medical assistance. I can help. Stay here!"

Ellie had one of the women follow her to the door and lock it behind her. "Don't open it for anyone you don't know."

With that, she ran up the street, following the crowd. Stopping at her own residence, she picked up her medical bag while running back toward the door. She instructed everyone to stay inside and keep the door locked, as she had at the Burke's. This time, she hesitated momentarily.

Turning to Tabitha, she asked, "Would you like to go? There will likely be many injuries that you can help me tend."

Tabitha's eyes got big, and she nodded emphatically. Ellie did not wait. As soon as the girl had her cloak, they headed out the door, running up the street.

Ellie had expected to be going to the Fields again as that always seemed to be the source of the protests and riots. But the sounds of a fight were so much closer than she had expected. Ellie and Tabitha only had to go two blocks before they came across the melee blocking the street of Golden Hill.

The narrow passageway was crammed with people. Blood soaked the snow on both sides of the street. A man tried attacking a soldier with a club-like stick, but he lost his weapon as he swung. When he could not retrieve it, he ran. Soldiers pursued him down the street and caught up to him standing in a doorway on the corner. The soldier struck the man with his cutlass, leaving a gash across his right cheek.

Another man driving a tea water cart was attacked and cut while a boy running toward the safety of a house was struck on the head and a woman waiting for the boy in the entry was stabbed with a bayonet. A sailor was struck in the head and hand while another was also stabbed with a bayonet. The soldiers and angry mob were attacking indiscriminately. If a man wore a red coat, he was attacked by the citizens with clubs, sticks, and rocks. If any person, regardless of age or gender was present on the street, the soldiers attacked with cutlass or bayonet. People with sticks helped protect those without as much as they could.

Ellie was momentarily at a loss as to where to begin. She had seen battle before, but her patients typically came to her after it was over. Conscious of Tabitha's presence, she knew she needed to keep the girl safe. It would not do anyone any good if they dove into the fray and were injured themselves. Looking around, Ellie found a clearing at the end of the street, where there was no fighting taking place. She ordered Tabitha to stay there with her medical kit while she ran in and quickly assessed the two individuals who had been stabbed. The woman's injuries were not fatal, so Ellie pointed toward Tabitha and told the woman to go see her for help. The man was in far worse condition.

As two men passed by away from the fight, she grabbed one by the sleeve, stopping him. The other man stopped along with him.

"I need your help," she said. "I need to get this man out of here so I can treat his wounds."

The men looked at her, then down at the man. "This were your husband?" one asked.

Ellie shook her head. "I don't know who he is. But his injuries won't wait. He needs help now. I can give it to him, but I need to get him out of the middle of the fight to do so."

As she spoke, a stick swung in her direction, and she had to duck to miss it. The men nodded and helped carry the injured man down the hill towards Tabitha. They set him down on the ground and Ellie immediately got to work, trying to stop the bleeding while assessing the severity of his injuries, certain she could save him as long as infection did not set in. She set about cleaning his wounds, explaining everything she was doing to Tabitha as she worked. Though she would clean them out as best she could, that was no guarantee of anything. Once he was properly cleaned and the bleeding had slowed, she set about stitching him up.

Ellie worked quickly, moving from person to person that arrived, working both soldiers and civilians, doing what she could for them. Thankfully, none of the injuries had been fatal and her and Tabitha were able to help a number of people. Other women slowly came out to assist as well, many being family of the injured.

As they worked, they heard the story of what had started it all that day. Several soldiers from the 16th

Regiment were posting handbills around Fly Market when Isaac Sears and Walter Quackerbos came upon them. Sears seized the one posting the handbills while Quackerbos took hold of the one carrying the stack of them. The other soldiers with them departed quickly and the two captured soldiers were taken to the mayor's office, the men demanding that they be arrested.

The soldiers who had run had gone back for reinforcements and soon, twenty additional soldiers armed with cutlasses and bayonets had arrived. Drawing their swords and bayonets, they demanded that their compatriots be released. Some even attempted to get inside. A captain stopped them, saying the soldiers were before the mayor now and would receive justice. The captain told them to put up their arms and return to their barracks.

Word quickly spread and the soldiers soon found themselves outnumbered. In no time, there was a large crowd of both civilians and soldiers gathered outside the mayor's office. Mayor Whitehead Hicks ordered the soldiers to return to their barracks, attempting to defuse the tense situation as best he could.

As the troops made their way up Golden Hill, one of the highest points in the city, a crowd gathered around them and stayed close behind them in order to escort them back to the barracks. The rumors that the soldiers had drawn their swords had caused the crowd to follow them. The mob tried to intimidate the soldiers, closing in around them and wrenching stakes and clubs from anything they passed to be used as weapons. The people did not trust the soldiers to be left unattended after having already drawn their swords outside the mayor's office and were worried the soldiers would become violent against innocent citizens. As they crested the hill, soldiers from the other barracks joined them.

The second group of soldiers was led by someone dressed as an officer, though most people Ellie treated swore he was not an officer, merely a soldier in disguise. The citizens were unconcerned initially but soon realized that additional soldiers had arrived behind them as well. They were now trapped in the narrow passageway of Golden Hill between soldiers on either end.

The soldier dressed in an officer's uniform saw the reinforcements and commanded, "Soldiers, draw your bayonets and cut your way through them."

Those on the front line had nothing but the clubs and sticks they had gathered along the way from the mayor's office. Many in the crowd did not even have that much. Soldiers began firing into the crowd as they wreaked vengeance on the inhabitants of New York for the embarrassments they had suffered. The people in the crowd began punching the soldiers and throwing things at them as the soldiers yelled, "Where are your Sons of Liberty now?"

Word spread to every store and shop within the city. More people joined in, causing the riot to grow and spill over into the side streets and into the Fly Market. City officials and army officers soon arrived, trying to quell the melee and unarmed citizens eventually began to disperse. After a time, the officers and city officials forced the soldiers back to their barracks, but not before leaving significant injuries on both sides.

Ellie stood from working on a woman with a large gash in her leg and took in the scene before her.

Papers flew by on the wind, and she grabbed one, looking at it, recognizing it as the one the soldiers had been posting. It began with a poem about God and a soldier. She put the paper in her pocket to read later. Tabitha continued to work on injured as they trickled past. Most of the injured had gone home to have family members tend to them. A mildly injured soldier had stayed to help keep peace in Ellie's make-shift triage station. As she thanked him, she heard the horses approaching behind her and knew without looking that some of the officers had finally made their way over to her. Likely, they were there to collect the remaining soldiers and order them back to their barracks.

When she turned around, Robert and Thomas were dismounting and walking angrily toward her. Taking in her blood-soaked dress, Thomas spoke first.

"What the devil do you think you are doing here?"

"I'm helping. What does it look like I'm doing?" She could not help the sarcastic and defensive tone in response to his anger and insinuation that she should not be there.

"You could have been hurt." Thomas turned his irate gaze toward Tabitha. "I know you care not for your own safety, but what of her? You would deliberately put Tabitha in harm's way?"

Robert came to stand directly beside Thomas with his arms folded across his chest, glaring at her, a united front. Ellie had the sudden urge to laugh. She barked out a howl and turned around, making her way to Tabitha to assist the girl in stitching up another cut.

Tabitha's eyes were wide as she looked between Ellie and the two angry army officers standing in front of them. She knew Ellie knew both men but was shocked to see the way she ignored and laughed at them. Thomas threw his hands up in the air and went back to his horse, mounting him smoothly and efficiently before riding away.

Robert moved in closer and took Ellie by the hands, pulling her to her feet. Ellie quickly pulled her hands away as soon as she was standing.

"This day was not without difficulties for us, Miss Ellie. You must understand our concern."

"Why?" she demanded. "Why must *I* understand *your* concern? Why can't *you* understand I'm not some helpless, fragile flower who's going to break at the first sign of hardship and blood? I'm perfectly capable of taking care of not only myself, but others as well."

"You are a woman. A beautiful, young woman of whom many would take advantage. You're not a soldier, nor are you a man. It's not proper for you to be on your own, nor is it safe. Particularly not in the middle of a riot," he growled.

"I don't give a flying fuck what's proper. And I'll worry about my own safety. I certainly don't need a man to keep people from taking advantage of me."

"You've already taken an arrow to the chest and were abducted. When will it be enough?"

Their voices were getting higher, and they moved closer to each other with every sentence.

"And I came out of that situation just fine! Without a man's help!" Ellie was not about to admit Dajoji had helped by agreeing to take her with them, then helped keep the Abenaki from taking her. She would have managed without his help, and Robert did not need to know that. She was really getting tired of being treated like she was incompetent simply because she was a woman.

Ellie was toe to toe with Robert now. He was nearly a full foot taller than her, being the same height as Thomas, but she did not back down. She had to tilt her head to look up at him, but with hands on her hips, she gave him her fiercest scowl.

"Mistress, I think we's done got all the injuries," Tabitha said timidly, interrupting the two stubborn people, neither of whom were about to back down.

With one last growl at Robert, Ellie turned to look at Tabitha. Everyone around them had left and the girl had packed Ellie's medical kit. She stood nearby, clutching it in front of her with both hands. Ellie held her hand out for the bag and placed her other hand on Tabitha's arm, guiding her away, careful to not take her anger out on Tabitha. They walked down the street together and though he did not say a word, Robert followed on his horse until he saw them home and safe inside.

Ellie turned one last time to glare at him as she went in before closing the door on him and shutting out the world.

---

## Saturday, January 20, 1770

The riots and unrest continued. Before the night was over, soldiers attacked the lamplighters as well. One received a cut on the head and another had a ladder pulled out from underneath him. On Saturday, another skirmish broke out around noon as soldiers clashed with a group of sailors on Nassau Street.

Mayor Hicks ordered them to disperse once again, and his order was ignored. The Sons of Liberty came to the aid of the sailors and the soldiers retreated after the officers again got involved. Later in the afternoon, there were three more incidents. One involved another sailor, another was directed at a woman going to the market, and the third was at a gathering in the Fields. Yet again, when the troops attacked, they were driven back to their quarters by the officers.

Ellie stayed away this time, though not intentionally. The melees were all over quickly and there were only minor injuries. She had not even heard of the first two until well after the fact. Instead, she stayed at the Burke residence and continued working on the quilt.

When they finished, the women all filed out but Ellie stayed behind to help Lucy with the cleanup. Mrs. Toole and Jenny did most of the work while her and Lucy packed up all of the sewing accoutrements and the quilting frame.

"I'm surprised Mrs. Emerson wasn't here today to see us finish the quilt," Ellie observed of Adelaide's absence. She had been there every day until the very last one.

"Mr. Emerson is in port. She's spending a few days with him," Lucy explained.

Ellie smiled. "That must be nice for her. It's so seldom he's ever here."

"Mmm. Sometimes, I envy her that."

Surprised by the confession, Ellie had noticed a strain between Lucy and Thomas. She had attributed it to her own presence in their lives, but perhaps that was narcissistic. Thomas had been far more curt and easy to temper than she remembered him being. Could that be it? She wondered fleetingly if he raised his hands to Lucy. Thomas had never seemed the type before, but he was clearly not the same person she had once loved. He was haunted and physical punishment was commonplace there. No one thought twice about a man who raised a fist to his wife. It was not only a man's right, but his duty to correct his wife's behavior, by any means necessary. She hated even thinking of Thomas that way but wondered if this was the case. She was almost afraid to ask. Lucy must have sensed her curiosity.

"You've something on your mind, Mrs. Russell. Out with it."

Ellie hated that she was so transparent. Picking some loose threads from the floor, she gathered up her courage to ask her friend about what had her concerned.

"Is he," Ellie paused, trying to find the words, "does he hit you?"

It felt like a betrayal to even ask it. She was quite relieved when Lucy said, "Never. Major Burke has always been unconventional with me. Even when I give him cause, he's never corrected me in that manner. He calls it 'bodily autonomy.' Is that not the queerest notion you've ever heard?"

Ellie hated the woman's acceptance of physical abuse as a suitable means of punishment from a husband to a wife and wanted to argue. Knowing it would fall on deaf ears, she kept her mouth shut. But her words did give Ellie some degree of comfort, and she had to keep from smirking at the mention of bodily autonomy. It was something she had taught Thomas all those years ago. It warmed her to think he took her ideas to heart.

"He is rather moody of late, though. All this business with the Liberty Boys has put them all in a foul state of mind. It's all simply exhausting. There's even talk of bringing extra troops over from England to help quell some of the rebellions. Providence only knows where we'll house them all. I imagine you'll end up with quite a few in the extra space you have."

The women heard the door open then, and Thomas came in to find them. He mumbled a brief hello and began to leave when Lucy called him back.

"We were just speaking of the recent rebellious acts. Do come tell Mrs. Russell what you told me last evening of the extra troops that may be coming from England."

Thomas sighed reluctantly and sat in the chair nearest his wife as Mrs. Toole brought in a tray with brandy and a glass for him.

Exhausted, he looked at Ellie and said, "There may be extra troops coming in from England," as if he had just revealed new information.

He poured himself some brandy without adding anything further. Ellie almost laughed at his sarcasm.

Lucy tried plying him for more and he slowly began contributing to the conversation. When one of the children needed attention, Lucy stepped away and Ellie took the opportunity to bring up her part in the melee from the day before.

"I wanted to tell you that I appreciate your concern over my safety, but it's really not necessary. I was perfectly safe yesterday. I made sure we were far enough away from the action that neither myself nor Tabitha would be injured."

Thomas grunted and shook his head. "You're not invincible, Mrs. Russell."

"I don't think I am, Thomas. But I need you to trust me. I'm aware of my limitations."

"Trust you?" he scoffed. "When have I ever been able to trust you, Ellie?"

The words cut her deeply and she dropped into the nearest seat. She tried to see it from his perspective. She had never told him about her past, despite him asking repeatedly. He had opened his heart to her only to have her stomp all over it. She had helped Lucy when she gave birth to Caitlyn, but did that cancel all of the other ways he felt she had betrayed him? She decided to not argue the point.

"I'm sorry you feel that way," she said with remorse.

She was trying to keep it simple, and not say anything even more provoking. Thomas leaned forward in his chair, ran his hand through his hair, then rested both elbows on his knees. Instead of looking at her, he rubbed his eyebrows as if to stave off a headache. For a moment, Ellie saw her Thomas; the Thomas she had fallen in love with. She desperately wanted to run to him and hold him in her arms, erasing all of his troubles in the world and easing his pain. It was all she could do to stay in her seat.

Just as quickly, the vulnerability was gone, and his mask was back in place.

"I must apologize," he said. "I should not say such things. The years of repeated unrest are taking their toll. We thought that upstart Prendergast was to be the last of it, but I'm afraid it shall only continue. These latest brawls with the Sons is proof of that. I fear they will continue to become more brazen in their attacks. There were only cuts and bruises this time, but what will happen next time? Will they not be satisfied until someone is killed?"

Ellie gasped at his words as she suddenly remembered the Boston Massacre. What was the date of that? She never was good at dates, but was almost certain it would be this year, spring, she thought.

Thomas was suddenly sitting up as well, watching her to see what had alarmed her. He looked around to determine if it was something she had seen and asked her what was wrong. Ellie tried to relax her posture and said, "Sorry. I thought I saw something outside."

Thomas laughed bitterly. "Do you think I know not when you're lying to me?"

"March 1770," she declared aloud before she realized the words were out of her mouth. Thomas was visibly confused as she clasped her hands over her traitorous mouth.

"Two months from now? What's March 1770?" he asked.

Ellie shook her head, standing abruptly to leave. "I'm sorry. I have to go. Please tell Lucy I had a lovely time."

Thomas stood and grabbed her arm, stopping her.

"What is March 1770, Miss Ellie?"

The look on his face was a warning. She knew he would never hurt her, so it was an empty threat, but she had caused him enough pain. When she looked at his hand on her arm, he let her go immediately, albeit reluctantly. In return, she told him, "The Boston Massacre."

Thomas called after her as she escaped out of the house. He wanted more information, but there was nothing more she could give him. He would have to wait until news of the massacre hit the papers in a few weeks.

## Chapter 35

*February 1770*

"A captain has come forward who may purchase my commission," Robert announced at Sunday dinner after a day spent in church.

"That's fantastic," Ellie said.

Lucy gasped excitedly. "Are you promoting?"

Robert shook his head, looking sheepish. He stole a quick glance at his friend who showed no reaction. Apparently Thomas had not told Lucy of Robert's plan.

"No. I'm going to leave the army to practice law."

Lucy looked at her husband in question who did not say a word. Thomas continued to eat while not participating in the conversation.

"Congratulations," she said uncertainly.

"The captain is looking to his purse, but if he can manage it, I may be free of the army rather soon. I'd not expected it to happen this quickly. I've been too busy corralling soldiers and breaking up fights with the Sons of Liberty to work toward my own goals. There's still much to do."

"Well, I'll be glad when you're out of the army and no longer obliged to the King," Ellie said almost absently.

Everyone at the table stopped and turned their focus onto her. Her fork stopped midway to her mouth as she realized they were all looking at her.

"What?" she asked.

"What makes you think he would no longer be obliged to the King simply because he's no longer in the army?" Thomas asked.

"Is that what I said? I just meant that you've both done your time. Honestly, I wish you'd consider selling your commission, too. I don't want to see either of you have to go back to war again."

Everyone started arguing with her, but it was Thomas who said, "Surely, you don't think it shall come to that? A few insurgents are no match for the British Empire."

Ellie looked to Robert but knew he could not help her. She was the one with knowledge of the future and some days, she was not even certain that Robert believed her about the Revolution.

"You know what? Forget I said anything. You're right, of course."

Thomas set his own fork down and leaned back in his chair.

"I shall not forget it. When you agree so readily, it means you don't wish to discuss it, not that you concede the other party to be correct. Pray tell, what makes you so certain there shall be a war? A war the Crown will somehow lose to a bunch of farmers who don't wish to pay their taxes?"

Thomas took a large pull from his wine and Ellie realized she always saw him with a drink in his hand these days. She knew it was not unusual for this period as the water was terrible, but she briefly questioned if his intake had increased.

"I just hate the thought of you two having to go through that," she said evasively. "The last war was bad enough."

"The war you spent hidden away with the red man? What do you know of it or what we went through?"

"Thomas, that's enough," Robert warned.

Ellie closed her eyes, trying to rein in her own temper. She knew he was hurting from the thought of losing his friend as soon as Robert sold his commission and moved to Boston with her. It probably did not help that she was the one to whom he would be losing him. Setting her napkin on her plate, she stood, thanking Lucy for the meal and saying goodnight to her and Adelaide as she headed to the door.

Robert was quickly behind her, walking her home through the snowy streets. He tried making excuses for Thomas, but Ellie stopped him.

"I get it, Rob. You don't have to apologize for him. He's got a lot on his plate right now and it can't be easy to hear that his best friend is planning on moving away with his... well, it's bound to be difficult for him. I'm just an easy target."

"I've not yet told him about Boston, Ell. It's more than that. You don't know what we went through after you... left. It changed him. He's got a lot of anger."

She patted him on the chest as they stopped at her door. "I'm sorry for it, Rob. But I'm a big girl. I can handle his anger. Better me than Lucy."

"Neither of you deserves it. I know not what's gotten into him recently. I shall speak with him."

Ellie smiled and wished him goodnight.

---

## February 6, 1770

*Gentlemen,*

*It's well known that nations erect monuments to preserve the memory of a grand event. Experience has proven that these monuments have had a good effect on the future generations of those who raised them. Taking this into consideration, a number of the Friends of Liberty in this city erected a Pole in the Fields as a temporary memorial of the unanimous opposition to the detestable Stamp Act. With the Pole having been destroyed by some disgruntled persons, a number of the citizens decided to erect another and made several pleas to the mayor. Knowing that some might be opposed to the erection of the pole, the citizens offered to make it a present to the city when it was finished, provided they would allow it to be erected where the other stood near Mr. Van De Bergh's.*

*And now gentlemen, seeing that we are denied the privilege of public ground on which to erect the Pole, we have purchased a place for it close to where the last one stood. Your attendance and approval are desired at nine o'clock on Tuesday morning the 6th*

*at Mr. Crommelin's Wharf, in order for it
to be raised.*

When the Sons of Liberty petitioned the Mayor and
Common Council for permission to erect yet another
Liberty Pole on city ground, it was denied. This led
to John Lamb and William Cunningham purchasing
a small piece of land near the location of the previous
poles. They raised up another Liberty Pole, sinking it
deep into the ground and encasing two-thirds of its
forty-six feet of length with iron bands and hoops
riveted together. It had a gilt vane with the inscrip-
tion "Liberty and Property." An invitation to attend
the raising of the pole was sent out to Sons of Liberty
members across the city.

After having no response to the reward for the
author of the December broadsheet signed by 'Brutus,' the governor issued orders for all of the printers
in the city to be arrested and jailed. During the ar-
rests, a printer named James Parker was identified as
a person of interest in the case. He finally revealed
the name of the author as being Alexander McDougall. McDougall was accused of seditious libel against
the Crown and was arrested.

## February 8, 1770

When Alexander McDougall was arrested on a
charge of malicious, seditious libel for the article he
authored, he refused to post bail. He appeared in the

court at his bail hearing, but instead of paying bail, he informed the court that he would rather go to jail for "the cause of liberty and freedom." The court obliged and sent him to the Wall Street Gaol.

Every afternoon, his supporters gathered at his window and cheered forty-five times. They brought forty-five pounds of beef which was cooked and shared amongst the spectators and rum was passed around and used to toast him forty-five times. On another day, a group of women brought a side of venison stamped with the number forty-five. A spit was built outside the jail, and it was roasted then shared with everyone present. On the forty-fifth day of McDougall's imprisonment, the Sons of Liberty brought forty-five alleged virgins dressed in white who all sang the forty-fifth Psalm in his honor. This began a debate in the newspapers as to whether or not there were forty-five virgins in all of New York City.

The number forty-five had become a rally cry against unlawful imprisonment after a warrant was issued for a member of Parliament in 1763. With tension over the plan to tax the colonies in order to pay off the debt from the war, John Wilkes had opposed the King in his publication. He was not only a member of Parliament, but also editor of *The North Briton* newspaper. He was critical of both King George III and Parliament, with the most critical issue being printed in issue number forty-five. The number was deliberately used as a reminder of the Jacobite Uprising of 1745, which had commonly been referred to as *The 45 Rebellion* or simply *45*. The King had been personally offended by the publication and issued a warrant for Wilkes' arrest. With the publicity surrounding his arrest, "Wilkes, Liberty, Number 45," became a rallying cry which carried across the sea to the colonies.

McDougall now sat in the jail, with no trial date in sight. With the attention he was receiving and his popularity ever-growing, no one wanted to prosecute him. He regularly published letters written by him and those of his supporters in the *New York Journal* and the *General Advertiser*. A Loyalist newspaper published those of his detractors. Everyday McDougall spent in jail, there was debate in the newspapers.

The papers were not the only place the case was debated. Everyone in the city discussed it, taking one side or the other. Of course, most at dinner in the Burke house agreed with the Crown, while Ellie tried to argue for freedom of speech.

"He did nothing wrong. He merely spoke his mind, saying how he felt about the current state of things in the city right now," Ellie argued.

"He spoke maliciously about assemblymen and the lieutenant governor. He even said Parliament was behaving tyrannically. That is sedition!" Thomas exclaimed.

"It was only his opinion," Ellie shrugged. "He was not calling people to overthrow the King or Parliament. He was simply trying to say that they have not been living up to their own constitution and responsibilities to their people. If a person is only allowed to speak his mind about his government if his words are favorable, then that government *is* tyrannical."

"Words have power, Mrs. Russell. One must have a care what one says."

Ellie could not help but wonder if that was a direct jab at her.

"And I fail to see how it's your concern," he added, "given how you're not a British subject as you so like to point out."

Ellie huffed. "It affects me more than you'll ever know."

"Please, do elaborate," he said over his drink, swinging his other arm wide as if to give her the floor.

"You couldn't possibly grasp what I know of the situation."

Ellie had not meant to challenge him with that as she had no intention of expanding on her knowledge or where it came from, but he was getting on her nerves, and she was not about to let him barrel over her.

Before the conversation could escalate any more than it already had, Robert jumped in and changed the subject. Dinner proceeded with tension filling the air. Lucy and Robert dominated the conversation while Ellie and Thomas stewed quietly.

After dinner, Thomas retired to his study while the rest of them moved to the parlor for drinks. It had become their new ritual, and Thomas had begun making a habit of leaving the rest of the party to themselves. He was becoming more reclusive while they all visited. The longer he remained in Ellie's presence, the more they argued or bickered. He was exhausted by her secrets, doling out small bits of information as she deemed necessary while withholding others. It was becoming harder and harder to keep their truce. It was easier to not be around her.

"I don't think she's coming back," Ellie observed after Lucy had been gone longer than it should have taken her to check on the children.

That week, Jack Emerson was away at sea again and Adelaide was home nursing sick children. Ellie found herself alone with Robert and had not even realized it, though it was not the first time it had happened.

"No, I don't think she is," Robert agreed. "She seems to disappear every time we start talking."

"Are we that boring?" Ellie asked, slightly offended.

Robert laughed. "I hardly think she's concerned with being bored."

Ellie was confused.

"I think she's a nosy goosecap who is up to no good," Robert said in explanation, though it was still lost on her.

"I don't understand," Ellie admitted.

Robert laughed at her obtuseness. The woman was incredibly intelligent and observant, yet when it came to herself, she willfully ignored how others saw her. She had missed Lucy's obvious attempts at manipulation.

"She's giving us time alone, Ell."

"Why?" she began. Then, looking at his face, she said, "Oh."

Robert saw the realization finally enter Ellie's bright eyes as the slight flush spread across her cheeks. As beautiful as she was, she did not even see it, often downplaying her looks. She never did anything to draw attention to her appearance, but she did not need to. She had a youthful appearance and a natural beauty that did not need any enhancements. It took a lot to make her blush, and Robert enjoyed seeing the color in her cheeks now.

Robert moved from his chair to sit beside her on the settee. He took her hand in his and asked, "Would it be so bad?" He brushed a hair from her forehead and added, "Spending time alone with me?"

Ellie's heart was racing. Though she had always found Robert attractive, his attentions were entirely unexpected. She had no idea he thought of her as anything but a friend. They had been alone together plenty of times in the past, but this was different. Suddenly aware of how close he was, she could smell him and feel the warmth emanating from him. Ellie was at a loss to say anything.

To her relief, Robert did not pressure her. He looked down at her small hand in his large one as he rubbed her fingers with his thumb. She fought to not jerk her hand away from his. It was far too intimate a gesture, leaving her uncomfortable.

"I'm not asking you for anything, Ell. I merely wish you to consider the idea. I could make you happy."

Pulling her hand from his nonchalantly, she placed it on his cheek instead and said with a smile, "Rob, you do make me happy. I love our time together. I always have."

Robert leaned in then and kissed her. Ellie was not expecting it, but after her initial surprise wore off, she leaned into it; into him. Her hand had moved from his cheek when he leaned in and was now around his neck. His slid around to her low back. Robert's kiss was sweet and gentle, like he wanted to savor everything about it. There was a need behind it, but it was not urgent. It was almost as if he was seeking approval, though for what, she could not imagine. Ellie felt almost dizzy when he finally released her.

Robert walked her home, where he kissed her hand before leaving. He did not try anything more than that and Ellie almost felt as though she imagined the need coming off of him when he had kissed her earlier. When she crawled into bed, it was a long time before sleep came.

"Everything looks as though it's progressing as it should," Ellie informed Addah Mawby after her checkup.

She and Tabitha cleaned up and began making their way out of the home. With the residence upstairs, they had to pass the shop as they did so, and Ellie took the opportunity to talk with Amos.

"Are you taking on apprentices?"

Amos Mawby eyed Ellie suspiciously, remembering the young Black boy who had come with her the last time she was there. After deciding her question was genuine, he replied, "'Tis again' de law here to train slaves in de trade."

"Well, it's a good thing I'm not asking you to train a slave, then."

"Who you asking for if not a slave. Was you not asking after de boy you brung last time that I showed around?"

"I am, yes. Harris would love to learn to be a cooper. But he's not a slave."

The suspicion on his face grew. "How's dat?"

"I assure you, he's free as is his sister," she said nodding to Tabitha. "And I want to help him make the most of his life. Will you help me with that?"

Amos glanced at Tabitha who stood holding Ellie's medical kit. He knew Ellie was training her to be a midwife.

"I don't got de space for 'nother person to live here right now."

"He can still live with me," Ellie waved off his concern. "That's not a problem."

"I don' know, miss. 'Tis a great deal of work to take someone on."

Ellie felt like she was losing the man and decided to try a new tactic. "I can't begin to pretend to know what it's like to be a person of color in this society. He needs a mentor; someone to teach him to be a man. If it happens that he can learn a trade in the process, all the better."

Amos nodded. "It a good t'ing what you do for those children. Send him 'round first t'ing tomorrow."

# Wednesday, March 27, 1770

"Robert, I don't wish to lose your friendship as well," Ellie informed him when he made his intentions clear.

He began coming around more frequently, inviting Ellie to the theater or dances in taverns. He even came to visit her after work on occasion, visiting not only her but the children as well, teaching Harris to play chess. Ellie was still not certain how to take his attentions. He wanted to try taking their relationship further, but she was still not certain if that was what she wanted. At least he was not rushing her into anything. Aside from spending more time with her, he had not pressured her for more. He had not even kissed her again. After her experience with Thomas and having spent more time there, she knew that was not uncommon. Dating was a more formal affair there and often went slowly.

They were having drinks in the parlor at Ellie's house when he let her know that he wanted to court her, which still sounded strange to her ears.

"Why would you lose that, Ell?"

Ellie sighed. "Marriage and children are not in my future, I'm afraid. I can only offer you companionship, and I fear even that will expire eventually. When it does, what will be left?"

"Miss Ellie, I care for you a great deal. I always have. I believe that shall never expire. You're far too special for that. If you'll accept my companionship, I'm happy to offer it." Robert looked at Ellie with wonder and awe as he so often did. His gaze was so intense, so full of veneration, it was difficult for her not to squirm.

They sat together on the settee, facing each other and Ellie had the urge to stand and walk around the room. Before she could, Robert took her hand in his. Alarm bells began going off in her head and she again fought to not yank her hand away from him. Why did she always react so strongly? For that matter, why did he constantly try to take her hand in his?

Reaching for her drink as an excuse, Ellie pulled her hand away. Taking a sip also gave her the opportunity to gather her thoughts while examining her reluctance. Did companionship mean something more there of which she was unaware? His reaction to that word was not what she had expected. She did not want to reject him outright. He was so attractive and she did care for him a great deal. When he smiled, his deep dimples flashed, and his chocolate eyes sparkled. His curly dark brown hair framed his round face. Any woman would be lucky to have him. He was strong and capable, protective, yet gentle. Maybe her reluctance was tied to his protective side. She did not mind a little protectiveness, even appreciated it, but Robert's was more overdeveloped than what she liked. Could she look past it for all of his better qualities? He was fun and jovial, and they had always gotten along well. She certainly had not hated kissing him. He knew some of her eccentricities and accepted them unquestioningly. Though, his veneration of her had a tendency to make her uncomfortable.

Ellie heard a thump from the drawing room upstairs and her eyes darted upward, hoping for a distraction. When footsteps unhurriedly walked down the hall into one of the bedrooms, she knew she was not needed. One of the kids must have knocked something over while getting up. Most likely, it was Harris. His leg had significantly improved, having all but healed, but he had a slight clumsy streak which she found endearing. Clumsiness ran in her family, leaving her no stranger to it.

Ellie had so little experience dating in any time period. Having always jumped into relationships with everything she had, it had never turned out so well for her. Her first marriage happened when she was barely out of high school and went downhill quickly. Her marriage to Dean had been forced but was not what she would have expected. They certainly had not dated before attaching themselves to one another.

Maybe taking it slow was what she needed for it to work out. Some of Ellie's hesitation was because of who he was. Ellie had always loved Robert. He had been like a brother to her and she was afraid to mess that up and destroy her relationship with him as she had with Thomas. But Thomas was another factor to consider. She did not want to come between the two men, though she feared she already had. They had been friends their entire lives, growing up together, then joining the army together. Ellie never wanted to be that woman who came between friends. She wanted to talk to Thomas about it but that ship had sailed. They were not exactly on friendly conversational terms. He was always there for their weekly dinners but made sure to be elsewhere whenever she was around otherwise if he could. If he could not, he begrudgingly spoke but kept it to a minimum. True to his word when they had made their truce nearly a year before, he seemed to be tolerating her and nothing more. Ellie missed the easy friendship they once had, but now those days were long gone. All she could do was continue moving forward. Perhaps Robert was part of her path forward.

With her concerns on the table, Ellie agreed to take things slowly and see where they led. Robert's smile split his face, and she was rewarded with those dimples again. He was so boyish when he smiled. She could not help the grin that slowly spread across her own face. He took her hand again, raising it to his lips and kissing it softly across her knuckles.

Ellie was trying to find a way to extract her hand when someone began pounding heavily at the door. Immediately alarmed, Robert told Ellie to stay where she was and he went to see who was there. Thomas was the last person he expected to see on the other side. When recognition entered Thomas's face, he was momentarily quieted before his rage flared again even higher. He did not need the reminder of Robert's intentions with Ellie after what he had just learned. He pushed Robert aside, entering the house as he stormed into the parlor to find Ellie. He stopped in front of her and threw some papers at her.

"Do you care to explain this?" he demanded.

Confused, Ellie bent to pick up one of the pages that was now on the floor. Robert followed Thomas in and stood behind Ellie as he read over her shoulder. She gasped as she looked at the image created by Paul Revere of British soldiers firing indiscriminately into a crowd of unarmed people and read, "The Bloody Massacre perpetrated in King Street, Boston on March 5th, 1770, by a party of the 29th Regiment."

The paper was a Patriot paper, surprising Ellie that Thomas would even be reading it instead of a Loyalist paper. With only five dead, it was likely the Loyalist papers were not even calling it a massacre.

"How did you come to know of this, Ellie?"

Robert tried calming his friend down while Ellie tried to collect herself and think of how to respond.

"Are you part of them? Are you with the Sons of Liberty? Is this why you're so eager to move to Boston? Did you know of their plans there? Have you known of them here?"

Ellie shook her head, "No. I'm not."

"Then how did you come to know of this before it happened?"

"Thomas," Robert began but was interrupted.

"No, Robert. She has likely been feeding them information from the beginning. The Sons, the Indians, probably the French. She cares not who gets hurt with her deceptions; only what she can gain from them. How many Abenaki, Robert? How many had to die because of her lies?"

Before Ellie could respond or ask questions, Robert moved around from behind Ellie and punched his friend in the face.

"Go home, Thomas. And dump that bottle when you get there."

While Thomas touched his cheek and wiped the blood from his split lip, Ellie walked away, fighting the tears that threatened to spill at Thomas's disgust. It killed her to see him like this. He had been drinking more and more, and it made his anger flow more freely. The anger she could handle. But his utter contempt for her cut straight through her.

Ellie heard their voices, then the door closed a few minutes later. She came back to an empty parlor. When she looked out the window, she saw that Robert was walking his friend home. She was not sure if she wanted him to come back after that, but when he did not, she put away their own drinks and went to bed.

## Chapter 37

*May 1770*

Summer came in slowly. With the days warming, Robert and Thomas decided to take the women to the country for a day. Robert stood on Ellie's doorstep and bowed low when she opened the door. He took her hand, kissing her knuckles. "Good morning, Miss Ellie. How do you fare this fine day?"

Ellie held back the giggle that tried to burst forth. No matter how long she was there, the formalities never ceased to amuse her.

"Good morning, Robert. I'm well."

"Shall we be on our way?"

Ellie smiled at him while taking his offered elbow the few steps to the street where a carriage was waiting. She released his elbow and took his offered hand as he helped her into the carriage where Thomas, Lucy, and Charles awaited them.

Once they were both inside and settled, Thomas signaled the driver, and they took off.

"Are Mr. and Mrs. Emerson joining us today?" Robert asked.

"They are. They're taking their chaise and shall meet us there," Lucy responded.

This immediately caught Ellie's attention. "Their chaise? As in, a chair?"

"Why yes, Mrs. Russell," Lucy answered.

"Should I have brought a chair then?"

Blank faces stared back at Ellie.

"Of course not. You're already here with us. We've plenty of room," Lucy finally replied.

Ellie's forehead creased in confusion. She looked around but did not see anywhere that chairs could have been stowed on the carriage. "But once we get there, will there be someplace to sit? I mean, I don't mind standing, but if I need a chair, I can run back to the house really quick and grab one. We're still close."

Lucy and Robert looked at Ellie with confusion while Thomas smirked, understanding her confusion as he was immediately taken back to their lesson about the difference between carts and wagons all those years ago.

"A chaise is a light carriage, Mrs. Russell. It only seats one or two people and may be pulled with as little as one horse."

"Oh." Ellie could not help the slight blush that crept across her face. At least her companions were not laughing at her ignorance.

"How is it after all these years, you still do not know the difference between carriages?"

Instead of being chiding, Thomas had a look of reluctant fondness on his face, as though he did not want to think of her that way but could not help himself. After a couple of weeks since learning of the Boston Massacre, he had finally let go of his anger at her over it, leaving her relieved. She would much rather see this side of him, even if she knew it would be short-lived. It was only a matter of time before she did something else to annoy him yet again, but she was desperately trying to remain civil with him.

She shrugged. "The Onöndowa'ga:' don't use carriages. And my years with Dean were spent with horses and pack mules. There hasn't been much need for me to learn."

"Well, we shall teach you everything you need know," Lucy informed her cheerily while patting her hand.

The ride to the country was pleasant enough. It only took a few minutes to get there, seeing as how the 'country' was only about three miles away.

As they approached, Lucy was leaning over, looking out the window. "We're approaching the kissing bridge," she said excitedly.

"The kissing bridge?" Ellie asked.

Lucy pulled her eyes from the window, but before she could explain it to Ellie, Thomas turned to Lucy and Robert turned to her. Both men gave the women a bow as best they could while in the seats of the cramped carriage. Robert took Ellie's hand and kissed the back of it again while Thomas leaned in and kissed Lucy on the cheek.

Ellie's eyes were wide in surprise when the men straightened and turned back into their seats.

"What was that?"

Lucy giggled. "It's proper etiquette for a gentleman in the company of a lady to salute his fair companion whenever atop a kissing bridge."

"I see."

Ellie could not help but glance at Thomas, who was pointedly looking out the window on his side.

They arrived at their destination along the East River where thirty or forty other people milled about. Some were fishing while others were conversing or playing games. They found Adelaide and Jack Emerson and joined them for tea in the grass. Charles stayed close to Ellie, and she pulled him into her lap while they had their tea. Afterwards, she played tag and hide-and-seek with him on the outskirts of the gathering, taking off her shoes while they did so. They laughed as they chased one another, a pregnant Adelaide looking on with disdain.

Thomas could not help but be jealous of Ellie's carefreeness and pleasure in such a simple experience. Her joy warmed his chest which caused him to look away. He had no right to feel that way and turned his attention to the conversation with his sister and brother-in-law. Jack caught them up on his latest journey while Thomas caught him up on everything he had missed in New York.

Jack had recently returned from a run to England after having been gone for about five months, leaving Adelaide a gift upon his departure that she discovered after he had been gone several weeks and her courses did not arrive. Despite Ellie renewing her professional exploits, she would not be serving as Adelaide's midwife. She still did not trust Ellie and preferred to retain Mrs. Erwin who had delivered her previous two children. Ellie was more than happy to leave it to Mrs. Erwin.

Robert approached Ellie, intercepting Charles before he could reach Ellie and lifting him up, setting Charles on his massive shoulders.

"Dinner shall be served shortly."

Ellie caught her breath and went to find her shoes, gathering them up and carrying them back with her instead of putting them on. She never got tired of walking barefoot in the grass and with the weather warming up, she took every chance she got to enjoy it.

As dinner was set out in front of them, Ellie had to ask what it was.

"It's turtle. They hold these turtle-feasts twice weekly. Have you never had it before?" Lucy asked.

Ellie shook her head. "I can't say I have."

Looking around, she saw that everyone was enjoying it. She was not opposed to trying it, but worried about how many turtles were killed every week for these feasts. Watching the whales in the bay had always tickled her while simultaneously making her sad that they would be hunted to near extinction very soon. She was certain the turtles would suffer the same fate.

"You've not yet tried it," Robert observed. "Is it not to your preference?"

Ellie picked at it, breaking off a small piece and putting it into her mouth. She took her time, letting it settle in her mouth as she tasted it. It had a firm texture with a slight sweetness to it.

"It tastes like alligator," Ellie said in surprise.

As everyone stared back at her, Ellie froze, her fork suspended in front of her. She suddenly felt self-conscious. "What?"

"You've tasted alligator?" Robert asked.

Her eyes darted amongst their group. "Yes?"

Ellie hated that it sounded like a question.

Jack slapped a hand on his leg. "It does taste like alligator, Mrs. Russell. I was trying to place it, but you're right; it's very much akin to alligator. I was unaware you'd spent any time in the south. Where were you that you had alligator?"

Ellie remembered that Jack had not been at the wedding in Long Island as he had been on another voyage at the time. Not wanting to recall all of her travels, she simply said, "I don't recall. I've been many different places and had it several times."

Though she had grown up in the south, it was not until she had lived in the desert that she had first tried alligator. She had taken a liking to it right away.

"Have you seen the beasts themselves, then?" he asked.

Ellie nodded while chewing the bite she had taken. She had only ever seen them up close at habitats but had stood on bridges and looked down on them or seen them on the side of the road while driving past various places.

"Frightening creatures," he said.

Ellie agreed politely but did not add much to the conversation. He did not seem to notice.

"You continue to intrigue me, Mrs. Russell," Lucy said in awe. "You've lived quite the adventurous life."

Trying to downplay her experiences, Ellie shrugged. She did not want to encourage Lucy to ask more about her past. "I've just lived the life in which I was presented."

"It never ceases to amaze me to hear of the places you've been and the experiences you've had."

Ellie looked around her and smiled tightly back at Lucy, giving her a polite, "Thank you." She did not know what else to say but hoped the woman would not continue to dig into her past. It was exhausting trying to constantly find the right words so as to not upset Thomas, raise suspicions, or make people think she was lying. She was trying her hardest to open up but still had to juggle how much to do so. It had almost been easier to keep her mouth shut and not say anything at all.

---

*July 1770*

Alexander McDougall was released from prison after twenty-three weeks. The printer, James Parker, had died in his sleep at the age of seventy-seven and there were no other witnesses to attest that McDougall had written the anonymous handbill. The prosecution had no choice but to drop the case. When McDougall was released, a parade was held in his honor and five hundred people walked him home. It had been quite a spectacle, leaving Ellie to navigate around the crowds during her walk around the city.

With the warmer temperatures and the drier roads, she took the horses out for rides on occasion as well, mixing up her routine and giving the horses some exercise. Harris had begun helping Ezra with the responsibilities in the stables and took them out periodically but never went far for fear that someone would accuse him of having stolen them and imprison him. He enjoyed riding and Ellie accompanied him whenever she could, giving him the opportunity to do so. With his new apprenticeship with the cooper, he no longer had much free time to enjoy the rides.

Robert had discovered Ellie's spot near Whitehall Slip, and he came to sit with her whenever he got a chance to get away. Her obsession with the spot became a topic of conversation at dinner. She suspected it was a diversion from having to talk about the captain who had been unable to secure the funds necessary to purchase Robert's commission. He was upset about it falling through and was trying to take his mind off of it.

"What is it that takes you there time after time?" Robert asked. "There are far more pleasant locales from which to watch the ships."

Like Thomas, he knew she loved the water and preferred being surrounded by greenery. Neither could understand why she would spend so much time on a sandy beach with little vegetation when she could be surrounded by the green she loved so much.

"It's a good view." Ellie shrugged.

"There's little difference between that and the view on the other side of the island, north of the fort," Robert argued.

"Oh no. There's a huge difference," she said without elaborating. She never offered more than that, only insisting that it was that view that drew her there.

When no one could get more out of her, Robert turned their attention to another matter. "Miss Ellie, you come to dinner every Sunday with us. Have you considered accompanying us to church as well?"

Ellie nearly choked on the drink she had just taken. Coughing until she could clear her throat, she looked at Robert incredulously.

"I don't do church."

When Lucy joined in Robert's attempt, Ellie turned her attention to the woman. Her eyes passed Thomas along the way, and she saw him trying to suppress a disinterested smirk. She glared at him for a moment before turning to Lucy who was trying to convince Ellie to attend, using the excuse of saving her soul. Adelaide was quick to join the attempt.

"I appreciate your concerns, but really, church and I do not mix well."

As they gathered in the parlor after dinner, Thomas made a rare appearance. Ellie noticed he had tea instead of his usual brandy. She recalled his drink at dinner which had been cider, but he had only drunk in moderation. He seemed to have been cutting back. She hated to think he had been on his way to becoming an alcoholic and was glad to see him refraining.

"You've such a lovely voice, Mrs. Russell. Will you sing something for us?" Lucy asked after her and Adelaide had taken turns playing instruments. They often took turns, with the women playing one week and the men playing on other weeks. Ellie had enjoyed hearing Thomas playing the pianoforte, a predecessor to the piano, again.

"Oh, I don't know any songs," Ellie protested, shooting a quick glance at Thomas who knew better.

"I've heard you sing to Charles," Lucy said. "You know at least one, even if it is a peculiar one."

"I don't really know any that you would be familiar with," she said slowly, choosing her words carefully. Ellie had always had an affinity for remembering lyrics and recipes. The recipes came in handy, though the lyrics were not always so useful. If anything, they usually ended up being earworms that burrowed in with no way for her to get them out anymore.

"That's perfect," Robert said. "It shall be new to us."

Ellie sighed. She was not getting out of this. They had shared their gifts with her; it was her turn to do so. She tried to think of a song that was not too heavily laden with twentieth or twenty-first century words or that needed a full band to accompany it. Finally, she settled on a song by Norah Jones. *Come Away with Me* had been one of her favorites for a long time and she knew it would sound decent even when sung *a capella.*

Thomas watched raptly as Ellie tried to focus her gaze on the window across the room. It was not long before her eyes had closed altogether as she sang, losing herself in the words. Having always loved her voice, he marveled now that she could elicit such an emotional response while being so void of emotions herself. He could almost swear he could see a range of emotions playing out on her face while she sang, but he knew better. The woman was incapable of any emotional depth. The deception put him in a foul mood.

Ellie opened her eyes to see everyone staring at her. They all clapped as soon as she finished. They tried to get her to sing another one, but she adamantly declined, saying the one was enough of a strain for her voice. It was not entirely true, but she was not comfortable singing in front of an audience. She loved music, but it was personal to her. Much like holding hands, sharing it this way felt rather intimate, and she was not yet ready for that.

Moving over to the fireplace where Robert stood beside Thomas, she looked between them, and asked, "How was that? Did it sound okay?"

"It was beautiful, Ell," Robert replied.

She beamed and turned to look at Thomas questioningly.

"It was. One could almost believe you capable of feeling after bearing witness to that."

The words were nothing she had not said of herself for decades, but coming from him, they were like a knife in the heart. Ellie tamped down on the pain slicing through her. If he needed to think her cold and emotionless, then so be it. She would not correct him. Instead, she tried to play it off.

"Ha. If only I was capable of such a thing."

Thomas gave Ellie a curt nod and moved away from her and Robert, going toward his wife. He could not be near Ellie right then and needed the reminder that he was married to Lucy. Standing behind her, he placed a hand on her shoulder, allowing the touch to ground him to her.

"I don't recall ever seeing you go to services at Fort Edward," Ellie said to Robert when he walked her home. She had been wondering about it since she ran into him again. He never missed a Sunday if he could help it and often tried to convince her to go with him. Thomas never missed either, but she suspected that was more for Lucy's sake than his own. She wondered what Robert's motivation was.

"I went when time permitted, though it was not often. In truth, your return has prompted a renewal of my faith," he responded.

"Me?" Ellie asked, aghast. She turned to look at him fully, twisting her arm in his to do so. "How the hell did I do that? And how do I take it back?"

Robert laughed as she had intended him to. Though she said it jokingly, she meant it.

"Ell, you've always been," he paused, trying to think of the right word, "more. You know of things no one else does and you've never quite fit into this world. I've lived more places than the average man and met people from yet even more places than I've seen. Yet I've never met anyone like you. Thomas said you died in front of him. He now believes he was mistaken about the severity of your injuries, yet I'm not certain how that could be. He's a good physician. He knows when a person has expired. And that's certainly a mistake he would *never* make with you. If there was even a chance that you would have still been alive, he would have fought for you." Ellie was not so certain, but she bit her lip to keep from saying anything and Robert continued, "You have a way about you, Ell. Almost as if you're an angel sent to us from heaven."

Ellie scoffed. "Make no mistake, Robbie. I'm no fucking angel."

Laughter erupted from Robert.

Though she joked, Robert's words concerned Ellie. Thomas had always put her up on a pedestal. He had worshipped her, even though he had seen her flaws. He had seen them and accepted her for who she was, regardless. Well, he had once anyways.

Robert was different. He worshiped her, too, but in an unhealthy way that made Ellie uncomfortable, as if he deified her. His adoration and many of his gestures were beginning to make sense. She felt as though he thought she was something she was not; as if he believed that she really was the angel he accused her of being like. It was as though he was blinded to reality. He revered her as though she was Jesus risen. That her very existence had renewed his own faith had her biting her lip in consternation as she contemplated what to do with this revelation.

## Chapter 38

*August 21, 1770*

"I don't understand," Ellie admitted. "If the colonists hate the King so much, why would they erect a statue of him?"

The *Britannia* had arrived in port at the beginning of June carrying statues of King George III and William Pitt along with a large bell for the Reformed Protestant Dutch Church. William Pitt had been instrumental in the repeal of the Stamp Act and when people wanted to celebrate him, it was realized that there was no statue of the King. It would have been improper for the colonists to erect a statue of Pitt without erecting one of the King, leading the Assembly to commission both statues.

Ellie had accompanied Robert to the unveiling at Bowling Green where they met up with Thomas and his family. She had been pleased to see the children there with them. With Caitlyn still so young, she was often left home with Anne while Charles was only allowed out on special occasions. The Emersons soon joined them, and her own children were there as well, though they had stayed quietly separated from the group. She tried to bring them in, but Tabitha and Harris continued to stay off to the side. When they saw the Mawbys there, they asked if they could join them, and Ellie obliged them on the caveat that they were not in the way of the Mawbys. They eagerly ran off to join the other family who welcomed them.

The families had all agreed to attend the ceremony and stay afterward for a picnic dinner. Of course, Ellie had needed to explain the word 'picnic' when she had suggested they do so, but the ladies were excited to participate. Everyone packed baskets full of foods they could eat while enjoying the late summer day.

The statue sat upon a heavy pedestal and plinth depicting King George III astride a horse. It was made of lead gilded with gold and stood about fifteen feet. A large gathering had formed for the unveiling and people cheered. Ellie was surprised by the reaction.

"The fault of our struggles does not lay with the King," Robert explained. "It's Parliament who has leveled the injustices upon us. They approved the Stamp Act, the Sugar Act, even the Quartering Act. It was they who discontinued the General Assembly. Everything we've suffered has been at their hands."

Ellie studied his face, searching for the truth of his words. She looked around at the faces of those in their party and they all seemed to be in agreement. She did not recall ever hearing this before. By her time in history, King George III was a villain. Americans tended to hate him. It was weird to think of him ever having been adored by the colonists.

"Do you disagree, Mrs. Russell?" Thomas challenged.

Ellie did not know how to answer him. She had no personal stake in this. As far as she was concerned, the course they were on was already written. Everything that would happen in the next several years had already been decided. It was all inevitable. She could care less if the responsibility lay at the hands of Parliament or King George III. It was done and there was no turning back now.

"I was merely surprised," Ellie tried to be diplomatic. "I'd not heard that perspective."

"You've heard it said the King is at fault? With whom are you speaking that say such things?" he demanded.

"At ease, Major," she said dryly. "I'm not speaking with anyone. It's only my own misunderstanding of current politics."

Thomas snorted, not believing her in the least. She was fully capable of understanding politics. Again, he suspected she knew more than she was letting on and was simply trying to get out of discussing it. Given the occasion, he let it go, trying to avoid yet another fight.

The group stayed in the Green for a while, trying to get in for a closer look. The crowd was thick, and they had to squeeze in. Seeing the circular shape around the statue, Ellie was put in mind of the park she had once visited in her own time that had a similar circular shape. When she had visited the area before, there had been an iron fence surrounding flowers which bordered a large fountain. Cocking her head in remembrance, as if trying to get a better view, she had a sudden flashback, remembering the sign on the outside of the fence. When her brow furrowed in concentration, Robert took her by the elbow and pulled her back from the crowd.

"Are you well?" he asked.

Ellie nodded mutely as she tried to find her voice. "I remember a plaque. A fence will be put up soon but the statue won't stand for long. It gets torn down during the war."

Robert nodded, looking at Ellie with awe and reverence once again. She shook herself, taking in their surroundings, glad he had pulled her away from everyone, but now he was looking at her weirdly again. She shoved him back playfully as if to break the spell that had fallen over them. He caught her hand easily as it made contact with his chest, and he brought it to his mouth. Instead of kissing her knuckles as she had expected, he pretended to start nibbling on her hand, making her laugh. She twisted in his grip, trying to pull her hand free while the laughter continued to bubble forth.

The rest of their group rejoined them, and Robert released her. They wandered through Bowling Green until they found a little spot for their picnic. Each family set out a blanket on the ground and the women began pulling food out of their baskets. Tabitha and Harris had made their way back to Ellie, which made her feel warm. The Mawbys had gone home, and Ellie had half expected the kids to do so as well, but they stayed with her, joining her on the blanket. She began handing them loaves of bread, cheeses, fruits, and other items she had brought.

When Ellie pulled out the brownies she had made, she passed them around and everyone took one. They were not quite the same as the brownies she made in her own time, but they were pretty close. She had used honey instead of sugar and cooked them over the fire, grateful to Mehitabel Prendergast for showing her the nuances of using the fire to get different temperatures. She was rather proud that they turned out as well as they had.

Everyone examined their brownie closely, unsure what to think about it. Thomas smelled his, Lucy put it gently to her lips before slowly sticking out her tongue to lick it and Robert dove right in, taking a bite.

"These are utterly delightful," Lucy said. "I've never heard of anyone using chocolate to make anything other than a drink. Wherever did you get the idea for these?"

"Just something I thought I'd try."

She was holding back yet again, but Thomas knew whatever it was, she would keep it to herself. This was simply one more example of her eccentricity that set her so far apart from anyone he had ever met. It both infuriated him and intrigued him.

The group talked while they dined, and the conversation stayed light. Perhaps it was the sunshine and fresh air, but they all managed to get along and not bicker. Probably because she was in her last weeks of pregnancy and could not be bothered with it, but even Adelaide had limited her snarky comments to Ellie, despite Ellie's copious improprieties.

First, Ellie removed her shoes and stockings in order to walk through the grass barefoot. Then, she played with Charles, even going so far as to climb the tree they were all sitting under, much to the horror of everyone there. Ellie could hear them talking below her.

"Where did Mrs. Russell and Charles get off too?" Adelaide asked.

Charles started giggling from his perch beside El-lie, giving away their position. Adelaide looked up and immediately began screeching. "Mrs. Russell! Come down from there at once!"

Ellie started chuckling at Adelaide's horror.

"Really. That is *not* how a lady should behave at all!" Her face was turning red with anger and disgust.

"I never claimed to be a lady," Ellie called down teasingly.

Robert and Thomas joined in at that, both trying to urge her down. Thomas demanded Charles get down and he looked to Ellie for a second before complying. As he scurried down, Thomas could not stop from staring at Ellie's bare feet and her tattoos there which were nearly at eye level to him. Ellie stayed up on her branch a little longer, ignoring everyone. Once Charles was no longer up there with her, it was not as fun, but she would not come down now simply because she would not give the men the satisfaction of compliance after they made demands on her.

"Ell, you really ought to come down before you fall," Robert said looking up at her.

"I'll come down when I'm ready," she replied.

Robert went over to the trunk and began looking for footholds.

"Robert, don't you dare," Ellie called out. "This branch won't hold both of our weights. Stay down."

"I'll stay down if you come down." Robert paused to look up at her.

"What are you going to do once you get up here? You going to throw me down?"

"Miss Ellie, please come down," Robert asked again.

Thomas whispered something in Charles's ear, then the boy called up to Ellie, "Miss Russell, won't you please come down and play with me down here?"

"Damn it," Ellie exclaimed while narrowing her eyes and pursing her lips at Thomas. The man certainly knew how to manipulate her. What choice did she have now? Ellie slowly made her way down, and as soon as she reached the ground, she touched Charles on the shoulder, calling out, "Tag. You're it."

Ellie ran away quickly with Charles laughing and following her. This was a game they played often, and he always enjoyed it. Ellie loved that she was physically able to do it. It had been years since she had been able to run like this before she fell through time.

When Charles tired of playing tag, Ellie pulled a length of rope from her basket and gave it to him. "Do you know how to jump rope?"

He looked at her quizzically, saying, "No."

Ellie stood and took the rope back from him, demonstrating to the best of her abilities while in her skirts, petticoats, and stays. It was a wonder she could do it at all, let alone nearly ten jumps before getting the rope caught in her voluminous skirts. She handed the rope back to him and told him to try. He struggled to get the right force to propel the rope over his head at first. It took several tries, and she did her best to help him, holding his hands while going through the motions. Once he got the hang of it, he struggled to coordinate his feet with his hands and got tangled up in the rope often. His little face screwed up in determination and he kept trying. Finally, he cleared the rope, and his face lit up in triumph. Ellie clapped and cheered while everyone else looked on. They gave him words of encouragement, but Ellie had been the only one to do so robustly.

While Charles jumped rope, Thomas sat with Caitlyn in his lap on a blanket across from Ellie. Turning to her, he commented, "You managed to obtain another tattoo."

Ellie pulled up her skirt a little to look at her ankle. Smiling fondly at her newest ink, she responded, "My Onöndowa'ga:' sister gave it to me before I was taken from the village. It's the Haudenosaunee symbol for time with a broken link."

"It suits you. I'm pleased you were able to find something to represent your time there."

It was hard to suppress the chill that ran through her at his words. It reminded her of the night she had told him what each of her tattoos had meant. He had kissed each one as she spoke, working his way around her body. Her blood heated at the memory and she had to pull her gaze from his and focus on where they were.

As the day wore on, the leisurely afternoon came to an end. They packed up their things and began making their way back up the street. The men carried the baskets as they walked. Ellie took Caitlyn to give Lucy a break while also holding Charles's hand as they walked.

"Mrs. Russell, you're so good with the children," Lucy observed. "You've had two husbands, have you not?"

When Ellie nodded in agreement, Adelaide added, "And you've no children from either?"

"Nope," she said simply.

Lucy was not about to give up so easily. "Do you not wish to have children of your own? Surely, that's worth marrying again?"

Ellie let out a deep breath, knowing they would only keep asking. These women would not let it go. As part of her efforts to continue to open up to people, she figured now was as good a time as any. With a deep inhale, she said, "I can't have kids."

The women gasped. Lucy asked, "Are you certain?"

Ellie laughed bitterly. "Oh, I'm quite certain."

Thomas was stunned. He wanted to reach out to Ellie and pull her into his arms and hold her tight or even just take her hand. Motherhood was every woman's purpose in life.

When Ellie noticed the silence around her, she looked up from the baby she had been making faces at to see everyone staring at her and laughed.

"It's alright, really. I came to terms with it long ago."

It was not entirely true, but she was not about to go into any more detail on it. Instead, she offered, "My youngest brother was my baby. I was seven when Kevin was born. He was the sweetest kid. I used to take care of him. I'd change his diapers–his clouts–and read to him every night. He'd curl up into me as he fell asleep."

It was difficult to think of her brother now. They had been close once but had become estranged when she married. They had been trying to redevelop a relationship when she left. Now, she would probably never get the chance to do so.

When they reached the Burke's house, Ellie took the kids upstairs. Lucy followed her, taking Caitlyn to put her in her bassinet. When they turned around, Charles was standing, bent at the waist with his head on his bed. In the amount of time it took the women to put Caitlyn down, he had fallen asleep, still half-standing. Ellie wanted to scoop him up and cuddle him. The women both chuckled softly and Lucy went to him to get him into bed.

"It's been an exciting day. Poor dear is exhausted," Lucy said quietly.

"I can't say I blame him," Ellie said on a yawn. "I think I'm about ready for bed myself."

It was not late, but it had been an eventful day spent in the sun. That was always enough to tire her out. As Ellie reflected on the day, she found she had really enjoyed it. These people were starting to feel more and more like her family. As long as she was not bickering with Thomas or being scolded by Adelaide, she enjoyed the time they all spent together. She even started questioning whether she still wanted to go to Boston.

## Chapter 39

*Fall 1770*

Ellie was uneasy. She had walked past this church countless times but had never been inside. Unable to shake the feeling for anything, she spent the entire service fidgeting. Why had she let Robert talk her into going to a church service? Of all things, *church*? What was she thinking? The last time she had been to church for service was with Dean, and she had fought him on going at all. Ellie had always been more spiritual over religious and had always hated organized religion and attending services. Yet, somehow, there she was, sitting in a pew beside Robert with Thomas and his family on the other side of him, Adelaide and her children directly behind them while her new baby was at home with the nanny.

While Ellie had always held a disdain for religion, she loved visiting old churches. The architecture was truly a work of art. This building was no different. The two-story chapel was beautiful both inside and out. White columns lined the sides of the main floor, leading into the arched ceiling and holding the balconies that ran the length of the chapel. The altar and small pulpit were covered in ornate details that Ellie wanted to explore more closely. She tried to focus on the details to calm her frazzled nerves, but it did not help.

Robert took her hand, trying to offer her comfort while Thomas leaned forward to glare at her. Neither helped, and her leg had not stopped bouncing since she had arrived. When Ellie removed her hand from his, Robert instead placed it on her knee gently in an attempt to still her, but the other knee just started bouncing in its stead while she traced the edges of her ankh, playing with the necklace nervously. Though she hated going, she had never felt like this when she had attended services with Dean. Ellie could not understand why she was as uneasy as she was. She had felt something as soon as she walked into the chapel but could not place it.

Charles sat between Thomas and Robert and the boy kept looking over at Ellie and trying to whisper to her or switch seats to sit beside her. He was excited that she came but wanted to play instead of pay attention. She would much rather have spent her time with the five-year-old than sitting through a service. Unfortunately, Thomas was not amused by his son's antics and kept scolding him to sit still and be quiet. Every time Charles got a stern look, another was reserved for Ellie, which made her squirm even more.

When the service finally finished, Ellie shot up out of her seat, wanting to make it to the exit as quickly as she could. Unfortunately, there were far too many people between her and the door, and none of them seemed to have anywhere to go.

The reverend made his way toward their little group, shaking hands with the men and nodding to the women.

"I see you've brought a guest, Major Jensen."

Robert placed his hand on Ellie's back and introduced her. Ellie nodded a greeting. She was trying to be polite but was far too frazzled to worry about niceties.

"Did you enjoy the service?" the reverend asked.

"I'm not really very religious, I'm afraid. But this building is beautiful," she said while looking around, hoping she could take the attention away from the religious talk and her fidgeting by discussing the architecture. It felt somehow safer. Despite the service being over, her unease had not settled, and she was still feeling antsy. She was not the only one. Now that the service was over, Charles was trying to get away to play, and Thomas scolded him again. By the look he gave her, she suspected he desperately wanted to scold her, too.

She was hardly listening when she caught the words 'Saint Paul's Chapel.' This got her attention.

"I'm sorry, what did you say?"

"I was saying how fortunate we are to have this second location to help ease the burden on the original Trinity Church down the street. It really was getting too crowded there for everyone to attend meetings. We've only been open four years, but hopefully, Saint Paul's shall serve us for a long time. It's so new, in fact, we're still taking donations to build a steeple. We've not yet been able to add one."

Images filled Ellie's mind as she stared at the reverend with wide eyes and a slack jaw. She actually felt the color drain from her face. Hearing the name was like putting on a pair of corrective lenses. Everything became sharp and clear as she understood where her unease was coming from, and she suddenly saw the chapel as it had been the first time she saw it more than two hundred years in the future. It was yet another reminder that she was trapped in this place so far from her friends, family, and everything she had ever known. She thought she had gotten used to her situation, but much like grief, it still managed to take her by surprise on occasion. In addition to the guttural feelings this place elicited by itself, Ellie suddenly felt completely alone.

Ellie could hear Robert talking, and it took a moment to realize he was talking to her. She felt as though she was locked in a soundproof vacuum. Everyone in the group was staring at her with concern. Even Adelaide asked if she was well.

"I... I'm sorry," she stammered. "I need some air."

Pushing past everyone, Ellie squeezed her way through the crowds and out the door. She thought she had moved past feeling like this, but apparently, she was wrong.

When she got outside, Ellie walked around the grounds, trying to calm herself. It only made it worse. Now that she saw them with a fresh eye, she recognized the grounds more than she had the interior of the building. The steeple was missing, and the interior had some slight differences, but the grounds were unmistakable. How long had she spent photographing these very grounds and the tombstones within it? In its current environment and condition, Ellie had not recognized the church until now. If she had seen the Occulus, the World Trade Center Memorial, or even the new Freedom Tower, she would have instantly recognized where she was. Today, it was not until she heard the name of the chapel that she had realized the significance. This was the 'Church that Stood.'

One of the only buildings in the immediate area of ground zero that survived with no damage when the twin towers fell on that horrible day that the terrorists attacked New York City in 2001, the church immediately became a symbol of recovery and hope. It had housed countless first responders in the days immediately following the attack, and for many years after, it was a memorial before the official one could be built. Though she had walked the grounds many times afterwards, the temporary memorial she visited in 2011 was the only time she had ever been inside the building.

The memory of the well-used fireman's empty turnout gear sitting upright on one of the pews had haunted her. A place of rest, the white back of the pew had been scuffed by the numerous rescue and recovery workers who worked relentlessly for months after the attacks. Someone had placed a pair of worn black boots on the floor in front of the pew and an empty firefighter's coat on the dark brown seat above them. The placement of the coat with the top leaning against the back of the pew and the skirt sitting on the bench, the cuffs resting in the lap, made it appear as if the person who had worn the gear had simply fallen asleep while leaning against the pew then shriveled into nothing inside of it without taking it all off first. The once-black coat had become more charcoal colored, covered in dirt, soot, and ash. The reflective yellow stripes across the sleeves, waist, and skirt peaked out against the blackness covering it. The simple display had stirred something inside Ellie when she had first seen it. The feeling of sheer exhaustion and grief had been palpable, and she had been unable to take her eyes off of the display.

When Robert finally made his way out to Ellie, the tears were silently falling down her face. She was inspecting the new tombstones which she had appreciated so much in her own time, having always enjoyed old cemeteries and the peaceful feeling she got while in them. Though all of these grave markers were now new, they had been hundreds of years old when she had first seen them. There was no peace for her there now.

Ellie's back was to Robert, and he sounded confused and irritated when he called out to her. The irritation was probably in part due to the fact that she did not turn around or acknowledge him when he called out to her. When he came up beside her, he spun her to face him, about to give her some sort of lecture when he saw her tears and he immediately softened. Wrapping his big arms around her, he pulled her head to his strong chest. She let him hold her momentarily while she allowed herself a moment of self-pity and mourning for everything she had lost. This was yet another reminder of a life to which she would never return.

When she finally let go of the self-pity, she gathered herself and pulled away, wiping at her eyes.

"Sorry." It was all she could manage.

"Do you wish to tell me what happened?" he prodded gently.

Ellie shook her head. In a quiet voice, she said, "Too many ghosts."

Robert was visibly confused. "Ghosts? The church is but four years old, younger than Charles is now. How can it be filled with ghosts?"

Ellie did not answer. Instead, she shook her head and started wandering slowly through the graves. He followed closely behind her.

"Ell?"

"The reverend would be happy to know the church will be around for a very long time," she said by way of explanation. "It will survive the unimaginable and become a beacon of hope to hundreds of thousands."

Robert stopped in his tracks. "Is this one of your visions?" he asked reverently.

Ellie looked down at the headstone in front of her. "You could say that."

Robert immediately dropped down to one knee in front of her, taking her hand in his. He looked up at her with reverence, but there was more. Was that fear she saw in his eyes? Exaltation? Glorification? This was such a different reaction from what he normally had whenever he witnessed her have a 'vision.' She thought perhaps because it had to do with where they were and the fact that it pertained to a church this time. It did not matter. She could not handle Robert's veneration of her at the moment. Ellie pulled her hand from his and turned away to stare at the headstones. When she turned around, he stood, remaining behind her like a bodyguard.

While she stood there at a random grave, Charles came up to Ellie with a dandelion flower he had picked. Ellie bent to be eye to eye with him, leaving Robert to hover over her helplessly.

With his hand outstretched to her with his offering, Charles whispered, "I wish you to not be sad."

Ellie's heart melted. She kneeled and pulled the small boy into a hug, holding him tight for a moment. He wrapped his little arms around her neck.

"Thank you, sweet boy. That makes me happy."

With one arm around his waist, Ellie slid the dandelion stem into her bodice so that the flower stuck out over the top. When she looked up, she saw Thomas watching her. Lucy and Adelaide were chatting nearby with the rest of Adelaide's kids behind them.

Thomas knew that tortured look on Ellie's face. It was the same look she had the first time they came through New York City on the way to Williamsburg, then again when they had arrived in Williamsburg. It was the same look she had when he took her to the ball at the governor's palace that Christmas. There was a recognition there each of those times, as there was now. But it was more than recognition. There was panic, sadness, and pain. He had never understood what had haunted her all those years ago, or how it had haunted her from so many places, but apparently it was still there. Seeing it killed him as much now as it had then.

Thomas wanted to hold her and comfort her like he once had, but she was not his to comfort now. He envied his son. Even Robert stood behind her with a hand on her shoulder. A gesture so simple, yet something he could never again offer her.

Lucy moved closer to look up at Thomas with pleading eyes, urging him to take them home. Caitlyn had not been feeling well and they were on their way when Charles ran off to go see Ellie. Thomas did not wish to yell across the churchyard and released his wife to chase after his child. As soon as he was in closer proximity, he said, "Come, Charles. We must return home. Your sister ails."

"I wish to stay, papa," Charles begged. "Miss Russell needs me."

This nearly broke Ellie's heart. Fighting the tears from falling anew, she pulled Charles back into her and said, "You go Charles. I do need you, but I'll be alright."

"No," he cried as he squeezed her tighter with his little arms.

Ellie looked up to see the indecision and turmoil on Thomas's face.

"I must apologize, Mrs. Russell. He's not usually so disobedient," he said, hesitating before reaching to grab his son. He did not want to break them apart as they both looked as though they needed the moment. The tear that rolled down Ellie's cheek nearly undid him.

"I don't think it's disobedience, so much as him following his heart," Ellie said, rubbing Charles's back while wiping at her eye.

Did he not wish he could do the same?

"Why don't I bring him home? You go. Get Lucy and Caitlyn home. I'll follow along with Charles."

"I do not wish to burden you with my child, Mrs. Russell."

In a whisper, Ellie said, "Your children could never be a burden to me, Thomas."

---

When Ellie brought Charles home, she had no intention of staying for dinner. Her emotional turmoil and grief had taken a toll on her, and she was exhausted.

She wanted nothing more than to crawl into bed and let sleep overtake her.

Of course, Lucy had other plans. When Ellie tried to decline, Lucy looked at Robert and would not hear of it. When nothing else seemed to convince Ellie, Lucy had offered to allow Charles to stay and dine with them. This was a special treat and Charles was immediately excited, begging Ellie to stay. There was no denying they had a special bond. She adored him and he favored her as well. He pulled her by the hand to the table and sat next to her throughout the meal, behaving as a perfect gentleman. He even pulled her chair out for her before sitting. Ellie tried to stifle the laughter that bubbled up at his chivalry and at Robert's annoyance that he was being shown up by a five-year-old.

Lucy asked, "What did you think of the service, Mrs. Russell?"

Ellie was trying to avoid contributing to the conversation, but this question was directed right at her. She tried to keep her answer vague and not divulge the fact that she had not paid any attention to the service at all.

"It wasn't for me. I've never been much for religion."

Ellie had every intention of leaving it at that when Charles announced, "It made her sad. But my flower made her happy."

He was smiling as big as could be as he pointed to the dandelion still displayed on Ellie's bosom. Ellie gave her own sad smile at that, saying, "It did make me happy. Thank you ever so much, Charles."

Lucy looked concerned. "It made you sad? Why on earth would it make you sad." She had been too distracted by the ailing Caitlyn to have noticed her despair, only that she had paled before leaving the chapel.

Robert tried to come to her aid. "It put her in mind of something from her past."

Unfortunately, this did not help. Thomas immediately questioned, "Something from your past?" He looked from Ellie to Robert then, adding, "What do you know of her past?"

Thomas looked both pissed and surprised. Ellie was quick to say, "It was nothing. It just brought back some difficult memories."

"Is that why you appeared ill after the service?" Lucy asked.

Ellie nodded without adding anything more.

"I suppose that's a comfort. I thought perhaps you'd caught whatever it is that has Caitlyn out of sorts," Lucy said.

Ellie shook her head. "No. I've not come down with anything. Do you need me to check in on Caitlyn? How is she?"

Ellie's attempt to change the subject worked well. She did not contribute much more to the conversation and once the dinner ended, Ellie headed home. Needing some time alone, she did not stay for drinks afterward this time.

## December 1770

The frigid air circled around them between the market stalls, blowing in even more cold. Ellie looked to the gray clouds on the horizon and asked, "Do you think we'll have more snow soon?"

Was she really talking about the weather? Ellie had been out shopping when she ran into Thomas. They had each been out on their own and without anyone else around, they were both suddenly awkward. At least it meant he did not lecture her for being out unescorted, for which she was grateful. Between him and Robert, the overprotectiveness was starting to grate. She was not sure why he was suddenly maladroit around her, but it had made her awkward in return. Finally, he seemed to find his confidence and offered to escort her home. Hesitant to accept, she ultimately decided to let him.

Ellie burrowed into her cloak, gathering it tighter around her as they walked in silence. Thomas seemed to have something on his mind, but whatever it was, he was keeping it to himself. She did not pry. Finally, after three blocks, he broke the silence.

"You believe not in marriage or love, nor are you able to have children. Is this why you would not marry me?"

Surprised by both the question and the candor, Ellie looked at him, trying to decide how to explain. He was not looking at her, keeping his eyes ahead of them. She had no idea how to answer him without sounding dismissive.

"Partly."

Before she could say more, he asked, "Why did you not tell me?"

At the time, she had kept quiet out of fear of rejection. She remembered Genetaska's and Dajoji's words about letting Thomas in, and considered doing so, but now it seemed pointless. She would answer any questions he had but did not feel a need to volunteer anything. Perhaps she was still hiding, afraid to open up, but now there was a reason not to do so. She needed to maintain the distance between them to remind her that he was happy with Lucy. There was nothing she could offer him.

"Because what I told you was also true. I wasn't certain about the children at the time, though I suspected. And I knew how much you wanted them, so…" she shrugged, letting her sentence hang there.

"How can you be certain? Perhaps it was your husbands who were unable to have them?"

Ellie shook her head. She could not explain that she had always been on birth control as it did not exist in this time, but birth control was no longer the reason she could not have them.

"Not at this point."

"At what point?"

She sighed, realizing he was going to make her say it. With her youthful appearance, Ellie liked to pretend she was not as old as she was, and she did not like the reminder. She also hated the reminder that the age gap between them was so large.

"It's called menopause, Thomas."

"Menopause? I've not heard of that."

"Of course you haven't," she said, frustrated, trying to think of a way to explain it that he would understand. It had not occurred to her that the word was not in use there. She had been trying to be sarcastic, but it did not matter since he had never heard the word. "I no longer have my courses."

"Are you trying to say that you've gone through the change of life?" he asked skeptically.

Ellie stopped walking to look at him and he stopped along with her.

"That's exactly what I'm saying." At his surprised and confused expression, she added, "I know you never believed me when I said I'm older than I look, but it was always true. I'm an old woman. And you were so young, but the way you looked at me, the way you made me feel..." Ellie closed her eyes in remembrance. "It was intoxicating. I got caught up in it and wanted more. I never meant for things to go as far as they did. I never expected the emotions."

"You mean you merely wanted to slake your lust?"

"I wanted to feel desired," she corrected. "I wanted to feel passion. I just wanted to feel."

Ellie had been so numb for so long, being with Thomas had been a novelty. She had felt alive with him. Knowing they had been walking a fine line, she had foolishly thought she could control it and no one had to get hurt. She had been wrong.

"So long as it meant not feeling too much," he accused. "Because love is a myth. That is what you said?" His voice hardened as he continued walking.

"Thomas…"

"I don't believe love is a myth, Ellie. And it doesn't merely end."

Was he trying to tell her that he still loved her? He could not possibly. She decided that he was talking about Lucy. Of course he loved her; he had married her, after all.

"I'm sorry I didn't tell you, Thomas. I… I was not capable of it at the time." She knew it sounded like an excuse, but it was as close to the truth as she could get.

Thomas merely grunted as he resumed walking. After a few minutes of quiet, he asked, "And what of Robert?"

"What about Robert?" she asked defensively.

"You've no intention of being wed, yet you allow him to court you."

"What? So, I'm supposed to be a spinster and spend my days alone simply because I have no interest in marriage?"

"That was not my meaning."

"Robert knows what this is."

Thomas immediately pictured her lying naked in his arms, but then the image flashed to her with Robert, and it nearly undid him. "And what exactly is it Miss Ellie? More meaningless intercourse?"

It felt like he was boring a hole right through her. She looked away, unable to meet his steel gaze.

Shrugging, she tried for a nonchalance that she did not feel. "Not that it's any of your business, I told him I had no interest in marriage. We're just seeing where things lead. Maybe by the time we get to Boston, something will change, but I don't foresee that being the case right now."

Thomas stopped walking again. His arm shot out to grab hers, though he did not look at her. "When *'we'* get to Boston?"

He finally turned his hard eyes to hers and Ellie's lips parted in surprise at the pain and confusion she saw.

"Shit. He hasn't told you, has he?"

Thomas shook his head slowly. "No. He has not told me."

Looking up at the overcast sky, Thomas tried to gather his thoughts and control the storm brewing within him. Robert was moving to Boston with Ellie? How could he? And why had neither of them told him? He felt the rage bubbling up inside and fought to contain it. The rage felt better than the hurt that was coursing through him, but he was not about to lose his temper.

"Thomas," Ellie began, putting her gloved hand gently on his forearm. One look at his face had her quickly removing the hand. "I'm sorry. I thought he told you. I didn't mean to just blurt it out like that."

"Yet you did. So, tell me this. Why are you so set on Boston? And why is Robert selling his commission to go with you?"

Ellie shook her head while looking away and began to say something, but he cut her off. "I'll have the truth for once, Ellie."

She lifted her head to look at him and squared her shoulders. "Fine. The truth is, Boston is calling me and I'm answering. I want to see the events of history as they unfold. Boston just happens to be where they unfold. As for why Robert is going with me, I can't answer that. That was his choice, and quite frankly, as much as I'd love to have a friend with me, I'm not sure our friendship will survive his overprotective streak. I hope I'm wrong, but I'm not sure I am."

Ellie was more concerned with surviving his deification of her, but she was not about to say that to Thomas. It was easier to blame his overprotectiveness.

"Why sell his commission? He could put in for a transfer and go with you. There are plenty of troops in Boston at the present. How have you managed to convince him to leave the army?"

Ellie shook her head. "I didn't convince him of anything. He made that choice all on his own."

"I find that rather doubtful."

Ellie scoffed. "If I had that kind of power, Thomas, I'd have you selling your commission as well."

Thomas's head jerked back in surprise. "Would you now?"

Ellie had not had any intention of trying to convince him to do so anytime soon, but she saw her opportunity and seized it.

"Yes. I would. This is not the time to be part of the British Army. What's happened here these last few years is nothing compared to what's to come. Please, Thomas. Reconsider your career path. Leave the military. Go back to being a physician."

His brow furrowed as he tried to understand Ellie's request. "Why would I do that?"

"Because you'll be safe."

"Safe from what? Is this the same as the so-called massacre that occurred in Boston earlier this year? What are the Sons planning next?"

The hope she had only moments before of convincing him were gone and her shoulders slumped. Ellie turned to continue walking home.

"I'm tired of trying to convince you, Thomas. I'll say it one more time, and one more time only. I'm not with the Sons of Liberty."

"I should hope not, Miss Ellie."

---

Lucy Burke decided to have her Christmas ball once again. Everyone came out for it and Ellie tried to enjoy herself, but she kept thinking back to the conversation she had with Thomas on their way back from the market. She watched him and Robert who barely spoke to one another. When they did, it was brief and curt. She really hoped she was not coming between them. It was the last thing she wanted.

The night after the ball, Lucy had them over for a more intimate family affair. Jack Emerson was in port and accompanied his wife and children. They had a feast, then visited in the parlor afterward. They took turns entertaining each other, playing instruments, singing, and telling stories. Thomas asked Ellie to tell her *Princess Bride* story, but she decided on one better suited for the holiday and told them *A Christmas Carol.*

Robert sat by her side with his arm around her shoulders all night. Ellie tried not to feel smothered by it. At least he was not grabbing her hand to hold it anymore. He seemed to have given up on that. She was grateful she had not had to explain herself to him about it.

Adelaide and Jack were the first to leave. As they stood in the doorway saying their goodbyes, Ellie and Robert grabbed their cloaks and made ready to leave as well. Standing in the corner of the hallway, Robert turned his attention to something hanging from the ceiling and when Ellie looked up, she saw the mistletoe at which he was staring. He smirked, then reached up and grabbed a berry before kissing her. It reminded her so much of her kiss with Thomas all those years ago, her chest ached. She pulled back, opening her eyes to see Thomas standing behind them. He locked eyes with her briefly then turned and walked away without a word. Ellie's cheeks flamed and she felt as though she had been caught doing something she was not supposed to be doing.

As they said their goodbyes, Thomas was nowhere to be seen.

## Chapter 41

February 1771

Tabitha and Harris seemed to be adjusting to life as free persons well. Tabitha was picking up what she needed to be a good midwife, getting more patients after having helped deliver Addah Mawby of her baby. Harris was doing well under Amos's tutelage. He came home one night with the news that Amos was being harassed by other coopers for training him, leaving him worried that he was going to have to stop learning from the man. Ellie tried to reassure him that it would not come to that.

Ellie had given the kids as many choices as she could, allowing them to make their own decisions as often as possible. When the topic of church came up, she allowed them to decide whether they wanted to go at all. When they expressed an interest, she gave them the choice to decide which one they wanted to attend. They both opted to attend with the Mawbys. Both of them spent more and more time with the Mawbys and Ellie was grateful they had that connection. She did not begrudge them their time with the other family. She wished they could have been more like a traditional family themselves, but in that world, it was not something that was going to happen. Lucy and Adelaide had not been as openly racist or opposed to the situation as they were initially, but they had not fully accepted the children either. It chafed, but Ellie continued to try intermingling the groups as much as she could. At Thomas's insistence, Lucy even allowed them to join them for dinner on occasion and they would visit in the parlor afterwards. Robert had begun teaching Harris to play chess and when they went to the Burke's, he played with both Thomas and Robert.

Along with their traditional chores, Ellie encouraged the children to both learn other tasks that were seen as belonging to that of the other gender. She taught Harris to sew, do laundry, and cook, at which Tabitha and Ezra had laughed hysterically while Harris grumbled.

"Why you 'spect me to learn this?" he complained.

"What will you do if you tear your shirt, and you don't have me or Tabitha around to help you mend it? You need to be able to take care of yourself."

After that, Ezra sat in on some of the lessons as well.

With the new year, Ellie started feeling restless in New York. She felt the time slipping away from her and began to become eager to get to Boston again. She had enjoyed her time in New York City over the last two years, but something within her felt like it was coming to an end. She had gotten to see the Battle of Golden Hill play out, though she had missed out on the Boston Massacre. However, after seeing it play out in the broadsheets, she realized it had not been much of a massacre. There was no question that it had been a tragic event, but she was not certain five people qualified as a massacre. The citizens of Boston had started the conflict, throwing rocks and ice at the soldiers, egging them on and trying to goad them into firing on them.

Ellie did not want to miss out on the Boston Tea Party or Lexington and Concord. There were still many events on the horizon that she wanted to see. Not only the events themselves, but she wanted to see the lead up to them. Golden Hill had made her realize that. It was one thing to hear about a battle or a skirmish, but to see the buildup play out for weeks before the climax gave it so much more depth. That was the experience she was looking for in Boston. But how could she leave the children now while they were only just establishing themselves. Was it fair to pick them up and take them with her? Life was so much simpler when she was first widowed, and she only had herself for which to be responsible.

---

"You're rather quiet this afternoon Mrs. Russell," Lucy observed at dinner.

Ellie looked up from her plate when she realized she had not been listening. Her name had pulled her from her thoughts.

"Sorry. Just have a lot on my mind."

"Anything you'd like to share?" she encouraged.

Ellie sighed and picked up her glass, more for something to do with her hands than out of a desire to drink anything. "It's nothing." She forced a smile. "Tell me, how are Charles's lessons going?"

The change of topic went unnoticed, and Lucy gushed as she shared his progress with the rest of them. He had recently started learning to read and write and do math. Ellie enjoyed hearing about how well he was doing.

"He'll be beginning Latin and French soon," she said proudly. Thomas and Lucy were both fluent in French and spoke it often in the home, so Charles was already speaking it a little. Thomas spoke Latin as well, but he did not have anyone to converse with, so Charles had not picked up on as much of that.

"That's exciting," Ellie said. "I always wanted to learn French."

"You don't speak French?" Adelaide asked, surprised.

"No. I only speak Onöndowa'ga:', English, and very poor English," she joked. "I do know a few words in Spanish, but only the bad ones."

"How is it you do not speak Latin, given your medical knowledge?" Robert asked.

"It's not taught where I'm from." Ellie briefly glanced apologetically at Thomas, not meaning to bring up her past, but other than a flinch, he did not react. "Latin is not necessary for medical training where I learned."

Before anyone could ask further questions that he knew she would not answer, Thomas interjected. "Have you considered learning them now?"

Ellie's eyes widened. Latin had never been something she had considered, though she had taken a semester of French in high school. It had not taken. Should she try again?

"I tried my hand at French once, but it was brief, and I didn't retain much of it. Maybe I should try again. Who are you going through to teach Charles? Maybe I could take lessons with him," she half-joked.

Robert, Lucy, and Adelaide laughed uproariously, but Thomas knew she meant what she said. "We'll see that you get the instructor's information," he offered.

"Thank you," she replied while inclining her head at him.

After dinner, everyone seemed to disperse. Adelaide went home right away while Thomas disappeared into his study. Lucy stayed for a while but soon disappeared as well. Ellie found herself alone with Robert again.

He had been a perfect gentleman and taken things slowly, for which she was grateful. They sat on the settee together in the parlor. The conversation lulled and he leaned in to kiss her. She tried to shut off her mind and just feel, wanting to be in the moment and enjoy his attentions. Scooting in closer, she deepened the kiss, and he welcomed her. His hands roamed her back and waist but never went further. Hers slid through his hair and along his neck.

Ellie heard footsteps behind them and opened her eyes to see Thomas standing in the doorway. He looked pained yet could not seem to pull himself away from the scene in front of him. Ellie disentangled herself from Robert and his eyes followed hers to Thomas, who was finally walking away.

Robert pulled Ellie in for another kiss, but she slid back. "It's getting late. I should be getting home," she said without looking at him.

Putting his hand under her chin, Robert turned her head gently to face him, her eyes immediately looking down. Releasing her, he sat back, running his hand through his dark curls as he sighed, realization dawning on him. He had been avoiding acknowledging it, but he could no longer do so.

"He shall always be between us, will he not?" He could not stop himself from asking, though he already knew the answer.

"You're his best friend, Robert," Ellie evaded. "I think he's afraid I'm going to steal you away from him. I've given him enough reason to hate me, I'll not give him more."

Robert shook his head. "He hates you not, Ell."

Ellie laughed. "It's pretty damn obvious that he does."

"You are blind."

Ellie did not say anything to that. What could she say? He was wrong. She knew it, but there was no point in arguing with him over it.

"I, on the other hand, am not blind. I see it plain as day, Ellie. Is this why you plan to never marry? Is it why you did not wish me to court you?"

Shaking her head, Ellie tried to argue. Robert was having none of it. "Please say it, Ell. I may be capable of handling a great many things but lie to me not."

She released a heavy breath, turning in the settee. "I'm sorry, Rob. I'm just not a forever kind of girl. It has nothing to do with Thomas or anyone else. I'm glad he found Lucy and has the family he always wanted. I want you both to be happy, but I'm afraid I'm not the person who can make that happen for either of you. Thomas moved on long ago, but maybe it's time for you to as well."

The words cut through Robert. He could never simply move on from her as she suggested. "Is that what you believe yourself to have done, Miss Ellie? Have you truly moved on from him or are you merely laboring under the false pretense that you have?"

"I let him go a long time ago, Rob. I had a life after I left the fort and he was not part of it. I had to let him go. Seeing him again was a shock, certainly, and it stirred up a lot of old feelings, but I assure you, those feelings are long gone. I will always care for him, but my feelings for him are not the same as they once were. I simply miss his friendship and worry I'll ruin your friendship with him as well."

"He gave me his blessing to pursue you."

Robert was not certain why he was telling her this now. Perhaps because he did not believe her claim to have gotten over Thomas and he wanted her to know that despite how she likely still felt, Thomas was not something she should let stand in her way.

Thomas's constant bickering and avoidance of her had been bad enough, but Ellie felt like she had been stabbed in the chest with this revelation. She did not know why it had that effect on her. She certainly could not expect him to still have feelings for her after all these years. They had both moved on. He had gotten married and had kids, taking the life he had always wanted. It was everything she had wanted for him. Yet, a small, selfish part of her wished he still felt something for her.

No one had ever made her feel protected, worshipped, and cherished as he once had. He had adored her once and it had been addicting. Thomas had been kind, generous, open to new ideas, and intelligent. He had accepted her quirks and her differences, even when they drove him nuts. He had made her feel for the first time in twenty years, even when she did not want to. She had fought to contain her feelings all those years ago, but he had gotten under her skin.

That he would give his blessing, misplaced as it was, spoke volumes about how he felt about her now. There was nothing left between them, not even friendship. He merely tolerated her presence now. As much as it hurt, it was for the best.

Chapter 42

*May 17, 1771*

"There's been a battle in North Carolina. The governor finally marched against a bunch of seditious farmers," Thomas informed them as they walked through Ranaleigh Gardens Thursday night.

Attending the concerts in the garden was a favorite pastime of their little group and even though her and Robert were no longer courting, they still spent time together. He had distanced himself from her at first. She would go weeks without seeing him, but eventually, he started coming around again. The city was not that large and they had all the same friends. It was inevitable.

Everyone asked what had happened, but Ellie had no answers. She simply told them that they agreed to end it because it could go nowhere. She had no interest in marriage, so it was pointless. It was close enough to the truth.

"The Regulators," Ellie nodded absently. "At the Battle of Alamance."

"You've already read the broadsheets?" Thomas asked, making Ellie realize that she had spoken aloud.

"Governor Tryon will be on his way here soon," she said by way of answer. Instead of helping, it only made it worse. Ironically, she had never heard of Governor Tryon or the Battle of Alamance in school or any museum she had visited, despite having lived in North Carolina when she was young. She also had not read the broadsheets now. Those bits of information had been obtained from a popular television show in her time.

"That information was not in the broadsheets," Thomas frowned. "How is it you've already heard news of it when we've only received word of late?"

Robert saw the slightly panicked look on Ellie's face and knew exactly how she had come by the information. Obviously, she had experienced another vision.

"She must have heard me mention it," Robert said, coming to her rescue.

He knew she did not tell people about her gift. As far as he knew, he was still the only one she had ever told. He liked it that way. It made him feel special, even if they were no longer courting. The grateful look she shot him was thanks enough for him and he nodded briefly at her, giving her a small smile.

Ellie focused on keeping her mouth shut as Thomas relayed the details of the battle. "The militia marched against rebel farmers in Hillsborough near the Alamance Creek. They only numbered one thousand to the rebel's two thousand, yet the farmers were no match for the militia. Alas, nine of the King's militia were killed and as many as sixty-one wounded, but the Regulator losses have been reported to have been much higher. Governor Tryon took fifteen prisoners and hung seven."

"Are we not lucky to be getting such a distinguished governor?" Lucy asked in awe.

Their party continued to talk while they roamed the Gardens, weaving their way through the shrubbery and trees, hedges, and flower gardens. It was a beautiful setting and exactly where Thomas and Robert had always pictured Ellie spending her time. She would have preferred it, were it not for the copious amount of people who always filled the space. It was a favorite amongst the people of New York City, and they came to enjoy not only the gardens, but the drinks and ice cream offered there. Ice cream was a huge novelty that could not be obtained just anywhere, so it was a big draw.

"The reverend at Saint Paul's informed me you donated to their fund for a steeple," Thomas said quietly when he found himself beside Ellie, everyone else engaged in conversation.

Ellie made a noise of acknowledgment without adding anything further.

"He thought it peculiar given you are not one of his congregation. Why would you do so if you wish to have nothing to do with the church?"

Letting out a long exhale, Ellie corrected, "I don't want to have anything to do with religion. The building itself means something to a lot of people. And it will for a long time."

Thomas wanted to ask more but the concert was about to get underway. He dropped the matter as they found their seating. Ellie wanted to sit in the grass, but there were chairs set out and she had learned early on that sitting in the grass was

unacceptable for a lady at these events. She had ignored the stares the first time she had done it, but
when someone from the venue came out and asked
if everything was alright, she had assured him it was.
He could not understand why she was not sitting in
a chair if that was the case and had made it plainly
clear that sitting in the grass was not an option if she
wanted to stay. With a huff, she had picked herself
up and plopped down in a chair. People were so rigid
there.

Robert walked Ellie home after the concert. He
was still a gentleman, and they were working on
maintaining their friendship. She had warned him
this was a possibility. Though he had hoped she was
wrong, now he understood. Unlike Thomas, if she
could not give him more, he would accept what he
could get from her. He could not see her being out
of his life again now that she had returned. He would
do whatever it took to keep her there, even if it was
not in the manner of his choosing.

"I would still accompany you to Boston, if you'll
allow me," he said as they approached her house.

"What about the army?" she asked, opening the
door. "You can't just walk away from them and no
one has been able to purchase your commission."

Robert looked around them, then grabbed her
arm and pulled her inside the house. He closed the
door, ensuring it was shut tight before looking
around for servants or kids. He pulled Ellie in close
then and whispered, "Do not fret. I shall find someone to purchase my commission. If what you say is
to come to pass, I wish not to be on this side of it. If
there is to be a revolution, I would fight for the cause

of liberty. Until then, I may practice law. I've already been endeavoring to do that, taking on cases on occasion."

Ellie searched for the truth on his face. He was completely earnest. She nodded. "I'd like having you there."

---

"Mrs. Russell. T'ank you for comin'," Amos said as she walked into his drawing room.

He had sent word with Harris that he wanted to meet with her, so she came as soon as she could. Addah brought them some tea and they all sat down.

"I don' know how much longer I can train Harris. He a good boy, but de othe' coopers don' want me trainin' him. By law, they limit how many Negro folk can learn de trade, cuz de othe's don' want de competition. Now they harassin' me somethin' fierce."

Ellie let out a heavy sigh. This would devastate Harris. He loved his lessons with Amos. "Is there really nothing you can do?"

Amos looked to Addah next to him before turning back to Ellie. "There is one t'ing. I have a cousin who a cooper, too. He could take de boy on and teach 'im."

Ellie wanted to be relieved, but she sensed there was a 'but' coming. "Alright. How do we make that happen?"

"He willing to teach de boy. I wrote to him already and he be happy to have Harris come. But he in Boston."

Ellie laughed, causing the Mawbys to look at her with concern.

"Are you alright, missus?" Addah asked.

Ellie sobered and summed up the situation. "You can't continue teaching Harris the trade, but your cousin can, but you're worried because he's in Boston? Is your cousin a good man?"

"That de gist of it," Amos said. "He a fair man. Ezekiel won' beat de child or not'ing. He teach him real well."

Ellie nodded. If this was not a sign that it was time for her to go to Boston, she did not know what was. As much as she had been enjoying her time there, it was becoming more and more obvious to her that she needed to put some distance between her and Thomas. She had thought they could be cordial to one another and that with time, they may even find their way back to being friends. But it was getting harder and harder to be around him all the time. He never looked happy to see her and while they had moments of friendliness, they were far from being friends. If anything, his constant hot and cold with her was confusing and more than a little exhausting. She pictured him as being happy whenever she was not around then immediately becoming grumpy as soon as she showed up. Her presence was obviously disturbing him. Much like their time at the fort together, the time had come when it was better that she left.

"How do we make this happen?"

Chapter 43

*July 1771*

With the sun shining and the weather holding, Ellie, Tabitha, and Harris made it to Boston in a week's time. The waters were calm, and Ellie once again spent as much time as possible on the ship's deck. She had always loved the water and while she had enjoyed the journey to Williamsburg with Thomas and Robert years ago, this trip was so much better. The last one had been bitterly cold, and she had nearly frozen while trying to stay on deck. This time, the weather was perfect, and Ellie could not have asked for a better trip.

It felt good to get out and do some traveling. She had always loved traveling and visiting new places and had not done so since arriving in New York City. Before then, Ellie had primarily only traveled through New York. She was excited to finally be able to see Boston, even if she was not planning on staying just yet. Though Ellie wanted to make the move as soon as possible, it was too soon to make it happen. She would have to write to the Armstrongs and let them know she was leaving and make arrangements to transport all of the belongings she and the kids had accumulated. For now, this was merely a scouting trip. This journey would not only serve to scope out Harris's prospects but would help pave the way for them all to move there. Ellie planned on looking for lodging and feeling out Tabitha's prospects for midwifing.

Ellie told Lucy and Adelaide she was going, but not until the morning of their departure. Not wanting them to try talking her out of going alone, she had not told Robert or Thomas. She was not going to rely on Robert or change her plans and wait for him to take a furlough to be able to join her. Ellie did not need a keeper and would do fine on her own. They would have to accept her apologies after she returned.

As soon as they landed, Ellie arranged for a carriage to transport them and their luggage to a local inn. She had gotten recommendations on the journey as to where to stay. The inn situated in the North End of Boston sounded perfect for them. She rented two adjacent rooms, taking one and putting the kids in the other. They were still more comfortable when they were able to stay together, despite Tabitha now being eighteen and Harris being fifteen by their best guess. Ellie was not going to complain if it meant having to only purchase two rooms while getting one to herself.

"We'll go by Mr. Hencher's after breakfast and let him know we've arrived. After we meet with him, we can explore the city a little," Ellie explained to

Tabitha and Harris while sitting down to eat at the inn.

The siblings nodded and talked excitedly about what they might see.

"Does you think it much like New York City?" Harris asked.

Ellie grinned. She knew the two cities held many similarities but also just as many differences in her own time. She was nearly as excited to see the changes in the city as they both were to see it for the first time. They had never been outside of New York City and this was an entirely new adventure for them.

"I think a lot of things will be quite similar, but many will be–"

"I will have what's mine," a man exclaimed across the room, interrupting their conversation.

All three heads turned in the direction of the angry male voice. At the sight of an older man with a potbelly hovering over a cowering woman, the siblings quickly turned and looked away. Ellie glowered at the man, waiting to see if he was going to get physical with the woman. His fingers were in her face, but so far he was not touching her. He said something low that Ellie could not hear from where they sat then stormed out abruptly.

Ellie watched for another minute to make sure everything was alright. The aging innkeeper caught Ellie's eye as she wiped her cheeks. Ellie gave her a small smile and nod of solidarity then turned back to her breakfast, not wanting to make the woman uncomfortable by prolonging her stare.

Once they made their way outside, Harris could hardly contain his excitement. He practically ran down the street with the women following behind, laughing at his enthusiasm.

Once they arrived, Ezekiel Hencher invited them inside.

"Me cousin tol' me all 'bout you," he said.

"Mr. Mawby said you might be able to take Harris on as an apprentice. He's a little older than most apprentices begin, but he's already been working with Mr. Mawby for over a year."

Ezekiel nodded. They talked a little more, then he took the boy into the workshop and walked him around, quizzing him on various items. When he was satisfied, he came back out to meet with Ellie and Tabitha.

"He'll do," he said with a single nod. "I take 'im on. You be here tomorrow morn," he added, looking at Harris.

Ellie could not hide her surprise. Her eyes widened and her voice pitched slightly. "You wish him to start right away?"

"Is dat a problem?"

Ellie looked at Harris who was staring back at her with pleading eyes. She was glad to see that he was excited to start and not discouraged by jumping right in.

"No. That'll be fine," Ellie agreed. "We'll make sure he's here."

They discussed the details about where he would live and what his life would entail. Ellie reluctantly agreed to allow him to stay when she and Tabitha went back to New York, but only if Harris still wanted to by the time they departed. The women would stay for a few weeks, and this would be a trial run for them all to make sure it would be a good fit for everyone.

They spent the day wandering around the city, enjoying the little bit of free time Harris had before he was to begin his work the next day. Much like New York City, Ellie was struck by how familiar, yet how foreign it was. She kept looking down while they walked, trying to find the Freedom Trail, even though she knew it was not there. It was built into her subconscious as much as it was built into the sidewalks in her own time. She had walked it twice before and both times had kept looking down for the red bricks in the sidewalks to make sure she was still on it. Part of her half expected to find it around the corner. When they passed the Old North Church, she looked for it, then found herself seeking out Paul Revere's house. She giggled to herself when she found it easily, though it blended into its surroundings far better than any other time she had seen it.

At the end of the long day, the innkeeper was sweeping the steps when they approached. The siblings went inside, and Ellie hung back.

"Are you well, madam?" Ellie asked.

Lydia Colton's eyes were red and blotchy, and Ellie wondered if the dour old man had been back to bother her again.

"Only, I was thinking on my late husband," she said.

Ellie put on a sympathetic smile, "I'm sorry for your loss. How long ago did he pass?"

"Four months now, it's been. In truth, sometimes it feels much longer. I know not how I've managed this long without him." The woman had stopped sweeping and was staring at something in the distance only she could see. "Nor how I'll ever manage on my own at all."

Ellie patted her arm as Lydia's tears started fresh. "I know it feels that way now, but you'll find a way. I'm sure you're stronger than you realize."

The woman sniffled and wiped away the tears once again. She stiffened her spine and gave Ellie a nod and a sad smile. Ellie left her to her work and went inside to her room, calling it a night.

---

As planned, Harris went to Ezekiel Hencher's first thing in the morning. The women spent the day wandering further around the city, taking a carriage for much of it as they explored the South End and other surrounding areas.

The following days were much the same, but after the first two days, they began asking around about the situation for midwives.

"We've several, but there's always need for more," Lydia said as she served their breakfast one morning. The women had become fast friends, talking every morning over breakfast and late at night when Ellie could not sleep.

"That's one of the reasons I recommended midwifery," Ellie said looking at Tabitha. The girl nodded and smiled shyly. Though she had begun to open up a little with Ellie, she still spoke very little when others were around.

"You might try–"

"Mrs. Colton!" Before Lydia could say anything more, the dour man from a few days before returned, storming in like a freight train. "Your deadline is only a day away. Have you any news for me?"

The smile vanished from Lydia's face along with the color. She stood from the chair she had been sitting in next to Ellie and looked at the floor as she stammered out a response.

"I–I don't... I mean, I still have until tomorrow..."

The man sneered at her. "It matters not. One more day will change nothing. If you've nothing for me today, then you shall have nothing for me tomorrow." He was leaning in, practically spitting in her face as he spoke.

Ellie could not help herself. Standing, she placed herself between them, pushing Lydia behind her. She stuck out her hand to shake with him as she introduced herself. They were standing so close, her hand jutted out from her breast, but of course, he did not take it. He merely looked down at it as if it were a worm.

"May I be of any assistance here?" Ellie asked when he did not introduce himself.

The man looked at her, then back at Lydia again. "You have until one o'clock tomorrow."

He turned and stormed out once again without a backward glance. As soon as he was gone, Lydia crumpled to the chair, resting her elbows on the table and her face in her hands.

Ellie sat next to her and rubbed the woman's back while she sobbed. When she finished, Ellie asked, "What's going on Mrs. Colton? What's tomorrow?"

Lydia looked down at her hands which were now in her lap. "I fear my late husband owed far more than I knew. Mr. Walklate was one of his creditors. I'm going to lose the inn and have no way to support myself." With the last, her sobs began anew.

Tabitha excused herself to give the women some privacy and Lydia told Ellie everything. All she had left was the inn. Her sons had both been sailors and had long ago passed away while out at sea. Having thought they were doing well, when her husband died, she found out that he had run up more debt than what they were bringing in. The inn did well, but not as well as the late Mr. Colton had imagined. Lydia had tried raising the money but had not been successful. Her only option had been to remarry, but at her age, she had little prospects. Now she was facing a life of destitution.

"Would you mind if I look at your books?" Ellie asked. "Maybe I can find something."

Lydia nodded between sobs and took Ellie back to the office where Ellie sat at the desk and started going through the numbers. After pouring over them, she finally looked up at Lydia apologetically.

"I'm sorry. I don't see how you can find the extra money you need by tomorrow."

"Thank you for looking. It's mighty kind of you to try."

Feeling unhelpful, Ellie tossed and turned all night, trying to come up with a solution. Women there were only granted a third of their late husband's estates after death if there were living children and one-half if there were no children. It was with the express intent that the wife would be able to 'support herself' in his absence, though one-half was never enough, one-third even less so. The trades were prohibited to them, limiting what professions they could find to support themselves. Women were pressured to remarry as quickly as possible, and in some colonies were required to remarry within seven years. Their lives were not their own at all. It irked Ellie more than anything else in this time period.

Ellie realized again how lucky she had been in marrying Dean. Having consumption had given him the foresight to create a will in which he left Ellie everything. Had he not done so, she could have easily ended up in a similar situation to what Lydia now found herself. Instead, she had not been required to give up anything, though she chose to do so herself, giving Dean's physical assets from his business to his factor. She had kept the rest of his fortune, which gave her more freedom than many widows enjoyed in the era.

Lydia Colton was a mess of nerves the next morning. Breakfast came out slow and often burned. People were complaining throughout the dining hall.

"I may have come up with a solution," Ellie said, taking Lydia by the elbow to her office.

Shutting the door, she gestured for Lydia to sit. She proceeded to tell the woman her plan and Lydia smiled for the first time in days. "I know not how to thank you," she said excitedly.

Ellie held her hands up. "We don't know if Mr. Walklate will accept the offer. Wait to thank me until after it's over."

True to his word, Mr. Walklate came walking in at one o'clock with another man in tow, whom he did not introduce. He looked around the place as if sizing it up as his newest property. If Ellie could not pull this off, it may well be.

"Do you have my money?" he began the second they got back to the office.

Ellie finished pushing the door closed while she watched a confident Lydia Colton walk across the office and place a coin purse down on the table. Her head held high, she dared him to take objection to it.

"I've all but the last twenty pounds," Lydia said. "If you give me one more month, I shall have the rest of it."

The man looked down at the purse and sputtered. He looked up at Lydia, then back at Ellie, refusing to reach for the purse. The other man that had come in with him nudged him.

"Are you not going to take the coin?" he asked.

Mr. Walklate begrudgingly snatched the purse and opened it up, snidely saying, "I said all of it, Mrs. Colton. Not merely some of it. The deadline has come and gone."

"Now, now, Mr. Walklate. Mrs. Colton has just handed you over two hundred pounds."

"Sterling," Lydia interjected in case they thought it was Boston money.

"Sterling," the man acknowledged with a nod to Lydia. "Surely we may count this as good faith and give her another thirty days for the last twenty pounds?"

"'Tis doubtful there's that much here at all," Mr. Walklate said snidely. "It's not possible you were able to raise that kind of money overnight. She's probably only trying to make us think that she has paid us that much of it."

Lydia continued to hold her head high, challenging him now. "Perhaps you would prefer to count it?"

His eyes narrowed and he replied, "I absolutely will. Have no doubt to the contrary."

Mr. Walklate proceeded to pour the contents of the purse into his hand and count out the British sterling pounds one by one, setting the counted coins on the desk beside him. The man beside him whom Ellie was beginning to think was his partner or possibly a boss of some sort counted at the same time. When they reached the last of the coin, the other man smiled at Lydia.

"Well done, Mrs. Colton. You have your thirty days. Until then, the inn shall remain yours."

Turning to the seething Mr. Walklate, he placed a hand on the man's shoulder while holding out his other arm in a gesture toward the door. Ellie immediately caught on and opened the door.

"Mr. Walklate, after you."

The man's face was red as he glared at Lydia. For a moment, Ellie did not think he was going to leave. With the other man's hand on his shoulder, he finally turned toward the door. He spared a glower for Ellie as he walked out and Ellie shut the door behind the men.

The women cheered and Lydia wrapped Ellie in a tight hug. "How shall I ever repay you?"

Ellie smiled. "Just run the inn properly and keep it in the black. If you have any issues, you write me immediately. I'll send you the rest as soon as I get back to New York. Then, I'll be back as soon as I can and will help you run it."

It was a good investment. After looking over the books trying to find a way to pay off the late Mr. Colton's debts, Ellie had seen what the inn brought in. By itself, it did well. However, she knew food at inns was notoriously bad and she ventured to guess that they could easily improve revenue if they improved the food offered. It might bring in more locals for dining. It had been the only solution she could think of the night before and when she offered to buy out Lydia's late husband's debt in exchange for partnership in the business, Lydia had been more than happy to accept her help.

It had taken nearly everything Ellie had brought with her, leaving only enough to get home now. Ellie hated traveling with that much cash, but she had not known how much she would need for travel expenses, food, lodging, or to pay Ezekiel Hencher for taking on Harris, so she had brought a substantial purse. She would have to make another trip to the cave near Albany to replenish her personal bank as soon as she got back to New York.

Ellie had been more than happy to make the investment. Not only would it save Lydia, but she knew she would see it back, and it also gave her a more solid reason to get moved to Boston sooner rather than later. No more excuses. It was time. As soon as she got back to New York, she would write to the Armstrongs and let them know she would be leaving. Once she heard back from them, she would make the journey. Excitement fluttered through Ellie, followed by a brief bit of sorrow that she tamped down. She would not let her emotions deter her from this.

September 1771

"Pray, where have you been?" Robert asked as he quickly dismounted his horse only feet from Ellie.

She had only been home a day and had been on her way back from the market when he rode past. Upon seeing her, he had pulled on the reins, bringing his horse to a stop and turning around.

"Did Lucy not tell you?" Ellie asked in confusion.

She had asked both her and Adelaide to let Robert know that she would be gone for several weeks. She would have asked them to inform Thomas as well, but Ellie decided it would be deemed 'improper' for her to ask such a thing. Instead, she assumed Lucy or Robert would mention it at some point.

Robert stalked toward her and grabbed her by the shoulders. He was not sure if he wanted to shake her or hug her. A little of both, he decided.

"She did. Though, why did I have need to hear it from her? Why did you not tell me yourself?"

"It all happened rather fast. I didn't have time to let you know," Ellie lied.

She had known of the possibility for a few weeks as they waited for word from Ezekiel but had chosen not to tell anyone. It was only at the last minute that she had told Lucy and Adelaide. She had not wanted to tell anyone before they received confirmation that Ezekiel would see them, and once they had it, she had not wanted anyone talking her out of going.

Robert pulled Ellie in for a hug, holding her close. "I thought you promised you'd not leave without saying goodbye?" he asked over her head.

Being held felt good and she wanted to relish it. Slowly, she eventually pulled back. "I didn't leave. I'm still here. I only went to scope things out."

"Miss Ellie, something could have happened, and I never would have known."

"Come inside while I put all this away," she said on a sigh, gesturing to her shopping baskets.

Ellie did not apologize for not telling him she was leaving but instead told him of Harris's new apprenticeship and Ezekiel. They had stayed long enough that Ellie felt comfortable leaving Harris with him. He had been excited every night after spending the day working and had nothing but good things to say about the man. Even Tabitha had felt better about leaving him there. Knowing they would be returning soon helped alleviate some of her concern as well.

"And I sort of bought into an inn," Ellie said.

"You did what?"

Ellie finished putting things away and pulled Robert into the parlor with her. They sat down and she explained what had happened with Lydia.

"Now I need to get back as soon as I can," she said sheepishly.

Robert ran a hand across the back of his neck and turned away from her. He stood, then sat back down again. "You'll not wait for me? Do you not wish me to join you now?"

Ellie took a deep breath. "Robert, I meant it when I said I'd be happy to have you join me. That's not changed. What has changed is that I just can't wait. I still have to get in touch with the Armstrongs and let them know, so you still have some time. I'm not leaving right away. If you can sell your commission before I go, then you'll come with me." She shrugged. "If you can't, you'll meet me there. This doesn't change any of that. It only changes how soon I'll be going."

Robert nodded slowly, taking in her words. "Very well, Ellie. I'll do what I can."

Ellie smiled reassuringly and pulled him in for a hug. "I'm glad you'll be there with me. I missed you these past weeks."

"Did you now?" he asked with a wolfish smile on his face. He knew nothing could ever happen between them, but it would never stop him from flirting with her. She would always mean the world to him, and he could not imagine ever not loving her.

Ellie slapped him playfully on the arm. "Of course I did. How many best friends do you think I have?"

It killed him to hear her call him that, but he would take it over being nothing at all. "Well, apparently now you have one more by the sounds of it," he teased.

The corner of Ellie's lip turned up in a lopsided smile. "Lydia is great. You'll like her."

A fleeting thought passed through Ellie's mind. She had guessed the woman to be in her late forties. Robert and Thomas were now forty-one. Maybe she could arrange something between her and Robert once he arrived in Boston. Lydia was a nice enough woman and women in this time period fared much better with a man to protect them, though Ellie would never admit that she fell under that category as well. She did not need anyone. And Ellie could see that Robert was lonely, despite his claims to the contrary. This could work out for the both of them. Ellie would have to keep an eye open for an opportunity once they all settled in.

*October 1771*

"Why me?" Ellie asked as Lucy guided her around the market.

"Whatever do you mean?" Lucy asked innocently.

Giving her a dubious look, Ellie asked, "Why did you ever decide that we must be friends to begin with? Surely you had plenty of friends already. Friends who don't have the history I do."

Ellie had been referring to her history with Thomas but could not bring herself to say it outright. She had not needed to. Lucy knew what she meant. The question had been on her mind for two years now. She had always wondered but never asked. This seemed the perfect opportunity.

"One may never have too many friends," she diverted while picking up an apple.

At the look Ellie gave her, Lucy set the apple down with a thump. She sighed and said, "Oh, alright. I wanted to like you not. I even tried not to be your friend. Yet, when Thomas's siblings found out you were well and you were here, they all wrote, asking after you. They all adore you. And they're not the only ones. Robert does as well. I thought to make a match between you two, then leave you be, but it did not turn out that way. I admit I was jealous at first, yet I could see they were all correct about you. You did not have to attend me when I was in my travails, yet you did. You bought those two Negro children when you oppose slavery, with the sole purpose of setting them free. I understand you not, Mrs. Russell, yet you are a good person. You always put other's needs ahead of yours and you're so esoteric and daring, I never know what you shall say or do next. Life with you around is always interesting."

"Oh. Well. Glad I can amuse you," Ellie said sarcastically while disagreeing with the woman's assessment of her being daring.

Lucy laughed. "You shall be my midwife then?"

"You still haven't told me why you want me as your midwife."

Lucy thought she was about two months pregnant and for some reason Ellie could not fathom she wanted Ellie to be her midwife. She had been taken by surprise at the request. First, she had been surprised that Lucy would want her to do it, but she was also surprised by the sharp pain she felt tugging at her heart. They were married. Of course they would be having sex. But it did not make it any easier to swallow. This was exactly why Ellie needed to leave New York. She could not sit around and be this close to Thomas and his family and watch them. Ellie truly wanted him to be happy but watching it was far too difficult. It was a constant reminder of everything she would never have. She felt as though she had been in a constant state of mourning since her arrival in New York City, longing for a life that could never exist for her. She had felt more alone during her time in the city than she had since she first fell into the past and she needed an escape from it, from the emotions that were constantly trying to drown her.

"I did. Because you're my friend. Honestly, must we repeat the whole conversation?"

Ellie stopped walking and turned to her friend, "That's just reason for me not to do it. There's a reason doctors don't practice on their friends and family."

"What doctors don't do that? You'll find none of those here in the colonies."

Ellie sighed. "You're avoiding the answer again, Lucy. Did you have a row with Mrs. Erwin?"

Lucy turned away from Ellie as if pouting. "I trust her not. She was not there for me when I needed her last time, and even had she been, you made it go much more pleasantly. I'll admit I was skeptical about kneeling and so many other of your methods, yet it seemed to go so much better than my first delivery. I trust your knowledge and ability more than anyone else."

"Are you worried about this birth, Mrs. Burke?"

"All women are worried about giving birth, Mrs. Russell. I've been terrified every time. Sometimes I think you fortunate that you are unable to have children. I know that's awful of me to say, but I'm grateful you'll never face the possibility of dying during the process."

Ellie had not considered that. The death rate during childbirth was high for both mother and baby during this period, but that fact had always been nothing but statistics to her. It just became personal. Ellie gave a murmur of agreement.

Lucy continued sheepishly, "After Caitlyn was born, I withheld my wifely duties to Major Burke far longer than I should have. I know it was wicked of me, but I was afraid of getting caught again. He didn't seem to mind. He told me to take whatever time I needed. In truth, I thought to never lie with him again. I do find the act rather… uncomfortable. And I love him, but the man is not easy to be with in that manner."

That had not been Ellie's experience with him. She wondered not for the first time if Lucy knew the extent of her previous relationship with Thomas. Did the woman know they had been together sexually? Ellie did not want to know about Thomas's sex life with his wife, but the woman took Ellie's silence as permission to continue.

"He insists on engaging in unholy acts," she said, almost in a whisper as they walked slowly between market stalls. "I'm sorry, but there is no reason for one's mouth to make contact with such unclean parts. As if that were not bad enough, he likes to pull me on top of him. It's undignified."

Ellie was trying to suppress a laugh. Clearly, this woman had no idea what she had or how to use it. She had loved sex with Thomas. He had been quite adept with his tongue and had always enjoyed it when she used hers. Maybe not always. The first few times she tried, he had been taken aback, thinking only prostitutes engaged in such acts and could not be-lieve Ellie was willing to do so. She was not only will-ing, she enjoyed it. Ellie had always found pleasure in giving her partners pleasure. There was nothing sexier than knowing she was the reason they were reacting the way they were. He did have some hang-ups about sex, but they were reflections of his time. Thomas had been reserved and afraid to open up to her when she had first bedded him. It took her a while to break through his barriers, but she finally did, making him understand that he was not disrespecting her by asking for what he wanted or for enjoying sex with her. Ellie also had to teach him that it was okay for a woman to touch herself and actively pursue what she wanted without it being sinful or making her a whore; nor was it a reflection on him and his abilities. Once she had made it a safe space and encouraged him, he had really opened up to his desires and hers. It had not been the case with Dean, nor had she ever been with anyone else with whom she was so attuned in that manner. She missed that compatibility.

Ellie had known plenty of women even in her own time who did not enjoy sex. She had never been one of them. Though this woman's horror at her husband's 'wanton desire' as she was now calling it amused Ellie, she simultaneously felt sad for both Lucy and Thomas. Had he spent these last years married to someone who hated sex? Ellie could certainly relate to being rejected sexually by one's spouse and her heart went out to Thomas. The thought curbed any remaining mirth she had about Lucy's descriptions and horror about sex. Between that and his career, she wondered if he was as happy as she thought him to be.

"Oh, I know I must seem innocent and naïve," she continued. "Adelaide insists it's pleasurable, but honestly, my grandmother taught me a woman's pleasure is a mortal sin. With the discomfort I feel, I can't help believing that to be true."

"My last husband didn't care much for it either," Ellie offered. "Oral sex, I mean."

Lucy blushed at Ellie's candor but was grateful for her sharing that little bit to make her feel less isolated and abnormal. It was her duty to lay with her husband and do as he asked, even if she did not enjoy it, but it was difficult to force herself to do so. With the extent of his understanding on the matter, it was all that much easier to avoid it altogether. He never pressured her or pushed her. Of course, the last two times they had coupled, Lucy had ended up pregnant. It did nothing to help encourage her to engage in the activity, but it did provide her an excuse to further avoid his affections.

She put her arm through Ellie's as she so often did. Ellie had to admit, it was nice having a girlfriend that she was close with. She missed her cousins fiercely and as much as she hated to admit it, she would miss Lucy when she finally left for Boston.

"It brings me pleasure to be able to speak with someone about this," Lucy said. "Adelaide shares her secrets with me, but it doesn't feel right for me to do so with her. Anything I tell her is about her brother, which simply does not sit well."

"Yeah, no. I get it. A girl needs someone to talk to about anything."

Ellie really did not want to be that person for Lucy, but she could see how much the woman needed it. She was entirely capable of putting her own feelings aside for the comfort of others. If Lucy needed someone to talk to, she could listen. It was a small thing for Ellie to do, but huge for Lucy.

"You are so right. And if there's anything you ever wish to share, I shall be that for you, too."

Ellie nearly laughed. She would not be sharing. Not with Lucy.

Lucy realized Ellie still had not answered her question and asked again.

Ellie breathed out deeply and stopped walking, turning to look at Lucy. "I'll be your midwife. I'll stay only as long as it takes for you to deliver. After the baby is born in May, I'll make my way to Boston. This will be the last thing I do before I leave."

Lucy cheered, saying thank you, then added, "Oh, I do wish you would stay. It's been lovely to have you here."

Thanking her, Ellie shook her head. "I appreciate that, but I can't stay here. I fear I'm only a source for discontent and it's not fair for any of us. Thomas and Robert both deserve peace and as long as I'm here, that will never happen."

## Chapter 46

# *March 1772*

"**M**y apologies, Mrs. Russell. I was not expecting you today," a confused Thomas said as he stopped in the hallway after Mrs. Toole had let her in.

"Lucy asked me to come," Ellie responded, just as confused. Had she gotten the date wrong? She tried to picture the handwritten invitation Lucy had sent, but she could swear it had been for that day. It was Charles's birthday, was it not?

Before he could respond, Lucy walked past and he stopped her, giving her a pointed look. "Sweetheart, I thought it was to be only family today."

Ellie felt his words like a dagger to her heart.

"It is only family today, darling."

Thomas lifted his eyes to Ellie then looked back at his wife.

"Mrs. Russell *is* family," Lucy insisted. "We both know Charles would be devastated were she not here. And what of Robert?"

Thomas shook his head in surrender and walked away. As soon as he did, Ellie heard a new voice coming from the stairs.

"Mrs. Sorenson? Is that you?"

Ellie turned to see a handsome young man approaching. He looked remarkably like Thomas had when they met. It was obvious this was one of his brothers, but the age gave away which one.

"Christopher?" Ellie questioned, not entirely certain he was not a nephew or some other relation. The last time she had seen him, he was seven years old. At twenty-one, he was now a full-grown man.

His face split into a smile as he came within her reach, and she immediately pulled him in for a hug. Startled, he was not sure whether or not to hug her back, resulting in his arms stretching out at his sides momentarily. After a minute, he gave in and returned her embrace while laughing at her informality.

"It's so good to see you," Ellie said when she released him. "You grew up. You're so tall now." Like with Thomas, she had to stretch onto her toes as far as she could to hug him.

Christopher's smile was that of someone who knew how to charm women. He was warm and open, his smile inviting. "That's what happens after fourteen years. Though I dare say you've not aged a bit."

Placing a hand on his arm playfully to respond, she heard a throat being cleared behind her. Ellie turned to see Martha Burke scowling at her. Adelaide had obviously learned from the best.

"Mother, father, you recall Mrs. Sorenson?" Christopher asked with a hand on Ellie's back.

"It's Mrs. Russell now," Thomas said curtly as he came back down the hallway, not caring to see his youngest brother being so familiar with Ellie.

"You married?" Martha asked, a hint of surprise and relief in her voice.

If she were married, the girl would not be a threat to her family, though she wondered at her sudden appearance now after having been thought dead years ago. At least her son was also married now, preventing him from chasing after the destitute wretch. Though, if the way her youngest son was watching her was any indication, she would have to keep a close eye on him. The woman had already destroyed Thomas and Martha did not want to have to pick up the remaining pieces of another son.

"Briefly," Ellie replied. "I'm widowed now."

"Again?" James Burke asked. "I'm sorry to hear it."

"Thank you."

Once everyone had arrived, they settled in the parlor, Jenny and Mrs. Toole setting out refreshments for everyone to enjoy. Ellie found a seat far away from Thomas's parents and Christopher came to sit beside her.

"Ignore mother," he leaned over to whisper quietly to her.

The daggers Martha was shooting at Ellie from across the room were enough to have her squirming in her seat. Thomas's parents and brother had traveled up from Virginia with Lucy's parents in order to attend the breeching ceremony for Charles. He would be getting his first set of men's clothing today, leaving behind the long skirts of childhood. It was a grand occasion that had family members coming in from afar. Most of Thomas's siblings she had once met were married and busy with their own families now, but his youngest brother had joined their parents for the journey. Ellie spent most of the afternoon with him and Robert while avoiding Thomas's parents.

When Lucy had invited Ellie to the ceremony, she had not been expecting such a big affair. She had heard of breeching ceremonies since her arrival in the past but had never attended one. The Prendergasts had two children that had undergone the tradition, but both occurred long before Ellie met them. Boys underwent the ceremony at different ages depending on a variety of factors. For the Prendergasts, the boys were needed for working the farm, so they had undergone the ceremony early. With no chores pressing down on him, Charles was allowed to remain a child much longer, holding onto the gown of youth. Lucy wanted to postpone the transition, wanting to keep him as her baby as long as she could. Now that he was turning seven, she could not put it off any longer.

It was good to see Thomas's brother again, even if it meant having to deal with his mother who clearly hated her as much now as she had when they first met, the difference being that the woman did nothing to hide it now as she had the last time. With Lucy and Thomas busy, Ellie welcomed Christopher's company now. He was excited to see her, welcoming her back from the dead. They talked about what had happened to her and he listened with understanding and sadness as Ellie briefly explained her decision to go with the Onöndowa'ga:'. Mr. and Mrs. Burke were not as understanding.

"I'm trying," she replied. "That woman has never liked me."

The corners of Christopher's mouth turned up. "No, she has not. You never did fit into her picture of what a genteel woman should be. I dare say that is precisely what drew my brother to you."

Ellie raised a brow and shot him a look, but her attention was quickly drawn away by a very pregnant Lucy escorting Charles into the room. She had two more months until her due date, then Ellie would be free to go to Boston.

Charles was still in the unisex dress that all small children wore in this time. Being escorted around the room, he made his rounds, then was sat in a chair while the barber cut his hair into a more masculine style. His shorn blonde locks were collected and given to the attendees.

Lucy escorted him back out where they went upstairs to his room. Leaving Charles with Thomas's valet, Hugh Pomeroy assisted him in changing into his new linen shirt, trousers, jacket, socks, and shoes.

"My boy is no longer my baby," Lucy mourned as she spoke with her family and friends during the wait.

While he was dressed, his parents made their way around the room, Lucy lamenting the loss of her son's youth while Thomas preened and looked forward to being able to begin his son's education on riding, hunting, and other manly endeavors.

Charles came back in his new trousers and was proudly presented by his father. Jenny and Mrs. Toole restocked the food and drinks while Charles now made his way around the room unescorted. As he did, people slipped him coins and banknotes that went into his pockets while they congratulated him on his new status.

When he made his way to Robert, the man pulled out a toy sword, handing it to the boy with a big grin. Charles's eyes lit up and he smiled excitedly as he took his new toy and immediately pretended to stab Robert with it. Robert played along, grabbing his stomach and doubling over, causing Charles and everyone around the room to laugh and cheer.

***

*April 1772*

"Is that your favorite now?" Ellie asked as she watched Charles play with his new toy sword. She had been watching and joining him as he played with his toy soldiers for the last four years and no matter what new toys he received, he never seemed to tire of the soldiers, until now. The soldiers forgotten, he waved the sword in the air as if trying to fend off an unseen foe.

"Yes," he said. "I'm going to be an officer like father." Along with the adult clothing, the terms 'mama' and 'papa' were also discarded in favor of 'mother' and 'father.'

Ellie did the math. He would only be ten at the start of the war, but eighteen by the end of it. If she were in her own time, she would not worry. However, men in this time often enlisted as young teenagers. Her heart broke at the thought.

"Oh, Charles. That's really honorable. Do you want to be a doctor like him, too?

"He's not a doctor. He's a soldier. Soldiers are brave. I'm brave, too."

Ellie grinned at his comments. "I believe you are brave, Charles. But you don't have to be a soldier to be brave. Your daddy was a doctor first. He's one of the best doctors there ever was. It takes a really smart and brave man to be a doctor, too."

"Are you trying to convince my son to not be a soldier?"

Ellie jumped, placing a hand to her heart. She turned to see Thomas standing in the doorway of the drawing room. "You startled me, Major. I didn't hear you."

Thomas folded his arms across his chest as he hovered in the doorway. She was sitting on the settee, and he entered the room, but did not yet sit down. He stared at her a long moment then finally took a seat across from her, fanning out his coat tails as he sat.

"I apologize for startling you, Mrs. Russell. What was it you were discussing with my son?" Thomas crossed his legs at the ankle and leaned back in the chair, waiting to hear what Ellie had to say for herself.

"I was just asking him about his soldiers."

"Were you? Because it sounded as though you were trying to convince him to be a physician rather than a soldier."

Looking over at Charles who had stopped playing and was watching them intently, she sighed. "I only thought to give him options he may not have considered."

Thomas scoffed. "You merely hate the army, thinking us all scoundrels who were responsible for removing you from the Seneca."

"I don't hate the army, Major."

Ellie had grown up as a military brat and had almost joined up herself. The only reason she had not was because she had gotten married instead and Johnny had been dead set against it. She was young and disillusioned enough that she had acquiesced. However, she still had a healthy respect for the military. It was only history and her own personal experience with the British soldiers she had interacted with since her arrival in the period that jaded her views on the soldiers by which she found herself surrounded now.

"I do take exception to the practices of the British," she said, "but that does not mean I have a problem with the men who serve. In any other circumstances, I would happily see Charles take up the mantle. I only wish to see him safe from war."

Thomas chortled. "There is unrest, but this is nothing new. We are not at war, Mrs. Russell."

"Not yet."

Thomas shook his head. "There's no reason to believe that shall change. You can't worry everyday about what *might* happen."

"But in this case it's true," she argued. "You don't know what's coming."

"Nor do you."

She wanted to argue that she did, but that would lead down a road she was not prepared to take. Ellie remained quiet instead.

"You can't stop living because you're afraid of what might happen," Thomas scolded while giving her a pointed look.

Ellie suddenly thought they were no longer talking about war or Charles or the future. This was a jab at her and what he perceived as her reason for not marrying him all those years ago. Maybe he was right. She had been afraid. There was more to it than that, but underneath all of her other reasons for not marrying him, she had been afraid. Of course, she would not admit that anytime soon.

"Well, I won't be your problem much longer," Ellie said. "I heard back from the Armstrongs. They're going to return home this fall. I let them know I was leaving as soon as Lucy has the baby. Once I'm gone, you won't have to worry about what I am or am not afraid of."

Thomas sat up in his chair, leaning forward with his elbows on his knees. "You're really going then?"

Ellie could not decipher the look on his face. It was not the relief she expected to see there, but she was not sure what it was. She nodded.

"I'm really going. I need to get to Boston to help Lydia with the inn and make sure Harris is doing well. Tabitha is anxious to be closer to her brother again."

Thomas nodded slowly while looking down. She had told them about the inn when she returned from her impromptu trip. Her excitement had been difficult to watch. He was happy for her, but could not imagine her once again not being part of his life anymore. It had been difficult having her there, but would it be more difficult not seeing her ever again?

"Ellie, you were never a problem," he said softly.

Ellie did not believe him for an instant. She searched Thomas's face, trying to understand what he was trying to tell her. When she did not answer, he continued, "Lucy and the kids have loved having you here. Would you not consider staying?"

"Lucy and the kids? Are they the only ones?" Ellie surprised herself by voicing the question aloud. It came out before she could think better of it. Before he could answer, she shook her head as if to clear the words away. "I'm sorry. I should not have asked that. I must go. I can't stay here. History awaits no man. Boston is calling me, and I'm answering the call."

"Am I the reason you're leaving once again?"

Ellie's heart was breaking all over again. How had she managed to cause this man so much pain merely by existing? Being near him seemed to only cause him pain, yet now the thought of her leaving made him look as though someone just told him his dog died. Ellie wanted to go to him and pull him into her arms to give him comfort. She wanted to tell him that she would give him the world if she could. Instead, she stayed where she was, sitting on the settee across from him, unsure what to say to him.

"Thomas, I—"

Before she could continue, he interrupted her, afraid of what her answer to his question might be. "I do wish you would have talked to me at the fort. Why have you only now begun sharing more of yourself with everyone else when you would not do so with me all those years ago? I know you still have your secrets, but you've spoken more of yourself in these last years than you ever used to."

"I couldn't," Ellie said with a shake of her head. Unable to look at him, she looked down as she mindlessly played with one of Charles's toys. "I've been broken for a really long time. When I was at the fort, I was unable to give anything of myself. It was never about you. I'm still learning how to do so but I am truly sorry that you got caught up in my strife." Ellie forced herself to look at him. "I honestly never meant to hurt you. I genuinely thought you'd be better off without me in your life."

"Yet you came back."

The corner of Ellie's mouth lifted in a sardonic smirk. "Purely by accident. Had I known you were here, I would not have come," she said in an attempt to use humor to soften the truth. "I considered going to Virginia but thought you'd have gone back there and immediately ruled it out."

To Ellie's delight, Thomas did not scowl at her or take her meaning to be an insult. A sad smile of understanding broke across his face as he nodded.

"I doubt you not."

"I promise you're not the reason I'm leaving," she lied.

He was, but not in the way he thought. Hoping that with time, they could resume their friendship, she had once thought staying was a good thing. She saw now that was not meant to be and knew they would never again be friends as they once had been. That thought alone killed her. More than that, she could not stand to see the pain she caused him simply by being there. They spent more of their time arguing than anything else. Ellie was not an argumentative person, and the constant turmoil added to already frayed emotions that she had been trying so hard to smooth and she needed some distance.

## Chapter 47

*May 1772*

"What do you think of this one?" Adelaide asked as she modeled the hat for Lucy and Ellie. It was a wide-brimmed straw hat like most of the others they looked at, but this one had black and white ribbons around the thin crown with a long trail of black ribbon down the back.

"I like it," replied Ellie. "Very pretty."

Adelaide looked at herself in the mirror, unsure. Not trusting Ellie's opinion, she turned to Lucy to see that the woman looked pale.

"Mrs. Burke, are you quite well?"

Ellie's head snapped over to Lucy in time to see her legs give out from under her. The shop they were in was quite small, so Ellie was within reaching distance and grabbed Lucy by the arm, trying to hold her up, or at least keep her from hitting the ground hard. Adelaide was immediately on her other side, grabbing her other arm.

Ellie checked her pulse and felt her forehead for her temperature. Her pulse was a little fast, but she did not seem to be running a fever. She asked the shopkeeper for a juice, who happily obliged. Lucy sat in a chair and drank it until she was able to stand again. Unsteady on her feet, the women helped her out of the shop and down the street. Along the way, Lucy doubled over, screaming in pain as a contraction hit her. Ellie immediately pulled out her pocket watch and began timing it.

Ellie had worried about allowing Lucy to go shopping as far along as she was, but she still had about three weeks to go, so she thought the woman would be fine. To be safe, she had decided to accompany her, glad now that she did. As they walked slowly down the street, Lucy had several more contractions, each getting closer together. The baby was coming. Fast.

Ellie turned back to Jenny who had been following them. "Go fetch Major Burke and let him know it's time."

Jenny gave a slight nod and ran off down the street toward Fort George. The women continued down Queen Street but had to keep stopping. At this rate, Lucy was going to give birth on the street. A few houses away from Ellie's, she made a decision.

"We're not going to make it back to your place, Mrs. Burke. We'll stop at my house."

Lucy nodded at her while taking deep breaths. Adelaide began to argue but saw that Ellie was right. Even if they went all the way back to the Burke residence, Ellie would need her birthing kit which was at her house.

The second they made it into the front door, Ellie shouted for Tabitha and Hannah. She instructed them both on what she needed, and the women went their separate directions to begin their tasks. As Ellie's apprentice, Tabitha would assist with the birth. Ellie was grateful to have the assistance, even if she had only limited experience.

Getting Lucy into the house had been difficult but getting her up the stairs was even harder. They took their time and supported her the whole way, finally making it to the top after stopping on each step. Ellie guided them down the hall into a spare room that was not in use. Ezra had come in after hearing all the commotion and Ellie sent him to intercept Thomas and Jenny and let them know they were there instead of at his house.

Adelaide and Hannah began stripping Lucy down to her shift while Tabitha and Ellie started prepping the room, laying down the waterproof drop cloths. One was placed on the bed and another on the floor. They all worked hurriedly as Lucy's contractions were getting closer and closer together.

They managed to get Lucy undressed, but as they guided her to the bed, her water broke. Immediately after the flood of water came a gush of bright red blood. Everyone immediately stopped and stared at the sticky mess on the floor, concern spreading across every face in the room. They helped the now crying Lucy onto the bed.

Ellie's normal anxiety during deliveries skyrocketed after seeing the mass of blood, but she took a deep breath and put on her most calming demeanor. She may have been panicking inside, but it would not do for Lucy and the other women to see it.

With Lucy on the bed, Ellie leaned in for an examination. She felt her stomach and was happy to see the baby was in the correct position. When she lifted her shift to check Lucy's cervix, she was no longer so optimistic. She was already dilated to about a four, but there was so much blood, it was difficult to see anything. It did not look as though the bleeding was ready to stop anytime soon. Ellie tried wiping it away, but it kept coming.

"What's happening?" Lucy asked in a panic. "Why is there so much blood?"

"I'm trying to see that now," Ellie said.

There were several possibilities, none of which were good. Her most pressing concern at the moment was getting the bleeding to stop. If she could not stop it soon, Lucy would be in trouble. While she worked, Lucy continued to dilate. It was moving so fast, Ellie was certain the baby would be there in minutes.

Adelaide stood by Lucy, wiping the sweat from her face and holding her hand. She looked down at Ellie often, trying to see for herself what was going on.

"Are you quite certain you know what you're doing?" she asked Ellie. "Perhaps we should send for Mrs. Erwin."

Ellie looked up long enough to scowl at Adelaide. "There's nothing Mrs. Erwin would be able to do that I'm not already doing."

"How can you be so certain. You're still so young, she has far more experience than you do."

"Damn it, Adelaide. I have plenty of experience. More than Mrs. Erwin could ever hope to imagine. Now shut up and let me do my job."

The woman huffed, but she did not say anything more to Ellie.

Tabitha was by Ellie's side the entire time and Ellie was giving her instructions as best she could while she worked. Keeping her voice low, she did not tell Tabitha everything. She hated limiting the girl's education like that, but it was best if Lucy did not hear her doubts.

With Lucy dilated to a seven, Ellie was able to clear away enough of the blood to finally see the obstruction. Instead of seeing the baby's head, she saw only a deep red tissue. Tears filled her eyes at the implication and she tried her hardest to bite them back. If she only had an ultrasound and modern equipment, Lucy and the baby could both come out of this easily.

They heard a commotion downstairs and with the booming voice, they all knew that Thomas had arrived. Ellie felt an unexpected relief at his presence. Initially, she had thought it was merely the comfort that his presence typically brought her, until he started being disagreeable anyways, but her brain kicked in and she knew it was more than that. Excusing herself to go talk to him, she left instructions with Tabitha to prep her instruments and to not let Lucy push in her absence.

Thomas watched as Ellie ran down the stairs, wiping away tears as she approached him. These were not the same tears that she had shed after delivering Caitlyn. Judging by Lucy's screams upstairs, the baby had not yet been delivered, so why was Ellie taking the time now to come talk to him instead of tending to his wife?

"Thomas," Ellie began while shaking her head.

"No, Mrs. Russell. Whatever you're about to tell me, don't say it. Just go back upstairs and help Lucy."

Ellie stared at him, not sure how to tell him what she needed to say. He had been even more distant these last few months than ever before. She did not relish having this conversation with him now. Gathering herself, she spat it out.

"I need you. There's a complication."

Thomas shook his head, looking up the stairs towards the sounds coming from his wife. "Men don't go into the birthing chamber."

"You know I don't give a rat's ass about any of that stuff. Lucy's got placenta previa. She can't deliver vaginally."

Thomas looked at her blankly. She had no idea when the terminology came into use or if he would have heard of the condition even if it had been in use. As a male who did not do midwifery, it was entirely possible that he knew nothing about it.

"The placenta is located low in the uterus, completely blocking the cervix. As she dilates, the blood vessels connecting the placenta to the uterus are tearing."

"What are you saying, Ellie?" he asked quietly.

"I need to do a C-section." When he did not respond, she added, "Thomas, I can't do it by myself. I need your help."

"A C-section will kill her. Women don't survive those," he said in a shaky voice as the color drained from his face.

"No," she said urgently. "Women can survive them, but we need to do it quickly. She's been dilating extremely fast and if we don't get up there soon, she's going to try to deliver vaginally, which she won't survive."

Ellie inflected as much confidence in her voice as she could muster. She had only ever watched C-sections done during her clinical trainings and was not qualified to do them. However, it was the only option. If she did nothing, they would absolutely lose both Lucy and the baby.

"I no longer practice medicine. I've not done so in years."

"That doesn't matter. You're brilliant. I can guide you through it."

"Then you can guide Tabitha through it." Thomas knew she was training the girl to be a midwife and if anyone needed the instruction, it was her. Surely she could not expect him to cut into his wife?

"Tabitha doesn't have the medical foundation you do. Please, Thomas. I would not ask this of you if it was not absolutely necessary."

Finally, Thomas nodded quietly, gathered every ounce of strength he had, and followed her up the stairs.

Hannah had a wash basin set up and Ellie rewashed her hands while Thomas went over to sit by Lucy. With one look at her, Thomas knew they were too late. Lucy was dying. She had already lost far too much blood. He laid down next to her, stroking her head and kissing her pale face. He could not bear to see her this way. He bit back the tears that threatened to form, not wanting to scare Lucy any more than she already was. She tried to talk but was too weak to do so.

"Shh," he whispered, his mouth against her forehead. "All will be well, sweetheart. We're going to take care of you."

Thomas stayed by her side a moment longer, telling her he loved her and reassuring her that they would take care of everything. He finally gathered his resolve and went over to the wash basin, scrubbing his hands while he transformed from the concerned husband into the surgeon he once was. If he could not save his wife, he could at least save his child.

"Lucy," he heard Ellie say. "We need to take the baby from your stomach. We'll have to cut into you to get to it."

Lucy was no longer pushing or screaming, not having the energy for either. Instead, she was moaning in pain and could barely hear what Ellie was saying.

Ellie had instructed Tabitha to scrub in and now the three of them prepared to cut Lucy open. While fighting to control the shakiness she felt, Ellie made an incision in her friend's abdomen. While Ellie focused on the C-section, Thomas focused on Lucy. Tabitha and Thomas assisted wherever they were needed, the three of them working quickly and effectively together as a team, as if they had practiced this many times before.

Shortly after cutting into her, Lucy slipped away. Thomas had kept an eye on Lucy while he assisted Ellie who worked to deliver the baby. She had been so preoccupied with her task, she had not noticed Lucy passing, having left her under Thomas's care.

"How's mom doing?" Ellie asked Thomas while she focused on what was immediately in front of her.

"She's well," he said in as calm a voice as he could muster.

Ellie nodded and continued working. He caught Adelaide's eye and when she opened her mouth to protest, he shook his head.

When they got the baby free, Ellie handed her over to Tabitha who took her to clear her airway and clean her up. She and Thomas remained, and Ellie began to close Lucy up.

Thomas watched as Ellie unnecessarily stitched his wife's uterus closed. He let her place the first three stitches before he put his hand over hers, stopping her from continuing. She looked up at him and he shook his head. Her eyes got big, and she finally turned to look at Lucy.

"No!" she screamed.

Ellie moved up on the bed and began to do chest compressions on Lucy. The woman was gone, but she could not just give up. She had to do something. Adelaide watched in horror but did not say anything or try to stop her. Instead, she looked expectantly at Thomas to do so. He understood what Ellie was doing and knew she needed to try. He let her do CPR for a few minutes, assisting her where he could, without putting any real effort behind it. He knew it was far too late. After Ellie showed no sign of stopping, he finally came around the other side of the bed and put his arms around her from behind, pulling her away from the bed.

Ellie fought to get away from Thomas. "No! I have to help her," she cried. "I promised I would take care of her. I told her she'd be okay."

Tears rolled down her cheeks and Thomas continued to hold her from behind, putting his forehead to the back of her head.

"She's gone," he whispered. "There's nothing more you can do for her."

Finally letting go, Ellie doubled over in grief. Thomas gently lowered her to the ground and her knees folded underneath her as she sat on the floor. He kept his arms around her while she sat there and cried. It only took Ellie a minute to realize she was being selfish. This was Thomas's wife. Instead of grieving his own loss, he was comforting her. She immediately collected herself and pulled free from his embrace. With a hand on the bed, she pulled herself up, wiping the tears from her eyes and returned to working on Lucy. It was not necessary to stitch her up now, but Ellie did not want to leave her like that. She did not stitch her as closely as she would have had the woman still been alive, but she pulled the skin of her abdomen together and closed her up. Thomas stood behind her and paused for a moment to watch her, then moved to the bed and curled up beside his wife. They each pretended the other was not there and Adelaide went to assist Tabitha with the new baby girl.

## Chapter 48

*May 1772*

"I'm so sorry, Thomas."

Ellie found him in the parlor downstairs while the women worked to clean Lucy's body and the surrounding room. She did not even try to stop her tears from falling. What could she have done differently? Did she try hard enough? If only she could have done a blood transfusion. If she had done the C-section immediately when they got back to the house, could she have prevented the death? Ellie was wracked with questions. Not knowing only served to increase her guilt over not being able to save Lucy. But having to face Thomas fueled the guilt even more. It did not matter. She deserved the guilt. She should have worked harder to save Lucy.

Thomas kept his back to her and continued staring out the window. There was nothing he could say.

Trying to understand, Ellie went over everything again and again. When replaying the labor and delivery was not enough, she replayed Lucy's entire pregnancy, looking for any indication she may have missed. Ellie remembered Lucy's previous admission that she found sex to be uncomfortable. At the time, Ellie had thought she meant it to be psychologically uncomfortable, not physically uncomfortable. Now she was not so certain.

"Did she ever have pain or bleeding during intercourse?" she asked while coming deeper into the room.

Thomas finally turned to look at her. He stared at her as if she had just grown another head. "I'll not discuss my marriage bed with you."

"Damn it, do you really think I want to hear about it? I'm not asking because of some morbid curiosity. I'm trying to understand what happened. I need you to tell me."

"I thought you already knew what happened. Did you not tell me the placenta was blocking the cervix?"

"Yeah, no. It was. I know it was placenta previa, but I didn't know that's what it was until she dilated enough for me to see the placenta. By then, it was too late. She'd already lost too much blood. What if I'd known before? Maybe I could have saved her. I could have done the C-section sooner, before she lost that much blood. Please, Thomas. I need to understand what happened."

He stared at her for another moment. When he saw the look in her eye, he reluctantly admitted, "She never said anything, though I oft wondered if I was causing her pain. When I asked, she always said she was well."

"Of course she did. Women aren't supposed to talk about that stuff. They're taught to just suck it up and do it anyways." Ellie could not keep the bitterness from her voice as she flopped down on the settee, rubbing her hands over her face as she tilted her head back. She was pissed at the needless suffering Lucy had inflicted upon herself. If she had said something, maybe Ellie could have done something to help. Logically, she knew that was not likely, but she needed somewhere to direct her anger.

"And does having that information help you? Does it change what you would have done?"

"I don't know." Ellie was quiet while she considered it. When that did not help, she talked through it. "Placenta previa usually occurs in women a little older than her or in those who've given birth several times already, but if she had uterine fibroids, it could account for both the placenta previa and pain during sex."

"What are fibroids?" he asked, watching her work through her puzzle, grateful for anything else on which to direct his attention.

"They're growths in the wall or lining of the uterus."

He nodded. "Could you have prevented this had you known she had these fibroids?"

Ellie shook her head, letting out a sigh. "I don't know. I'm not sure I would've made the connection. It's uncommon. Women give birth with fibroids all the time with no complications. Without an ultrasound, there was just no way to know the placenta was in the wrong place."

"An ultrasound?"

"Never mind," she said, shaking her head.

Robert came barreling through the door at that moment. He headed directly for the stairs, then stopped when he passed the parlor and saw Ellie and Thomas inside.

"How's the babe? Is it a boy?" he asked with a grin.

As Robert looked between the faces of the people before him, he instantly knew the worst had happened. "No. The babe?"

"The baby is fine. It's a girl," Ellie said somberly.

"Then what–Lucy?" Robert's face went ashen, and he began shaking his head in disbelief.

"I couldn't save her," Ellie whispered as the tears threatened to fall again. She took a deep breath, fighting them back. If she started crying, she would not stop.

"No!" Robert paced while fighting tears of his own. He came to a stop and looked at Thomas with sorrow. He clapped Thomas on the shoulder. "I'm so sorry, my friend."

Thomas nodded.

Adelaide came down to let them know that they were finished with Lucy upstairs and that they needed to decide on a plan. With Adelaide having a baby of her own, she had fed the newborn, who was now sleeping. But there was still much to do. They needed to make arrangements for burial and figure out the best plan of action to keep the baby fed and all of the children cared for.

Thomas left the room with Adelaide and Robert spun on Ellie. "Could you not bring her back, Miss Ellie?"

Ellie jerked back in surprise and stared at Robert, her forehead drawn in confusion. "She's gone, Rob. I can't bring her back from the dead."

"Can you not? Or will you not?"

"I can't. I did everything I could for her."

Robert stepped closer to Ellie, towering over her. "Did you? You still harbor feelings for Thomas. Would you do it for his sake? Or is that *why* you let her die?"

Ellie reached out and slapped Robert before she even thought about it. She was seething. "How dare you? You weren't there and you know nothing of medicine. I did what I could."

"I may know nothing of medicine, but I know you survived death once before. You've been sent from beyond, Miss Ellie. You could bring her back if you wished to do so."

Closing her eyes, Ellie shook her head, trying to gather strength. "I told you I'm not a fucking angel, Robert. I'm not what you think I am, and I certainly don't have any powers beyond what you have yourself. If you think it's possible, why don't you go raise Lucy from the dead?"

Ellie stormed out at that, unable to be around people any longer. Having reached her breaking point, she did not want anyone around when it happened. She had already been feeling guilty enough before Robert's words, but now, the guilt ate at her very core. If even he could see that she was responsible, maybe she was not wrong to feel that way.

## Chapter 49

*May 1772*

"Y ou must be pleased," Adelaide said coldly when Ellie arrived at the Burke residence.

"Excuse me?" Ellie exclaimed, stopping inside the door to stare at the woman.

Adelaide grabbed her by the arm and pulled her further into the house and closed the door. "With Lucy out of the way, you shall finally have what you've always wanted."

"I'm going to pretend you did not just say that." Ellie pulled her arm free and resumed heading upstairs to the bedroom where Lucy's body now lay. It had been two days since she had died, and Thomas and Robert had taken her home after the birth. Adelaide and the other women in Lucy's church had prepared her funeral clothing. The women were gathering together today to clean and dress Lucy's body for burial.

"When will you marry?" Adelaide called after her as they ascended the stairs.

Ellie looked around, though she knew Jenny and Mrs. Toole were the only other people in the house. Thomas had taken the children and gone to stay with Adelaide until after the funeral. He needed her help with the children, particularly the new baby whom Adelaide was nursing along with her own baby.

Ellie stopped and turned back to look at Adelaide. "Excuse me? Marry who? I'm not planning on marrying anyone."

"Is it not what you've always wanted; why you changed your plans to move to Boston after your first winter here? With Lucy out of the way, my brother is now free to wed another."

Ellie could not believe this woman. At least it explained why she had always hated Ellie. The woman thought she had been there to steal Thomas away from Lucy this whole time.

"Adelaide, I had my chance to marry your brother. If it was what I always wanted, I would've accepted his proposal fourteen years ago."

Adelaide's eyes opened wide in surprise.

"You didn't know he proposed?" Ellie asked.

"I knew," she replied. "I knew not that you refused him. I thought you were not together because you were taken by the savages before you could wed."

Ellie cringed at the derogatory term the woman continued to use.

"You couldn't be more wrong," Ellie spat. She really did not want to share anything this personal with this woman, but she knew Adelaide was not finished. "I turned him down because I knew I couldn't make him happy. He deserved more than I could give him. When the Onöndowa'ga:' came along, they didn't take me captive. I went with them of my own accord. They were trying to take Thomas, and I gladly traded my life for his. I didn't believe he would've survived the ordeal."

The other woman turned away for a moment, looking down the stairs behind them. They had made it to the top of the stairs but had not gone further.

"I knew not," she said quietly.

"Why would you? It's no one else's business."

After a moment, Adelaide held her head up and said, "Yes, well, that merely proves my point that you are the best person to step into Lucy's role and become Thomas's next wife."

The laugh that escaped Ellie was bitter. "What makes you think that's what either of us even wants?"

"One would have to be blind not to see it."

Ellie shook her head in disbelief, playing with her necklace. "It doesn't matter what anyone else thinks they see." She threw her hands up in the air in exasperation. "Jesus, Adelaide, your friend isn't even cold and in the ground yet, and you're trying to marry off her husband. What is wrong with you?"

It was not uncommon for people in that era to remarry within less than a year after losing a spouse, particularly if there were children involved. However, this was ridiculous. It had been two days! Ellie could not believe Adelaide's gall. To make matters worse, they were discussing this with Lucy's body only feet away down the hall. Ellie closed her eyes in an attempt to collect herself.

"Nothing is wrong with me at all. I'm thinking of what's best. Thomas is in no condition to do so, but he needs a wife, and his children need a mother. Like it or not, you're the best option."

"Oh, great. *Your friend just died at your hand. Congratulations, you now get to raise her children with her husband who hates you.*" Ellie said sarcastically. "Yeah. That sounds like just the life I want. Sign me up." Ellie turned to go down the hallway to where she knew Lucy would be waiting.

"You may pretend all you like. Thomas most certainly does not hate you. And I know you care for both him and his children. If you truly have their best interests at heart, you shall marry him."

Ellie spun on the woman. "I'll not be goaded into marrying anyone, Adelaide. And I'll not be a rebound. I know people here remarry immediately after the death of a spouse, but Thomas needs time to grieve. Once he is in a position to open his heart again, he'll be perfectly capable of finding a woman of his own choosing. He doesn't need you meddling in his affairs, trapping him with someone for whom he doesn't care."

"You're wrong," she said. "I only hope you'll come to see it in time to do what's best."

Ellie was spared having to respond by a knock at the door. The other women had arrived. Jenny answered the door to let them in and they all headed upstairs to join Ellie and Adelaide. The women proceeded to prepare Lucy's body in near silence.

They spoke very little, for which Ellie was grateful. Tears streamed down her face as they worked. Ellie had handled more dead bodies than she could count, but this one hit hard. She could not help but feel responsible for Lucy's death. While washing her, Ellie replayed the birth in her mind for the thousandth time, reviewing every minute in an attempt to figure out what she could have done differently. If only she had done a C-section to begin with. She should have done a more thorough digital examination. Maybe she could have felt the placenta and realized what had happened. There would never be a time in which Ellie did not blame herself for Lucy's death.

Once Lucy's body was finished, the women spent the rest of the day preparing the house while Mrs. Toole worked on food for the mourners who would come the following day. They wrapped all of the paintings and mirrors in the house in black. A table on which the coffin would rest was draped in black cloth with black crepe strung from it. The window shutters were shut and held closed with black ribbon. The house would remain draped for the next year. Ellie marveled at the thought that Adelaide could even consider her proposal when even the house would still be in a state of mourning for the next twelve months.

***

The preparations continued into the next afternoon. The cabinetmaker brought a coffin in which Lucy's body was placed and carried down the stairs by Thomas, Robert, and the other pall bearers Thomas had arranged. Food was finished and set out along with some drinks and everyone prepared for the arrival of guests. Lucy had been active in the church and the neighborhood and had made many friends over the years. There would be a large gathering of people inside the parlor.

"Mrs. Russell, a word?" Thomas asked as Ellie was carrying some last-minute dishes into the parlor. Setting them down, she followed him up the stairs into the drawing room with no idea what he could possibly want with her. As she entered the room, she saw they were the only people there. Had Adelaide been talking to him as well? Ellie was suddenly nervous.

Standing there wringing her hands in front of her, Thomas stood with his back to her, staring into the cold fireplace. He leaned against the mantel and Ellie wished she could offer him some amount of comfort but knew there was nothing she could do. She waited as patiently as she could, then he finally turned around.

Thomas moved to a small box on the table and opened it, pulling something out of it. As he walked closer, Ellie could see a pair of white gloves in his hands. He held them out to her and she looked at him questioningly.

"They're mourning gloves," he said in explanation. "Have you not come across this in all your years?"

Ellie shook her head as he pushed them forward to her. She took them slowly, still unsure what she was supposed to do.

"Am I to wear them then?"

Thomas chuckled hollowly. Even his laughter sounded tired and now that he was standing closer, Ellie could see the dark rings under his eyes. She doubted he was sleeping.

"If you wish," he replied. "They are to commemorate Lucy's life. As is this." Thomas pulled out a ring from his pocket and held it in his open hand. Ellie looked at him, then back at the ring and picked it up to examine it more closely. It was silver with a skull on it. The engraving read 'Death Conquers All.'

"It's beautiful," Ellie said as she tried to hand it back to him.

Thomas shook his head. "Those are yours. Her closest friends and family shall all receive their own. Keep them and remember Lucy."

A tear escaped Ellie's eye, but she quickly wiped it away. The last thing Thomas needed was her guilt and sorrow on top of his own grief.

"Thank you, Thomas," Ellie said, her throat thick.

Thomas nodded and Ellie quickly left before she could break down.

The guests arrived in the evening, viewed the body, left notes for Lucy on the table beside the coffin, then had some food or drink before making their way back outside to make room for new mourners. They chatted outside but inside was quiet. Ellie did what she could to help, trying to stay busy. Adelaide and Robert stood by Thomas's side in support as he met with guest after guest.

"How do you fare?" Robert asked, taking a break from the throngs of people.

"I'm alright," Ellie replied, setting down the dirty dishes she was about to take to the kitchen.

Robert looked at the plates she was setting down, then back at her. "There are people to take care of that."

Ellie looked down at the plates as well. "I know," she said on an exhale. "But I need to stay busy, and I want to help."

"You're helping by being here. You need let the servants take care of these matters."

Ellie put a hand on her hip and looked up at Robert, then nodded in Thomas's direction. "Go help

Thomas. He looks as though that woman is going to talk his ear off."

Robert turned to look, then groaned. He grabbed Ellie's wrists and pulled her with him towards Thomas and Adelaide. Interjecting themselves into the conversation, Robert redirected it and the woman moved on, leaving them momentarily without guests to greet. Thomas thanked Robert for his assistance, then turned to Ellie.

"We have servants, Mrs. Russell. They shall take care of the dishes."

"I only wish to help, Major Burke."

"I believe we've had this discussion before. I'll not have it again."

Before Ellie could respond, more people approached. Ellie stayed there for a little while but felt distinctly out of place. She was not family and had no right to be standing in a receiving line. As the line filled once again, she slipped away and resumed her previous activities, trying to stay out of sight of the line.

After the guests had all gone through the receiving line, the procession began as they moved Lucy's body to Saint Paul's Chapel under a darkening sky and the peal of the church bells. Ellie followed behind, staying close to Charles. He had tried to stay with her at the house but was required to be in the receiving line between his father and Adelaide. Now, Thomas was a pallbearer and Adelaide had her hands full with the other children. Jack assisted the men in carrying the coffin, leaving the women to help tend the children. Ellie carried the three-year-old Caitlyn while holding Charles's hand. Anne carried the baby and helped with Adelaide's children.

The walk to the church was long and tiresome. At nearly a mile to the church, the pallbearers had to stop and rest halfway there. Ellie took advantage of the respite as well, not eager to go to Saint Paul's. It was the last place she wanted to be. She had not been back since she went with Robert for the service and was not eager for a repeat of the emotional onslaught the building had stirred in her. Under the circumstances, Ellie knew it would only be worse today. It was going to take everything in her to remain collected and in control. She took a few calming breaths before the procession started up again.

Finally, they made it to the graveyard beside the chapel. The reverend spoke of Lucy's many good deeds, then talked of the afterlife where she would be awaiting her loved ones. To Ellie's relief, he kept his words relatively short, and the funeral was soon over. Guests slowly dispersed as the sky grew ever darker. Ellie stood by her friend's gravesite for a time, never letting go of Charles's hand. Much like his father, he had not cried while they laid his mother to rest. The tight grip with which he clutched Ellie's hand was his only giveaway as to how much he was hurting.

With the other guests gone, Ellie finally knelt down, pulling Charles into her arms. He buried his face in her neck and clung to her as he finally cried. She rubbed his back while he let his grief wash over him. Thomas watched the scene and wished he was in his son's place. He allowed it to continue until Charles was all cried out, then gathered himself up and went to retrieve his son.

They all walked back toward the house together where Robert left Thomas and the children to escort

Ellie home, then returned to help Thomas settle back in at home to start the new life that lay before him.

*June 1772*

As Ellie packed up her few belongings in her bedroom, there was a knock at the door. She heard Hannah downstairs answering it, then the footsteps on the stairs. When she walked into the hallway, she was surprised to see Thomas standing there at the top of the stairway. He looked as though he was just as surprised. She invited him into the drawing room, and he looked around nervously before sitting down on the edge of the settee. Ellie nodded to Hannah who was on her way to church with her brother. Tabitha had already left to accompany the Mawbys to church, leaving Ellie alone in the house with Thomas. Hannah hesitated at the top of the stairs, but Ellie brushed her away, letting her know they would be fine.

As Ellie came into the room, Thomas lifted a sheet of canvas that he had brought with him and handed it to her.

"Lucy wished for you to have this. She was planning on giving it to you to show her appreciation for helping with the birth."

Ellie took the beautiful painting he held out and looked at it closely, admiring the artistry. She recognized the image immediately. It was a view from Whitehall of the rivers and Brooklyn beyond. She gasped, covering her mouth as tears sprang to her eyes. She was not even aware of sitting on the settee beside Thomas while she studied the painting.

"Thank you. It's beautiful. How did she know?"

"After we discussed it being your favorite spot at dinner, she wanted to know where it was." When Ellie only nodded, he continued, "Though I never could understand why. What was so special about that place, Miss Ellie? It's not the type of environment for which you usually care."

"It was never about what was beside me. It was always about the view."

"There are plenty of views around the island even more spectacular than that one," he argued.

Ellie shrugged. "I can't explain it to you. I wish I could, but I just can't."

Thomas nodded and an awkward silence fell over them. Suddenly remembering her manners, Ellie stood. "Can I get you some tea?" she asked. She needed something with which to busy herself.

She set the painting down on a table, but before she could leave to get the tea service, Thomas burst out, "How do you do it, Miss Ellie? How do you go through life being so unaffected?"

"Unaffected?" she asked, unsure what he was talking about.

"Nothing ever causes you concern or unease," he replied. "You walk away from me as though I matter not for anything. You disappear for ten years, allowing me to think you dead. Then you show up here and befriend my wife and my children. You court my best friend, then walk away from him as well. You even watch your friend die. All without a care. How do you do it?"

Ellie was stunned into silence. He could not be more wrong, but she deserved his anger. She would let him unload it on her and she would take it all. It was her penance for killing his wife. He deserved everything good, and she would hold all the bad for him. If he wanted to think she was cold and emotionless, she would let him. Not responding, she simply stood there waiting for him to unload more.

"I wish to understand," he continued. "I want not to feel anything anymore. Tell me how you do it. Tell me how you go through life feeling nothing. You make everyone love you and you simply walk away. You're completely unaffected. How is it you care so little?"

Thomas was studying her face. What Ellie saw there was not anger. It was hurt and anguish and despair. Not blaming her or accusing her of anything, he genuinely wanted to know.

"Oh Thomas, you have no idea how wrong you are. Just because I don't share my feelings, it doesn't mean I don't have them," she replied softly. "Instead, I choose to ignore them. I've had a lifetime with which to bury them down deep. You, my friend, are cursed with strong emotions. It's not entirely a bad thing. Sometimes I wish I could feel as deeply as you do."

Thomas continued studying her for a moment more, then turned away and broke down. His head was in his hands, but Ellie could see and hear the quiet sobs wracking his body. She immediately went to him, her heart breaking yet again. Standing in front of him, she wrapped her arms around him, pulling him into her. As she had done with Charles only days ago, she stroked his back and ran her hand over his hair, kissing the top of his head. She would give anything to take away his pain. She would carry it for him if she could. In that moment, she knew she had been fooling herself in thinking that they were nothing more than acquaintances with mutual friends these last four years. She was in love with him and always would be.

It had taken years to get over Thomas, but she had done so during her time with the Onöndowa'ga:'. Though she never stopped loving him, that love had changed. She had moved on, accepting the fact that they were not meant to be together. Since her arrival in New York City, she had told herself that she only cared for him as a friend; that while she still loved him, she was no longer in love with him. It was merely the constant reminder of her situation that had made being around him all the time so difficult. Now, she found that not only was she still in love with the man he used to be, she had somehow managed to fall in love with him all over again, despite the best efforts of them both to hate one another these last few years.

Unlike Dean, the only thing Thomas had ever expected from her was honesty. A true man of the Age of Enlightenment, he was driven by intellectual pursuits; always curious, open to new ideas, and eager to learn new things. Despite the years apart, this had not changed and it drew her in, even now.

Ellie cradled him until he had nothing more to release.

He sat up tall then and looked at her, studying her face. Thomas saw no judgment or pity there as he would have expected from any other woman. He would not get that from her, which was why he came to her in the first place. All he saw was her own sorrow and something else. He saw affection. He had felt like he was drowning again, and when he saw the affection in her eyes, something came over him. He leaned in and kissed her like he had wanted to do since she showed up in his parlor alive nearly four years ago. His kiss was urgent, desperate. He clung to her with everything he had. When she answered in kind, he stood, hauling her with him, never pulling his mouth from hers. Lifting her into his arms without a thought, she wrapped her legs around his waist and he carried her down the hallway, following her directions to her bedroom.

Thomas barely managed to make it into the room and close the door. Instead of moving forward to the bed, he leaned her against the wall beside the door, her legs still around his waist, and proceeded to unfasten her bodice hurriedly and lift her skirts. As eager as he, she helped him as much as she could, both with her own clothes as well as his. They did not get very far, leaving most of their clothes on as they came together, her back against the wall, him supporting her weight.

In that moment, Ellie was more grateful than ever that underwear was non-existent in that era. Though, she was certain that if it had been, hers would have simply melted off from the heat between her and Thomas.

Sliding into Ellie felt like coming home. Thomas closed his eyes and paused for a moment to collect himself so he did not spill his seed instantly. His forehead to hers, his mouth hovered over hers, mere centimeters apart as their breaths mingled and he slowly started to move, building up to meet the need he felt to consume this woman who had been so close yet so far away these last years.

Their coupling was urgent, frenzied, a release from everything over the previous years. It felt good to be in his arms again, though Ellie knew it would only add to her guilt when it was over. At that moment, she did not care. Grateful everyone was away from the house, she took everything he had to give as he worked his years of frustration and anger out on her. Pinned between his powerful body and the wall, she gave as good as she got, and when they both climaxed, she was certain the entire city could hear their cries of pleasure and feel the earth quake beneath them.

Finally carrying her over to the bed before his legs gave out on him, Thomas held her in his arms as if he was afraid to let go for fear she would disappear. Ellie understood how he felt and was afraid to think about what came next. In that moment, she blocked out all thought of everything but the here and now and simply enjoyed the feel of Thomas's arms wrapped around her, his breath on her hair. It did not take long before she fell into a sound sleep, more peaceful than she had experienced in some time.

When she woke, Thomas was gone. She should have known; it was the exact same thing she had done to him the first time they had spent the night together. Sexual relations outside marriage were complicated in this time period. Hannah, Ezra, and Tabitha would all be home soon, and it would be extremely scandalous for him to be seen leaving her bed chamber. He also could not very well spend the night at her house. Not only did he have responsibilities at home, but it would not be proper for him to be seen leaving there in the early hours of the morning. Propriety aside, she knew he still hated her. This was nothing more than a release for him. Ellie understood, even if it did hurt.

*June 1772*

Thomas made himself scarce when Ellie arrived for her French lesson with Charles, not yet ready to face her. He had told her he no longer wanted to feel anything, and it had been the truth. She was able to have sex without it meaning anything and he thought he could learn that from her. He had been wrong. Instead, their time together brought everything rushing back to him as if it were their first time together. It only served to add to his guilt. He had betrayed Lucy on more than one level. She had deserved so much more than him. Hearing Ellie's voice down the hall from his study was too much and he decided to go outside for a walk until the lesson would be finished.

As Thomas headed back to his house, Ellie came down the street towards him. Apparently he was wrong to think he had stayed out long enough. He looked around for an escape, but there was none to be had. Swearing under his breath, he gathered up his courage to face her.

"I must apologize for losing control last night," he said while avoiding looking at her. "I was not myself, and it was not my intention to take advantage of you."

Thomas's words felt like the arrow that had once pierced her heart. She knew at the time of their joining that it was nothing more than grief, and she had been okay with that, despite knowing how much it would hurt later. However, she had not been prepared to hear the coldness of his words regarding the matter.

"You didn't. There's absolutely nothing for which you need to apologize. Look, you're just feeling guilty, but you have nothing to feel guilty for. What happened between us last night was a perfectly normal reaction to a highly emotional situation. I was just a proxy, and I'm okay with that. It doesn't mean you loved her any less." Ellie was not sure if she was trying to convince him or herself. Maybe it was both.

Thomas finally looked at her, his eyes narrowed, and his mouth set in a grim line. "No, it doesn't. I did–I *do* love my wife."

"I never said you didn't," Ellie said as calmly as she could, as if trying to sooth a predator about to pounce. "I'm well aware of that fact. I'm trying to say that this doesn't change that."

Thomas went back to looking away.

"It doesn't matter anyway," Ellie sighed. "I'll be gone soon enough. Then you won't have to worry about me bothering you anymore."

As she turned to leave, Thomas finally looked at her again, this time with surprise on his face. "You still mean to leave after this?"

Her eyebrows bunched together in confusion. "Why wouldn't I?"

"I thought perchance you might have changed your mind."

"I can't stay."

Thomas nodded once and looked away. "It's probably for the best."

Ellie could feel the tears prickling the backs of her eyes and left before he could say anything else. He was grieving and now feeling guilty on top of it, but it did not ease how much his words hurt. If she had any doubts about leaving, he had just allayed them. The constant back and forth with him was far more difficult than had he remained in a constant state of anger and hatred towards her. Every time he was nice to her for even a moment, her heart perked up. But he inevitably always turned back to being angry, cutting her open. She could not do it anymore, even though she deserved his anger, more so now than ever before. Realizing she was in love with him only further complicated the situation. She needed to protect what was left of her heart. Leaving was the only thing left for her now.

***

"Will you come, mistress? It's Charles." Jenny stood at Ellie's door, slightly out of breath.

"What is it?" Ellie was immediately alarmed and went for her medical bag. "What's happened? Is he hurt? Sick?"

"No, mistress. He's inconsolable. We've tried everything. The only thing left of which I could think to do was fetch you."

Ellie stopped in her tracks. "Does Major Burke know you've called on me?"

"No, mistress," she replied hesitantly.

Letting out a deep breath, Ellie responded slowly, "I'm not sure this is a good idea. He doesn't want me there."

"Whether he does or not, Charles needs you. I shall take responsibility for calling on you."

Still hesitant, Ellie followed.

Charles's cries could be heard from outside the house.

"He's been crying for an age, mistress," Jenny told her.

Ellie went inside where Thomas was holding a screaming Charles against his chest, bouncing him gently as he paced the room. The boy was no longer as small as he once was, but with Thomas being so tall, Charles looked entirely like the child he was.

Thomas turned to see Ellie standing in the door, but before he could say anything, Charles was squirming to get away from him. The boy held out his arms to Ellie, and she came to him. Were those tears in her eyes? Thomas thought he had to be imagining it. Ellie was far too unemotional for that. He had watched her cry for Lucy, held her in his arms while she did, but her tears had dried up more quickly than he could have imagined possible and she had once again become the stoic, unfeeling woman he knew her to be. Something as simple as this surely could not be affecting her.

Despite his size, Ellie scooped Charles up with ease and sat with him on the sofa. Nearly as tall as her now, he was far too big for her to stand while holding him. He curled up into her, putting his head under her chin while she stroked his back and his hair.

"Tell me what's wrong, sweetie."

Between sobs, the boy managed to get out, "I want mother."

"I know you do, honey." Ellie kissed his forehead. "I think she probably wants you, too. I know she never wanted to leave you. She would happily have stayed with you always."

"Will you sing the rainbow song?" he asked, choking down his cries.

Ellie closed her eyes, and a tear fell down her cheek. Thomas watched as she sang to his son, providing the comfort he could not. When her voice cracked, she sang more quietly, almost on a whisper. What would he do the next time this happened, and she was not there to comfort Charles? They had formed a bond over these last years that could not be ignored. Yet, how could he ask her to stay? He had already betrayed Lucy. If Ellie stayed, he knew it would happen again. His control around her had always been tenuous at best, and he knew she would not marry him, even if he was capable of offering it. Ellie had long since put him behind her, not that she ever had any intention of staying with him to begin with. She had made that perfectly clear.

Charles's sobs slowed to sniffles. He stayed curled into Ellie, and she started into another song when she finished the first, her eyes never opening, her cheek resting on his head. She and Charles were entirely alone in the universe together as the rest of the world fell away around them. Thomas felt like an intruder but could not make himself leave, could not tear his eyes away from the sight before him. Charles eventually fell asleep, and Thomas stood to take him to his bed.

When he leaned over to pick up the boy, Ellie shook her head. In a soft whisper, she said, "He's okay here. Let me just hold him a while longer."

Nodding, Thomas sat across the room from her, needing to keep as much distance between them as he could at that moment. If he could not make himself leave, he would have to sit across from her.

"Are you quite certain you must leave?" he heard himself ask quietly.

Ellie looked up from Charles at that and nodded sadly. "I'm certain."

"He'll miss you fiercely," Thomas said, looking at his son asleep in her arms.

"I'll miss him, too," she said as the tears rolled down her cheeks.

Ellie loved Charles immensely. It broke her heart to leave him so soon after losing his mother. She desperately wanted to stay and be there for both Thomas and his children, as Adelaide had suggested. But that was not an option. Thomas did not want her there, and she needed to respect that. It was not lost on Ellie that he had said Charles would miss her; not that he would.

Even had Thomas wanted her there, Ellie needed her own time to grieve for the friend she had killed. Every time she looked at Lucy's children, she would be reminded that the woman was dead because of her. There was no choice but to leave.

"Ellie," Thomas started hesitantly, "Lucy would have understood if you stayed for the children. She knew how much you love them, and she would have wanted someone to care for them as she did in her stead."

"Is that not why you have Anne? Your children already have a governess. They don't need another one."

"That's not what I... I thought... the other night... in time, perhaps we could..."

Thomas could not seem to find the right words. He stopped for a minute to collect himself the best he could and tried again. "Not a governess. Miss Ellie, you'd make a wonderful mother. The children... the children and I would... we'd be fortunate to have you."

Ellie was confused by Thomas's words. Was he trying to say what she thought he was? Was this his idea of a proposal? Again? He was asking her to be a mother to his children? Ellie was acutely aware of the words he was not saying, yet she was still stunned. Not only by the suggestion and the fact that it was coming from Thomas who had spent the last four years hating her, but by his approach. This was not the confident, romantic poet she had come to love all those years ago. This was a cold business arrangement by someone desperate to find a suitable mother figure to care for his children.

The irony was not lost on her. When he proposed the first time, she was incapable of being what he needed. Now he was the one incapable of being what she needed. Staying would only drive the wedge further between them. She had to have misunderstood his meaning or was simply overthinking his words.

Ellie shook her head sadly. "We both need time to grieve, Thomas. I can't be a replacement for Lucy. You would only end up resenting me even more. Like you said before: it's best that I go."

Thomas could kick himself for saying that to her. He had been feeling guilty and could not handle her being nice to him. It had only added to his guilt. Taking it out on her seemed like a good idea at the time, but now he regretted it; almost as much as he had regretted the words he had just spoken. He had been at a loss and wanted to ask her to stay, to be with him, but he could not seem to find the words. Despite the truth about Lucy understanding, asking Ellie for more so soon seemed like an even bigger betrayal to his wife than he had already committed.

Even Thomas could not fault Ellie for refusing him this time. Not even certain what he was asking her or if he meant it, he felt as though he was floundering. He was on unstable ground and could not find solid footing. Why was this so difficult? Ellie seemed to sense his struggle. She stood, careful not to wake the boy in her arms. Thomas quickly stood and came over to collect him.

"I should go," she said, stroking Charles's hair one last time.

When she kissed the top of his head, Thomas once again found himself jealous of his own son. He had missed being on the receiving end of the affection Ellie showered on those she loved, knowing she was not the cold, unfeeling person he had accused her of being. It was simply a means for him to protect himself. If she had left him because she was incapable of feeling anything, then it meant it was not because she simply did not love *him*. Though she was not one for expressing her emotions, and rarely spoke of them aloud, she was generous with her affections when she felt them. It was one of the things he had always loved about her.

"Thank you for being here," he said softly.

"Anytime," Ellie said, wishing it could be true.

## Chapter 52

*June 1772*

"Why are you still leaving?" Robert asked while watching Ellie pack up the remaining items she still had in the drawing room. "I thought you still loved him."

Ellie looked down at her knitting basket. She would leave it out, so she had something to do aboard the ship on the way to Boston. Knowing who Robert was talking about, she could not admit it; not now. Days ago, she would not admit her feelings even to herself. She certainly was not about to admit them to Robert, even though he had been accusing her of it for more than a year.

"I have to go, Rob. I never did belong here; that hasn't changed."

"Everything's changed," he said vehemently. "What's stopping you from finally being together now?" He had lost her because she had still been in love with Thomas, yet now she was walking away again when they could finally be together. Robert did not understand his friends at all.

"Um. How 'bout the fact that he doesn't want me?" she replied sarcastically.

Robert scoffed. "He wants you so badly he knows not what to do with it. Is it not also what you want?"

Though Ellie did not know what she wanted, it was obviously not what Thomas wanted. She was not blind. He had his one fling with her while he was deep in his grief, but that was all it would ever be. However, there was no point in arguing it. Robert saw what he wanted to see. There would be no changing his mind.

"It doesn't matter who wants what. I can't, Rob. Not like this. We both need time to grieve. Even if he did want me, I won't be a rebound. He'd only come to resent me." She laughed, but there was no humor in it. "Even more than he already does."

"Why can you not see that he resents you not? You both care for one another. Is that not enough?"

"No. It's not. I don't believe in 'love conquers all,' Rob. It takes a lot of work, and there are some things that love just can't withstand. And I'm not strong enough to put myself through that again. I'd rather walk away, holding onto the way I feel now than try to force something that isn't reciprocated, leaving us hating each other in the end." Ellie turned away from him to grab her books that were still in the drawing room.

"You are two of the most stubborn fools I've ever had the misfortune to know. Did you not comfort him after the funeral? I know he called on you."

Surprised he knew about that, Ellie shook her head. "That was never about me. He's hurting right now and just seeking comfort in the familiar. I could have been anyone that night."

Exasperated, Robert threw his arms in the air. There would be no convincing her not to go to Boston. At least not by him.

"Are you still going to join me?" Ellie asked, pausing in her packing to see his reaction.

Robert rubbed the back of his neck. "I need to stay a while, Ell. Thomas needs someone here to help him."

Ellie felt the stab that he meant the comment to be, but she understood. "I'm glad he'll still have you and Adelaide."

Robert nodded but wanted to argue that it should be her staying. He knew there was nothing he could say to change her mind.

---

"I wanted to come say goodbye," Ellie said sheepishly to Thomas while standing in the hallway of his home. "We're leaving in the morning. I wanted to make sure I didn't miss seeing Charles before I go."

Playing with her necklace nervously, Ellie was unsure how Thomas would react or if he would even let her see his son. He certainly had no reason to. Thomas stood so stoically, she could not read him. For a moment, she did not think he would let her past the hallway. Finally stepping to the side, he gestured her toward the nursery upstairs.

Charles and Caitlyn played with their toys while the baby slept peacefully when she found them. Seeing the baby brought tears to her eyes that she fought back. This was going to be difficult enough. She did not need to lose control already.

Ellie sat down on the floor beside Charles who had pulled out a cloth bag. "What are you playing?"

"Jacks," he answered, pouring the contents onto the floor.

Smiling, Ellie played with him for a few minutes while three-year-old Caitlyn joined in.

Robert arrived then and Ellie looked up to see him standing in the doorway with Thomas, unable to keep from staring at the sight they presented. The pair had both always been exceptionally good-looking. Despite the good looks, they were not men to be trifled with. Both slightly taller than average with a menacing air when they chose to use it, they intimidated many, even occasionally, those superior to them in rank within the army. They had been her family when she had first arrived there in the past. When she lived with the Onöndowa'ga:', she had thought of them often, missing them both terribly. Though Robert would be joining her in Boston, they did not know how long it would be before he would arrive. Thomas, on the other hand, Ellie did not know when or even if she would see him again. Her throat closed at the thought, and she shut her eyes against the pain of it. Was she doing the right thing? She thought she had better get on with her goodbyes or she was going to lose her nerve and stay forever.

"Charles, I have to go away for a while," she said. Her throat was so constricted, she could barely get the words out.

Charles stopped playing and looked up at her. "Where are you going?" he asked, unperturbed.

"I'm going to Boston. Do you know where that is?"

Charles nodded solemnly. "It's the capital of Massachewsis," he said innocently, making Ellie laugh softly. "It's north of here," he added proudly.

"That's right," Ellie said.

He was an intelligent child, much like his father. Thomas would see to it that he got the best education. And there were the tears again.

"How long shall you be away?" he asked.

Charles looked innocently at her with his big blue eyes, waiting for her to tell him that she would return to him. After him losing his mother, Ellie had almost stayed just for Charles. This was not going to be easy for him.

"I don't know," she whispered.

Ellie wiped at the tears she could no longer keep at bay. The small boy came over to her and wrapped his little arms around her neck. Ellie pulled him into her lap, and he rested his head on her chest while she stroked his hair.

"I promise I'll do what I can to come see you again, alright?" Ellie could only whisper now. "But I want you to keep practicing your letters. Use them to write to me. Whenever you miss me, you just write it all down and give it to your dad. He'll make sure it gets to me, okay?"

Ellie looked up to make eye contact with Thomas, who nodded in agreement. His own eyes were red with unshed tears. Ellie had to look away.

Charles nodded his own agreement. Ellie could hear his soft sobs and feel his tears falling onto her chest.

"Only, I don't want you to go," he cried.

"I know, sweetie. I don't want to go, either. But I have to."

Ellie pulled back, forcing Charles to look at her.

"Listen, if I could stay just for you, I would. You'll always be my most favorite person in the whole wide world. But I want you to be a good boy and help your dad. Be strong and take care of your sisters. Deal?"

"Deal," he nodded sadly.

Ellie pulled him in for another hug. "I love you, sweetie," she whispered.

By the time Ellie finished saying goodbye to the kids, she had to run out of the house. Unable to face either Thomas or Robert, who had both offered to escort her home, she barely acknowledged either and ran out as fast as she could. It was not until she got home and closed the door behind her that she realized she had not said goodbye to Thomas. Well, that was for the best. She was certain they had already said everything they had to say to each other. Anything more would likely have ended in a fight or more awkwardness, and she was far too shattered to deal with that at the moment.

"You must make her stay," Robert yelled as soon as Ellie ran out the door.

Both men were utterly ruined after the scene they had just witnessed. They went to the drawing room where Robert poured them each a small glass of brandy. Thomas rarely ever drank anymore, but he needed it tonight.

"I know not what makes you think I have any say in what she does," Thomas yelled back, matching Robert's anger.

"You're the only person who can make her stay," Robert continued yelling.

He was not opposed to going to Boston himself, but he did not want to see Ellie put herself in harm's way while she waited for him to join her, which was exactly what she was doing if her visions had any merit. Thus far, they had. If he could find a way to keep her in New York, he would. He felt no shame in using Thomas to accomplish this goal. But more than that, everything changed with Lucy's death. How much more pain could they all take?

"I cannot make her do anything, Robert. Have you not met the woman? She is the most stubborn, pig-headed woman I've ever met. She's never listened to me before; why would she now?" Thomas's brows knitted in confusion and suspicion. "I thought you were to go with her. Have you changed your mind?"

Robert shook his head. "I'm still waiting for my commission to sell before I can leave. She's in a hurry to go, so I'll meet her there once I'm free of the army. Besides, you need me here now."

"Why the hurry? She's waited this long. Why not wait for you to be free? Surely the inn may wait a little longer?"

Robert shook his head. "She's not moving because of me. My plans do not affect hers. She would move regardless of whether or not I am there."

Thomas nodded and took a drink. Looking into his glass, he said. "Well, I did ask her to stay. She declined. She'd not stay even for Charles."

Her goodbye to Charles had been heartbreaking for them both to watch. It was hard enough for them to know she was leaving but watching the interaction between her and Charles had been devastating. She truly cared about Thomas's son, and the boy was en-amored with her.

They were quiet for a moment as they each re-flected on what they had witnessed.

"Do you love her still?" Robert asked quietly while staring into his own glass. He already knew the answer and could not look at Thomas when he heard it. If he heard it. He was trying to make Thomas con-front his feelings for Ellie before it was too late.

"Christ, Robert. Lucy's barely been dead a fort-night. How can I possibly think about that now?"

They both knew he was deliberately avoiding putting a voice to an answer.

"You may want to start thinking about it if you wish not to lose her again."

## Chapter 53

*June 1772*

Robert escorted Ellie and Tabitha to the docks. They arrived early and the ship was not scheduled to leave for several minutes. Ellie wanted to spend as much of it as she could with her friend before departing. Excited about the adventure ahead of her, it also saddened her to be leaving her only friend in the world behind, once again. She could not even think about what else she was leaving behind. As if on cue, Thomas came running up.

Slightly out of breath, he said, "I was concerned I might miss you."

Confused, Ellie said, "We still have a few minutes. Why are you here?"

Thomas jerked back as if slapped. "Do you think so little of me as to think I would not come to send you off?"

"Sorry. I didn't mean it like that. I just... No. I did mean it like that. Are you just here to make sure I actually leave?" Ellie stubbornly crossed her arms in front of her.

Sighing, Thomas looked at Robert. Something passed between them, and Robert huffed and turned away, taking Tabitha and the horses to board the ship while giving them some privacy.

Thomas was almost surprised to be there. He was not planning to come see her off, thinking it would be too hard to bear. However, no matter what he did, he could not get Robert's words out of his head. Thomas was not yet ready to be with anyone else, but if he did not act now, he might lose the only chance he had to finally be with Ellie. If there was any chance they could be together, however small, he needed to know. He needed to do whatever he could to not lose that chance. As much as he felt he was betraying Lucy, the guilt was less than the weight of not knowing.

Thomas stood with his arms behind his back, looking at the ship that would take Ellie and Tabitha to Boston. "Miss Ellie, we may never see one another again. Please do not think this easy for me."

"Boston's not so far away," she said quietly, letting down her guard if only a little. "You never know what the future could hold."

"No. One certainly does not," he agreed. "If you do not like it up there, will you consider returning here?"

"I hadn't even thought about that. I don't think I will dislike it, though."

Ellie had been to Boston before in her own time. After walking the Freedom Trail and exploring the area, she had fallen in love with the city. She had even considered moving there at one point but did not want to live somewhere quite that cold. Utah winters had been bad enough. Despite the cold, she looked forward to living there now and seeing what would come of being part-owner of an inn. Too many of the last years had been filled with pain and she needed the fresh start this would provide her.

Thomas had sounded hopeful, and she wanted to give him something, anything, to hold onto. She almost told him that she would come back, but she knew what was to come. Even if she came back, he would not likely be there. He would go off with his regiment wherever they had a need for him. She bit back the anxiety brought on by the thought and hoped he would be safe during the upcoming war. Should she warn him as she had Robert? Would he even believe her if she did?

"I feel as though I'll never see you again," he said quietly.

"I'm sorry," Ellie added. "I wish it could be different, but I need to do this. It won't be forever, though. I only need to stay until 'seventy-five or 'seventy-six," she said absently. Originally, she only wanted to be in Boston for the events leading up to the Revolutionary War, but it was more than that now. Ellie needed the time to grieve for her friend. "After that, I don't really know where I'll be."

"That's oddly specific. Why until 'seventy-five or 'seventy-six? What is it that is keeping you there until then but allowing you to leave after that?"

"I don't know how to explain it. It's just something I need to do."

"Perhaps you might consider returning here to New York. I've no plans to go anywhere."

A dark cloud passed over Ellie's face and she could not stop the frown from forming. She placed a hand on his arm. "I really hope you don't have to go anywhere. But if you want that to be the case, you need to consider leaving the army."

"The army needs people here at the present to quell the insurgents and their activities, but I'm certain it shall all be behind us by then."

Ellie bit her lip while she considered what to say to Thomas, not sure if she should tell him. Before she could make up her mind, he saw the indecision on her face.

"What is it, Miss Ellie? Clearly there's something on your mind and you're trying to figure out how to tell me. Say whatever it is."

She was not sure if she liked how well he knew her.

"Thomas, war is coming. It will be full blown by then. The army will not be staying only in New York."

"This again? You cannot truly believe that?" he asked, his eyes widened in surprise.

A sailor approached to let Ellie know they would be getting underway in twenty minutes. Ellie was nearly out of time. Thomas looked dejected at not having been able to change her mind. He was quiet for a minute before asking, "May I write you?"

Confused, Ellie replied, "Of course. Why would you even ask? You don't need my permission for that."

"I suppose I don't. Yet I would have it regardless. I wish not to be a nuisance to you in your new life."

Ellie closed the gap between them. The distance, both physical and emotional, had been killing her. She put a hand on his arm, saying, "You could never be a nuisance to me."

Thomas laughed bitterly at that. "Is that not what I've been these last years?"

Smiling mischievously, she said, "Okay, so you've been a complete pain in my ass." She became serious before adding, "But you're not a nuisance."

Thomas cocked his head, looking around to Ellie's rear with one eyebrow raised in doubt. The gesture made Ellie laugh, which brought a smile to his face. It was good to laugh with Thomas again, even if only for a moment. They had spent far too much time at odds, and it had eaten at Ellie.

"And were I to promise to stop being such a pain in your ass," he said mockingly, "would you stay?"

Ellie sighed, shaking her head. "I wish I could, Thomas."

"I've chased you away, yet again," he said sadly. "I am deeply sorry for the way I've behaved." Thomas was looking at the ground, avoiding Ellie's gaze.

"Gods no, you haven't. This is just something I need to do."

"Are you saying that you'd be leaving regardless of whether or not I was even here?" he asked doubtfully. Ellie heard the disbelief in his tone.

"Yes. I would. I was already planning on going to Boston when I arrived here. If you recall, I was only planning on staying for that first winter. Then I let Robert talk me out of it."

A dark shadow passed over Thomas's face as his brows furrowed. "Why Robert, Miss Ellie?" he asked quietly. At Ellie's confused stare, he added, "Why do you confide in him things in which you never confided to me? Why did you stay for him? Why is he joining you in Boston? Do you love him? Why him and not me, Ellie?"

Ellie had not been expecting that line of questioning. Apparently, neither had Thomas. His face changed, and he quickly looked around, saying, "Never mind. It matters not. I do not wish to know."

Ellie answered anyway. "I do love him. I always have."

Thomas looked as though she had just gutted him. Ellie quickly put a hand to his arm and added, "Not like you think. He's always been like a brother to me. Did he tell you why we stopped courting?"

When Thomas shook his head, Ellie told him, "Because I never could get past that. I could never see him as a romantic partner. I tried, but I just never felt that way about him." she shrugged, leaving off the part of the breakup that was due to Robert's suspicion of her feelings for Thomas. "He's the closest thing I have to family here. I never wished to come between you two. I'm sorry he's leaving you to come meet me in Boston, but please don't be upset with him over the decision. I know the only reason he's coming is because he thinks he needs to protect me after what happened at the fort. He somehow feels responsible for my leaving with Dajoji all those years ago."

Ellie was rambling. Almost out of time, she did not know what else to say. This somehow felt safer than talking about anything else.

"I'm pleased he shall be there to look after you," Thomas said softly.

He knew that was not the reason Robert was going. Thomas knew how Robert felt about Ellie. Though it was a relief to hear that his feelings were not reciprocated by her, it did not change the fact that Robert would be in Boston with Ellie while he was stuck in New York City, hundreds of miles away.

If he wanted a chance with Ellie, there was more he needed to say to her. Thomas had been building up the courage to do so but was running out of time and decided to take the plunge.

"Miss Ellie, I know I've not been the most agreeable since you returned, yet neither time nor distance has done anything to erase you from my heart, despite all of my endeavors to the contrary. These last few years have not been easy. Everywhere I went, there you were. At every turn, you drew the interest of every man around, leaving me to wonder if this would be the man to win your affections. Then, you were with Robert, and I'm ashamed to say I wished him ill every time he touched you. Ellie, I've been in hell."

Thomas had not been able to look at her while he confessed his feelings. He had turned sideways and stared at the ship while he spoke, but when he said the last, he hung his head in sorrow.

Ellie moved closer to him. Turning him to face her, she wrapped her arms around him. She had almost forgotten how much taller he was than her as she strained her neck to look up at him from that close.

"I have, too. Seeing you every day with Lucy nearly ripped my heart out. I thought it was because I could no longer count you as my friend now that you had a new life but it was so much more than that. Thomas, I am truly sorry for how much I hurt you when I turned down your proposal, even if it was the best thing for us both. If I'd said yes, I would've just ended up hurting you even worse. I'm so sorry. I thought someone like her could make you happy. Happier than I ever could."

Thomas wrapped his arms around her tiny frame, and they stood there holding each other. Ellie rested her head on his chest, taking comfort from the sound of his heartbeat while Thomas buried his face in her hair, kissing the top of her head.

"Please stay, Ellie," he begged on a whisper.

Pulling back, Ellie wiped the tears from her eyes. Staying to be with Lucy's widower would only confirm that she had, in fact, let her friend die; that Ellie had not done enough to fight for her and save her life. Had Lucy known that Ellie let her die in the hope of stealing her husband? No. Ellie would leave if that was the only way to prove to herself that was not what had happened.

"I have to go, Thomas," she said, shaking her head. "Please understand. I can't stay just because we had sex. We both need time to grieve. And we won't do that if I stay. If I stay, you'll never move past the guilt. You'll come to resent me." Ellie could not resist adding on a laugh, "Even more than you have these past few years."

"I have never once resented you, Ellie. I could never."

Regardless of what the norm was there, being with Thomas at that point was not something Ellie could do. The least she could do for her friend was not disrespect her memory by jumping into a relationship with her husband only days after her death. At his downtrodden expression, she felt a need to reassure him.

"But this is not forever." Ellie grabbed his collar. "Do you hear me? This is not like the last time. You know I'll still be alive. I'll only be in Boston, okay?"

Thomas tightened his arms around her and pulled her in again, kissing her lightly on the forehead. "Okay," he said exaggeratedly.

The modern word sounded strange to her ears coming from his lips, but he could not help mocking her speech patterns. It worked, lightening the mood slightly and causing her to giggle. Despite the joviality of the moment, he still looked miserable.

"Come with me," she said suddenly, surprising even herself. Ellie had not been planning on asking that of him. It had never even crossed her mind before.

"Excuse me?" Thomas let her go and stepped back to get a good look at her.

"I mean, I know you can't just leave right now, but you could sell your commission just like Robert and meet me there," Ellie said hopefully, the idea taking root.

"My life is here or wherever the army sends me."

"I wasn't going to say more, but I'm running out of time to convince you, Thomas. This is not the time to be part of the British Army. Please, Thomas. Please sell your commission. Do it for your children."

"For my children? Miss Ellie, you're not making any sense. What makes now any different from the last seventeen years in which I've served?"

"Because of what's to come. The next decade will be unlike anything anyone has ever known."

Thomas snorted. "Because of the war which you believe is coming? Do you know the future now, Miss Ellie?"

This was her opportunity. Would he believe her? "Yes. I do. And it's not pretty."

He laughed. "You always did have the most peculiar notions. My family and I shall be well."

"Thomas, you don't understand. Just let me–"

Thomas was already shaking his head. "Go now. Send me word that you've arrived safely in Boston."

"But–"

The sailor approached again to let Ellie know they were ready to depart, and Thomas closed his eyes against it, willing time to stop. He wanted more time with Ellie. Why had he been such an ass? How could he let her go once again?

As if reading his mind, Ellie said sadly, "We never seem to be on the same page at the same time, do we? I'll look forward to receiving your letters."

Robert came back over then to say goodbye. When he took her hand to kiss the back of it, she pulled it back and threw her arms around his neck, kissing his cheek. She held onto him for a minute while he lifted her off her feet, hugging her tightly, making her squeal and giggle a little. Things may have been awkward between them when they had first broken up but they had slowly gone back to normal. When he set her down, she drew up on her toes and kissed his cheek again, saying, "I love you, my friend."

He kissed her cheek as well. "I love you, too, Ell."

Robert released her and walked away, waiting for Thomas down the street a little bit.

Ellie and Thomas watched Robert for a moment then she leaned in, pulling Thomas into a hug. He held her tightly in his arms, not wanting to let her go.

"This isn't forever," she whispered.

As she pulled away, she looked into his eyes, putting a hand on his cheek. He leaned into her warmth, closing his eyes to relish her touch. Not knowing when she would see him again made her brave.

"Just so you know, I may love Robert but you're the one I'm in love with. I've always loved you, Thomas. I love the man you are. I love your integrity and honor and your uncompromising principles that also infuriate me." She smiled teasingly before continuing while he watched her, a surprised expression on his face. "I love the way you are with your children and those you love. I love your curiosity and intelligence and your desire to constantly learn and improve yourself. I love the way you treat others with fairness and respect. I love everything about you."

Stretching up onto her toes, she kissed his cheek and whispered, "I am madly in love with you, Thomas."

When she slid from his arms, Ellie had tears sliding down her cheeks. Thomas tried to hold on, but she was already out of his grasp and running toward the ship before he could stop her. He had been too stunned by her words to even respond. What would he have even said to her? Did he still love her? Of course, he did. But could he say it aloud? Did it matter if he did? He wanted to run after her and stop her, to make her stay. He was surprised to find a tear rolling down his own cheek as his heart clenched.

When he had thought Ellie dead, he had turned to Lucy in his grief and while everything was good in the beginning, it did not last. He continuously compared her to Ellie and found all the ways in which his wife came up short. Though this was not the same, he had a much better understanding of grief now than he did then, and he knew Ellie was right. They both needed time to grieve Lucy's death, and if she stayed, neither would. His guilt would eat at him, and he would take it out on her. Their past record had not been the smoothest, and with the added complication of Lucy, a relationship with Ellie now would only end once again in disaster. He knew all of this, yet his heart wanted to try it anyway. When he saw Robert coming back, he wiped away the tears that had come unbidden. The two friends stood on the dock and watched as the ship got underway, taking the love of his life away from him one more time. Neither moved until long after it had passed from view. Finally, Robert had to drag his friend away, back to his now-empty home.

I thoroughly enjoyed getting to know eighteenth century New York City. The Ratzer Map (*Plan of the City of New York, in North America: Surveyed in the Years 1766 & 1767* by Bernard Ratzer), *New York City Neighborhoods: The 18th Century* by Nan A. Rothschild, *Black and White Manhattan: The History of Racial Formation in Colonial New York City* by Thelma Wills Foote, *The Sons of Liberty in New York* by Henry B. Dawson, and *In the Shadow of Slavery: African Americans in New York City, 1626-1863* by Leslie M. Harris really helped bring it to life for me.

I tried to keep as much of the original wording from the broadsheets as I could. However, eighteenth century writing can be difficult for the modern reader to understand and I reworded parts of them for better flow and ease of reading. I did retain the original spelling of names in the broadsheets, even when they were misspelled.

The Battle of Golden Hill or the Riot on Golden Hill is considered to be the first bloodshed of the American Revolution. It occurred six weeks prior to the Boston Massacre, but because no one died, it is often overlooked. There were reports of at least one person having died in the conflict, though there has never been any evidence of this having actually occurred.

This battle was not an event I had heard of until I began my research into New York City during this time period. Trying to stay as true to the historical record as possible, the events unfolded as I wrote, while inserting our characters into the conflict. The other names mentioned as leaders, instigators, or those otherwise involved were all real people.

Like the rest of the colonies, New York had a long history of slavery. An official market opened on Wall Street near the East River in 1711 where humans were sold as chattel. With 42% of the population owning slaves by 1730, New York City had a higher percentage of people who owned enslaved than any other city in the colonies with the exception of Charleston, South Carolina. Enslaved persons consisted of 15-20% of the total population.

An alleged slave rebellion, known as The Conspiracy of 1741 or the Slave Insurrection of 1741, coincided with several fires being set over several days. Afterwards, approximately thirty Black and four White persons were executed while another eighty were exiled. There is a lot of debate as to whether or not this rebellion actually occurred or if it was merely paranoia and a witch hunt as no evidence of any conspiracy or plot was ever uncovered. However, the event had some very real consequences for Black persons in New York City after 1741. Laws restricted the movements of Black persons, whether free or enslaved and made it illegal for White people to entertain them.

By 1762, the slave market on Wall Street closed, but Black people were still bought and sold throughout the city. Age made no difference as to whether a person was sold; children were often torn from their mothers. I imagine these markets to be something truly terrible to witness. It would be difficult to ignore, even more so when children were on the block. While my intention was not to make Ellie some sort of White savior, I wanted to show her affinity for helping others and the extremes in which she would go to in order to do so. The introduction of Tabitha and Harris also allowed me to explore how others viewed the issue in the era and how Ellie had once influenced Thomas.

While I tried to keep things as close to historical as possible, I have taken liberties with some of the issues surrounding slavery. It was not my intent to focus on the practice or explore it in depth. One of the things I took liberty with was the emancipation of Tabitha and Harris. Though I could not find anything specific to New York, it was not uncommon in the colonies for enslaved children under eighteen years old to not be allowed to be emancipated. They were not legal adults and therefore could not support themselves. Freeing them would only be seen as leaving a drain on society.

Like free or enslaved Black persons, women also had limited rights during this era. Widows were given more freedoms than unmarried women, but they were also quite restricted. They could manage estates, create legal documents, and bring lawsuits, whereas unmarried women could not do any of those things.

Inheritance laws were complicated then as they are now. A man could choose to leave as much as he wanted, up to everything he owned, to his widow but could not leave less than the law required. In most colonies, this minimum was one-third of a husband's land and property if there were children, one-half if there were no children. The remaining portions went to any other legal heirs, with priority usually going to sons. If there were no children, other male heirs including brothers, nephews, and even uncles benefitted. A widow could not legally sell or dispose of any of the property without the consent of her husband's heirs. In many places, they only received an inheritance until they remarried, then it either reverted back to his heirs named in the will or it went to the new husband. This resulted in women being pressured to remarry as quickly as possible with some colonies requiring women to remarry within a specific amount of time. However, approximately 80% of women between ages thirty-five and forty-nine did not remarry.

It was fascinating to learn about the funeral service and death rituals observed during this period. Eulogies focused on the deceased were not typical. Instead, sermons focused on the inherently sinful nature of humanity and were designed to leave the attendees considering their own fate. These sermons were typically held at the burial beside the grave.

Commemorative objects were commonly distributed to ministers, friends, and family of the deceased. Due to the expense, mourning rings were more common amongst the wealthy. The most important people who were closest to the deceased would receive theirs first before they were distributed to others. It was not uncommon for individuals to receive these objects in the mail if they could not attend the service in person. Gloves were sometimes given out before the service as an invitation to the funeral. These objects were cherished and often passed down through the family.

# ACKNOWLEDGMENTS

Thanks to David Sorum who allowed me to bounce ideas around and helped me work through the concepts on which I got stuck. I appreciate the time you've spent on the artwork for this.

To Marki Henricksen and Mason McNamara, I appreciate both of you reviewing the medical scenarios for me and helping me make them better and bring them to life. Thank you for your time and your feedback.

A huge thanks to Lisa Lambert and Billy Romero who gave me continuous feedback throughout working on this story and discussed ideas with me at length, letting me ramble on and on endlessly.

To Rick and Kristen White, thank you for putting up with my obsession to work on this story and giving me the space to do so on two separate vacations. Your support and understanding made it easy to get the words out when they threatened to consume me.

A special thanks to all those who helped encourage me and gave me input to improve the story. It would not be what it is without the contributions of each of you.

To my readers, I appreciate you taking the time to read my works. I hope you enjoy them as much as I have.

**Also by Veronique Holloway**

<u>Ichabod's Curse Endures: The Headless Horseman
Rides Again</u>

**<u>Time and Other Lies</u>**
Volume 1: Pulled Through Time
Volume 2: Time of the White Raven
Volume 3: Time Alone
Volume 4: A Time of Madness
Volume 5: A Time of War
Volume 6: Forward in Time
Volume 7: Learning Time
Volume 8: At Home in Time

**For additional information, maps, and insights,
visit <u>VHBooks.net</u>**